THE
BOY
AT
THE
DOOR

Alex Dahl is a half-American, half-Norwegian
author. Born in Oslo, she wrote *The Boy at
the Door* while living in Sandefjord. Her next
novel, *The Heart Keeper*, will be published by
Head of Zeus this summer.

THE
BOY
AT
THE
DOOR

ALEX DAHL

HEAD
ZEUS

First published in the UK in 2018 by Head of Zeus Ltd
This paperback edition first published in 2019 by Head of Zeus Ltd

9 7 5 3 1 2 4 6 8

A catalogue record for this book is available
from the British Library

ISBN (PB): 9781786699251
ISBN (E): 9781786699220

Printed and bound in Great Britain by
CPI Group (UK) Ltd, Croydon CR0 4YY

Head of Zeus Ltd
First Floor East
5–8 Hardwick Street
London EC1R 4RG
WWW.HEADOFZEUS.COM

For Oscar and Anastasia, with love

PART ONE

CHAPTER 1

TUESDAY, I WAKE angry. I often do, if I'm honest, but today it's worse than usual. Firstly, because I wake alone – Johan has gone off to London for the third time this month – and secondly, because it's October and it will be completely dark until almost nine o'clock. I reluctantly get out of bed and stand awhile by the window looking out onto the harbor. It's not yet seven, but across the bay, cars are moving in a slow line towards the motorway. The water in the harbor is dully reflecting the moonlight through a thin, eerie layer of ice. Downstairs, my daughters have already started fighting. I glance at my phone and it's full of messages and missed calls, but I just can't face dealing with them right now. With everything going on, I've hardly been in the office the last week, but I am going in today.

I take a few exaggeratedly deep breaths and keep my gaze on the moon, still high in the sky; mindfulness is the way forward, I've heard. I try to see Sandefjord the way it is in summer, when it really is a joy to stand at this window, looking out over the balmy, calm inner harbor full of leisure boats, and that bright, late-evening light. We get more sun than almost anywhere else in Norway, but I must say the winters are especially wet and drab. According to the weather report, we can expect another onslaught of torrential rain this afternoon, but for now, it's cool and clear. I take another couple of deep breaths, mentally steeling myself for the day ahead. I guess everyone feels like the world is a dark place sometimes.

*

Tuesday is a crap day in my world. Especially now that Marialuz has decided to leave us halfway through her contract and I'm stuck with no au pair. It's like you can't win with those people. I don't particularly enjoy having a stranger in the house but I most certainly don't enjoy having to do all the work myself either. It just isn't possible. Especially on Tuesdays, when the girls both have after-school activities in opposite parts of town. Nicoline dances ballet at five, and Hermine swims at six. Because Nicoline finishes at six thirty p.m. I then have to drive into town to collect her, and bring her back to the pool, where we sit on ugly plastic chairs watching small children bob around in the water until seven fifteen. Nicoline whines for the full half hour we're there, unless I let her watch YouTube makeup tutorials on my phone and buy her candy, which I do. Obviously.

Tonight I'm in a particularly stressed-out, irritable mood, as things didn't exactly go to plan at work. I bend over backwards for my clients, sometimes literally, and still they complain. Angela Salomonsen had the nerve to email me today, saying that the violet raw-silk cushions I commissioned handmade in Lyon look dove-gray in the particular light of her conservatory, and could I call her immediately so we could discuss this situation. These are the kinds of things I have to deal with as interior stylist in a wealthy town full of spoilt, bored wives. Sometimes I think it is a miracle that I work at all, considering I have two small children and my husband is always traveling

4

and I have no au pair. It's not really like I have to, but I quite like what I do, and being me is very expensive. Also, in my circles, it's definitely looked upon as a bit lazy to stay at home. Unless you have a cupcake business from the kitchen counter and blog about it, which I don't, as I hate cupcakes *and* blogs.

It's raining hard outside, and as I watch volleys of rain slam against the floor-to-ceiling windows beyond the pool, it occurs to me that I don't remember the last day it didn't rain. I suppose October is like that in many places, but I think I'm one of those people who is particularly sensitive to dreary skies and wet wind – I am a Taurus, and I prefer my surroundings to be beautiful at all times.

A little boy catches my eye as the children line up at the one-meter diving board. I'm not sure why. He's significantly smaller than the other children and his skin is a deep olive-brown and smooth. He's bouncing up and down on his heels, rubbing his arms, but his face is completely void of the goofy expressions of the other children waiting their turn. He looks frightened. I look around at the other parents who are waiting in the steamy, overheated room for someone who might be the boy's parents – I don't remember seeing him here before. There's chubby Sara's fat mother who I always try not to have to talk to – I've heard from several people that she's really needy and the last thing I need is some cling-on mummy friend. There's Emrik's father – a good-looking guy I went to school with back in the day who is now a police officer, and who I occasionally glance up at before quickly looking away. I can feel his eyes on me now but wait ten seconds longer than I want to before meeting his eyes. I give him a very faint smile and he immediately returns it, like a grateful puppy. I'm a good girl these days, though it doesn't come easily to me; there was a time when I would have felt giddy with excitement at this little game, perhaps easing the top button of my blouse open, running my tongue slowly along the backs of my teeth. I scan the few remaining people for the little boy's parents, now pointedly ignoring Emrik's dad's wanting gaze.

There are the grandparents of Hermine's best friend from school, Amalie, sitting closely together and sharing biscuits from an old, faded, red cake tin. There is also a slim, ginger woman sitting close to the door, a heat flush creeping across her freckled white chest. She, too, is watching the boy intently, and I suppose she must be the mother, though it faintly surprises me that she must have had the child with someone pretty ethnic; the kid is so dark the father must be even darker, and she doesn't immediately strike me as someone with such exotic tastes.

There's nobody else here; I imagine the other parents are out in the parking lot, preferring their own rain-battered cocoons and a newspaper to listening to kids' screeching voices cutting through the clammy, hot air.

Finally, Hermine's class finishes after two rather underwhelming attempts at diving, and she walks over to where Nicoline and I are sitting.

'Did you see that?' She beams, exposing the wide, fleshy gash in her mouth from six simultaneously missing teeth.

'Fabulous,' I say, standing up, gathering our things together and nudging Nicoline, who is watching a ten-year-old in America apply a thick layer of foundation before expertly contouring her elfin face. 'Hurry up in the changing rooms. We'll wait in the foyer.'

Hermine does not hurry up in the changing rooms, and Nicoline and I wait impatiently in the brick-clad foyer, staring out at columns of rain moving back and forth across the parking lot like dancers in a ballroom. I keep checking my watch and it's already past 7.30 when Hermine appears, freshly blow-dried and with a lick of pink lip gloss in spite of the fact that she's about to step into a torrent.

I can practically feel the thin, cool stem of the wine glass in my hand and am slightly hysterical at the thought of having to deal with the girls for much longer today. They begin to argue over something as we walk out the door, and over the sounds of their high-pitched squabbling and the crash of the rain, I don't pick out the other sound until I've taken several steps outside. I briefly turn around, and there is the receptionist, an older, tired-looking woman with tight gray curls and a sweater that reads 'Happy Halloween'. She's shouting my name into the downpour, motioning for me to come back inside, and it's so typical – one of the girls must have left something behind.

'Cecilia, right?' she asks as I step back inside, already drenched. I notice the little boy again, the one who'd caught my eye at the pool. He's sitting on a bench, staring at the floor, his hair dripping onto the brown tiles.

'Yes?'

'I… I was wondering if you could possibly take this little boy home? Nobody has come for him.'

'What do you mean, nobody's come for him?'

The receptionist comes over to where I'm standing near the door and lowers her voice to a near-whisper, indicating the little boy on the bench.

'Maybe there's a misunderstanding… He knows where he lives. It's over on Østerøya; I looked at the list, it doesn't seem too far from where you are.'

'I'm sorry, it's really inconvenient,' I say, glancing back out at the black, wet night, longingly now. 'Isn't there anyone else who can take him? There was a woman in there I thought was his mother.'

'I'm afraid it can't have been; they've all gone.' Damn Hermine and her blow-dry.

'Have you called the parents?'

'Yes. The number he gave goes straight to voicemail.'

'Can't he take a bus or something?' The receptionist gives me a slightly cold look and pointedly looks over my shoulder to the downpour outside.

Nicoline and Hermine stare with open mouths from me to the boy to the receptionist, and back to me. The idea of not actually being collected by anyone from their activities is clearly unfathomable to them, as it very well should be. What kind of parents would not turn up to pick up their child? Some people really should be prevented from reproducing in the first place.

'Fine,' I say. 'Of course I'll take him.' I look at the boy, expecting him to get up and follow us to the car, but he remains sitting, staring at the floor.

'I've never seen him here before,' I say to the receptionist. 'What's his name?'

'Tobias,' she says. 'He only started a few weeks ago. He's eight, but as he's quite little for his age and hasn't swum much previously, we moved him in with the seven-year-olds.'

'I see.' I try not to think of the extra half hour this kid's parents' fuck-up is going to cost me and my plans for a very large glass of Chablis by the fire before Johan comes home. I walk over to where he's sitting.

'Come on,' I say, but realize my voice sounds harsh. I kneel down next to him, and only then does he look up at me. He's like a sparrow, with jittery, nervous eyes, but a soft, sweet face, framed by defined, dark brows. He's tiny – it seems impossible

8

that he can be a year older than my solid, tall Hermine. There's something serious and un-childlike about him, and it throws me for a moment, but then I try to empathize – it must be a result of coming from a family that forgets to pick up an eight-year-old from the swimming pool on a bitingly cold, wet October evening. 'Come,' I say again, softer now. He doesn't take my outstretched hand, but does stand up, gathering his things together.

In the car, the girls are completely silent for once, and the only sound is the repetitive, fast swoosh of the windscreen wipers. Nicoline sits up front with me, staring out at the twinkling lights of the harbor as we drive through town on our way to Østerøya. I glance in the mirror and see that Hermine is looking unselfconsciously at Tobias, whose wan little face is turned away from her, to the window. Hermine begins to draw shapes in the gathering steam on her own window; hearts with arrows through them, her initials – H.W. – little bunnies with smiling faces.

'Mum?' says Nicoline.

'Yes?'

'Can you drop us at our house before you take that boy home?'

Our home is only a two-minute detour, and it would be good for the girls to get a head start on the evening routine. 'Sure. Daddy isn't home yet, though. He's landing at ten.'

'Okay.'

'I won't be more than twenty minutes, so you can get changed into your pajamas and brush your teeth.' I turn into our long driveway and glance at the boy again as our house comes into view. It's quite an impressive sight with its shiny black roof, numerous softly lit windows, a triple garage, swimming pool

9

just discernible through the hedges, panoramic sea views and welcoming red door. I wonder whether the boy has ever been to a home like this before, but his neutral expression betrays nothing. Back on the road, I try to make some conversation with him.

'So, which school do you go to?'

Silence.

'Tobias?'

Silence.

'Are you in... umm, second grade? Third?'

Silence. I give up.

I pull up at the address the receptionist wrote down on the back of a Sandefjord Svømmeklubb business card: Østerøysvingen 8, but there doesn't seem to be anything here. I glance back at Tobias, but he sits immobile, as though he's never been here before.

'Tobias? Is this where you live?' He nods slightly, and finally, through the dark and the rain, I make out the outline of a structure set back from the road atop a rocky crag. 'Okay, bye, then,' I say, but the boy doesn't move.

'Umm, would you like me to walk you to the door?' Slowly the boy raises his eyes to meet mine and there's something in the way that he looks at me that makes me anxious. He nods. I look away, back up at what looks like a small, huddled wooden house, cursing this turn of events. I could be at home now, my feet up on the new InDesign footstool, a glass of crispy wine in my hand, flicking through *Scandinavian Homes*, my cashmere Missoni throw across my knees, listening to the snap of flames and the howl of the wind. Instead I'm here in the crashing rain with a mute, strange child, trying to find his parents. I run from the car up a steep gravel path to the door of the little house, the boy trailing behind me, seemingly oblivious to the onslaught of icy water. I knock on the flimsy door with peeling blue paint, but as I do, it opens a crack, as though it was never properly closed. I'm not sure whether the booming sound rising above the hammering rain is coming from my heart or from something inside the house.

'Hello?' I say loudly with fake confidence, pushing the door open all the way. The door opens straight into a living room, but the house is clearly unlived in – there is no furniture except the bare wooden bones of a sofa in the middle of the room. There are mounds of dust everywhere, cobwebs descending from dark, moist corners, and mouse droppings scattered about. I turn around fast, to the boy standing in the doorway, no longer in doubt that the booming sound is indeed coming from my heart.

'Tobias,' I say, taking hold of his bony shoulders with both of my hands. 'Is this your house?' He nods.

'Where are your parents?' No reaction.

'Tobias, look at me! You have to explain to me what's going on here! Do you live in this house? It doesn't look like anyone lives here.' He still does not answer but I follow his eyes up a narrow staircase. I run up the stairs and my steps reverberate in the hollow, empty space. I shudder to think of him just standing there downstairs, in the dark, by himself. For a brief moment I am grateful for my own two girls. For all their shortcomings and the constant annoyance of listening to their never-ending squabbles, they are nowhere near as weird as this kid.

At the top of the stairs is a white, clean-looking IKEA lamp, unplugged, but seemingly recently placed amid the thick dust. I plug it in and look around in the pool of light. There are two rooms upstairs, one on either side of the stairwell, and a small water basin. In one of the rooms is a dirty mattress, propped up against the wall, and in the corner stands a bin liner overflowing with clothes. In the other room a smaller mattress is placed against the window and a postcard hangs from a nail – Krakow. I turn it over but nothing is written on it.

Downstairs, Tobias is where I left him, standing motionless in the doorway, not letting his eyes wander around the room. I kneel down in front of him, determined to find a way to communicate with him.

'Tobias, you need to tell me what's going on, right now. Do you live in this house?' He nods.

'Where are your parents, Tobias?' No response.

'Look, I'm going to have to call the police.'

'No!' he shouts, and I'm surprised by how forceful his voice is – I would have imagined it to be a fragile mewl, judging by the rest of the kid.

'I have to, Tobias. Obviously I can't leave you here in this… this empty house. Where are your parents, sweetie?' I reach into my pocket for my iPhone, only to realize Nicoline still has it.

'Look, we're going to go back to my house and make a few calls. You don't need to worry, Tobias. You're a child, and you haven't done anything wrong. There has probably just been some kind of misunderstanding. Okay?' He shakes his head curtly and his indifferent expression of earlier is replaced by a scowl. I stand back up and reach for his hand, which is cold and wet. 'Come on, sweetheart. It's going to be okay. I'm going to help you.' He looks me square in the eye and nods slightly, eyes distant and sad.

At home, I park outside the garage because most likely

I'm going to have to spend the rest of the evening driving this forlorn little boy around when the police find out where his parents actually are, because they sure as hell aren't at home in their squat. I switch off the ignition, look quickly in the rearview mirror, and freeze, my hand on the door handle. Tobias is crying silently, big droplets rolling from his eyes and hovering a moment on his chin before dropping off onto his already-soaked jeans.

'Hey...' I say. 'Hey... Come on inside. I'll fix you a hot chocolate and you can watch a movie with my girls until we figure something out, okay?' I think he shakes his head but his sobs are so violent that I can't be sure he isn't just shaking all over.

'Please,' he whispers finally. 'Please can I stay here tonight? Just tonight? They'll come back tomorrow. I promise. I promise! Just tonight! Please don't call the police!'

'But, Tobias, where are they? *Who* are they? Your parents?'

'Yes.'

'Where are they?'

'They're coming back tomorrow.'

'How do you know?'

'They said.' At this, I let out a sharp little sigh. Judging by the state of their living quarters, I wouldn't take Tobias's parents' word on anything.

'Please,' he says again, and there's something so raw and urgent in his eyes that I wait a moment before I speak. I have to say no. This kid can't just stay here. It must be illegal to just take some kid in overnight without at least alerting the authorities. I could call now, and they'd come straight here; serious-looking men and women with briefcases sitting around my living room all night questioning this mostly mute boy.

There would be phone calls, crying, pleading, the astonished expression on Johan's face when he gets home from the airport less than two hours from now. Or... or I could put him up in the guest room, just for tonight, and drop him at his school first thing tomorrow morning and that would be that. Then the school could deal with him if the parents don't return.

'Okay,' I say. 'Of course you can stay here tonight. But just one night.' He nods and smiles a tight little smile at me as we walk the last few steps to the front door. Next to it hangs a wooden heart, made and painted by Nicoline, which reads: 'Welcome to the Wilborg family!' Tobias pauses next to it for several long moments and there is something in his focused, serious expression that unsettles me. There is something else, too; something about his smile – it looks familiar, like I have seen him somewhere before. This is a small town. I could have seen him anywhere, at any time. It isn't so strange. But there was something about his smile... something familiar.

'Welcome,' I say, holding the door open for him, smiling stiffly, and he nods, stepping into the hallway.

*

Sometimes, if I wake in the quietest hour of the night, when the house seems to gently buzz with all that sweet normality, I pad across the hallway and stand awhile in one of the girls' rooms. I stand still, listening to the rise and fall of soft, slow breath. In spite of the hell they put me through sometimes, and in spite of the fact that, really, I'm just another working mother trying to hold it all together at an astronomical cost, I am so very grateful for them. That somebody as perfect and wonderful as those two should have chosen Johan and me as parents is astonishing.

Hermine is contrary, sharp-mouthed and utterly beautiful. She is witty and independent, and has mastered sarcasm since she was tiny. Nicoline takes after Johan – she is truly kind, both in actions and in thoughts, and I don't say that lightly, because nobody else in this family is as completely and uncomplicatedly kind as those two. Nicoline just wants us all to get along all the time, and easily senses when something is even slightly awry. One day, she'll make an incredible mother. The kind who lives for the glee on dirty, sugar-crusted little faces. The kind of mother I'm just not.

I love my girls, wildly, but often my intentions surpass my practical ability. I want to be the kind of parent who reads to them for hours after spending the afternoon baking glittery pink, gluten-free unicorn oat biscuits. I want to be the mother whose facial expression is calm and harmonious even when they shout 'Mommy' for the seventh time – in that minute. 'Mommy, mommy, mommy!' 'Yes,' I want to smile, 'here I am.' A one-woman comfort station, a one-stop shop for food, fun and endless reassurance. But I'm not that mother, most of the time. I'm the mother who fantasizes about a *piscine de champagne* on Mala Beach, the one who wants to smash stuff when they fight and shout, the one whose maternal patience just isn't all that.

But I do adore them. And especially in those silent, dark hours, when their faces are vulnerable and bare by the light of the moon, their breath uncontrolled and peaceful, their little hands clasped to their chins beneath unguarded faces, lingering at the very end of childhood.

Tonight everything is different. For several hours, I lie in bed, unable to sleep, just focusing on syncing my breath to Johan's soft, regular rhythm. A part of me wants to go and stand in one of the girls' rooms, to make sure that they really are there, that they are safe. I want to walk quietly around the house, making sure everything is okay, that everything is how it should be, but I don't, because everything is strange and different, and I know I'll burst into tears if I move even an inch.

CHAPTER 2

HERE IN SANDEFJORD we have everything. Or, rather, we don't – and that is my point exactly. We don't have any of the undesirable components that make life so unpalatable in many other places: pollution, poverty, property crises, excessive crime, immigration issues – I could go on and on. This is not the kind of place where little boys turn up out of the blue, with empty eyes, no parents and nothing but a plastic bag containing a pair of Batman swimming trunks and a frayed baby-blue towel. Sandefjord isn't that kind of place. Wasn't.

Sandefjord is the kind of place people want to live. Postcard-pretty, snug and sheltered at the top of its fjord, Sandefjord is the kind of place less attractive places bad-mouth. Can't blame them, of course – it's not everybody's privilege to be able to live somewhere like this. Here, everybody has a nice home that they own, a new car in the garage, a well-paid job, numerous foreign holidays a year and a mountain cabin, too. Everyone I know, at least.

The call came at lunchtime. I'd only just begun to relax after the events of the last twenty-four hours and though I'd only been at the office for an hour, I decided to take an early lunch break so I could get my eyelash extensions done – Johan likes them. Walking from my office in Kilen, past the fish shop and the boats pulled up for winter, and the steel-gray water of the inner harbor, it occurred to me that the whole town resembled how I felt; cold and drained from all the rain. I checked my phone a couple of times as I walked along; I'm not sure why, really. And then, when I lay atop the table and the young girl was working painstakingly on my new, feathered lashes, I heard my phone vibrate from where it lay in my bag. Again and again. It couldn't be work – nothing I do is urgent enough to merit repeated missed calls. The eyelash girl stopped for a moment and asked if I wanted to pick up. 'Nope,' I said, trying to fight off waves of annoyance. Did I, on some level, know then what I know now?

'Cecilia Wilborg?' said a smooth, female voice when I picked up on the sixth attempt, walking back out of the salon into the bleak day.

'Yes?'

'Hi. This is Vera Jensrud calling from Østerøyparken School. I'm glad I've got hold of you. Finding your number wasn't exactly easy. Presumably you know why I'm calling?'

'I'm afraid I don't. I'm… uh, actually in the middle of something here,' I lied, picking at my cuticles. 'How can I help you?'

'Is it correct that you dropped off a little boy here at the school this morning?'

'Yes. Yes, it is.'

'May I ask what your relationship to the child is, Mrs Wilborg?'

'None. None whatsoever. Now, I'm afraid I'll have to…'

Vera Jensrud interrupted me. 'But Tobias lives with you and your family, is that correct?'

I burst out laughing, an exaggerated, outraged squawk. 'Excuse me?'

'Look. This boy does not attend this school.'

'So which school does he attend?'

'We don't know. He refuses to say. You can only imagine how upsetting this is for everyone, most of all, of course, this little child. Now, we need to immediately establish who he is and where he belongs, and the only thing we have been able to get out of him is that he lives with you.'

I glanced briefly up at my office building, trying to stop myself from screaming. 'He most certainly doesn't live with me! I don't know this child!'

'But you dropped him off here this morning?'

'Well, yes, but I met him for the first time last night.'

'Right.' Vera Jensrud sounded uncertain, as though she didn't quite know whether to believe the half-mute eight-year-old or me. 'Wait. You say you met him last night? But he stayed at your house?'

I hesitated. Fear seeped into me, ugly and cool, like poison through the pores of my skin. The wind ripped at my jacket and I ran the short distance back to the office. 'Yes. Look, it was a very strange situation. He told me he attends your school, so I figured it would just be best to drop him off there.'

'Presumably you spoke with his parents last night before taking him back to your house? That's why I'm calling, really, to see whether you'd be aware of some way of getting in touch with them.'

'I... uh... The lady at the pool tried calling them several times and they didn't pick up the phone.'

'What about when you tried, later, from home?'

'I... I didn't. Tobias asked me explicitly not to.'

'Mrs Wilborg, this is a boy no more than eight years old. Did it not occur to you to call the parents before taking in a small child overnight?'

'I'm sorry I wasn't able to help you. I'm afraid I'm going to have to go now...' I stuttered, and hung up the phone. It began ringing again before the screen had even gone dark, and when I realized I was being watched by the guys in the office across from mine, I picked up. I pushed my chest out but turned my face away from them so they wouldn't notice my intense annoyance.

'What? I've said I can't help you!'

'Mrs Wilborg, this is Police Inspector Thor Ellefsen. I'm sitting here with Vera Jensrud, the social environment teacher at Østerøyparken School, as well as a representative from social services. We really need you to come down here as soon as you can so that we can discuss this situation.'

'Look,' I said as pleasantly as I could manage, though by then a full panic had set in and I could feel my mind receding into a blank, numb state. 'Of course I wish to help you, and I feel desperately sorry for this poor child. I just don't think I'm able to add anything at all to your... your investigation.'

'He says he lives with you.'

'Well, he doesn't.'

'This really is the strangest situation I have encountered. Will you be able to be here in fifteen minutes, do you think? We think you should bring your husband as well.'

'Johan? Oh. Oh no. That's really not necessary.'

'In cases like this, we prefer both partners being present. We'd appreciate any help you and your husband can give us. We're quite happy to call him to explain, if you'd rather?'

'No. No, I'll call.' Irritation gave way to the most profound rage. After we'd hung up, I stared out at the slightly churning sea, at the rows of pretty little houses along its shore, at the white-gray, low-hanging sky, at the swathes of ochre, downtrodden leaves in the park across the road.

I've loved this town my whole life, but in those moments I hated it and wanted to barge through it like a giant, smashing and burning everything in my way until only charred splinters remained. And now, driving slowly and distractedly back to the school where I dropped Tobias this morning, I feel no less unhinged. I can see Johan's car a few cars ahead of mine and imagine him, serious and pensive behind the wheel, glancing around for me, anxious at having been summoned by the police. He'll be worrying about the child, wringing his hands and stressing about how the situation will affect me. Before he spots me, and for the last few minutes before I get there, I have to run through the rest of the events of last night and this morning to make sure I get the wording exactly right.

By the time Johan got home from the airport, I had managed to re-establish a semblance of normality at home. The girls had meekly gone straight to bed, jolted by the presence of the boy; a sense of strangeness lingered on the air in the house. I put Tobias into Marialuz's old room in the cellar apartment, and momentarily felt bad for leaving him two whole floors away from us, and especially on such an unsettled night. I had to do what felt right for my own family, didn't I?

I heard the door downstairs shut softly, followed by the familiar thud of Johan's footsteps. When he appeared at the top of the stairs, I turned from where I was sitting on the chaise longue by the floor-to-ceiling windows and gave him my most dazzling smile. I'd lit candles in countless little metallic jars, and a shy fire was flickering in the fireplace. On the table stood an open bottle of Johan's favorite red, a Côte de Beaune-Villages. I poured him a glass and watched him settle exhaustedly into the sofa, rubbing his eyes. I positioned myself close to him and gave him my best adoring-wife expression.

The thing about men, I find, is to treat them with a carefully honed combination of casual aloofness, sharp reproach and unadulterated adoration. It throws them, keeps them on their feet – you can't be nice all the time. Big mistake.

'Baby,' I whispered, 'you look exhausted. Let's get you to bed in a minute...' I narrowed my eyes slightly and laid a hand at the top of his thigh. 'I've missed you...' Johan smiled, his handsome face bright and grateful for this warm welcome home. I'm not always that pleasant – to put it mildly – when he's jetted off somewhere for four days, leaving me alone with the kids.

'I have to tell you something,' I continued. 'A friend of Hermine's from the swimming club is staying the night, okay? He's downstairs, in Marialuz's bed.'

'On a school night?'

'Yes... Well, I think there was some sort of family issue, so I figured it would be okay.'

Johan nodded thoughtfully. 'But why didn't you put him upstairs in one of the guest rooms on our floor?'

'Hermine and Nicoline were terrible this evening, fighting and shouting at each other. I thought it would be best if he had his privacy.' I forced a little laugh. 'It's not like he's not under the same roof. Besides, he looks very tired. He's a tiny little thing.'

'What kind of family issue did you say the kid had, honey?' Johan gazed into the ruby dregs at the bottom of his wine glass, frowning.

'Oh, I'm not really sure. I didn't want to get too involved, to be honest. Here,' I took the wine glass from his hand and pretend-pulled him to his feet. I stood on my tiptoes and tilted my face up for a kiss. Johan still looked preoccupied, but leant in and kissed me chastely on the lips. I pulled him in closer and slipped my tongue into his mouth, pressing my body against his. He pulled back after a while and looked at me, dazed but happy.

'Baby...' he whispered.

'Shhh,' I said, and together we half ran up the stairs in the soft darkness. As I walked ahead of him down the hall towards our bedroom, I glanced briefly out of the skylight, and saw the face of a strange and unsettling full moon appear from behind a dense cloud, blurred by rushing rain. Suddenly my mind darted to that place I never allow it to go; to another cold, dark night, the darkest of all my life.

I could practically hear the sound of flames snapping, the wind wailing outside, my own short breath interspersed with an occasional high-pitched, involuntary howl as the pain crashed over me again. I still can't believe that I survived... I am not someone who is easily thrown, but in that moment, struggling to reciprocate Johan's eager kisses, I felt a surge of panic, and had to swallow back tears. The fear did not subside, and as Johan climbed on top of me, I had to reach over and switch on the bedside lamp so that I could see that it really was him.

Afterwards, when his breath had settled into a slow, steady purr, I lay a long while on my back, trying to keep hot tears from scattering down the sides of my face. They were no longer for bad, old memories, or for myself, but for a tiny boy.

*

Johan is waiting for me in the parking lot and I clumsily park across two bays next to his Tesla. He is smiling, but his eyes are serious.

'This is about that little boy, they said.'

'Yeah, apparently,' I say, walking up the gravel path towards the merry yellow school building.

'I'm not sure you mentioned last night what kind of family problems he'd had.'

'Come on, Johan, they're waiting for us. I told you, I don't know. I just wanted to help him last night and assumed the school would be able to sort out whatever the issue is today.'

'So... so why are we here?'

'It would appear he doesn't actually go to this school.'

'But... but he said he goes here. Where does he actually go, then?'

'Well, that seems to be what everybody wants to know.' Just then, a man and a woman appear in the doorway of a smaller building next to the main school building, waving for us to come that way.

'Let me do the talking, okay, babe?' I say in a low voice and smile reassuringly at my husband.

Inside, we are introduced to Police Inspector Thor Ellefsen, social environment teacher Vera Jensrud, and a representative of social services, Laila Engebretsen. The latter looks vaguely familiar, and it takes me a while to realize why; she used to be called Laila Hansen, and we went to primary school together. Back then she was a timid, chubby girl with messy pigtails and hand-me-down clothes, and she's not really that different now. *Scruffy* is the word that comes to mind. I must admit that she's gone from awkwardly tall and 'big-boned' to what I suppose some people might call statuesque, but she most definitely retains that gangly, clownish presence I remember from childhood. I'm surprised that she's got married and changed her name and wonder what kind of man would be drawn to someone as void of sexiness as this chunky missy.

She smiles at us, a genuine smile, before her features settle into a sad seriousness. She nods towards a little window, through which we see another room where Tobias sits on the floor, watching a cartoon among piles of merry IKEA cushions shaped as animal heads. He is looking evenly at the screen, though he must be aware of the window, of people peering at him worriedly. A knot appears in the pit of my stomach, like a hand twisting at my intestines. I turn away and face Vera, Laila and Thor, trying to mirror the social worker's expression of concern and empathy.

'Cecilia, Johan,' says Laila, 'thank you both so much for coming, and especially at such short notice.' I raise an eyebrow and purse my lips in agreement – short notice, indeed, but then I remember that the impression we are going for here is helpfulness and concern.

'Oh, but of course,' I say. 'We are very concerned about Tobias.'

'Yes,' says Vera Jensrud.

'This is, quite frankly, a highly unusual situation,' adds Thor Ellefsen. 'I've been a Sandefjord policeman for thirty-two years, and I can honestly say nothing like this has ever happened before. We are at a bit of a loss, and hope you can help us piece together some crucial information.' Johan and I both nod. Sitting down on a low, green sofa, I lose sight of Tobias through the window, but he is vividly here, in my mind, as though my brain has memorized every last characteristic of this little stranger; the smooth olive-brown skin; the floppy black hair; the grown-up, but expressionless eyes; the sharp, too-big teeth that seem to only just have come through; the thin, small hands held close to his sides in fists.

'Could you please talk us through the events of last night that led to Tobias spending the night at your family home?' continues Ellefsen.

I nod, clear my throat and begin to speak. I tell them about how I first noticed Tobias at the pool, how he'd seemed afraid. I tell them about the receptionist saying nobody had turned up for him, and that the number she had for his parents went straight to voicemail. How she'd asked me to please drop the boy at the address on Østerøya. I pause, nervous because of how they are all looking at me.

'What was the address?'

'Østerøysvingen 8.'

Laila Engebretsen nods. 'That is the same address he gave us,' she says softly. 'The poor boy. He's traumatized. Doesn't trust adults. It took me two hours to get him to breathe a single word.'

'The trouble is,' says Inspector Ellefsen, 'the house at Østerøysvingen 8 has been empty since 2010 when the owner, an old lady, died. Her son, who inherited it, lives in Kristiansund and never comes here.'

'But... I went inside. With the boy. And, uh, it seemed to me that someone had used it recently. There were mattresses upstairs, a new lamp...'

'It has come to our attention that the building may have been used as a squat on a couple of occasions. We've stopped by there two or three times and always found it empty. There were some Latvians here last winter, doing odd jobs, who were unaccounted for, housing-wise. Also, as you may know, we've had some Eastern European beggars here in Sandefjord the last few years. Romanians. We wondered whether they might sleep in that house occasionally.'

'But what about Tobias?' asks Johan, his face red and splotchy. He gets like that with indignation, and I can only imagine the thoughts churning through his mind at the moment – he's so kindhearted and sensitive, my Johan. 'Who is going to take care of Tobias?' I press my leg discreetly but firmly against Johan's. He needs to understand that I'm the one who does the talking here.

'He must be the squatters' son?' I ask.

'We're looking into that, but we have not had any reports over the years of any of the transient Eastern European groups having children with them. Also, his Norwegian is flawless.'

'He *looks* like a gypsy,' I say.

'A gypsy?' asks Laila, her docile eyes suddenly sharp on me.

'Well, yes. You mentioned there have been issues with Romanians coming here to beg. It seems quite likely to me that he could be one of them.' Laila writes something on her notepad. I can see it, from where I'm sitting: *Romanian?*

'Okay, back to last night. What did you do when you realized there was nobody at Østerøysvingen 8?' Inspector Ellefsen holds my gaze a long while and I feel irrationally nervous; after all, I haven't done anything wrong.

'I… I was going to call someone.'

'Who were you going to call?'

'I guess I was going to call the lady at the swimming pool. If I couldn't get hold of her, I would have tried the police or social services.'

'But you didn't?'

'Well, I would have, but I realized the phone was at home, with my eldest daughter. She'd been playing Minecraft on it in the car.'

'Okay. So what did you do next?'

'Well, if I'm honest, it was quite a frightening thing that happened. The house… it was so empty and cold. It was freezing and stormy outside, I was exhausted after a long day, my Tuesdays are terrible. And the boy, Tobias, I mean, well – I felt so desperately sorry for him. He didn't look surprised at the abandoned house. He looked empty, broken, dejected. We got back in the car and drove to my house. I thought I'd get him a hot chocolate and a snack. I was planning on making a few calls...'

'But you didn't.'

I swallow hard and try to recover my harmless-and-concerned expression, but my mind is receding back to that irrational, black panic, and I want to stand up and crash through the door, running to the car, leaving these polite faces and sharp eyes and constant questions behind. 'No, I didn't.'

'And why was that, Cecilia?' Laila asked kindly.

'Like I said, I was tired. Confused. When we got to the house, Tobias asked if he could stay the night. Begged, in fact. I said I'd have to make a few calls, figure this out, but he became so distressed and upset that I just didn't know what to do. I suppose I couldn't see the harm in letting him stay just the one night. He told me he goes to this school, and so I felt reassured that you would be able to help him if there really was a more serious family situation.'

'I would have thought you'd come inside the school with Tobias this morning, just to make sure everything really was okay' Vera Jensrud spoke slowly, watching me as though she were about to frame some criminal rather than ask a concerned mother some routine questions. Bitch.

'Well, I would have, but he asked me not to, actually,' I say. 'He said, "Thank you, but I'll be fine from here." That's what he said.' Actually, he had asked me to walk him in, and I'd said I was in a rush, and leant across him to open the back door, filling the car with crisp air. Then I'd stared out the window until I'd heard him move, and then closed the door with a very soft thud. My face feels hot. My feet are itching. I glance quickly at

Johan and find him looking at me, an expression of sympathy on his face, but mixed with something else – shock.

'But he's seven,' says Vera Jensrud, writing something down on a notepad. I want to smack her in her plain, wrinkled face.

'Eight,' I say.

A long silence follows. I feel Johan's eyes still on me. Laila Engebretsen rustles the papers in her notebook, most likely to break the tension. 'In any case, we're glad you're here now.'

'So… so, what happens to the poor child now?' I ask.

Laila Engebretsen exchanges a quick glance with Inspector Ellefsen. 'Well, we are obviously doing absolutely everything we can to determine the boy's origins and to locate his family. In the short term, he will stay in a safe family setting here in Sandefjord.'

I nod. 'And in the longer term?'

'Well, we certainly hope we can solve this and give Tobias the best possible chance at a stable family life.'

'So, you've found him somewhere for the short term?' Johan asks, his face tight with worry.

'Due to the international migrant situation, where Norway has seen hundreds, if not thousands, of children arriving unaccompanied, our short-term foster families are unfortunately completely exhausted in this region. In this phase of a traumatizing situation like this, it is of the utmost importance to limit the changes a child is exposed to as much as possible. We'd like to ask whether you'd consider the possibility of taking Tobias in for a short while, maybe a few weeks. He seems to have taken to you. And, of course, we know you will be able to provide him with a secure family environment while we sort this out.'

Laila Engebretsen looks at me expectantly, as if she's asking me a perfectly reasonable favor like watering her plants or picking up her mail while she's off to Tenerife. I am, for once, actually speechless. I shake my head hard, but as I do, I realize that Johan is nodding. Up and down his head goes and I want to reach across and punch him, the utter goon; his lip is wobbling and his eyes are even glinting with tears.

'Of course we'll have him,' he says, and then, 'thank you. Thank you.'

KRYSZ ALWAYS SAYS that if a person sees me then they will shoot me or at the very least shove me into a small hole in the ground where I'd have to sit staring at mud walls, eating stale bread and drinking slimy water. Nobody ever saw me because I know every stone and every tree near the houses I have lived in. When Anni and Krysz go away all day, or sometimes many days, I am outside in the woods where people rarely go anyway, but if they did, I would know where to hide. I'm not allowed to stay inside the house, in case police come. It has happened, that I've seen people and hid. Once, I was picking little red fruits from a bush when a man came running very fast on the path a few meters below where I stood. He was very red in the face and spluttering. He had headphones in his ears for his music and he wore a bright yellow vest and shiny, tight black shorts. He didn't look dangerous and I didn't think he would have shot me even if he had seen me. He didn't because I stood very still against the trunk of the tree, stroking it gently the way I like to do. Sometimes I feel a murmur in return against my fingertips. Krysz says it isn't true and it isn't possible but it is.

A few days ago Anni and Krysz were very angry with each other. They shouted. Krysz put his things into an old brown bag and the things that didn't fit he put into some plastic bags. Anni shouted while he did this, the fat smoke hanging from the side of her mouth, unlit. When he was finished he said, *Goodbye, Anni.* He's done this before; they both have, so I wasn't very afraid. I was only afraid of the shouting, because it often comes before smashing or worse. Instead of more shouting, Anni was quiet. She stared at the bags and at Krysz, who had sat down on the bare floor in the bedroom. She stared at me, hovering in the stairwell outside, and I tried to flatten myself up against the wall the way I do against tree trunks when I'm outside, but it's much easier in the woods, and I wasn't able to stop her looking at me in a cold, angry way. *I'm leaving,* he said. *You're leaving,* said Anni, laughing, but not nice laughing. *Yeah,* said Krysz. *What about the boy?* said Anni. *What about the fucking boy?* Anni said: *You can take him with you.* Krysz said: *Fuck, no.* Anni said: *Well, then he goes back to where he came from.* Krysz said: *What the fuck does that even mean?* Anni didn't say anything else, but walked over to where I still stood in the stairwell and for a moment I thought she might spit at me the way she sometimes does when she's angry, but she just looked at me, up close. Her lips were pulled back, she was sneering like a wolf, revealing her brown half-teeth and the black gashes in between them. *Come,* she said.

*

Once when I was smaller, I asked Anni if I could call her *Mother.* She said no. Then she laughed, showing me her half-teeth and the long red gums over them. *Why would you want to call me that? I'm not your mother,* she said, and I did ask her then, again, *who is,* but she just shrugged and turned away. I guess my mother must have died, so Anni and Krysz couldn't bring me to her like they were supposed to after Moffa died. It's the only reason I can think of but I still don't know why they bothered keeping me until now.

The voices of the other children holler around me like stones bouncing on a lake. I have almost never been this close to other children before. The water is such a special blue that I have to stare at. It is wonderful. I know how to swim a little because Moffa taught me, in the lake. No! I mustn't let Moffa into my mind. I know not to think about him because it's sad and if you think about one sad thing, you'll probably think about *all* the sad things. Krysz told me this once when he wasn't drunk, when he took me fishing, very early in the morning, when the sky was pink and gray at the same time and heavy birds flew close together, feet almost touching the water, which looked like a giant mirror.

Where are we going? I asked as Anni set off down the driveway, walking so fast I had to run to keep up. After all the shouting, more bad things had happened, very bad things, and now Anni had a bright smear of blood on her cheek. It was afternoon and black clouds hung low over the trees. *To the town*, she said, lighting a cigarette. She was crying, but only with her eyes. Her face was frozen, like a statue face. Anni and Krysz never took me to the town, except a couple of times in the car with their friend Pawel, who's a baddy, because he has kicked me many times. I had to lie down on the floor in the back, but still, I'd been able to see pretty white houses, fountains, big boats, children playing on some strange, tall machines. If I made a noise, Pawel would turn around and hiss at me, like a tiger. *If anyone sees you, they'll put you in a hole or worse*, they always say. Now, we walked fast along the side of the road until we reached the top of a hill, and from there we could see the beginnings of the town – gloomy church spires and a few redbrick buildings that were taller than all the others. *You'll stay with Fatma for a couple of days*, said Anni. *She owes me. Big time. I need to think*.

Anni talked fast all the way to the town, which was quite a long walk. It wasn't important things she talked about, like what had just happened, but strange stories of when she was a child, before she became like this. I hoped it would begin to rain because it bothers Anni and it doesn't bother me. She'd swear and fall silent if it rained, and inside my head I could laugh a little bit about how her mud-colored hair would fall limp into her eyes and how the black on her eyes would wash away down her face like soot and how her cigarette would keep going out. But it didn't rain. And Anni kept talking like everything might still be okay, but I could see that she was afraid and that she had smoked her special smoke because her eyes were so hard.

In the town we walked along the water promenade and I struggled to keep up with Anni because there were so many things to look at, things I'd never seen before. A huge boat was docked, so big that cars were driving into it in a line. On its side was a photograph of a family laughing in a shiny black car. The children sat smiling behind their parents, probably on nice car seats, holding fizzy drinks, with cameras slung around their necks. Further along the way was a skateboard ramp, but there was nobody there now and a pool of black water had collected at the bottom. I saw an airplane coming in low over the water, and as it passed, its landing wheels came out and I craned my neck all the way back to follow its path, but Anni yanked my arm hard and hissed in my ear, *Come!* I also counted nine dogs and they all looked nice and funny, with open mouths, long tongues and kind eyes, but none of them were as nice as Baby. Baby was me and Moffa's dog.

Fatma's house was a flat on the seventh floor of a gray building. It was noisy at her house, because there were many children. Anni waited for a bit after we arrived, and spoke quietly with Fatma in the kitchen, which really was just a bare room with a microwave and a sink full of plates and pans. *Okay, bye, then,* she said, turning away from me so quickly she was out the door before I had said *bye* back. A boy who looked a couple of years older than me came over to where I stood, and smiled. He had a narrow face and a long skull with dense black curls. *Abdi,* he said, and pointed to his chest. *Tobias,* I whispered, and he smiled and I couldn't stop looking at his teeth because they were very white and all perfectly in line with each other, not like Anni's brown half-teeth, or Krysz's yellow ones. Maybe he knew that I didn't want to talk, or maybe he even knew that I had almost never spoken to anyone besides Anni and Krysz and Moffa, or maybe Abdi didn't like talking much either, anyway we sat down on the bottom bunk bed and played a football game. I had never played before and it made me really happy but really angry in a way, too. I had seen TVs before, because although we didn't have one in Østerøysvingen 8, we had one in the house before then, and in the Poland-house, and at Moffa's house. Most of the things I know about people, I have learned from TVs.

In the room with Abdi and me were his brothers and sisters, or maybe some of them were cousins, because I don't think one lady can have that many children. I counted eleven, and they sat all around us – on the floor in front of the television, on the upper bunk, one on the window sill, watching us play the game. Abdi looked like the oldest one, but then I noticed two girls sitting on the floor by the door, reading, wearing purple headscarves and round glasses, and they looked older than Abdi. Occasionally the smaller children got up and walked out of the room and came back after a while. Many of the small ones had on T-shirts and only nappies, the kind you pull on like underpants. They all had the same dark skin, narrow faces and long skulls like Abdi, and they seemed to smile a lot. They all looked so much like Fatma, it was almost like one big person had been divided into many small bodies.

After a while, Fatma came in with a tray of white bread rolls. We all had one, and when the tray was empty she came back with a new tray of chopped carrots and very small tomatoes I had never seen before, not even on television. When that tray was empty, she came back with a new one, this one heaped full of potato crisps and cookies. I wished I could live with them in that flat. Maybe that was what Anni had arranged?

It was very late by the time the flat quietened down. I could see the glow of the moon high on the sky, behind a thin cloud. I was lying next to Abdi on the bottom bunk, and at our feet lay another boy, a younger brother, curled into a ball. Fatma came in and turned off the lights and she gave me a really big smile and I could see in her eyes that she felt sorry for me, and that was nice but it also made me angry. I prayed in the night that I could stay there with them and I almost managed to convince myself that that was what Anni had arranged, because if you already have eleven children, you really might as well have twelve.

When I woke the next morning, Abdi and the two girls with purple headscarves and at least another couple of the children had gone. *School*, said Fatma and smiled that kind smile again. *Soon you will go to school, too*, she said, and put a steaming bowl of something down on the table in front of me. My heart shuddered. School. I wanted to ask her questions like: *Can I live here? Where is Anni? Is Anni coming back? Have they found Krysz? Why did you say I will go to school? How can someone like me go to school?* Instead I said nothing, because if you ask too many questions people will know that you know nothing. If you don't say anything, they don't know what you know. *Will you help me here today?* asked Fatma, and I nodded, because what else could I do? I ate the bowl of sweet, watery porridge with bits of chicken floating in it, and it was nicer than it sounds. After breakfast, I helped Fatma to iron some sheets and then some curtains, holding the edges up and off the apartment's floor, which was covered in small bits of food, bits of children's plastic toys and balls of dust, while she ironed.

We bathed three of the small boys and she sang to them in another language while running a sponge across their thin backs. Their ribs showed through their skin, and their fingernails were long. They stared at me and splashed in the shallow water and wailed when they had to come back up. This reminded me of how Moffa used to bathe me in a birch-wood tub outside on the lawn overlooking the lake every evening in summer, singing *Kaptein Sabeltann*'s pirate song in a funny voice while swatting at buzzing swarms of mosquitoes, tickling me with the coarse old sponge tied to a stick from the apple tree.

Fatma gave me a plate of pasta with ketchup and peas, and I sat on the bunk and played the football game alone while the small children napped. Then Abdi and the older children came back from school and we played the game together again.

For two or maybe three days it was like that. The other big kids went to school, but I stayed in the apartment with Fatma and helped her. I asked her how she knew Anni and she said, *Anni and me used to live together in Karlstad*. I never knew Anni had lived in Karlstad, but I guess I never knew anything about her before I knew her anyway. I asked her why she owed Anni big-time and she looked down at her own hands peeling carrots and said in a very soft voice, *Because Anni and Krysz helped me and my children across the border to Norway.*

Today is Tuesday, and after I heard the church bells from the church across the road ring five, Fatma came into the room and said, *Yamal, you have to get ready for swim club.* I told her I had to go, too, because I also have swimming club on Tuesday, even though it's not the same group as Yamal. I know this because it's the only time I have to be somewhere, and Anni says I'm really bloody lucky to go there. Fatma said I couldn't go to swim club. It made me really sad and then she said, *Okay, you can go, but I'm going to tell Anni she has to get you from there.* I asked, *Can't I come back here?* but Fatma shook her head and picked up one of the small boys, who screamed and cried. Outside on the street, walking through really hard rain with Yamal, I regretted saying I wanted to go to swim club. I wanted to stay in the warm flat with all the children. The rain is still coming down now; it's washing down and across the big windows here at the swimming pool. I'm shivering. I don't want to jump into the water from the green board. I look across the pool to where some parents are sitting, but of course there is nobody I know. A woman is staring at me, and I quickly look away, so used to trying to not be seen. *If anyone sees you, they'll shoot you or put you in a small, black hole...* Before we left the apartment, Fatma handed me a plastic bag with a frayed old towel and some swimming shorts with Batman on them. *Did Anni say she will pick me up?* I asked and she smiled and put a hand on my shoulder. *Don't worry*, she said, in her careful, strange Norwegian. *I've sent her three messages. She'll be there.*

*

The water in the shower is amazing – fast-flowing and properly hot. I stay under the stream for a long while, trying to make a plan for what to do next. I suppose I could just wander back down to the town with Yamal and go back to the flat with him as though that's what Fatma told me to do. But she didn't. The last thing she said to me before she shut the door behind us earlier was: *Just wait*. I know what's going to happen next. Anni will come and get me. She has to, eventually. When I stayed at Fatma's, maybe Anni went and found some money so she could get her hit, and maybe she made a good plan. Getting hits is what Anni and Krysz want. When they have money and can get their hits, they are as nice as anybody else. Anni sometimes tells me stories of when she was little and she lived on a farm and she knew how to speak to horses. *For real*, she'd always add, as though I didn't believe her. Krysz sometimes tells me about when he was little, too, and how he and his friends used to hunt in deep forests and fish in wild rivers, but I'm not sure that this is true because I've been to the house where Krysz was a child, and I lived there, even, and it's just a normal little house with lots of other houses around it in a city, and I never saw a forest or a river at all.

Yamal has gone when I come back out to the changing rooms. It's horrible, having to put my rained-on clothes back on – my jeans are so wet I have to try three times before I manage to pull them over my knees, and so cold that they make me shake with it. I go out into the reception and sit down on a bench. The only sounds are the tap-tap from the reception lady's keyboard and the falling rain outside. *Is it your mummy or your daddy who's picking you up?* asks the reception lady. I shrug and glance around, as though Anni might be standing somewhere, quietly waiting for me. *I've tried calling the number*, she says.

It's so wet out there. After a while, a lady and a little girl appear. They stand waiting, and the woman seems annoyed, looking down the hall towards the changing rooms, out through the glass doors to the dark, wet parking lot, and back down the hall. I feel her eyes on me and I imagine looking up at her, just staring at her face, how she'd probably be shocked. Krysz once said I have the ability to look right through people.

Another little girl appears, with bouncy blonde hair and nice clothes, like she is on TV to sell something, and the mother sighs heavily and pulls her towards the door. When they've left, the reception lady looks up, sees me still sitting there and lets out a big sigh, too, and half runs over to the double doors. *Cecilia*, she shouts into the loud rainstorm. *Cecilia!* I hear the woman and her girls come back into the hall, whispering with the reception lady. I keep my eyes trained to the floor, to where my dripping hair has made a pool on the brown tiles, like the rainwater at the bottom of the skateboard ramp, and focus all I can on that name. *Cecilia*. I know this name.

CHAPTER 4

IF MY LIFE were a Hollywood movie, then Johan would be the one-dimensional, classic male lead of the high-school movie genre; the wealthy, good-looking, sporty guy who also loves puppies. He just can't help it; he's inherently decent. Perhaps it has something to do with the fact that he was raised in this sweet and safe little town by wealthy, good-looking, sporty parents who love puppies and who donate substantial amounts to charity and are still happily married forty years later. He's by no means perfect, but his imperfections are of the rather innocent type; toilet seat up, cycling shorts flung on the floor, an occasional belch in my presence, insisting on a couple of drunken weekends a year away with his buddies, too many evenings spent at the gym, not liking oysters and whistling in the car.

We've known each other since childhood, and I remember him as the older, floppy-haired boy up the road who was always nice to us little rope-skipping girls. He used to play football on the street with his brother and friends and sometimes we little girls would be allowed to join in. Once, I tripped over and grazed my knee, and Johan scooped me up rather graciously and carried me all the way into my house, delivering me onto the sofa and into the care of my impressed mother. It can't have been more than a minute, but I never forgot that episode; the feeling of complete security as he carried me, the taste of tears at the back of my throat, his face worried, sweaty at the hairline, my throbbing knee and the scent of freshly shorn grass on the evening air.

When he became a father, Johan continued in the same vein, not afraid to adopt all the Scandinavian stereotypes for modern fatherhood; he practically breastfed. He strolled around Sandefjord proudly with Nicoline, and then Hermine, in their pink strollers, expertly feeding and burping and changing them. He got up in the night and walked around the dark house in circles, holding a little girl carefully, his lower arm pressing gently against a sore tummy, while Mommy slept, night after night. He complimented me and made me feel loved when I hated myself and my crumbling, chubby, post-baby body. He came to prenatal couples' yoga and sat there straight-faced and serious while the other dads-to-be stared awkwardly down at their meaty hands and hairy winter legs bared to the world.

All in all, Johan is a pretty okay man. That doesn't mean I don't get angry with him sometimes. Some people might even say I get disproportionately angry with him a disproportionate amount, but I genuinely believe men need to meet some resistance, or they get bored. They need to not entirely know where they've got you, even whether they've truly got you at all. Build them up and shower them with so much sex and affection that they become completely obsessed with you, and then tear them down. Boom. Hooked. Repeat. This strategy has certainly worked for me – I have been married to the most desirable man in Sandefjord for twelve years now, and he could have had anybody.

I've been angry with Johan so many times and for so many different reasons, but I haven't ever been angry like *this* before; not with him nor with anybody else, ever. In the car on the way home, nobody speaks. We've left my car at the school and are returning home in Johan's Tesla together, which Johan insisted on as a display of unity. Tobias is in the back seat. I clench and unclench my fists so hard I leave vivid red marks on my skin. This isn't normal anger, I recognize that; it is true fury, the kind when you might actually murder someone. Images flit through my mind of clawing at eyes, ripping hair from skulls, sinking knives into soft bellies, kicking faces to a pulp. I want to kill Johan. I want to scream, but I know that if I open my mouth, not a sound will come. He stops at a red light, smiles reassuringly at Tobias in the rearview mirror, and I want to bolt from the car, running down the near-empty streets, shrieking and howling.

'We believe the best thing to do would be to take Tobias home with you now,' said Vera Jensrud in her pedagogical, soothing voice, after Johan had thanked them (thanked them!) for asking us to take this kid in. 'And then this afternoon, Laila and a colleague will come to your house and you can work out a plan together. They will have a quick chat with Tobias as well, and then in the next few days we'll schedule in some in-depth assessments.'

'Should he be in school?' asked Johan, his face still bright with the prospect of lending himself to such a good cause as a lost, poor little boy.

'Yes, of course,' said Laila Fucking Engebretsen. 'But as he'll be registered on your address in the short term, he will no longer be in the catchment area of this particular school, so he'll attend your local school. I'm thinking that Monday would be a good day to start for him, that way he has a couple of days and a weekend to acclimatize to his new surroundings.'

'Oh, good. Our daughters will be able to help him settle in, and they can all walk to school together. They'll be delighted that we are going to host Tobias,' said Johan, and I shot him an ice-cold glance, but modified it a little when I realized Vera and Laila were both looking at me carefully.

'Of course, we can give you some time to discuss this between yourselves…' Laila said. 'It is a big decision, and it's really important that you are both on board. It would be traumatizing for Tobias to have to move twice while we attempt to solve his long-term plan.'

'Yes,' I said, at the exact same time as Johan said, 'No, I think we agree on this, Cecilia?' In the end, Vera ushered us into a small office across the hall from the one we'd been sitting in, and as soon as the door shut, I turned to Johan, who, judging from his relaxed and open facial expression, had not expected my fury.

'Are you out of your fucking mind?'

'What?'

'Are you completely fucking crazy, is what I'm asking.'

'Cecilia… what… what are you talking about?'

'You do understand that we will not, under any circumstances, host that kid in *our* house?'

'Why ever not?'

'Why not? Please tell me you're joking? Why *not*?' I wanted to shout, but was obviously aware of the social worker and police across the hall, so I made do with a loud hiss and grasped Johan's arm, digging my nails painfully into his flesh. Then he did something that surprised me, for once in his life. He grabbed my hand off his arm and held it hard to my side, and forced me to meet his eyes.

'Listen to me. You're a bitch. You can be so much more than that, and you know I love you dearly, but sometimes you really are a bitch. Cecilia, this is the right thing to do. For God's sake, imagine if it was your own kid. Stranded somewhere, for whatever reason, completely at the mercy of the kindness of strangers. Wouldn't you want someone kind to take them in and help them until we could be found?'

'This would never happen to my children. They're from a good family,' I said, but heard my voice falter as I spoke. Bad things can happen in good families, I know all too well. Truth is, I'm afraid. I'm terrified of what this could do to us as a family. And especially now, when I've finally arrived at a point where a harmonious family life seemed within reach.

'There are no such things as good or bad families, Cecilia, and least of all good or bad children. He's a little kid, honey. Think about how he must feel. Do you really think it will cost us so much to take him in for a short while?'

'I'm extremely stressed at the moment. You clearly don't understand how much pressure I'm under! It's more work for me. We don't even have an au pair now!'

'Honey, what kind of pressure? I mean, I know you're busy with the kids, but you only work part-time…'

'Only? Are you fucking kidding me?'

'I didn't mean it like that, baby, you know that…'

'I need help, Johan! I work around the clock trying to keep things together for the girls at home, as well as working. You're always on a plane or at the office.'

'If that's what you are worried about, let's just get a new au pair?'

'It's not enough to just get a new au pair. I'm not in a position to give an abandoned child what he needs.'

'You're an incredible mother. Give yourself some credit. You're always talking yourself down; it's like you don't think you're good enough. I wish you could see what everyone else sees.'

'Johan—'

'Cecilia. Think about *him*. In there, alone. We can help him, we really can. Stop obsessing over details, and just… let your heart do the rest.'

I glared at my husband and walked out of the room and back into Vera Jensrud's office, giving the three people waiting a cool smile. 'Very well,' I said, trying and failing to keep the slight tremble out of my voice. 'We will have Tobias until you find his parents or long-term foster care. How long do you imagine it would take to find foster parents, if that's what it comes to?'

'As we mentioned, due to the migration crisis, we are terribly short of foster families at the moment, but in a case as grave as this, we'd hope to have him placed in a couple of months at the longest.'

*

'Johan, can you please drop me here?' I say as we approach Kilen. I can see my modern office building at the water's edge from here.

'What? We're heading home.'

'I realized that I need to get some papers from the office. It won't take that long – maybe half an hour. Then I'll walk back up to the school and pick up my car.'

'Cecilia,' says Johan, a thin vein pulsing on the side of his head. He gently indicates to the back seat with his eyes. 'Don't you think you should…'

'Here would be great,' I say as we reach the roundabout where we go right for my office or straight across for home. I reach over fast and flick Johan's indicator to the right. He looks angry, but pulls over.

It begins raining again as I walk away from the car, and I stop for a moment and look up at dark, swirling clouds, letting fat drops slap my face. What's really shocking is that Johan seems to be angry with *me* for not wanting to let some kid into our family home. I mean, I empathize as much as the next person, but my consideration is obviously more for my own family and its harmony. I won't let anything threaten it; I never have.

When I reach the door to my office, I change my mind and turn back around. I don't really need anything from here; what I need is some time alone. Rain is falling heavily now, and my mind goes to those last few moments last night, when I walked Hermine and Nicoline out into the wet parking lot, when I still didn't know of the little boy's plight, when he was still someone else's problem. I let the rain slick my hair to my scalp and run down my face, and I head towards the town center. What I really want is a drink; a huge glass of white wine, then another, and another. Obviously that isn't an option as I'll be entertaining a couple of fucking social workers for hours on end in my house this afternoon, and it would hardly be advantageous if I stank of alcohol. My thoughts go to those years when Johan and I were students in Paris, how we used to make weekends extra fun with a line or two of coke. Right now, I would give anything for that clear-headed, in-control feeling, but how on earth would I go about finding someone to sell me cocaine in little old Sandefjord? I glance around the square outside the shopping center, but there's no one here; even the couple of old drunks who seemed to be permanent fixtures have given up in this rain. The one person I can possibly think of who might be able to get some is the one person I can't ask – typical. I decide on retail therapy instead and head towards Sandefjord's best ladies' boutique.

I may look like a drowned rat, but the shop assistants know very well who I am and that I have money to spend. I buy a Missoni throw like the one I already have, but with a metallic sheen. I also buy a pair of white mock-croc Hunter boots, and a black wool dress by Malene Birger. Clutching the bags, I cross the square and am looking around for a taxi, when someone shouts my name. I turn and see a woman in her fifties I vaguely recognize as the receptionist at the swimming pool, cowering from the rain underneath a shop awning. This is the stupid bitch who put me in this situation in the first place. I walk over to her and raise an eyebrow, waiting for her to speak – she doesn't even get a hello from me.

'Hi, Cecilia,' she says, smiling pleasantly, showing off a charming slick of coral lipstick on her teeth. Again, she is wearing something ridiculous – an oversized trench coat with drenched yellow faux fur, making her look like some freak animal. 'I hope everything was okay with the little boy, ah, Tobias, yesterday?'

I stare at her.

'Since when has Tobias been coming to the club?' I ask, coolly.

'Oh, uh, I think yesterday was the third or fourth time.'

'And you've met his parents, presumably?'

Fat chin quivering, bland blue eyes dropping from mine to the puddles on the ground. 'Well, yesterday he arrived with Yamal, another of the boys in the club. You probably know him.'

'No, I don't.'

'Right. The other couple of times he's arrived alone, but one time he was picked up by a woman.'

'His mother?'

'I would guess so.'

'What did she look like?'

The receptionist looks at me strangely for a moment, like I'm asking something very surprising. 'Is everything okay, Cecilia? You seem a bit—'

'I asked you a question. What did this woman look like?'

Blink, blink. Mouth opening and shutting, as if thinking requires some kind of facial effort. 'Well, she had shoulder-length light brown hair and was fairly tall, I suppose...'

'Did she look like a junkie?'

'Excuse me?'

'Did she look homeless, or like a drug addict?'

'No... Well, not homeless exactly. She was a little shabby, I suppose. She asked for a glass of water and when I gave it to her she smiled slightly and I noticed that her teeth were very decayed. Quite unusually so, áctually.'

'Right.'

'Why? Do you know her? Was she there when you dropped off the boy?'

I laugh incredulously, right in her face, then walk back into the rain, laughing some more at the thought of her still standing there, stunned, staring at me walking away from her. My heart is pounding so hard I hear it over the sound of the heavy rain. Could it be... ? *No*, I say to myself. *It isn't possible.* And yet. I run through the park, holding the huge shopping bag to my chest because its cardboard is disintegrating in the rain, and my laughter becomes sobs. I sit a moment on a bench at the edge of the park, by the sea, tilting my head back so that my tears run with the rain, listening to the distant clunk and whirr of a harbor crane. I'm overwhelmed by a sensation of the past as a slithering snake sneaking up on me, ready to unleash its poison on this immaculate life I've fought so hard for.

Next to the ferry terminal is a slightly shabby sports bar I've never been to, but seen from the car. I make my way there slowly, stunned, trying to think. I'm wrong. I *have* to be wrong. The bar is empty. I order a vodka shot, then another, watched by the bemused, tattooed barman. To hell with the social workers; after all, what is mouthwash for?

'My dog died,' I say as he wipes down a shelf above me, briefly exposing a taut, intricately inked stomach, and he nods.

'Sorry,' he says. 'That's really shit.' I stare at my hands, cradling the empty shot glass, not even attempting to stop the tears that drop from my eyes onto the slick, polished wood of the bar. I close my eyes for a very long time, and the images that rush at me are the ones I spend my life staving off. Then, a vague plan begins to form in my mind. I take my phone out, tapping in the number I know by heart, but haven't stored in my contacts.

*

It's a brisk walk home, and the combination of the warm vodka in my stomach and the rushing rain calms me down sufficiently to see more clearly. Maybe this won't be the end of the world. The kid will just stay a few weeks, and then everything will go back to normal. Maybe his presence won't trigger anything at all; maybe it won't dislodge those huge, black boulders inside of me and send them crashing onto this life I've managed to preserve against some hefty odds. Maybe I can just be kind to him and do my best to make him comfortable during his stay. He is, after all, just a small, lost boy, and he doesn't have the power to bring the past back out into the light. I have to believe that.

Johan meets me at the door. We both feel bad, and we fall into an awkward embrace across lines of rain boots and bags in the hallway. He moves in to kiss me but I turn away slightly – I'm afraid he'll smell the vodka on my breath in spite of the chewing gum.

'I'm sorry,' I say, and he says it at the exact same time. We both smile, tiredly.

'I've put Tobias in the blue room next to Nicoline, okay?'

'Okay.'

'I was thinking I might head into town and pick up a few things for him,' says Johan.

'Oh,' I say. I want to tell him that I need him here, that I'm afraid of being alone with the strange boy, of what this all means. But how do we ever tell anyone that we need them? I want him to know that inside of me there is a gash so deep and so black that it holds me in a perennial iron grip of anxiety and terror, and that it has been like that for me for a very long time. I want to tell him of that darkness, of all the nights spent awake, paralyzed with fear and regret, of the sensation of always walking atop the thinnest of glass floors laid across a tremendous abyss, but how could I? He wouldn't want me then. Perfect Johan loves perfect Cecilia, that's just how it is. Instead I pull out the Missoni throw and hold it up for him to see.

'Hey,' he says, and pulls me close. 'Why don't you sit down on the sofa with a nice cup of tea? I'll take Tobias with me to the shops; he might want to choose some stuff himself.'

*

I must have fallen asleep, because when I wake, the rain has let up. I feel disoriented, like I'm still in a dream. I can hear Johan's and Tobias's voices from upstairs. I check my phone, and it's full of missed calls and messages from clients I've been neglecting. I just can't face talking to Rita Hansen about her curtains today, or Emilie Herbert about the fact that her husband now basically hates their home after I convinced her to paint everything moss-green. I need to go get my car, too, but can't face getting up from the sofa just yet. I close my eyes again, and then I remember my dream, which wasn't really a dream at all, but a memory.

A train platform in rural Normandy, fifteen years ago: a group of five young Norwegian backpackers, about to start the long trip home after a summer spent hitchhiking around France. The sharp morning sun throwing dappled shadows onto the field beyond the train tracks, where cows grazed peacefully. Aleksander and Maja sat close together, sharing a cigarette, looking up at the distant rumbling sound of the train arriving. Julian listened to music on his Discman, staring at his feet, probably missing the French girl he'd just had to leave behind in Brittany. Johan sitting next to me, close to the edge of the platform, watching the steely glint of the locomotive as it rounded the bend ahead. All summer, and for several years before that moment, he had tried to get me to be interested in him, not realizing that I loved him and always had. He wasn't a pushy boy, and my rebuffs were gentle but firm. It's all about the timing, and I knew that even then, at nineteen. You've got to make them want you desperately before you give in. Aleksander and Maja stood up and began to gather their backpacks. Julian placed the headphones around his neck and smiled at us. I knew the repercussions of what I was about to say, and felt a sudden clutch of my heart, like a quick, dangerous hand.

I lit another cigarette with the new silver lighter inlaid with jade stones, the one I'd stolen in a bar in La Rochelle. The others stared at me uncomprehendingly. *But... the train...* It had stopped now and stood impatiently wheezing as the few passengers climbed on board. *I'm staying here*, I said, turning to Johan, who already had one foot on the lowest rung of the boarding steps, with my most dazzling smile. He stared at me with an open mouth, running through his options. He was about to go to university, his parents would kill him, we were about to run out of money… *Stay with me*, I said. Aleksander, Maja and Julian hung out of the open window of the carriage, staring, as if they knew that they were witnessing something life-changing and there was no point in saying anything. Johan stepped back onto the platform and the door immediately clanged shut behind him. He stood completely still, carrying his weighty backpack, watching me the way you would a creature who could easily kill you, and I burst out laughing at the craziness of the moment, of the missed train, my suddenly wild heart, the storm clouds gathering in the distance, the boy in front of me. I took both of his hands in mine as the train pulled away, and they were soft and warm, like a child's. *Hey*, I said, and as he looked at me, he started laughing, too, and then we were kissing like crazy, and laughing again, and kissing.

CHAPTER 5

Nine days later

Johan is sitting by the side of the bed when I wake, and it's still pitch-black dark outside. My mind darts wildly to scenarios of death. My mother? One of the girls? My mind is slow, achy.

'What is it?' I whisper, gripped by fear. 'What time is it?'

'It's just gone five a.m. The police just called.'

'Jesus. What the hell is going on?'

'A body has been found. Floating. In Kilen, late last night.'

'Floating? In the water?' I sit up fast.

'Yes.'

'They're still waiting for definite identification, but the police are working on the theory that it's Tobias's mother.'

'His mother?' My voice comes out shrill and strange in the hushed, soft darkness.

'Yes.'

'Why would they think that?'

'Apparently it's someone known to the police. A drug addict, maybe, or a petty criminal—'

'There aren't any criminals in Sandefjord!' Even as I say it, I realize how dumb I sound.

'Cecilia—'

'But they'd know if someone like that had a child?'

Johan looks at me, seemingly puzzled at my reaction. 'Cecilia, listen. They're... they're saying it's possibly... murder.'

'Murder? In Sandefjord? But... but that's not possible. It isn't necessarily murder just because someone is found floating in water, they could have fallen in, or jumped in, or...'

'Cecilia.' Johan is looking at me strangely. I stop talking. 'Don't breathe a word to Tobias until we know for sure, okay?'

Johan pulls me close, and it's a relief to bury my face in the soft fabric of his flannel pajamas so I don't have to censor my facial expressions as dense webs of thoughts spread out in my tired mind, fading in and out of each other. A woman dead – no, *murdered* – in Sandefjord. I see her, face down in the murky harbor water, bloated calves bobbing on the surface like discarded bottles, hair spread out, reaching, moving, like the stinging threads of a jellyfish, hands immobile and set forever in a half grip. The boy still here, and still no clues as to his background, until now... I see his little face, too; the way he seems to have acquired an ability to merge into any background like a chameleon so you entirely forget he's even there, watching, listening. I see his eyes, alert and quick like a soldier's, sad like nothing I've ever seen before, and his small hands, which he always keeps awkwardly pressed to his sides. He's stirring something in me, this boy, something I daren't even touch upon; his very presence threatens to unleash a wave of grief and regret so huge it would knock me down forever if I don't keep suppressing it at any cost. A small cry escapes me, a howl shooting up and out of me into Johan's flannel pajamas, and he pulls back and looks at me gently.

'Hey... hey, are you okay? It's been a little much for you recently, hasn't it?' I nod, and he pulls me close again, stroking my hair and kissing my hand, which he's clutching tight in his own. The last week has been the worst of my life. I haven't even stopped by the office – every moment of every day has been consumed by everything that is going on in my family, and now… this. My head hurts, and so does my hand, and I pull it from Johan's grip and slip it into my nightgown, above my heart. It's racing. It would be so easy now, in the hushed, black, early morning, to whisper the things I haven't told Johan into his ear. The things I've done. Maybe he'd keep holding me; maybe he'd still love me and stay with me… But maybe not. Most likely not. I try to control myself, but I'm sobbing silently now; all I can see is her, there in the harbor, floating on still, cold water. How could she have ended up there, in the merciless, freezing sea?

'Shhh, baby,' he whispers, lowering me gently back into the bed and lying down behind me in spoons. 'Shhhh…'

*

Last weekend, we took Tobias and the girls to visit my mother. She lives in the house where I grew up; a large waterfront villa on the southern tip of Vesterøya, the same peninsula we now live on, but closer to town. Like ours, it's a prestigious home, though definitely more old-school. From the gardens you can see all the way to Hvaler on a clear day, and when I was little, I loved to watch the boats cross back and forth, breaking the sea's steely surface in straight lines, churning up frothy wakes.

The girls sat silently, answering my mother's questions in monosyllables, barely glancing up from their iPads, until I became annoyed and took the screens away and made them go outside to play, even though it was cold and windy. I ushered Tobias outside with them and I watched from inside the house as Nicoline and Hermine began throwing fallen leaves at each other before collapsing on the ground in fits of laughter, wrestling, until Hermine's mittened pink hand shot up in surrender. Tobias didn't join the game, or even glance at the girls, though they were squealing and laughing; his eyes were trained firmly on the surging, unpredictable waves of Skagerak strait, an unreadable expression on his face. I noticed again how dark-skinned he is compared to the average Norwegian kid; he could easily pass for half-Indian, or perhaps Brazilian, or maybe... Cuban. His hair was ruffled by the wind and his cheeks already looked slightly chubbier and healthier than when he came to us. Watching him looking out to sea, I felt that deep, unsettled feeling again, and forced myself to look away from him, and stared down at my teacake instead, until I felt my mother's eyes on me.

'Is everything okay, Cecilia?' she asked.

'Yes. I'm just... a bit tired.'

'You seem preoccupied. It must be a big change for you all to have the boy come and live with you.' My heart clenched in my chest. I rubbed my neck; it was hurting where the collar of my sweater rubbed against it. I didn't want to be there, making small talk. I wanted to run, past the children, towards the lighthouse, into the crashing waves.

'Yes, well, for Cecilia it has been quite difficult, particularly,' Johan answered before I had a chance to speak. 'She does do most of the day-to-day stuff around the house because I'm away so much, and also, well, you know how sensitive she is.'

'Sensitive?' I asked, and again my voice sounded shriller and louder than I intended.

'Kindhearted,' continued Johan, after a careful pause. 'I know how much Tobias's plight unsettles and touches you, honey.'

'A beautiful boy,' said my mother, looking out the window to where he still stood, immobile. 'The poor, poor child. What wretched parents could leave a little boy behind?'

'I'm going to go and check on him,' I said, but when I reached the double doors that open up into the garden, it felt as though they couldn't be opened, that I didn't possess the strength needed to slide them apart, that a membrane separated me from the world in which this little boy existed. I turned around and saw that Johan and my mother were speaking intently, murmuring, probably about me and what a crazy lady I'd been this week. I could just make out Nicoline and Hermine down on the beach, almost at the lighthouse, running fast in their rain boots, darting in and out of licking waves. Such fiery children, those two; either best friends or sworn enemies prone to violence and screamed abuse.

I placed my hand on the door handle and mobilized all my strength to walk out there, in the wind, to him.

'Hey, you,' I said, crouching down on the hard, cool ground next to him, trying to get him to look at me, but his eyes stayed firmly on the gray waves. 'Do you want to come back inside with me? We could play a game or something.' No reaction. 'Do you know Snakes and Ladders?' It was like speaking to a statue; he just stood there, immobile. 'Tobias,' I said, surprising myself with what I was about to tell him, even trying to stop myself from going on, but finding I couldn't. 'When I was a little girl, I lived in this house. It was a wonderful place to grow up, and I used to do what my girls are doing right now, over there, look.' I paused, and realized I hadn't ever told my own children this. 'I loved the beach, and the garden, and the little woods over there. I'm an only child, and I used to invent friends I'd play with for hours, and they were completely real to me. I loved the house, too, but inside, it was sometimes difficult. My parents weren't happy with each other and they used to scream so loudly I'd wake up in the night from it. Other times they wouldn't speak to each other at all for many days, maybe they thought I didn't notice because I was little, but of course I did. Then, when I was only a little older than you, one day my father just disappeared. Gone. And he never came back.' Tobias turned slowly and looked at me. I took his hand, but he immediately pulled it back and held it to his side.

'Where did he go?' he whispered.

'Well, he had met another woman and he went to live with her. It was very difficult for me. I just couldn't understand how anyone could ever leave their child. But now that I'm grown-up, I've come to understand that sometimes people do terrible things when they are in difficult circumstances. I've been so afraid to admit that, Tobias, that people really can do some very bad things without necessarily being bad people. Do you understand?'

Tobias glanced back out at the sea, then towards the girls now running fast towards us, then at me. He nodded briefly. 'Did you never see your father again?'

'I did. When I was grown-up.'

'Are you friends now?'

My eyes were filling with tears and I turned quickly away from him, to the sea, wishing it would rain, so it wouldn't be so obvious that I was crying. 'Yes. Kind of.' A couple of tears escaped and rolled down my cheeks, and I wiped at them fast, about to stand up to go back inside – it was bone-chillingly cold outside and the wind seemed to rush about in circles, easing for a moment, looping and then slamming back into us full-force, but Tobias placed a hand on my shoulder and then leaned into me, putting his thin arms around me in a hug. I was so stunned I didn't immediately know what to do, but I managed to place my hands gingerly on his back and patted him gently. I looked up and saw Johan looking out at us from the window, and there was something in his expression that frightened me; it was as though he was happy and very sad at the same time, and also like he was thinking very hard about something.

*

I wake again just before nine, and Johan has taken all the children to school in the car; it's raining too hard for them to walk. For a long moment I stare at the bleak sky outside, consumed by the uncomfortable feeling that I've forgotten something important, and then this morning suddenly returns to me; Johan by the side of the bed, the impossible news of the murdered woman, the terrible images of her etched on my mind. I sit up fast and look around the room as though I have never seen it before. Already I can feel a void open up inside me, like a black hole that sucks in any constructive thought, any sliver of sanity. How did she end up like that, dead, in the water? I can't stop the vile images of her, bloated and lifeless... I scramble around in the bedside table for my pills and swallow them dry. Four little pills, but will they be enough today?

In less than an hour, I am meeting with an estate agent about a property I'm styling next week for a property magazine. I'm supposed to coherently explain my ideas for the color theme, and present a budget and timeline. How will I be able to string a single sentence together?

Then, at two o'clock I have a meeting with Laila Engebretsen at Sandefjord County social services. Needless to say, I'm feeling rather stressed about this, mostly because if anybody sees me there, they will surely think that there are problems in the Wilborg family, though there most certainly aren't. Rumors travel fast in this town and I certainly don't want a reputation as some kind of child neglecter; we're just not that kind of family. I suppose people have already heard that we are hosting the small, unclaimed boy, and – who knows? – perhaps this will all end up boosting my social profile. It is, after all, a very charitable thing to do. But then again, we're that kind of couple, Johan and I. The thing that worries me the most about looking after Tobias in the short term is that his presence could trigger those very unwelcome memories from the past; he could make me come completely undone, that little boy, and I just *have* to stop it from happening. I take another two pills; I'll probably feel drowsy for much of the day, but whatever it takes, right? I'll obviously leave the car when I go to meet with Laila, anyway – my bronze-colored Range Rover is quite a recognizable vehicle, and I just know what the women in Sandefjord are like: *You'll never guess what... I saw Cecilia Wilborg at social services today, and not for the first time either... Not so flawless after all, apparently, hahahaha...*

Is it every woman's misfortune to feel so judged by other mothers? In Norway we have so much freedom, it's almost restrictive. You can have it all; you can work, you can have children, you can be equal to your partner, but you'd better make sure you're doing all of those things – and doing them perfectly – or you're not good enough. Just don't be too completely perfect, because then we'll take you down. It's endlessly drilled into you that you can be anything you want, anything at all, but what is really being said is: You can be anything you want to be, as long as you want to be just like us. I've heard of mothers who were reported to social services because their child's packed lunch stood out – a chocolate chip cookie instead of the approved liver paté and the authorities come knocking. In this country, there is a formula for child-rearing, and you follow it, or else. I wonder if my own mother felt these pressures. I've never asked her.

I stand up but feel so woozy I have to sit back down on the bed for a moment. I close my eyes and take several deep breaths, but it is as though the airflow meets a wall of resistance at the top of my lungs, and it takes me several attempts to manage to breathe deeper into my stomach like Dr Friele taught me. *Allow yourself to be well, Cecilia*, she always says. But there *she* is again, in my mind; bloated, floating, staring into opaque, cold water... *Stop*, I tell myself. *Stop it*. I don't have to let her into my mind. *Allow yourself to be well*. But she won't go away. I see her ugly face, those brown, crumbling teeth exposed as she smiles menacingly at me, the greasy, limp hair creeping down her back like coils of wet rope. *Stop it*. Raw, thin fingers stained yellow by her roll-ups, held out in front of her, reaching into the black harbor water, no – reaching for me. Her scratchy voice chanting, *Cecilia, Cecilia, Cecilia, got you now, Cecilia*. Did a part of me always know she'd end up like this? God knows I've wished for it, but I've also always known that sometimes one disaster will bring an even bigger disaster, and I have never been able to figure out if she was more dangerous dead or alive. I still don't know if her death is cause for celebration or black panic. A sound breaks through my rushing thoughts and it takes me a while to realize it's my phone, ringing. I pick up, still trying to find a comfortable breathing pattern.

'Cecilia? Are you okay? This is Laila Engebretsen.'

'Oh, hi, Laila. We're, uh, still on for two o'clock presumably?'

'Actually, I'm calling to ask if we could move the meeting to the police station instead.'

'Uh, yes... Sure... Is there any more news?'

'Well, I can't really say over the telephone, but Inspector Ellefsen is ready to brief you at the station. How soon can you be there?'

I hang up and walk into the bathroom. I look at myself in the mirror and have to immediately look away; I look like somebody else. My eyes are haunted and wild, my hair sticks straight up in the front and my mouth is dragging at the sides in an ugly grimace.

I call the estate agent and say we're going to have to rearrange our meeting. I can tell he's annoyed – it's not like this is the first work assignment I've canceled or done half-heartedly in the last month. If I'm not careful, I'll lose all my clients, but maybe that would be a good thing – I am exhausted and stressed beyond imagining.

I splash water on my face over and over, and try to bring forth any thoughts other than the ugly, impossible ones. Johan and me, at the beginning, when everything was okay. When nobody had done terrible things. When there were no disastrous secrets. Walking away from the train station that day, finally, after having watched the train turn the bend in disbelief, holding hands and laughing, going nowhere and everywhere. We sat down at a pizzeria in the village and just kept laughing, holding hands over the table, getting drunk on Calvados and cheap white wine. Yes. These memories do calm me, because they remind me of what it is that I have to preserve in the midst of all this craziness. I go back into the bedroom and rifle through the drawers on Johan's side of the bed – I know he keeps a pen and paper in there. I write down my name, Tobias's and Anni's, trying to see connections or solutions, but after twenty minutes of staring at the paper, the only thing that is completely clear to me is that I need to know whether or not Tobias believes he's Anni's child.

*

Johan is waiting for me in the parking lot of the police station. He looks old, suddenly; his handsome face drawn and pale, new wrinkles carved on his forehead. He keeps running a hand through his hair, which I realize has thinned substantially over the last year, and I take his hand away and hold it in my own as we walk inside. We are met by Laila Engebretsen, Thor Ellefsen and a female officer introduced as Camilla Stensland. This Camilla character looks at me in the strangest of ways, and I'm not sure whether this is because she's very obviously a lesbian with her short hair and masculine air, or whether she has some kind of reason to suspect me of something. What, I can't imagine, but her gaze makes me uncomfortable.

'We had the identity of the dead woman confirmed this morning. She's Annika Lucasson, previously known to the police for some drug offenses, as well as a few break-ins over the past six months.'

I nod gravely, keeping my face completely blank, as though I were listening to the weather report.

'Are you at all familiar with this name?' asks Camilla Stensland.

'Annika Lucasson... No,' says Johan. 'I've never heard of her.'

'Cecilia?' Stensland's small blue eyes, trained on me again.

'No,' I say. 'No. I've never heard that name before either. Is she from Sandefjord?'

'No, she's originally Swedish, but she's been here for the past six months or so. She's received methadone here in Sandefjord since Easter, so we do have some records of her.'

'I see,' I say, keeping my eyes on Ellefsen's chubby fingers held together in a tight clasp, his wedding ring snug in swollen flesh like a string tied hard around the middle of a sausage.

'Did she drown?' asks Johan.

'While she was found in water, we are unable to divulge the cause of death at this time, but I will say the deceased bore some signs of violence. We have not yet found any possible murder weapon.'

I try to take a deep breath, but again, that wall of resistance seems to shut the air out from my lungs and I'm forced to take several noticeably short, strained breaths. Beady blue eyes staring. It might be even worse than I imagined – maybe she met a crazed stranger that dark night and was bludgeoned by a blunt object. Face cracked, bones glinting from underneath red and purple mangled flesh. I try to think if I'd ever imagined Anni's death like that, but I can't remember – I've imagined it in so many ways.

'Excuse me, could you please explain what this unfortunate woman's murder has to do with us, or Tobias?' I ask.

'We believe Annika Lucasson was Tobias's mother.'

'Why do you believe that?' I ask.

'There have been a couple of sightings of her with the boy in the last few days before Tobias was left at the pool,' says Thor Ellefsen. 'It is our theory that she may have hidden him during the time she spent in Norway.'

'But why would she do that?' asks Johan.

'She may have been hiding from a violent ex-partner, or been afraid that social services would take the child due to her drug addiction.'

'Which you would have done, and rightfully so,' Johan says. Laila Engebretsen nods. 'But why would anyone want to kill her?'

'Well, that's what we need to find out. Annika was believed to be in a relationship with a Polish man named Krysztof Mazur, also well known to the police for several counts of theft as well as drug-dealing offenses.'

'And have you arrested him?' I ask.

'It would seem that Mr Mazur left the country from Larvik on the Denmark-bound ferry on October twenty-first, four days after Tobias was left at the pool,' says Camilla Stensland. 'We've found CCTV footage showing his car. We do not believe that's a coincidence.'

'For… for how long has Annika Lucasson been dead?' I ask, my voice shaking now.

'We believe she has been dead and in the water for several days, judging by the state of her body when she was found last night.'

'So…'

'So, Krysztof Mazur may have dumped her there, and then left the country. Or he might have worked with an accomplice who placed her in the water after Mazur fled,' says Camilla Stensland. Beady blue eyes, hard on me.

'Which leads us to why it was so important that we could speak with you two as soon as possible,' says Laila Engebretsen, smiling her sad, pedagogical smile again. I want to hit her, and run out of this stuffy room, out into the fine drizzle sweeping across Sandefjord like a cool curtain of ash. 'From our conversations in the last week, it seems that Tobias is doing as well as can be expected and has settled well into your family, which is a most reassuring thing. Before the new developments with Annika Lucasson, it was our intention to just leave him be as much as possible, while we work behind the scenes, trying to uncover what his circumstances actually are, but now we will of course have to assist the police investigation, and that will mean speaking with Tobias.'

'Yes, of course,' says Johan.

'You know what? I just don't think that is a good idea,' I blurt out, and everyone turns to look at me. 'I mean… sure, eventually. But right away? This child is severely traumatized, barely speaks a word to Johan or me, and I just don't think that he should be subjected to intensive questioning at this time…'

Camilla Stensland interrupts me gently. 'We appreciate your concern for Tobias, but you can rest assured that any conversation with the child will be conducted with a child psychiatrist and a representative from social services present.'

'Strangers.'

'Excuse me?'

'Strangers to Tobias.'

'Tobias is the only person who can give us some information about Annika Lucasson and Krysztof Mazur. He would know who they know, and give us invaluable information about what has happened here,' continues Stensland. Johan nods, and takes my hand beneath the table. I remove it.

'First of all, we need to establish whether the child really is related to Lucasson. Today, after school, we need you to take Tobias to the doctor. He will take a blood sample so that we can run a DNA profile, as well as give him a general examination, something we would have scheduled for him anyway,' says Laila Engebretsen.

'What if he isn't Lucasson's child?' I ask.

'We are, due to a couple of very reliable sources, fairly certain he is.'

'But if he isn't?' Laila Engebretsen and Camilla Stensland exchange a fleeting glance here.

'There is, of course, the possibility that Tobias was in the care of Annika Lucasson without being biologically related to her,' says Thor Ellefsen, running a large finger across his russet mustache. 'He could have been snatched by her and Mazur. Or they could have been looking after him for someone, for whatever reason.'

'But who would leave their child in the care of a couple of criminal heroin addicts?' asks Johan, the telltale red splotches of indignation flaring up on his neck and face.

'Exactly,' says Stensland. We all sit in silence for a moment, pondering the implications of Anni's death and her possible connection to Tobias.

'Fuck,' says Johan, and everyone nods seriously. Finally we stand when Ellefsen stands, and make final arrangements for a doctor's visit this afternoon, and a meeting with Laila Engebretsen tomorrow afternoon, followed by police and the child psychiatrist. We walk back outside to the parking lot, and the drizzle has momentarily let up, exposing a small section of pale blue sky among bulbous, fast-moving black clouds. I look at Johan, who wears the stunned expression of someone who has just been woken up in the middle of the night. He shakes his head slowly, running a hand through his hair again, and this time I can't be bothered to stop him.

'Fuck,' he whispers, twice.

CHAPTER 6

SOME PEOPLE HAVE only ever lived in one house. *What's your house like?* The biggest one, Nicoline, asked me the day after I came here. *Which one?* I asked, and only when both she and Hermine looked up from their iPads to stare did I realize that they thought it was strange that I have lived in many different houses. But only one is home. *It's in the middle of a very big forest*, I said, and when I started talking, I could see my home inside my head because I know it better than anywhere else in the world. *It has a big lake full of fish and a field with two brown ponies in it. It is painted red but the paint peels off a bit when it gets hot in the summers. It has a shiny black roof. It has many windows, their sills painted white. The windows are like eyes and at night, when they're all lit, the house looks like a person. I have a big room on the first floor with a handmade carved wood bed. Next to it is a smaller replica of my bed, and on it sleeps Baby. Baby is a dog, but she can talk, and...*

Shut up, said the big sister. *You're a liar*, said the little one.

My room here is small and blue, with a slanted ceiling. Underneath the lowest part of the ceiling stands a too-big bed, and sometimes when I wake in the night, I sit up too fast and then I bang my head on the ceiling. I wake often. It's so quiet here. I like to switch on the lights in the night, the way

I have done my whole life, and sit on the floor and draw. The man gave me some drawing pencils and some paper, but a couple of days after I came here to stay, the very tall woman who smiles like she is going to cry soon came to talk to me, and when she left, she took away all the drawings I'd made. Without asking me. *I'll take these*, she said, and the man who lives here didn't say anything. So now I have to draw everything again.

I draw the pictures that hung on the wall in the Poland-house because they were funny: a dog that looked like a sausage, wearing a hat and smoking a cigar; a very angry duck with a sailor smock and no underpants screaming at three small duck boys; a train with a face blowing steam clouds from a tall chimney. Then I draw all the trees I can remember that stood around the house in Østerøysvingen 8, forty-one of them; the one with the broken, dead branch trailing downwards, the one with peeling white bark, the one with a gnarled, fat trunk that I like to sit beneath because I can always feel it whisper when I put my hands on it. My eyes feel tired, but I rub them and keep drawing. One night soon, I'm going to go back to the house to see the trees. The family is nice, but they almost never let me be alone, even though I know how to be alone.

I wake on the floor, stretched out on top of the drawing pad, still holding a green crayon. *Are you okay, Tobias?* asks the man, and I nod, but I feel very angry because I know that the burning feeling in my cheeks makes them really red, and he will think there is something wrong with me. I climb into the bed and turn towards the wall, waiting for him to go away, but he doesn't. Instead, he sits down on the edge of the bed and just waits. I wait, too, and I think I'm probably better than him at waiting, because after a while he gets back up and walks slowly to the door. I hear him pause for a moment before he speaks: *If, uh, you want to talk…* And then he's gone.

The girls are nice to me, at least most of the time, but not to each other. Every time Hermine says something, Nicoline rolls her eyes as if it isn't okay for her little sister to speak. When Nicoline speaks, Hermine sticks her tongue out, or shouts *Blablablabla*, so Nicoline has to hit her. I'm not really sure why they do this. Their mother and father get angry when they do this. One day when we were having breakfast before school, Hermine took a Cheerio from Nicoline's bowl. Nicoline slapped Hermine's small hand very hard, so she cried. Nicoline called her *You little bitch*. The mother didn't say anything but she looked into her coffee as if she couldn't hear them screaming and then she looked at me and said, *Sisters*. Then she stood up and walked out.

The mother is nice to me but she looks at me a lot. Sometimes when she looks at me it seems like she is about to say something to me, but doesn't. She's sad. I don't know why, because she has the things to make you happy, but she isn't. It's probably because I'm here. Or maybe it's because she's angry with the man. Sometimes when Krysz and Anni were fighting, they didn't talk for maybe two or three days. In this house, it's not like that exactly, more that sometimes the mother and father say things to each other, but they don't really *talk*. Or they say something but mean something else, like when the mother says, *Isn't that interesting?* when the father talks about his job things but what I think she really means is, *That isn't interesting*.

Moffa once said that I hear the things that people don't say. I told Anni this and she said she hears the things that people don't say, too, but then Krysz said, *Those are just the voices in your fucking head*. Once Anni and I went to the beach early in the morning. We threw rocks at the water, which was covered by a thin layer of ice, and watched it shatter into glassy shards, letting the black water surge up through the holes. She told me about the farm she lived on when she was a child and how one of the horses could speak with its thoughts. It told her that her mother would die, and it was true – the mother died, and then Anni had to go and live with her mother's aunt, who was very old and also very mean. She and her husband hit Anni every day and forced her to do things she hated, maybe even eating bark and things like that. When she was fourteen, she ran away and had to live on the street and ask people for money and that was why so many bad things happened to her.

I draw the bed Moffa made for me, and then Baby's small bed next to it, but when I have finished I feel very angry and very sad so I rip the drawing into small pieces and just then, the mother walks into the room. *Tobias*, she says, kneeling down next to me, looking at the torn-up pieces of paper, but not at me. *Laila is here to speak with you again. You remember Laila?* I get back in the bed and turn towards the wall and wait for her to go away. Maybe she is better at waiting than the man, and maybe even better than me, because when I haven't heard any noises in a very long time, I turn slowly back round, and see that she is still sitting there, on her knees on the floor, waiting. I am angry. Yesterday she made me go to a doctor. The doctor hurt me and took my blood. Then I had to speak to Laila. I know who she is and I don't want to speak to her any more times. There was a man and another woman in the room as well, but after maybe three hours of them trying to get me to say something, I had managed to say nothing and they gave up. *We'll try again tomorrow*, said Laila. Which is now.

I stare at the mother, forcing myself to keep staring even when she stares back, which feels strange. Krysz says I can see into people but it isn't true. *If you like, I'll come in with you,* she says. I shake my head. *Did they tell you yesterday why it is so important that they speak with you, sweetie?* she whispers, and picks up my drawing of the duck, turning it over as though there may be another drawing on the back. I shake my head again. *They think they've found your mother,* she whispers, close to my head now, her breath on my hair. I don't want to speak with her. Or with anyone. But I turn around. *What?* I ask, and sit up, but carefully so I don't bang my head. *Your mother,* she whispers. *Anni.* A small sound floats on the air and I am trying to figure out what it is when she moves closer and begins to rub my back gently, and whispers *Hey... hey...* The sound is coming from me. It's a little bit like the sound that came from the cat that almost died when it was hit by a car and Moffa had to kill it more. *Anni is not my mother,* I say. The mother in this house looks at me, and I want to look away because it is as though she can see behind my eyes, but I can't look away even if I want to. *Tobias, are you sure she's not your mother?* she asks. I nod. *Who is your mother? I don't know,* I say, *but I know it isn't Anni. If you don't know who it is, how do you know it isn't Anni? Because I remember her,* I say. For a moment she looks like I have hit her. *What...* she says but then she stops talking and presses her fingers in her eyes. Then she moves the different parts of her face around but it looks like it is difficult because I can tell she is angry even if she is trying to not look angry. I open my mouth to say something else, but just then, it is as though a giant vacuum pulls everything inside of my stomach out and I throw up everywhere: on the bed, on the floor, all over myself, all over Cecilia.

*

Your drawings are so beautiful, Tobias, says Laila. *Do you think you could draw something for us?* I do this thing where I just look at the table like nobody said anything. A hand slides a piece of paper and a new, nice set of colored pens across to me. The wooden table has an interesting pattern I want to run my finger across because it looks a lot like the pattern on a tree stump behind Moffa's house that I liked to sit on when I was small. I wonder if I'd be able to feel the tree whisper if I put my finger on it, but I think maybe not, because this tree is a table now, so it's dead. *Tobias?* The wood grain has long, soft lines in it that are nudged into swirls every two inches or so, like waves rising and falling on the surface of the sea.

The man and the woman took me and the girls to see the woman's mother. Her house was by the sea. The old lady had baked a cake but it was quite hard. We had Coca-Cola and that was really nice because I love it. We played on iPads and for once the sisters didn't fight – I think they were afraid of the old woman, who looked like someone hit her in the face every time someone spoke unexpectedly. I wanted to go and look at the gray waves and when I crossed the floor to the door I looked up at a shelf above the fireplace, where lots of photographs stood in gold frames. They were all of the same girl – first as a baby, then as a girl my age, then as a teenager and then as a grown-up. It was the mother in the house I live in now. I stopped and looked for quite a long time because there was something strange about the pictures. Now the mother looks like the ladies who are on posters selling things; the ones I have seen in magazines, smiling, wearing fluffy sweaters and high heels and swishy hair. She is beautiful, and I have not met someone who looks like that before. Anni looks very tired and old and her teeth aren't okay anymore. When we lived in the Poland-house I met some other ladies, but I don't remember them very well, except that they didn't look anything like the mother. She looks new and shiny even if she is a bit old, like a car that has had all its parts changed and polished.

In the pictures at the old lady's house, she looked different. It was like the eyes were more open and like she showed more of what she thought on her face. There was also something else about the pictures but I didn't have enough time to figure out what it was because the girls came running towards the door and scrambled to get outside, pulling me along with them. Out there, they played in the leaves and then ran along the beach, screeching the way girls do, and I decided to stand still and try to hold on to the strange feeling I had when I saw the pictures, but it never did come back to me. But now, watching the wood pattern on the table and remembering how similar it is to the pattern on that tree stump, I realize what it was I felt then, at the old lady's house – it was recognizing. The girl in the pictures looked like someone I know. But I don't know many people.

My heart suddenly feels quick and loud in my chest, and I stare as hard as I can at the lines in the wood, digging into my memory to uncover who it is she looks like. *Tobias*, says another voice, this one more insistent. It is a man talking now, and he repeats my name twice more, so finally I have to give up trying to find the face I know I've seen before, somewhere. *Can you tell me who this is?* says the man, sliding a picture of Krysz across the table. I shake my head. *What about this, Tobias?* he says gently and the next picture is of Anni. I shake my head again. *Please help us*, says Laila. *We are so sorry to have to tell you that Annika Lucasson has died*, says the man. That noise again, the cat screaming. *No*, I say. *Yes*, says Laila. The mother in the house I live in now moves closer to me and I let her take my hand. *No*, I say again. *Could you please help us find out what happened to her?* says Laila. *You can draw if you want.* I push the pens and paper away. *Can you please try to tell us how you know Annika Lucasson?* says the man, running a fat finger across his fuzzy jawline. He looks like a pirate, but his eyes are kind. *She's my mother*, I say, and the man sighs. Laila sighs, too, and the mother lets go of my hand and raises an eyebrow at the father in the house I live in now.

*

It's night. The father took away the bright floor lamp that I like to light in the night-time. *You need to sleep in the night, Tobias,* he said in a nice voice – the kind you use to speak to babies. I could turn on the overhead light but I don't like the way it casts shadows from the table and chair by the window onto the floor. Anyway, I don't mind the dark. They knew that Anni wasn't my mother. That's why they got angry. They didn't say they were angry; they pretended like it doesn't matter what I say and they'll be nice to me anyway, but it isn't true, and I know they got angry.

When I was small, I hoped my mother would come for me. But when I thought things like that, I felt bad, because wishing my mother would come for me was the same thing as wishing to not have Moffa. And she never came anyway, and now I don't have Moffa, so everything is much worse than I thought it could be when I was small. It was like my mind thought it was either Moffa or a nice mother, like I just couldn't understand that it is possible to have nothing. And it's Anni's fault, all of it. I'm not sad she's dead. I'm not going to help them find out how she died either, because she ruined everything. She deserves to be dead and when I asked how she became dead they wouldn't tell me, but I don't care because I know it anyway.

PART TWO

PART TWO

Annika L., Somewhere near Kjerringvik?, October 2017

It's early and I have to be fast if I'm going to get to the post office and back before he returns. I don't really know what time it is or even what date so I can't write it but it's October, maybe late October. I've been up the whole night to get everything ready, and I think everything is in order now, at least I hope so or it's not gonna make any sense. I've cried some, it isn't easy reading. I've done some writing too, adding bits at the end to what was already there, and that was even harder. I've had a very bitter black coffee and a smoke and my stomach is aching like it's bleeding on the inside and maybe it is. My vision's gone strange in the last week but maybe that isn't so strange. My temple above my left eye is still hurting real bad like maybe bits of bone have come loose and are floating around underneath the skin

I don't remember what I was wearing when I came here. I can't go anywhere wearing what I'm wearing now. My clothes must be in the bedroom anyway. No, now I remember – they're underneath what I'm wearing and I must have put this over my real clothes because it's cold – it is so very cold here. I'm looking at my hands writing this and it makes me want to cry, like how can it be that these are the same hands as when I was a little girl and the same hands my mother once held and the same hands that have done so many bad things? The strange old clock starts up in the next room and I count the hours – eight. No more time. On my way out of here I'll give my love a kiss on his forehead though the idea makes me feel sick now. I'll do it anyway, carefully, like he might suddenly lunge at me.

Annika L., Karlstad, April 2009

Ellen, my caseworker at Kungshemmet, always said I should keep a journal and write down what I'm doing and feeling. I thought it was stupid but I tried it anyway because I liked her and for a long while I wanted to become how she hoped I could be. And I liked it, so I haven't stopped. The good thing about writing is that when you read it a while later, the past and things that happened sometimes seem different than you remembered. I always remember things as worse than they were, and when I read my words from a while back, there are always nice or funny little episodes that make me smile. Like the time Tanja and I ran away from Kungshemmet and managed to hitchhike all the way to Arvika before we got caught. We spent a whole afternoon enjoying our newfound freedom, smoking pot with some older boys and running through a park, laughing hysterically.

Now that I have my freedom all the time I look back at Kungshemmet with a mixture of fear and sadness, like a bad dream, but I miss it also. The way the system works is – you can be as fucked-up and insane and addicted and dangerous as you want, but as long as you only harm yourself, you're out as soon as you turn eighteen. And so, after spending your teens fighting against the well-meaning carers and all the rules, and hating evening lockdown and everything else about it, you're suddenly out. Free. And you end up missing your prison. At least I do. Suddenly, nobody cares.

My mother always said that we shouldn't dismiss things like the stars and fate. Sometimes it seems like everybody tells you that if you just work hard and never give up and carpe diem and make good choices, then it will all be okay. You'll get a good job and a nice partner and maybe even some nice little children. But it isn't true. Sometimes you do all the right things and it's still all shit. Other times you do nothing right and it all works out anyways. My mother did everything the way you're supposed to – she worked hard and got an education, and had a husband and child, and then she died at thirty-four. I try not to think about her much. I try not to think about the first twelve years, or the next twelve, because it either hurts too much, or makes me want to give up. If my life has taught me one thing, it's this – don't look back, and don't look ahead, just do your best right now. It's all we've got.

It's my birthday today. Twenty-five, and that's a good few years more than anyone would have thought I'd live to see. I haven't told nobody, not even Sylvia or Roy. This morning I thought about something Ellen said. She said that writing about my life and my past would teach me to respect myself. So I thought I'd give it a shot. Twenty-five; for most people that's really young. They have a pretty clean slate and presumably a long life ahead of them. For me, I would guess this is towards the end of my life but inside my head it's confusing; some days I feel young and that there might be different lives for me yet, and other days it's like I am a single hit away from death.

So I'm going to write about my life now, on my twenty-fifth birthday, and how I got here. I woke this morning on a flimsy mattress on the floor of a garage. My home. The garage belongs to Sylvia and Roy, and they live across the courtyard in a yellow, run-down house. Sylvia is a fortune-teller and looks it. She is probably in her late fifties, and a large woman with jet-black hair parted severely down the middle and lots of black eye make-up. She has plump, smooth hands that like to rest on top of her crazy crystal ball. When she meets with clients, she wears a black robe with hand-stitched gold half-moons on it, and she is quite a sight. Sylvia has been paralyzed for nine years – she fell down a ladder after having visions of the future in the clouds and tried to get closer. Oliver, the neighbor's son, told me this. He comes round to the garage sometimes to smoke with me.

Anyway. Sylvia's paralyzed and can't do many things, and because Roy's a truck driver and away a lot, I live here and help her. Well, both of them. There are things Sylvia can't or won't do with Roy anymore, and so I do them as well. The deal is, I do what they want me to, and I live here for free and Roy gives me smack. Mostly it's easy things like cooking eggs and bacon, and bringing in mail and cleaning. Sometimes it's things like shoveling snow and feeding the cats and clearing out their litter trays. And sometimes it's letting Roy or one of his friends use my body. Like I said, I live for free and they give me smack. It means I don't need to live on the street or in a hostel like some people I know, and I also have time to do some other odd jobs when Sylvia and Roy don't need me. In the summer, I pick strawberries on some of the nearby farms, and though it's a killer on my knees, I like being outside all day and the feeling of earth on my hands. It reminds me of home. In the winter I shovel snow for a couple of the old people in the cul-de-sac and clear snow from their cars and things like that. The winters are quiet, though, because many of the neighbors are wary of me and probably don't believe that I'm a student lodger. So it's quite often more of Roy's friends to earn enough money and enough smack.

Yesterday Roy gave me more than usual and at first I thought it was because it's my birthday today and he was being nice, but then I remembered I hadn't told him that. Either way, it was a nice surprise, though it's not like I didn't have to work for it. But this is a good set-up, and most people I know would kill to have someone like Sylvia and Roy. I got meth, too, which I don't always, so everything is nice and smooth inside of me today. Glass, which is what Roy always calls it, is good like that – it gives you a good six hours of just… easy happy. I've already been into town; I took the bus and walked around like other girls my age, in and out of a couple of shops, but in H&M, where I wanted to buy a sweater I'd seen in the window, the security men came and told me to go away. I opened my handbag and showed the bundles of two-hundred-kroner bills to them but they still didn't let me come in, they just looked away like I wasn't even there, and pointed to the door. I ended up buying a stupid plain black sweater in another shop instead, because at least I was allowed in there, though the shop assistant clutched a phone to her ear the whole time, preparing herself to be threatened with a dirty needle and told to open the cash register.

When I came back, Sylvia said I could finish off the pizza I'd made for her lunch, and then I helped her into her bedroom like I do most afternoons.

'I had a strange customer today,' she said. 'A Hungarian woman in her eighties who wanted me to find out whether she'd live long enough for there to be any point in buying a time-share flat in Tenerife. I told her to spend her money on champagne and handbags instead.' Sylvia laughed so hard she began coughing, and she was still wheezing when I left the room and came back to my garage.

It's only seven and there isn't anything for me to do except write – Roy left this morning for Portugal and won't be back for over a week. Maybe Oliver down the road will come and smoke with me, but when he realizes how much I've done, he'll go away again because he likes it more when I haven't used, even though I'm hardly a charmer then, either. He sometimes tells me that it doesn't have to be like this, that it's possible to get clean and have a real house and work in a shop or something. Clearly he has no fucking idea what I came from. He said that I am pretty and nice and I told him to fuck off and find a nice little nursing student. Anyway.

Ellen said I should write about my life. I am trying, and it isn't so hard to write about my life now, but it is hard to write about the beginnings. The glass is starting to wear off a little and it's hard to concentrate, and to even remember things right. My mind feels like soup sometimes. Maybe I'll just write what I remember, even if it is out of context; I guess it doesn't matter much. Ellen says that thinking about the things that hurt make us grow, so I guess I need to prepare for that, but I'm not really that sure I want to grow. Because what would I grow into? It's okay where I am now, doing what I do. If I grow, like Ellen said, then everything might change, and if there is one thing I've learned, it is that change is just another word for everything getting even worse. But I'm gonna try – here goes.

*

I know I have to be careful with the sugarcoating. Now, everything about my first twelve years seems rosy, but I realize that can't have been the case. There would have been childhood accidents, upsets, disappointments and such things, I just don't remember any of them very clearly. Life began for me in a pretty decent way. I was born on a large, remote farm – a real *Värmlandsgård* in a forest clearing by a huge lake, a good twenty minutes' drive north from Munkfors. Värmland is a land of dense forests and beautiful lakes, with sweet little towns surrounded by agricultural land. My mother, Therese, and father, Samuel, mostly made money from timber. My mother also produced and sold apple juice from our special apples, which were rumored to be the best in all of Sweden, and her *äppelsaft* was even sold in a couple of nice cafés in Stockholm. My half brother, Ludwig, is fifteen years older than me, and had already left for university in Lund by the time I was old enough to really notice stuff. We don't have much to do with one another these days; he's the CEO of a technology company in Stockholm and finds his junkie sister embarrassing as hell, though he does give me money sometimes.

I used to help my mother with the apples. She had a small workshop in the barn with an old fruit press and several workstations where the pressed apples would pass through sifting cloths before being bottled into handblown glass bottles and labeled "*Mors Most*". I helped her rinse the cloths out in between each batch, following the brown apple particles with my eyes as they spun down the drain. We fed the snaky peelings to the pigs, and the cores were heaped on the compost. In my memories, it seems like it was always late summer, with swollen red apples dripping from the trees waiting to be picked and golden afternoon sun making the fields glow, followed by cool, clear evenings. I don't remember the winters as clearly, except for a kind of constant half darkness, and the roaring fire in the kitchen, where my mother and I would sit every evening, stitching or reading. I also don't remember my father well – he died in a timbering accident when I was seven, and although we missed him and mourned him, I also came to love the new life that emerged – just my mother and me on the farm.

She'd had me when she was only twenty-one and loved to play with me and take care of the animals on the farm. My horse, Besta, was an old *Värmlandshäst*, a workhorse breed native to this region, and he was my best friend. Because we lived so remotely and I didn't have any siblings close in age, I never did play much with other children. I had some friends from school, but they mostly lived near each other in the little town, and I ended up not being included in most of their social activities. I have wondered if anything would have been different if I hadn't always felt like an outsider. It seemed to me that Besta could communicate with me and that he was much more clever than people usually say horses can be. He and I had an easy understanding, and it was deepened by something that happened when I was nine; Besta had seemed unwell for a few days, and though the change in his behavior was slight, it was very noticeable to me. He was subdued, jittery and stayed back in the field when I came. I insisted to my mother that she call the vet, but she said we'd wait a day or two and see how he got on. He was, after all, an old horse and they do get stubborn with age, like men.

I remember walking away from the field he stood in with the other horses, my heart hammering, feeling in my very bones that I should turn around, that Besta was telling me something. Suddenly I was struck by an intense and overpowering sharp pain in my right thigh, and it was so acute that I crumpled to the ground in the middle of the lawn in front of the house. I felt my leg underneath my summer dress and it was rock-hard and swollen. I closed my eyes and began screaming for my mother and in the moments before she reached me, frantic, kneeling down in the dewy grass, I saw in my mind a large, black ball of coagulated blood. As soon as the vision had appeared, it evaporated, and with it the pain went, too. I lay in my mother's arms, breathing heavily and kept feeling my leg where the swelling had been, but it was smooth and soft, as usual.

'Besta has a blood clot!' I cried, and my mother nodded seriously. The vet said if the clot hadn't been discovered when it was, Besta would surely have died. And then, the winter I was about to turn twelve, I began to avoid my horse. I started spending every afternoon in my bedroom instead of in the stables, and my mother became very concerned. She tried to talk to me, and even brought me to see a doctor, but I couldn't tell her the real reason I was behaving so strangely. I should have; maybe it wouldn't have been too late. For several months, every time I went to see Besta, I had a clear and sudden image in my mind of my mother with a big, growing mass in her head. It was such a frightening image, and it only happened when I was with Besta, and how I wish I'd listened to what the old horse was trying to tell me, because even then, I knew it was true. By the time my mother's tumor was discovered after she began suffering seizures, it was already Grade Four and inoperable.

Damn Ellen and her writing and her pain and her growth. I shouldn't say damn Ellen, though, because she's pretty near the nicest person I've ever met. Even now, years after it was her job to deal with me, she meets with me every few months and we sit at a bakery in town and eat *kanelbullar* and she pretends not to notice that I'm high as a kite. I'm high now, too, and it's a good kind of trip, like when everything seems both mellow and clear at the same time, not fuzzy and confusing, which happens often. This is the kind of high when even though what I'm writing hurts, it doesn't quite reach me in the heart – like I'm in a cocoon.

I went to live with my mother's aunt, Marie, and her husband, Sven. They hated me and I hated them and I'm not sure I want to say that much more than that. This isn't one of those things where I might read these words back in a couple of months and be reminded of some funny or nice episodes that happened during that time – there weren't any. In the three years I lived there, I went from being a happy, well-adjusted girl who dreamed of becoming a vet, to a severely depressed, anorexic teenager. I became addicted to crystal meth, cocaine and, by the time Sven had grown tired of forcing himself upon a broken teenager, heroin. I won't lie. Drug addiction is not the worst thing that has ever happened to me, nor the many unpleasant things I've had to do to get hold of the next hit – that's what everyone gets wrong. *If only you could get clean* seems to be the consensus of every teacher, doctor, therapist, social worker I've ever met. They just don't get it. I don't *want* to get clean, never have. Smack is the only friend I have, even if it is a friend that wants to kill me and will most likely succeed.

Marie and Sven sold my farm and used up the money. How they got away with it, I don't know. I think this is the only thing Ludwig pities me for, and the only reason he still occasionally gives me money. Out of the five horses, four were sold to a neighboring farm, but they wouldn't have Besta because he was too old to work, so he was put down. I think I'll stop now for a while.

*

It's been a few days since I wrote anything here and it didn't feel like a very healthy thing for me to do. When the rush wore off and I reread my words they made me cry my eyes out, cry like I haven't in years, and it made me use even more than I normally do. I was in such a bad state that I called Ellen late in the evening and left a long message on her answerphone about how she'd promised me that I was strong enough to write about my life and then read about it and learn something and grow but she never called back and for the rest of the night I smoked so much meth I passed out while I was still holding the pipe, and when I woke, I had a bad burn on my arm, and Ellen was sitting on the upturned crate by my mattress, serious and pale. And so, yes, I have come to miss being locked up in a juvenile institution where, at least, there are people employed to care for you. Or maybe I just miss Ellen.

We went to walk by the river, but I wasn't able to walk very far, so we sat down on a bench, though it was covered by a layer of frost and our breath came out in white bursts when we spoke. Ellen told me about her oldest daughter, Vicky, who is my age, and lives in Australia, studying media. Ellen misses her and wants her to come home, and I felt so empty because nobody misses me or wants me to come home.

'Annika,' she said. 'Do you want to come and stay with me and Josef and Sofia for a while? A couple of weeks perhaps?' I shook my head and laughed, because although of course I would like to stay with Ellen and Josef and Sofia for a while, that is absolutely not an option. Ellen has known me since I was fifteen, and she is probably the only person living who cares about me. That's now, when she's sheltered from the darkest aspects of what I'm really like. She sees me every few months and looks concerned while I pick at a cinnamon bun. While she knows the extent of my using, she just hasn't seen it close up; the blood, the pain, the desperation, the men… She can't possibly understand how tired I really am, and I don't want her to know. She didn't press me on her offer to stay, but started to tell me about a program she'd heard about, a government-funded rehabilitation program in Arvika that she could inquire about on my behalf if I wanted, make a few calls…

'No,' I said, too forcefully, and she looked disappointed for a moment, but then assumed her professional expression of eternal patience, which I'm sure she needs in her line of work. This is what people don't get. I don't want to be clean.

Annika L., Karlstad, May 2010

Rereading those words frightens me to the core. Who is she? Who is that girl? I ask myself this question, over and over, and it seems impossible that she was me, just one short year ago. That dilapidated garage floor with the bloody, uncovered mattress, crazy old Sylvia, violent, dirty Roy, the constant cycle of meth and smack and fucking Roy and his friends for more smack and meth… Who was that girl? It doesn't matter, I've learned. Over the past year I have learned that I don't have to hold on to every incarnation of myself – it's okay to just be Anni as I am right now, today. Twenty-six now, and it doesn't feel like the end of the road. I can look back, able to hold the pain and process it, and while it doesn't go away, it exists inside me like the scars on my skin. My teeth are still bad, but I'm on the waiting list for restorative dental treatment. I still smoke, but no nasty junk – only Prince Mild now.

In Ellen and Josef's house there are rules. Many rules. No alcohol, boys, drugs obviously, video games or cigarettes. I follow all of them, except the one about cigarettes – occasionally I'll smoke out of the window in the dead of the night when the others are sleeping, and stand staring at the moon hanging full and sad above the trees, and at times like that I just can't believe that I'm there, in a normal home with a normal family. Ellen and Josef are always saying that they are lucky to have me. They ask me what I want to do next with my life. Only recently have I let myself think about how I used to want to be a vet, and it has occurred to me that I would still love that. I haven't said it out loud to anyone, because it still seems to me like saying you'd quite like to travel in time, or win the Nobel Prize. Ellen says that I can be who I want to be, but the problem with that is that I never wanted to be anyone at all particularly, so I have to think a lot about what my options are.

A month ago, I was invited to return to my old junior school, *Vasshettan Sekundär*, to talk about drug addiction and my way back to sobriety. It was a joint effort between Värmland County Educational Department and the hospital that treated me, orchestrated by Ellen. I was also interviewed by the local newspaper. Before I went back to the school, I had planned to at least try to look as nice as possible, though that is difficult when you've spent ten years on hard drugs, including crystal meth. It shows on my face, put it that way. But on the morning of the speech I decided to not try to cover up the way I look, or what smack and meth has done to me. When I walked onto the podium, I heard a small shocked gasp from some of the teenagers in the front at the sight of me, just a few years older than them, literally ravaged by drugs. A few of them have probably secretly smoked pot, or even dabbled with a line or two of coke, but perhaps meeting me will make them think twice. Afterwards, they asked me questions. *How did you finally manage to get clean? What was different this time? Somebody cared*, I said, and found Ellen's eyes in the crowd.

As a continuation of the intensive rehabilitation program I have been through, I am still in biweekly counseling sessions. My therapist, Dr Faber, tells me what Ellen told me back in the day at Kungshemmet; that frightening and painful memories hurt much less when we bring them into the light and give them a little bit of our attention, but not too much. Acknowledge them and accept that they cannot be changed, then let them go. Just let them go. I've decided to attempt to return to this journal now that my mind is a whole lot clearer and my heart stronger.

A couple of days after the speech at my old school, Ellen suggested that she and I go visit my mother's grave. When she said it, it occurred to me that I didn't know where it was. Marie and Sven had never told me, and I felt overcome by sadness again, for that girl I had been, and of course, for my mother. At first I didn't want to, and I suppose I was afraid of facing everything I have suppressed so hard for so many years, but because I have learned that doing as Ellen suggests is generally a good idea, I agreed. We drove to Munkfors, and it was surreal, passing through the streets I hadn't seen since I was a child. It seemed impossible that the farm I'd loved so much was only a short drive away, and that it still actually presumably exists in the real world, perhaps even much the same. I imagined what it would be like to drive there with Ellen, seeing the field empty of Besta and the other horses, the barn used for something other than *äppelsaft* brewing, the house lived in by someone other than my mother and me. This was difficult and it took a lot of effort to touch upon these thoughts and then just let them go. I had to bring forth Dr Faber's calm, brown eyes, her soothing voice always saying, *Let it go, Anni, just let it go...* But eventually it worked, and I managed to return my attention to Munkfors's empty mid-morning streets.

'Where are we going?' I asked Ellen as she turned onto the country road that I recognized as the one that led to my parents' farm, twenty minutes north.

'She's buried a few miles from Munkfors,' said Ellen, very gently.

'At... at my farm?'

'No, sweetie,' said Ellen. 'I don't know if you know it, but it's a small village called Eckfors. There's a little church there, on a hill overlooking the river. Your mother was christened there.' I had to swallow many times, keeping my eyes on the tall trees towering above the road outside. 'It wasn't easy to find out, but the priest in Munkfors suggested I check with Eckfors since they didn't have any record of Therese.' I nodded, but felt like I was balancing on the edge of a precipice at this sudden, unexpected information. Therese Lucasson, née Severin, christened and buried in a little church overlooking the river at Eckfors. How could I not have known this? How could it be, that for all the years I was lost in the murky sludge of heroin addiction, I had never once wondered about what had happened to my mother's remains? What kind of a person was that? *Let her go*, Dr Faber would say. *You are not you then, you can only ever be you now.* Still, I found it difficult in those moments to breathe, or think, or even just be.

Ellen realized, because that's the kind of person she is. She asked if I wanted to smoke a cigarette in the car before we walked up the hill to the church, but I said no.

My mother is buried next to her own mother and father. This brought me some unexpected comfort, more than I imagined. That she is with them made me cry, and I decided there and then that one day I, too, shall be buried in that same plot in Eckfors, overlooking the river, next to my mother forever. I said this to Ellen, and her face went from careful and sympathetic to alert and serious. I guess I can't blame her for always fearing a setback, a swift relapse to the shadowlands at the very edge of life. I told her that I didn't mean now, but someday, and she nodded and I think she wondered whether she'd outlive me, in spite of the fact that she's thirty years my senior.

I keep rereading my words, both the ones I just wrote, and the ones from last year, and I can't stop thinking about how it seems unbelievable that in this one year I have gone from that bench by the river when Ellen first spoke of the program, to that other bench by my mother's grave in Eckfors, overlooking a peaceful, slow-flowing river, sober and relatively capable, crying but not broken.

*

With all of these ~~improvements~~ changes, I came to miss some things that many others seem to have that I just didn't think could be an option for me. Like a partner. I had never had a boyfriend, or spent intimate time with a man other than for money or smack. It was always blatantly obvious that nobody could love someone like me. But then, Ellen does, and Josef, and Sofia, and a very small part of me started to think that maybe... maybe so could someone else. A couple of months after I finished the first stage of the program and began to feel that maybe I really could be squeaky clean, I sent Oliver, Sylvia and Roy's neighbor, a postcard from Arvika. On it, I wrote my telephone number and asked if perhaps he'd like to meet me for a walk and a smoke (no crack) one day. He came, and we ended up walking really far upstream, just talking and talking in a way I don't think we ever did back when I lived in the garage, and the thing is, Oliver is actually really funny. I don't remember that so much either, but then, it is true what they say – a heroin addict is never really interested in anything or anybody else. It's yourself and the smack, that's it.

Oliver is only twenty-one but he is so mature and knows what he wants his life to look like. *We*, he always says, like I'll always be in his life. We could go back to school, get some qualifications, maybe go to Poland for medical school or veterinary school, whatever you want, babe... When he talks like that I sometimes just have to laugh, and he laughs, too, but his eyes are serious. Ellen and Josef still have their rule about boys and although they really like Oliver and think he is a good influence on me, he isn't allowed to stay over at the house or join us on the weekends when we go to the country cabin and things like that. It's okay, though, because whenever I think about it, I am always surprised that Oliver hangs around in spite of not getting any sex for it. He seems happy to hold my hand, solemnly running his fingers across the mesh of scars on my arms. *We have all the time in the world, Anni,* he says, but I wonder how he can be so sure about this – it's like he doesn't know that terrible things can happen to you at any time.

*

Since the day I went to live with Ellen and Josef and Sofia, we travel every other weekend to their country house, a very basic *torp* an hour away, near the Norwegian border. The property consists of a small main house from the seventeenth century, painted a deep red with baby blue windows, and three tiny huts surrounding the main house. Inside the biggest dwelling – the *hovudstugu*, there is a basic kitchen with an open fireplace, and a living room with two ornate sofas handmade by Josef's grandfather. The three small annexes stand around the main house, and in each is a small bedroom with built-in bunk beds. The beds are covered by white-and-red crocheted bedspreads, made by Josef's grandmother. There is nothing on the plain pine-clad walls. The sparseness of the *torp* is quite incredible, and the first time I came, reeling with withdrawal, I just sat rocking back and forth on the bottom bunk in my annex, staring at the pine walls, itching all over. There is no running water, and the bathroom is a wooden shack with a hole in the floor. It doesn't exactly sound like paradise, but to me it is. I know that the time spent at the *torp*, just focusing on the very basics of life; heat, food, water, breathing – contributed to my recovery. Josef and I sit for hours at the edge of a floating pier on the lake, waiting for the sudden pull on the fishing line, and though it quite often doesn't happen and we end up eating tinned spaghetti by candlelight, there is something about the quiet beauty of the smooth, black lake water that reached me, even in the earliest days.

At the *torp*, Ellen likes to make wicker baskets. She walks out into the forest and collects armfuls of birch roots, then sits on a crocheted blanket on the grass in between the little houses and coils the thin roots in and out of the stakes until sweet little baskets take form. At first, I found it meditative and almost hypnotic to watch her, and then I began helping by handing Ellen the next root, until one day I just started making a basket of my own. I didn't think I'd be able to do it, because at first my hands shook so much it took a whole day to make a really small, ugly one, but it seems like it has actually helped with the shaking. Now, when we go there, I fish with Josef first thing in the morning and then I spend the afternoons coiling baskets.

Ellen must have known that these were things that could help. She has talked before of when she was younger and worked for a year in the Alps in a small alternative school for ~~troubled~~ disadvantaged teenagers. Some of the methods used there became really important in her own work at Kungshemmet, she says. The kids, who'd come from all over the world, and had a range of issues, from addiction to PTSD to various autism diagnoses to a history of terrible abuse, came to the school to learn to live in themselves, as Ellen put it. It was not a traditional school that placed much focus on classroom learning; rather, the kids were given a lot of responsibility and learned by doing. The school was a small, self-sufficient mountain farm, and the students had to entirely run it by themselves, only overseen and observed by adult 'guides'. They farmed vegetables, kept livestock, traded dairy at nearby markets, and so on. If they screwed up, they wouldn't eat, was the understanding.

But they didn't screw up – they got better, and many of the former students have gone on to forge proper careers and live stable lives.

I know the mountain farm must have inspired Ellen when she took on Project Annika, as I affectionately call it at home, because from the very beginning, she has insisted on me doing physical tasks every day. At first, it would be things like peeling potatoes or arranging the firewood in the hearth or making all the beds – things even I could master with my badly shaking hands. After a while, it became cooking full nutritious meals from scratch, and now even with vegetables Ellen and I have grown from seeds at the *torp*.

There is also a little dog, which is actually Ellen's sister's, but she is getting divorced, so little Billy stays with us quite often. He's a schnauzer and a strange little soul. He doesn't seem to be that interested in people generally but, for whatever reason, he loves me, and so now it is my job to walk him when he's here, and the long walks by the river or in the forests behind the *torp* are my favorite times. Billy can't see the aftermath of what I spent so many years doing to myself. He doesn't care about scars, inside or out, or about my brown, crumbling teeth, or about the way my hands still shake a lot sometimes when I fasten his lead. He just loves me anyway.

So these are some of the things that Ellen and Josef thought would work, but there is something else, too – something which I think is nearly as important as all the other factors combined: Sofia. She is seven years younger than me, nineteen now, and for some reason I feel like she is how I could have been if my mother hadn't died, if I hadn't had to live with Sven and Marie, if I hadn't felt that the only way I could keep living was cocooned inside a drugged haze. She's unsullied, sporty, kind and uncomplicated. We aren't friends, exactly; she's more like an older sister to me than anything else. I want to go back to having a chance, however slim, to be like her.

*

I haven't written in a few weeks, because so many things have happened – good things. Oliver got into a program where you can redo your grades from school in six months and a medical school in Krakow has said he can go there next year if he manages to get at least a B in every subject. When Ellen heard about this, she telephoned the program and explained about me and how I'd managed to turn my life around and that I should be given all the help available to continue to progress in my life, and then they said I could come as well. Ellen is trying to find a veterinary school in Krakow that can take me if I manage to get my exams in May. So now I spend most of my evenings in my room with the books. Sometimes I miss the comfort of all the physical tasks Ellen encouraged me to do in the evenings, but I know that this is the only chance I have to make things even better, and I have a lot of learning to do. It isn't as difficult as I thought, and lots of the things I'm reading are actually really interesting. It's sad, too, how many things I didn't know. Wars have been fought in my lifetime that I'd never heard about. Words that everyone else seems to know, I'd never even heard – you don't need sophisticated language to shoot up. *Apprehensive, atrocity, audacity, permeable, lucidity, theology, conceited, election, genre, mitigation*: all words found in my textbooks today that I had to look up and copy down in my notebook. Ellen says I shouldn't think of the notebook as a record of all the things I don't know, but as a collection of things I have now learned. I didn't even know who the prime minister of Sweden was until I read about him in my social studies book. It's Fredrik Reinfeldt, for the record.

Sofia asked at the stables where she rides whether I could volunteer to help with the horses, since I dream of becoming a vet. Every Thursday I go there and help muck out the boxes, brush the riding-school horses and change their water trays. There is one horse, an old *Värmlandshäst* called Spooky, who reminds me so much of Besta that it made me feel all choked up the first time I saw him. Then I started telling myself that it had all been a mistake and that it really is Besta, and so now, I whisper *Besta* in his ear, and it feels as though in the midst of this whole new life, I got to hold on to one small piece of the past, too.

Annika L., Krakow, January 2013

I imagine the experts would find it difficult to conclude whether it comes down to one massive wrong turn, or a series of ~~minor~~ bad decisions when it comes to a case like mine. I'm back on the smack, back on the meth, but on the upside, at least I'm still writing in this fucking journal, right? ~~All is not lost~~ – I've decided to write down some of the things that have led to what's going on now, because then I might be able to read back and see more clearly what I should do. It isn't easy to think clearly anymore. It's not that I can't think, but more that all the thoughts come at the same time. It's very late in the night, well into the hours that some people call morning, but it's still dark outside, because it is winter. I am standing by the window, resting this book on the window sill, because I've sold all of the furniture in the flat so there isn't anywhere to sit. Even the bed is gone, picked up by a couple of hefty guys soon after I put it online. I can see a few spread-out lights, but most of the houses still lie quiet and dark. I think about all the people inside, snug in their beds, peaceful in the last hour before the alarm goes off. Well, I'm high as fuck and don't intend to go anywhere tomorrow, so staying up all night isn't really a problem for me.

It's always loss, isn't it, that destabilizes everything and makes all the bricks inside of you come tumbling down. It's always the beginning or end of love that changes everything, that makes all the difference between happy and sad, capable and completely incapable. Ellen would say that isn't necessarily true, that we aren't slaves to external circumstances, that it is possible to build spaces inside ourselves that remain untouched by others, spaces that are only ours. But it's true for me.

We made it to Krakow. I can't be bothered now to read back all the entries in this journal from the early days here in Poland, because it's mostly stuff about how excited I was, how long I'd been clean for, how great Oliver is, and so on. Even though I must have thought writing things like that was a good idea at the time I wrote it, it is now pretty obvious that it wasn't. I must have thought that one day I'd read them back, happily remembering lots of little episodes of that new life with nostalgia, safe in my continued clean cocoon. I can't have imagined, then, that I would be so broken and so bitter that even rereading my own words would be impossible. I'm high on heroin. I've smoked crack with one of the guys from the club, and I'm about to smoke some more, and while I feel as lucid and cool as ever, the truth is, I've never been as high as I was in the two years after Ellen launched Project Annika. That's the truth. It's worse now, much worse than it ever was when I didn't know what it *could* be like, when I still thought smack was my friend. Some friend, I know that now. It's a fucking death sentence.

Krakow. Yes. We made it here, Oliver and I. It wasn't entirely uncomplicated. By the time we were ready to go, Oliver's parents had found out about our relationship, and were completely horrified. Before we sat for our final exams, we used to study together in my room (door wide open), or in Oliver's (door firmly shut...). Every time I got off the bus across the street from Oliver's house, I'd quickly glance up the road at Sylvia and Roy's house, and shudder at the thought of that disgusting garage and the bloody mattress and how, almost every night, there would be a knock on the door that I'd have to answer, or no smack. *How far I've come*, I used to think, letting myself into Oliver's basement room, which had a separate entrance. We'd kept our relationship secret from his parents, because he said they'd been aware of some seedy goings-on at Sylvia and Roy's, and just wouldn't understand if their son was involved in them. *Maybe someday*, Oliver said, *when you're a vet and I'm a doctor, and we come back home and build a house on Fritzgatan overlooking the river...* I didn't mind much, because I was still getting used to family life at Ellen and Josef's, and didn't really need having to adapt to another family.

But then one day, Roy saw me leaving Oliver's basement and he began shouting and swearing, right there on the streets, and saying things that weren't true about me anymore, things like *fucking whore* and *junkie bitch*. It had never occurred to me that Roy would be angry with me for leaving, but then I suppose I hadn't really given him or Sylvia much thought since that morning I'd woken up and Ellen had come for me. Oliver's parents came outside, and at the sight of me and Oliver and Roy all shouting and crying on the lawn in front of their house, put two and two together and had a total fit. In the end, they refused to speak to Oliver and didn't help him with any money even though they'd promised to, so he had to take a big student loan. As months went by and we got used to the new life in Poland, which was stressful and difficult but exciting, too, Oliver became almost obsessed about making up with his parents. Every attempt at contacting them would be met with the same cool rebuff, and even though he didn't tell me exactly what they said, it was pretty obvious that there was no hope for reconciliation unless he got rid of the junkie bitch.

So he left me. For another Swedish girl – preppy Åsa from Gothenburg, who's slightly cross-eyed and speaks real slow, but who has never, ever smoked crack or shot up smack in between her toes. Did I care that much? I probably didn't, in the grand scheme of things. If I'm honest, Oliver is probably far better suited to Åsa than he ever was to me, but what struck me hard was how loss seems to be so very random. Some people get to have everything and keep it, while some have very little and lose that, over and over. It made me angry. Looking back, I think what made me get clean in the first place had a lot to do with Dr Faber's theories on acceptance. After all the years of impenetrable drug-haze, confusion and bewilderment, becoming clean was only possible because Dr Faber and I focused so much on acceptance. Acceptance of myself and my shortcomings, but also of the past and the fact that I could never change it anyway.

It was a bit like prayer; it felt put-on and a bit silly, but it worked for a while in its simple innocence – *Just let it all go...*

When I got angry, I wanted revenge. Because I hadn't yet reached the next level on Dr Faber's magic recipe for recovery – self-love – I directed the anger and hurt and feelings of revenge towards myself. By now, of course, I knew that smack was no friend of mine, and I didn't have the nerve to go anywhere near it straight away, so instead I began to drink. Not a lot, but more than somebody like me could handle. I was doing well with my studies at that point, and had made a few friends, and instead of focusing mostly on my work and only occasionally socializing with them, I turned that balance around, and began going out drinking most nights. I'd wake up feeling terrible and hating myself, and I'd swear that I'd get it together and reach out and help someone else for a change. Ironically, that's how I met Krysz.

*

A faint light has appeared in the sky and I can see people walking towards the bus station by the park. I am so tired. Tired in my bones again. I want to be back at the *torp* with Ellen and Josef, fishing and making birch-root wicker baskets, but that will never happen now. If I told them I won't make it through veterinary school and that I want to come home and just do something else, they'd never judge me or pressurize me to stay in Krakow. But if I tell them that I've spent the past two months undoing everything they have spent so long building up, that I love smack more than I love them or myself, well, they'd turn away. It's a bleak day and that's a good thing because when you are thinking my kinds of thoughts, like how much longer until I kill myself or the smack does it for me because I'm out of options, you hardly want blue skies and sunshine, do you?

Krysz. He's at the door. I thought I'd have time to write about him first, but he's already here, hammering.

CHAPTER 7

IN ORDER TO stop speculation, and also due to the fact that I've turned down so many invitations in the last couple of weeks, I felt I had no choice but to invite the girls from the tennis club for dinner. I haven't seen them in weeks, ever since the night Tobias happened and everything was turned upside down. Usually, we meet every other Thursday for dinner, every Monday and Wednesday for tennis, and one Saturday a month for cocktails. We're active socially, to put it mildly. Since Tobias appeared, I have avoided the girls – not because I don't want to see them, exactly, but more because I just can't bear explaining. They're chatty ladies and they would bombard me with questions, and I have just felt so utterly unhinged, I couldn't face them until now. A couple of days ago, I received a WhatsApp message from Cornelia that clearly wasn't meant for me: *Haha, yes, soon they'll be running a whole orphanage up there on the hill*, it read. I don't like it when people talk about me, unless it's in such a way that it's obviously because of jealousy. They are jealous of me, my friends, always have been, and I intend to keep it that way, and that's why I decided to invite them over to show them that Cecilia Wilborg has everything perfectly under control, as always.

Johan left for London this morning, and is then going on to Singapore, so tonight is a good night for some company. I've had Luelle, the new au pair, clean every nook and cranny of this house. She's working out well so far, which is a little surprising as I've not been lucky with Filipinas in the past, however this one irons faultlessly, doesn't miss a speck of dust, tolerates children *and* knows how to make ponzu sauce. Such a find. The girls have been sent off on a sleepover to the Tandberg twins, and Tobias is in his room, as usual, drawing. If he makes so much as a peep, Luelle will deal with him, obviously. To my intense surprise and joy, the Dolce & Gabbana emerald gown that has hung morosely in the closet for over a year now, two sizes too small, suddenly slipped on beautifully when I tried it, on a whim, after my shower. I guessed that I'd lost a pound or two since the whole Tobias saga started, but apparently it's more than that, and so it would seem that it could be true, what they say about clouds and silver linings, etc.

The house looks spotless, I look rather okay considering the unbelievable stress I've been under this past month, the sashimi and ponzu sauce is all laid out downstairs and I've just done a last round, lighting all the little candles and fluffing cushions before the girls arrive. I'm in my bathroom on the top floor, placing a drop of Tom Ford behind my ears, when I am overwhelmed by a very strange sensation. It is as though I'm momentarily blinded in my right eye, and I have to reach out and support myself on the side of the basin. I blink repeatedly and eventually my vision returns, but a pulsating orange blob remains hovering in my line of vision, and no amount of blinking or rubbing will make it go away. I also feel tingly and numb in my fingertips, and just as the doorbell rings, that dreadful sensation of falling through layers of black smoke washes over me again, and before I can even think of opening the door, I have to take a tranquilizer, although I really shouldn't mix them with alcohol.

At the door is Cornelia, who insists on being called Coco, though no one has ever called her that. She's Johan's cousin, and one of my oldest friends. She is a trained nurse, but these days she runs a very successful business selling personalized diapers, and is also slim and beautiful. A lot of people compare us to one another, but I suppose I've always found that slightly unfair as I'm three years younger and, well, it shows. Anyway. She squeals and hands me a huge orchid.

'Where is he?' she whispers.

'Who?'

'Your new son!' I genuinely can't tell if she's joking or not, so I focus on untying the gold ribbons around the orchid and give a sad little smile.

'Come on, Cornelia. He's not our son. He's in bed. It's already late.' I've only just handed her a glass of champagne when the doorbell rings again, and at the sound of it, I feel even stranger than I did in the bathroom, like it's buzzing from inside my cranium. I down my glass in one and hope the medication will kick in soon.

Cornelia is looking at me carefully. 'What's wrong, Cecilia?'

'Nothing. I had a migraine the other day, and the pain has lingered on a bit. I'll be fine. Come on, let's open the door.'

This time it's Cathrine and Silje. They also both hand me large orchids. Five minutes later Fie and Tove have arrived, too, and we stand around the marble island in the kitchen, toasting. They have all commented on how incredible I look in the green dress, and on how great the house looks, and what a fabulous idea it was to serve salmon sashimi and ponzu as they're all on low-carb before the party season and their upcoming New Year sunshine breaks, and the pulsating light in my eye finally starts to recede and I feel calmer and more like myself again. As we eat, I have the sensation that everyone wants to ask about the last month, but nobody dares to bring it up. Instead, we talk about St. Barths vs. Mustique for New Year, how Fie is doing on the Birkin bag waiting list, and how stressful it is at this time of year, getting the mountain cabins ready for first snowfall and the start of the skiing season.

It's Silje who finally broaches the subject.

'Tell us about Tobias, Cecilia,' she says gently, and I appreciate how she sounds like she actually cares about what goes on in my life, rather than just wanting juicy gossip to dissect with the others behind my back, which is just what we do with most bits of juicy gossip. Though most people in Sandefjord have probably heard about the strange events of the little boy turning up out of the blue, and the unresolved murder of the woman who seemed to have been his caretaker, nobody has heard it straight from me, and all the girls lean forward, clutching their wine glasses. I tell them about the awful, dark, rainy October night when the boy was suddenly deposited randomly in my care, and about the unbelievable series of events that followed.

'How are Hermine and Nicoline taking it?' asks Fie. 'Do they feel resentful about getting less attention?'

'Well, I don't think they get any less attention, to be honest. We have a new girl working for us now, too, so I feel like I have the help I need, really. And Tobias is a very easy child.' This is true, according to every usual interpretation of an easy child. He does exactly what he's told, he doesn't argue with my girls, he picks up after himself, unlike Hermine and Nicoline, and he's polite and sweet. But still, it isn't easy to have him around – not for me. It's the empty expression and the careful way he carries himself that unsettles me so – like he knows he'll never be a normal little boy.

'So, what happens next?'

'Well, there is no trace of the parents. Tobias has been undergoing intense psychological evaluation, as it has been so difficult getting him to speak about his past and where he comes from, but the consensus at the moment seems to be that he doesn't know much more than we do. The woman who was found dead wasn't the mother, as you probably heard.'

'Annika Lucasson, right?' asks Cornelia. I nod. Neutral face. Still, the mention of her name makes me feel shaky. 'What I just don't understand is, how does a junkie manage to steal someone's kid and get away with it for years? Like, where did she hide him? How did she even provide for him?'

'Well, one theory seems to be that he could be the biological child of someone from Annika Lucasson's drug environment. I mean, she was in it for so many years, she would have known a lot of people with similar problems, and she drifted from Sweden to Poland and back, and then to Norway, so maybe the boy was placed in her care after his real mother died or something,' says Cathrine, absentmindedly looking at her reflection in one of the gleaming silver candlesticks.

'So, there is definitely no biological relationship between Tobias and Annika Lucasson?' asks Silje.

'No,' I say. 'I think the main priority of the police at the moment is to trace this guy, Krysztof Mazur, who they think had something to do with Annika's death.'

'So awful,' says Fie. 'You just can't imagine things like that happening here in Sandefjord.'

'You know, I've seen her around,' says Silje quietly, and everyone turns to look at her. She nods to herself. 'Yes, at Hvaltorvet. She used to sometimes sit by the fountain, drinking a beer or something. I remember her well, because she tried to speak to me on a couple of occasions.'

'Speak to you? Why? Oh, how creepy!' says Fie.

'Yes. She... Well, I remember one time in particular. She caught my eye as I was walking towards the entrance to the shopping center and stood up. And then she was like "Hey! Hey you! I need to speak with you." Absolutely crazy, poor woman.'

'I don't mean to sound cruel, but I just simply find it hard to sympathize with someone who throws away their whole life on drugs. I mean, think of what they cost the welfare system. It's my taxpayer's money and I just don't think it's right that they get council-assisted housing, methadone and whatever else they get, while people like us foot the bill,' I say, feeling myself flush red with anger. The girls all nod in agreement.

'So... so, do you think Tobias will stay here permanently?' asks Fie.

'What? Here? No, of course not.'

'But... where will he go?' asks Silje.

'Well, that is for social services to figure out. At present, the police are working with Interpol to determine whether Tobias could be one of the children missing from somewhere. There are, after all, hundreds of missing children, so it could still be that he has parents somewhere.'

'God, can you even imagine...' says Cornelia, pausing to finish the last of her Pouilly-Fuissé. 'Losing your child... Having him snatched away from you only to end up in the care of someone like that wretched Lucasson woman?'

'But what if he isn't one of the missing children and Interpol just can't find his parents?' asks Cathrine.

'Then I think social services will try to place him in a more permanent foster family,' I say.

'But you guys definitely won't keep him?'

'Well, no. We have no capacity to be a permanent foster family. Honestly, it would just be too much for us. He is, of course, a darling little boy, but neither Johan nor I have the competence to deal with a child who'll probably develop serious issues in his teens after what he's been through. I mean, God knows what this experience must do to a small child. First being left by your parents, then being raised by a junkie, who is then murdered. I mean... Jesus.' All the girls nod, and I begin to collect the plates. I feel like we're done talking about this now – I've done my part and explained to them what has been going on, and the result is that I feel restless and unsettled, as I always do if I let my mind linger on Tobias.

'But won't you find it just so hard giving him up now that you've bonded with him, and he's become a part of your family?' asks Fie. Fie is the one who always asks a little too much; it's a problem of hers. Some people just don't understand when a conversation is over. I feel a strange tingle, like an itch inside my brain. Is this woman judging me for not being in a position to take in another child, a boy who would change the dynamic of my family forever?

'No, I think that will be fine, to be honest with you.' I smile a brilliant smile and pour another round of wine, and though I expect all the girls to nod understandingly and move the conversation on to more pleasant subjects, no one says anything for several long moments, and I feel as though they are scrutinizing me, passing judgment. Just then, I hear the rumble of fast-moving steps from the staircase, and turn around in alarm. It's Luelle, and she looks as though she is about to burst into tears. I stand up fast and walk over to her, pulling her back into the hallway, so the girls don't overhear whatever it is she's about to say. Tobias has probably wet the bed again. It has happened at least ten times since he came here, and before Luelle started I was the one dealing with it.

'What? What is it?' I hiss. Can't she see that I'm entertaining guests? Luelle looks terrified, and for a moment I wonder whether Tobias has threatened her or something – traumatized children have been known to do all kinds of dangerous things, I've heard.

'It's Tobias,' she whispers. 'He's gone.'

'What the hell do you mean, he's gone?'

'I checked on him in his room after he had his bath around eight o'clock. He was in bed, closing his eyes, pretending to sleep although I'm pretty sure he wasn't actually asleep. Then I checked on him again now because I will go to bed in a minute, and the window was wide open and he's gone.' Cornelia has heard the commotion and has come out into the hallway, concern etched on her tight, shiny face.

'What is it, Cecilia?' she asks, and again, I am overwhelmed by the ridiculousness of everything that is happening to me. I want to run from this house, from these vacuous friends, and into the freezing black night, screaming.

'Tobias is gone, apparently. But don't worry, just go sit down, have some more wine. I'll… uh, I'll go and make a couple of calls.' I go upstairs to the guest room and, just like Luelle said, the window is wide open, letting the freezing November air into the room. Christmas is just over a month away and the temperature has drastically dropped in the last few days. I shiver and walk back out, closely followed by Luelle. '*Oh no,*' she's whispering. '*Oh no, oh no, oh no.*'

'Look,' I say, turning back around to face her at the bottom of the stairs. 'Just go downstairs to your room, okay? This isn't your fault. I'll find him.' I walk into the room where the girls are pretending not to listen. Just a few months ago, I would have been beyond livid at the thought of anything or anyone disturbing or interrupting one of my evenings with my friends, but tonight, my head throbbing and my heart aching, I want nothing but for them to go home. I want Johan and Nicoline and Hermine to come home, and I want to sit by the fire with my husband, watching the flames dance while the children sleep. As I begin to speak, I realize I want something else, too – I want Tobias to come home. I want to know that his tiny body is tucked in upstairs, I want to hear the constant scratch of his crayons through the door, and to see his little smile come out as I pop my head around the door to say goodnight. The smile that breaks my heart.

'You need to leave,' I say, too loudly, and they all look up at me. Suddenly sober, they begin to gather their things, whispering among themselves. 'Come on,' I say. 'Fast.'

'Cecilia, why don't you let us help you look for him?' says Silje.

'I think we should call the police,' says Fie.

'Or social services,' says Cornelia.

'Why don't we at least wait here until you've found him. Maybe he's just wandered off down the road or something; I've heard little boys do strange things like that sometimes,' says Cathrine, the only childless person present. 'That way we can continue when you come back.'

'It's ten o'clock and it's minus five outside. An eight-year-old boy is missing from his bed, and I am going to find him, right now.' I grab my car keys from the kitchen counter and I can feel the shocked glances exchanged behind my back.

'Cecilia, let us help,' says Silje. They are all hovering in the doorway, Fie and Cathrine still holding their wine glasses as though we might really continue.

'Okay,' I say, trying to stave off the returning blinding headache by breathing deeper, but my breath comes out in a strained whimper. 'Okay. Why don't you guys grab some down jackets from the rack over there and scour our garden and the neighbors'? I'm taking the car – he might have gone further.' They nod slowly, but nobody moves.

'I'm just going to, uh, quickly check with Petter that everything's okay at home,' says Silje. *Just like you would have if we were still sitting around the table, drinking my expensive wines and talking bullshit, huh?*

'Yes, me, too,' says Cornelia, like I don't know that they won't put ugly old jackets over their precious dresses to spend the rest of their evening shining torches into bushes, looking for the lost boy. I turn away from them, slamming the door shut behind me.

Reversing out the driveway, it is clear to me that I have certainly had too much to drink to drive safely. On the main road, I move slowly, and thankfully there aren't many other cars out tonight. I let my eyes travel back and forth across the road, over every bare tree and into every garden, but there is no sign of a thinly clad little boy. How long can he have been gone for? No more than two hours. But... Two hours outside in this temperature, wearing only pajamas – he could be dead. Another thought occurs to me – what if someone has seen him wandering alongside the road alone and called the police. He'd be in social services' custody by now, and it's just a question of time before they come knocking on my door wondering why I'm unable to look after an eight-year-old, only to find me drinking with my friends, or even worse – out on the road, drunk and incoherent. I begin to slow the car down even more, and then it occurs to me that I know where he is.

*

Tobias is a very beautiful child. There isn't any doubt about that, and I catch all three members of my family frequently gazing at him adoringly – he really is cute. I can tell that Johan loves having a boy around – Nicoline and Hermine have never once humored their father with ball-throwing, but Tobias does, though rather clumsily. Nicoline and Hermine, who some might say are a bit sullen, and more interested in YouTube make-up tutorials than anything else, have actually benefited from having Tobias around – they both think he's sweet and want to be his favorite, so they fight less when he's around. More than once, when I've gone to wake the children in the morning for school, I've found both girls fast asleep in Tobias's room, snuggled up to the tiny stranger. This, I must admit, I find strangely moving. Tobias doesn't smile often, but when he does, his whole face lights up and his otherwise expressionless eyes get a warm, lovely glow, and it feels like you just want to keep that kid smiling.

I park down by the road and run up the steep path on my heels, feeling my dress snag on some brambles on my way. Though I've only been here that one time before, it is as though I know the path well, and by the time I reach the door with its peeling blue paint, I feel a strong sense of déjà vu. The terror of that night, the crash of the rain, the abandoned boy... I raise my hand to knock, but decide against it. Instead, I listen awhile at the door, but can't pick out a single sound coming from within. It is a quiet, clear night, and bitterly cold. I shiver in my cocktail dress, but probably noticing less than I would, had I not been so tipsy. I put my hand on the door handle and think about how, as it turned out, this house was Annika's last home. How many times she would have trudged up that same path, in the morning, in the evening, in the middle of the night, probably. The door opens soundlessly and I step into complete darkness, trying to stave off the thoughts of Annika Lucasson floating on dark water. She haunts me, day and night, in death like she did in life. She would have liked that.

The house is as empty and scary as the first time I came here, but in the light from my iPhone screen I can make out small footsteps in the thick layer of dust. In the first couple of weeks after Tobias was found and Annika died, this house was cordoned off by the police; I know this because Johan and I drove past here a couple of times, just to see, really. Now, new dust has gathered and nothing remains of the police investigation, except half a roll of police tape in a corner in the living room. I follow the footsteps into the kitchen, where a drawing I recognize as Tobias's has been left on the dirty countertop. It is a drawing of many trees standing closely together, their distinctive trunks and branches meticulously and skillfully penciled. No sign of Tobias. I turn around and pick up the footsteps again, following them through the adjoining bare living room, then up the stairs.

Tobias is fast asleep on the floor in the smaller of the bedrooms, the one I'd assumed was his the first time we came here. He's inside a sleeping bag I recognize as Hermine's, which he must have found at home. Relief hits me so hard I feel tears spring to my eyes and run down my face. I sit down by his side, about to nudge him awake, but then I realize I'm too drunk to drive, and I just can't do it with a little child in the car. I have some blankets in the back of the car, so I run back outside and get them. In the bedroom, I sit against the wall, wrapped in the blankets, watching him sleep. I text Cornelia and Luelle to say I've found him and not to worry, and can feel my eyelids growing heavier and heavier.

*

When I wake, it's still night and so cold I sit up, gasping. My blankets have slipped off me and my arm is exposed, and so frozen I can barely feel it. My face feels tight and strange and I am so consumed by this that it takes a few moments for me to realize that Tobias, too, is awake. He is sitting up against the wall next to me, the sleeping bag zipper closed all the way up to his chin, watching me seriously.

'How did you know Anni?' he asks finally, his breath bursting out of him in puffy white frost clouds.

CHAPTER 8

THERE ARE ONLY two places we can go from here. I could tell
Tobias the truth, and my life, as I know it, would be over. I
can't imagine what life after that could look like. Or I could
tell him a lie. Another lie. I'm good at lying. Sometimes, in
life-changing moments, we are afforded at least a few minutes
to contemplate the stakes before making those crucial calls
that can alter the very course of our lives, but other times, a
moment's hesitation will give it all away. This is one of those
moments. I decide to be brave and take a chance on the slight,
ghoulish child levelly holding my gaze in the frigid night's
shimmery moonlight.

'How did you know Anni?' he asks again. He's clever in his
choice of words; had he simply asked *Did you know Anni?* I
would have chanced a straight-up lie, but he has already informed
me that he knows that I knew her.

I consider myself a collected kind of person, accustomed
not only to white lies, but pretty proficient also in the murkier
shades of fabrication. Still, hearing Anni's name spoken out
loud and having to acknowledge her and any connection to her
fills me with dread.

'Tobias,' I begin, in the calmest, lowest voice I can muster,
trying to copy Laila Engebretsen's ridiculously pedagogical
intonation. Tobias's gaze doesn't waver. 'Sometimes adults find

themselves in some very tricky situations. Very tricky. And, uh, you know, in situations that are so difficult you just couldn't possibly have even imagined them, you are forced to make decisions without even understanding what the consequences may be. Do you understand what I'm saying?' Slight nod. 'Sometimes, you're lucky and everything works out okay. But sometimes… sometimes everything is so unclear and difficult and impossible, and you end up making *one* single decision that makes everything that follows veer off course forever.'

I've got him. He is listening intently, his eyes still not leaving mine, but also glazing over slightly as he seems to consider my words in the context of whatever he is thinking about.

'You're very young, Tobias, and I don't expect you to understand everything I'm telling you, but you deserve to know the truth. Things that seem clear-cut and obvious when you're young don't always seem that clear when life has had its way with you. Anyway. Look. Johan and I have had some very big problems in our marriage for many years now. Problems that would make most people decide to end a relationship. But when you have children together, it is very difficult to make that decision, because as a mother, you just need to know that you are doing the best thing possible for your child. Tobias, I really believe that any mother does what she believes is best for her child, even though it doesn't necessarily seem that way at the time.' I pause for a long moment, and draw the blankets snugly around my shoulders, but still I'm shivering. Tobias is still looking at me closely, but not in the same confrontational way as when I woke.

'What kind of problems?' he asks, finally. 'Is Mr Wilborg angry with you?'

'No,' I say, accompanied by a sad little half laugh.

'But what? And what about Anni?'

'Tobias, I haven't told anyone what I'm about to tell you,' I say. A small hand appears at his chin, where the sleeping bag is tightly zipped shut. It emerges and he lets it rest a long moment on my shoulder before putting it back inside. I have to look away. 'I used to buy something very bad from Anni, that's why I knew her.'

'Is it smack?' The fact that Tobias, aged eight, knows what smack is makes me momentarily want to cry, and reverse the direction I've guided this conversation. I shake my head.

'No, sweetie. It isn't. But if I'm honest, it isn't so much better. It's not something that you're allowed to buy, and it is very bad for you.'

'Is it coke?'

'Ummm, yes. Yes, it is.'

'But... but why?'

'Like I said, I've had a very difficult time in my relationship with Johan, and although that is absolutely no excuse for substance abuse, I'm telling you as an explanation. I want you to feel that I am honest with you.' Tobias nods slowly, but his little face is scrunched up in a grimace.

'Does Mr Johan hit?'

'No, sweetie. No, he doesn't. Never.'

'But... what, then? It's nice in your home.'

'Yes. Yes, it is. It's just that... Between... between him and me, it's very difficult.'

'But... how?'

'Can I trust that this stays between you and me, Tobias? I haven't discussed these things with anyone before. And, like you probably know, buying the things that Anni sold isn't allowed. I could get problems with the police and everything.'

'I promise, I'll never, ever tell anyone!'

'Okay. Well, all right, I will tell you, though you probably won't entirely understand what I'm saying. Just please never repeat this. Not to anyone.' Head nodding furiously.

'My husband loves me but not in the way that most husbands love their wives. Because... because Johan likes men.'

'He's bad?'

'No. No, he isn't bad. At all. He just loves men.'

'So, he's bad.'

'No, Tobias, he isn't.'

'It's bad to... to be that.'

'Says who? It doesn't make him bad. It's just who he is. But... as his wife, it's been very difficult. He didn't know when he was younger, or when we met. Sometimes we find out things about ourselves that come as big surprises, even after we thought we were all grown up and thought we knew everything. And, sometimes, people change, and that is just how it is. I've changed, too. When I was younger, I used to be really relaxed and fun. I was always the one with the crazy ideas and the one who thought that life was just one really big adventure.'

'You're still fun,' says Tobias, and gives me that sweet, rare smile, the one I don't deserve. The smile I can't bear.

'No. Well, like most adults, I'm just... tired sometimes. Too tired, and too sad, and too weak, to change the things that could maybe be changed to make things better. And that is why I started buying the, uh, the stuff from Anni. I hope you know how terrible the consequences can be from taking things like what Anni used, and sold. I know I'm not the right person right now, to say that it's bad to do that when I've just told you I have done it myself. But... Everybody... everybody has hard things in their life. Most people find better ways of dealing with them. I guess I just made a really bad decision.'

Tobias nods. 'You... you just don't look like someone who shoots needles.'

'Oh God, I don't! Never any needles. Not that it matters. Or maybe it does. Yes, I think it does. Well, to me it does.' Tobias narrows his eyes and I realize that I'm rambling about drug use to an eight-year-old. He just looks very tired.

'Hey,' I say. 'What do you say we go home?'

After a long pause, Tobias nods.

'I liked this room and I liked the trees. I wanted to see it again.'

'I know,' I say. 'I understand that, sweetie. But do you think you can feel at home at our house, too?' Tobias looks down at the dusty floor, or maybe at my stilettos poking out from my woolen blanket.

'I came to look for something.'

'What was it?' For a moment, Tobias looks so pained, I wonder if he is going to cry.

'It... it was a little bear. Like a toy bear. My mother stitched it for me.' My heart pounds so loud I'm sure he can hear it.

'Your... your mother? Do you mean Anni?'

'No. My mother. She made me a little bear. And it's gone. Anni lost it but I wanted to see if it was here.'

'Did you find it?'

Small shake of his head.

'Tell you what. We'll go to the store and buy a new bear. I know it won't be the same, but maybe that will help.'

Tobias frowns, his dark eyebrows almost meeting in the middle. 'Can I ask you a question?'

'Sure.'

'If your husband likes men and it isn't a bad thing, why can't he be with a man? Why don't you find someone who likes you even if you're a girl?'

'Well, Tobias, it's more complicated than that. We have two daughters. It's important that they have both of us and a nice home.'

'But it's also important to be happy in your house.'

'Yes, it is.'

'I have one more question.'

'Of course, sweetie.'

'When did you last see Anni?'

'When did I last see Anni?' I repeat. Buy time, pretend to think. When *did* I last see Annika? 'I... I think it must have been right at the beginning of summer. Maybe... maybe, say, June. Yes, that must be it.' Tobias doesn't say anything, just keeps looking at me calmly, and it occurs to me again that I'm terrified by an eight-year-old. 'It's been a long time since I, uh... you know, used any of those things that Anni sold.' Finally Tobias nods, and two small hands appear at the top of the sleeping bag's zipper, and when he's undone it all the way, he steps out of it, wearing only his *Star Wars* pajamas, recently bought for him by Johan.

'Come,' I say, and lead him slowly towards the staircase, my hand on his shoulder. I'm not afraid of driving now, in spite of all the booze earlier – my head has never been this clear, though my heart is hammering. I need to think. I need to get Tobias home, and then I have to have a long, hot shower and a couple of espressos. With pharmaceuticals. And then, I'm going to have to come up with some kind of plan or otherwise my carefully curated life will erupt into the biggest shit show Sandefjord has ever seen, and that won't happen. Over my dead body.

*

My personal take on marriage is that it's nobody's fucking business how you conduct your life behind closed doors. Unfortunately, because Norway is such a normative society, I feel a lot of pressure to live life a certain way. It's all laid out for you here, how you're supposed to live. When I was younger, I felt so restricted by these norms. I had quite a wild phase during the years Johan and I lived in Paris, and deep down, I never wanted to return. Johan eventually wanted to go home, establish a real career, buy a house, be respectable parents, have a mountain cabin. Be like everybody else. So, we moved back, and I rebelled. Quietly, but still. I'd pursue little flings discreetly, living for those moments of intense exhilaration when I felt a new man's hand move slowly down my spine. I'd go back to Paris for occasional weekends, walking around our old neighborhood behind Panthéon, feeling stung by breathtaking regret for what I'd left behind. I'd do a line or two of coke with my wild university friends, who were still working in gloomy bars and dating numerous unsuitable people. Back then, Sandefjord often felt like death's antechamber. But then, as Johan's career took off, I got increasingly comfortable and it became clear to me that I no longer wanted the messy, hand-to-mouth life of a Parisian twenty-something. I wanted to be rich, and I wanted to be like a shiny picture – the perfect woman that everybody envied. And here I am. Sometimes I look at Johan and I see a middle-aged banker whose skin is prone to eczema and feel wild with longing for other men, for more excitement, for foreign cities, naked breakfasts in bed, inappropriate encounters. But here's the thing – and this might be the thing that has ensured I tend to come out on top when life gets tricky – I'm not stupid. I know what I have and I'll be damned if I let anything threaten it.

People want different things, that's just life. Some of my friends, like Cornelia, for example, want soppy romance and passionate *amore. Good luck with that*, I've always said, and it would seem that my cynical approach isn't so silly after all; Cornelia's love life is made up of an endless line-up of idiotic, lying, nasty clowns. And then there's Fie, who is married to Bent, a penniless substitute teacher for whom she left her first husband – dependable, wealthy, boring Arne. She's an imbecile. Three years down the line, when infatuation wears off, she'll realize she had it all and gave it up to live in a tiny, ugly house with an emasculated geek. And there I'll be, still, in my stable, content marriage with the most desirable man in Sandefjord, in my wonderful home, with our gorgeous daughters. It isn't a big price to pay, to live with moments of acute boredom. It's not like we don't love each other. We have sex occasionally, but less so, these days. It's not like I don't have my own pursuits – I have an active imagination and some very impressive toys to play with when Johan travels, and that is as far as I will go these days. Once bitten, forever shy.

At home, the poor boy finally fell asleep at gone four a.m., after I let him draw for half an hour while I was in the shower, trying to warm my frozen bones.

'I'm sorry,' he whispered, as I stood up to leave his room, after tucking him in tight. 'For running away and for saying that your husband is bad.' I nodded, and ruffled his hair a little, but he pulled away instinctively, then seemed to reconsider, and smiled sweetly.

'It's okay. But please don't run away again. We want you here, Tobias.' He opened his mouth as though he wanted to say something else, then decided against it and turned slightly towards the wall. If you lie to somebody all the time, are they less likely to suspect you of lying as they can't compare it to the truth?

CHAPTER 9

IN MY ROOM is a bed, a desk and a chair. The desk has three drawers on one side, and I always wanted a desk like that. It's nice to have somewhere to keep your things. I guess I didn't have many things before, but I do now because the family has bought a lot of things for me. *You need this and this and this*, they say, and bring me bags of things that I never knew I needed. Yesterday it was a folded pencil case with Yoda on it. The dad in the house knows I like *Star Wars*. He handed it to me wrapped in a white paper bag with red writing that said '*Changi Airport*'. Moffa and I used to watch *Star Wars* together, and he made me a lightsaber once, too. Inside the pencil case are lots of colored pens and pencils, each neatly placed in a little hoop so it's easy to find the color you want. In a separate compartment there's a ruler, an eraser, a compass and some plastic shapes with numbers on. A few days before that, the mother in this house gave me loads of small packets containing colored cards. Some were football cards and some were Pokémon cards. Many children at school have these cards, and I was very happy to get them. She also gave me some round glass balls. She said they're called marbles and that she used to play with them when she was small. Inside some of these balls are colored swirls, and in others there are air bubbles you only see if you hold them up to the light.

All of these things I've put into the top drawer. I like to sit on the chair and open the drawer and then close it again and then open it again, looking at the things and listening to the way the marbles roll back and forth. Other things the mother and father in this house have given me: a white-and-blue scooter, a green helmet, many clothes, an iPad, a noisy toothbrush with Luke Skywalker on it and a book about the planets.

It's nice here. Maybe nicer now than before because I don't have to meet the police and the other people every day anymore and answer questions. It made me angry because they asked me many questions I think they already knew the answers to. And the questions I did know the answers to, I didn't always want to say. After I went to Østerøysvingen 8 in the night to look for my bear, the mother in this house has been more nice to me. She was nice to me before, too, but in the kind of way when you have to, like at school to the teachers even if you don't like them very much. I thought she would shout at me when I woke up and saw that she was sitting next to me on the floor in a dress. The reason I didn't think she was so kind before was because she gets stressed and sad sometimes because of her problems and I didn't know about that so I thought she was just angry.

It's the weekend again and the dad in the house came back from another country yesterday. I've been here almost four weeks. The mother in the house has been more quiet than usual for many days, like she was thinking about other things, when the girls fight or talk to her. Then, when the father in the house came back, she put on nice clothes and made her hair curl and laughed a lot at the things he said about his trip. He said the place he went is so clean that you go to prison if you throw chewing gum on the ground. He said that the houses are so high you have to lean your head back all the way to see the tops of them.

And that it was hot and sticky, so he had to change his clothes three times a day. Here, it's cold now. It has already snowed a few times but it hasn't stayed on the ground. Soon it will be Christmas and all the kids talk about it every day, because they like to make decorations and get presents. I haven't made decorations before, but it is my class's job to make some bags to hang on the school tree, so I will next week.

The Christmas I had with Anni and Krysz was very bad. I still know what Christmas is supposed to be like because Moffa and me used to do it, and it was the nicest thing. We went into the forest after breakfast on Christmas Eve to get a tree, and Moffa always let me choose which one. *That one?* he'd say, and point to one that was really perfect, with no gaps in between the branches. I always liked to choose one that was a bit strange, because it's sad if those ones never get picked. Then, at home on Moffa's farm, Baby would run around the tree in circles and bark, because she thought it was strange that we took a tree into the house. We hung glass balls and little Santa figures on the tree and strung silver glitter garlands from the star on the top. Moffa always gave me a *julebrus* and I sat on the sofa drinking it with a red straw, watching cartoons while he made our Christmas dinner in the kitchen. After dinner, Moffa gave me my presents, and then he'd sit and listen to old records while I played with the things he gave me.

Krysz said that Christmas is stupid because it is just a way to make people buy many things. He said *fuck off* to Santa in the shopping center when we lived in the Poland-house and many people stared at us. On Christmas Eve when I was with Krysz and Anni, it was just me and Anni in the end because they had a very big fight and Krysz went somewhere the day before. Anni and me did Christmas a little bit, I don't think she hated Christmas as much as Krysz. We ate a whole grilled chicken and made a fire with one of those logs you can buy in the shop that burns a very long time. Anni gave me a Kinder egg and some pencils. She told me about when she was small and she had Christmases with her mother on their farm, and how they used to cut down a tree from their forest, too. They used to leave some milk and a cookie for Santa's reindeer in a big barn they had, and I told her Moffa and I used to do exactly the same thing. Anni always brought her horse, Besta, a big peeled carrot on Christmas Eve. After Christmas, before the New Year, Anni and her mother would ice-skate every day on a lake in the woods. Moffa and I had a lake, too, and I asked him many times if we could ice-skate there, and he'd shake his head like he was sad and say that because it is warmer now than it was when he was a boy, the ice isn't safe enough anymore. We'd walk around the lake, and though it was always frozen in the winter, it was true what he said about the ice, because close to the shore it was brown and see-through, even cracked in many places. Before I was born, Moffa knew a lady who had walked on the ice on our lake and fallen through, and it was four months before they managed to pull her out again.

Nobody has said anything about Christmas here. I don't want to ask them because it's not my family, and maybe they will have their Christmas and send me somewhere else. Hermine has made a list of what she wants and stuck it on the fridge door. It says: a horse, new iPad, iPhone 8, nail polish, eye shadow.

I open the drawer in my desk and look at the things in there. If I was going to write a list I don't know what I would write now that I have the Yoda pencil case and the cards. Maybe I would write *dog* but that would be stupid because I wouldn't get it. I'm trying to think of something else I could maybe want, but I keep thinking about Baby. She was small and white, with floppy ears and a brown spot on her back. She liked it when it snowed – she would chase the snowflakes and bark really loudly. She also liked pigs' ears and tummy-scratching and me. I asked Anni many times what happened to Baby, but she would never tell me and I think maybe she didn't know. Baby was not very old, so maybe she is still alive and living with someone else. I write *Baby* on a piece of paper and cross it out. I do it one more time but it was stupid because now I have thought about what it would be like if I opened a box and Baby was inside it. Someone knocks on the door.

Hey, kiddo, are you okay? says the dad in the house. I nod, but he's come just when I was thinking about Baby in a box, so he sees that I'm very sad. *Do you want to practice some hoops with me?* he asks. *It's not that cold this morning.* I don't want to play with a ball, but I don't want to say that because I still feel bad for what I said about him when the mother told me his secret. Moffa always said that if you are not sure about someone, listen to what your stomach says about them, because it usually knows. I think the dad in the house is a good man but Krysz says that men who like men are disgusting and should be shot. There was a man who used to come to the Poland-house. He was quite old and had different clothes to most people. He looked like a man in a play because he wore a suit and a tie and colorful scarves. He had a mustache that pointed sharply down at the ends, and a small dog who wore dresses. He used to come to look at the things that Anni and Krysz were selling, things like silver spoons and silver candlesticks, and old jewelry and watches, and then he would sometimes buy things to sell from his shop and Krysz and Anni would get money for smack. *Fucking faggot*, Krysz said every time the man left the house, leaving a strong mint smell from his perfume behind. I asked him once what that meant and he said it meant men who like men instead of women and that that was a wrong way to be and that in many countries men like that were rightfully punished. I never really thought about it again, until the mother in the house I live in now told me the secrets.

Yes, okay, I say and stand up. He's kind, and my stomach knows that. Anni was kind, too, but only sometimes. Krysz wasn't kind most of the time, but sometimes he taught me things, like drawing horses and dogs with one single line. Anni said that life had been very bad to Krysz so he forgot what it was like to be nice.

Outside, it is very cold even though it isn't snowing or raining. *It's Christmas in a few weeks,* says the man. *Have you thought about what you want?* I bounce the ball on the ground a few times and take a shot, but I miss. I shake my head and he looks at me, holding the ball in his hands. *Is everything okay today, Tobias?* I want to tell him that I like him and his whole family and that I want to stay with them when it's Christmas, and they don't have to buy me any presents because I only want Baby anyway. *Can I stay with your family at Christmas?* I ask in the end. The man looks at me strangely for a long moment and I realize that he thinks it's difficult to tell me that I can't stay here at Christmas because I'm not in their family, but then he throws the ball so it lands in a hedge on purpose and leans down to me, so his face is really close. *Hey,* he says, *hey. Did you think you weren't going to stay with us for Christmas? You don't have to worry, Tobias. We are going to have a really nice Christmas, all of us.*

*

135

I haven't told anyone about Moffa. Not one single person. The police and the tall lady who came many times to talk with me from social services asked me a hundred times about how long I was with Anni and Krysz, and I said, *Always*. I could have said everything I remember but I didn't. When I was small, no one knew about me, or that I lived with Moffa, but I don't know why. People know about most children, I think, but not me. Once, a car came driving up the driveway to the farm when Moffa and I were picking apples off the trees, and Baby was barking like a crazy dog because she thought it was a game and that the apples were balls. Moffa suddenly looked really serious when we heard the car's wheels crunch on the gravel in front of the house. *Quick!* he said. *Go to the barn.* I ran really fast to the barn and hid underneath a huge concrete bench with a heavy red wax cloth over it that stood against a wall. Nobody came for a very long time, but I stayed under the table until Moffa came and said, *You can come out now, Tobias,* in his nice, slow voice. *Who was it?* I asked, and he smiled and said, *Someone who wanted to sell me things I don't want.*

Some people did know about me, though. Moffa had a woman who was like a wife, but she wasn't his wife because she lived on another farm nearby. Her name was Carolin and she used to come to our house and sweep Moffa's kitchen and make waffles for me. One time I heard her ask Moffa, *How long is he staying this time?* and Moffa said that I would stay for a week, which was a strange thing to say because I stayed there the whole time. In the summer, some people came to help Moffa with the farm work, and they would see me around the farm. I don't remember many of them now, and I never spoke with them because they could not speak Swedish, or Norwegian, which is what Moffa and I spoke, even though it was Sweden we lived in. When Moffa had to go somewhere, like maybe the town, Baby looked after me and I looked after Baby. Before Krysz and Anni took me away from the farm, I had not seen anything that wasn't the farm.

The summer Krysz and Anni came to the farm, I was a bit more than seven, but not eight. Their job was to pick the strawberries in Moffa's field with some other people. Moffa gave them money to do it. They lived in a blue tent next to the barn, and there was also a red tent and a black one. In the barn, Moffa had made a shower for the people. Anni always said hello to me, and one time she came with me and Moffa to swim in the lake and I thought she was strange because when we walked back up the grass hill to the house she began to cry, but real quiet, and Moffa didn't see it.

Krysz hit Anni many times, and she always said he didn't, but one time, Moffa heard him hit her and stopped him and then Moffa and Krysz had very angry words outside of the tent. Krysz always used to say ugly things to people, like fucking faggot and fucking Santa and fucking Jew and fucking bitch and fucking paki but to Moffa he shouted *fucking pedo!* Moffa never got angry with anyone, at least not that I saw, not even me when I brought a dead bird to my room and it began to smell, but he got really angry then and made his voice very loud and shouted, *Leave this farm immediately, or I will call the police.* Krysz screamed many more ugly things and then he ripped the tent out from the ground and shoved it in the back of the old red car he and Anni had arrived in, without even folding it. *Come on*, he said to Anni, *let's go*. Anni cried, and Krysz pulled on her arm and then Moffa said, *You can stay here* to Anni. *Don't go*. Moffa said she could stay with us to help him with me so Anni moved into the yellow room in the attic because she didn't have the tent anymore.

For a long time Anni was sick so she couldn't help Moffa with me anyway. She stayed in the bed and I only saw her if I went up there to look at her from the door. She was always shaking and her face was as white as a ghost's. When I came up to the attic, she'd wave at me if she was awake, but I never went in the room, because she was frightening when she was so sick. After a while, she started to come downstairs and she drank tea in the kitchen every morning and evening. I didn't like it so much when she was there because I was used to it being Moffa and me and Baby. Now, when I went to sleep, I could hear them laughing downstairs. Moffa began talking about Anni, saying things like, *That poor girl* and, *What a lovely person she is* and, *Aren't we lucky that Anni came and Krysz went away.* But Krysz came back.

CHAPTER 10

I'M EXHAUSTED, TO the very bone. Perhaps it isn't so surprising, with everything going on, but I just can't seem to find a moment to clear my mind. This morning, after dropping the kids off, I decided to stop by the gym. Now I've finally lost that excess weight, I might as well take advantage and tone up as well. Something odd happened while I was there. I was on the cross-trainer, minding my own business, my eyes roaming between the TV high up on the wall, the mirror on the far side of the room and the sweaty faces of the other gym-goers, when a woman walked past outside. I saw her reflected in the mirror, walking fast with her head bent, a scarf drawn tight beneath her chin against the wind, and I could have sworn it was Anni. I craned my head to follow her as she rushed past, and I must have stopped abruptly, because suddenly the cross-trainer jerked my arm hard as the woman was lost from sight. I'd been at the gym for less than a half hour, but I couldn't bear to continue. In the changing room, I caught my own eyes in the mirror and realized they were brimming with tears. I was afraid to go outside and cross the parking lot in case I bumped into that woman, so I sat down on a hard wooden bench. Again, the images of her dead, face-down in the harbor water flooded my mind, and I closed my eyes, pressing my fingers firmly into their sockets, sending tears down my wrists. Still, she was there. In my mind.

Mouth open in a silent scream, eyes half-closed, looking straight at me, fingers reaching – reaching for me… My heart began to pound much harder than it had while I was working out and I lay a hand to my chest to calm it, but nothing worked and I sat there for a very long time, just trying to ride out wave after wave of panic. How had I got here? How had this impossible situation happened to someone like me?

I stepped carefully outside, as if I might be struck down by falling rocks. It was past nine, and the moon was only just slipping down the sky, leaving a foggy, wan morning behind. The parking lot was empty of people, and I began to run towards the Range Rover parked badly across two bays. As I got closer, I saw a yellow parking ticket snapping in the wind. Swearing to myself, I stuck my hand in my pocket to find the keys and realized the phone was ringing. It was Johan, calling from the office. I got in the car, slamming the door shut, sealing myself inside its cold, quiet space. My sense of unease increased and for a moment I felt completely overwhelmed by the impulse to get back out, fling the phone into the sea and just run away from the car, away, away, it wouldn't even matter where to; just away from this dark and rainy winter; this boring little town; my ungrateful, sluggish daughters; impossible Tobias; tormenting Anni; my insipid job; my spiteful friends – I wanted it all to be gone. For a mad moment, I even wanted to be like *her*; struck still forever, cold and immobile, held gently by the sea.

'What is it?' I said, realizing how tired and angry I sounded as I spoke. I tried to fix it immediately – if there is one thing I believe in, it is that with men, you have to accurately strike the chord between demanding diva and submissive sweetheart. 'Darling, sorry,' I whispered. 'I just fell on a patch of ice in the parking lot. It's so good to hear your voice, baby, are you okay?'

'Hi, uh, yeah.' Johan sounded flustered by my sudden change in tone. 'Are you okay?'

'Well, I've hurt myself, if I'm honest. But I'll be fine. Is everything okay?'

'Yeah. I, uh, called to see if you can organize playdates or sleepovers for tomorrow night. Remember how Morten said we really should prioritize our date nights? It's been a while.'

'You're right, it has. But, Johan, we have just taken in a random kid, and a lot's been going on.'

'Cecilia, I'd really like for us to talk, okay?' A bitter dread, like the smell of death, drifted into the car, threatening to strangle me.

'I... Okay, yes of course. I'll fix it.'

I leaned back against the cool leather seat and closed my eyes against another onslaught of irrational tears. Could it be that Johan was planning on leaving me? Had he already begun to separate himself from me and our life together, and all that remained was to tell me he was going? I focused on my breathing exercises and tried to envision Morten's face as he said, *This insecurity of yours is unfounded, Cecilia. It's in your head*. Morten is a marriage therapist Johan and I have spent tens of thousands of kroner on in a bid to strengthen our marriage. I do believe in preemptive measures, rather than little tweaks when it's already too late.

At home, I caught Luelle watching TV in the living room, the duster flung nonchalantly at her tiny feet. I glared at her until she scampered away, then made a triple macchiato. I took a couple of my pills and stood a long while at the window, staring out at the white wooden houses clinging to the rocky hills, like little boats riding enormous gray swells. Once, they were inhabited by whale fishermen who'd leave huge carcasses strung up to dry in their courtyards. These days, the whales have been replaced by Range Rovers and Porsche Cayennes.

A scraggly brown bird shot up from where it had been sitting on the recycling bin outside, and was rapidly devoured by the dreary, bulbous fog that came drifting towards the house from the sea. The temperature was just below zero, and a fine layer of ice crystals had settled on the road, the trees, the rocks that grow into steep crags at the back of the house, even the postbox. I felt wildly, irrationally angry, and were it not for the fact that Luelle was skulking around the house somewhere, pretending to dust, I would have flung something to the ground like I sometimes do. Instead, I did what I also sometimes do – I poured a generous measure of vodka into a water glass and sipped at it while I began making arrangements for the children.

It wasn't so much that I minded the idea of a date night, more that I felt generally unhinged and should have liked a moment to myself, rather than having to put on a show for Johan. For him, it would only involve showing up, but for me it would be bikini line, nails, lashes, self-tan – the whole works. And it made me angry that Johan seemed to think I could just pick up the phone and magically place three children, one of whom is a traumatized rescue-child who was raised by junkies until a month ago, with eager babysitters with one day's notice. Lucky for Johan, Cathinka Tandberg had little choice but to accept when I asked her to take the girls for a sleepover – she knows that's the price she has to pay for me to turn a blind eye to the fact that her Porsche Cayenne is unfailingly parked in next door's driveway every Tuesday and Thursday mornings. For hours. I don't think her husband would see the funny side if I were to WhatsApp him a picture. I couldn't exactly ask her to take Tobias as well, though, so there I was, faced with yet another way to adapt to this new life. I texted my mother and asked her to take him, even though she isn't exactly my first choice for child care, and must admit I was surprised when she responded saying she'd 'love to'.

*

It's almost six p.m. and I've just taken Tobias to my mother's. Like yesterday, today was another disgusting, stormy day, but my mood has nonetheless been significantly better. I even walked into town today, right past where Anni was found dead, without even particularly thinking about that wretched woman. I bought a new pair of sexy wine-red leather pants, which I will put on before Johan comes home. Whatever it is he wants to discuss with me, I'm going to make sure his mind is firmly on sex.

After dropping Tobias off, I slowly reverse back out of my mother's driveway – I can barely see three feet behind the car, it's raining so hard. For a moment, this feels like that awful night a month ago, when Tobias and I ran through the crashing rain to that dreadful little shack and found it empty. I turn the wheel all the way and maneuver the car back onto the road, and the headlights sweep across the kitchen windows. I see Tobias standing there, a small, dark silhouette looking straight out towards me in the car. I pause for a moment and wave at him, but he doesn't react. He must be able to see me, but I flash the lights twice in case he didn't. I wave again, but he turns around and walks slowly away from the window. A flash of cold in my stomach, sharp like a blade. Why is he acting like this? He'd seemed happy enough to be invited to my mother's house for a sleepover so 'she could get to know him better'. Could it be that he knows I lied to him? I've told so many lies. I simply can't remember all of them, and some lies I've told so many times they have solidified in my mind, replacing whatever may originally have been true, meaning I genuinely can't tell what's true and what is not. Everything I told Tobias was a lie. I don't have a cocaine addiction and I most certainly never bought a single gram of the white lady from Anni. My husband is not a homosexual, as far as I know. Why would I tell such blatant untruths to an eight-year-old? Because I would have told him anything – absolutely anything, no matter how outrageous, besides the truth. I worry that he might crack under pressure and speak to someone. And I'd much rather be caught out as a drug addict married to a gay man than as what I really am.

I drive home slowly, but even so, the road blurs and trembles in front of me – in spite of feeling better today I have had two of my special pills, and a very large glass of wine in the tub while the kids had dinner with Luelle. She was pleased and rather surprised to be offered a night off, and didn't quite know what to do with herself.

'Perhaps I'll just stay in my room and watch a movie,' she said when I asked what she planned to do.

'No,' I said. 'No, you must get out more. Have some fun. Spend the night away. I insist.'

'But… but, Madame, where?' she asked, almost frightened at my insistence, and it occurred to me that she wouldn't know a soul in this country. In the end, I booked her a room at Farris Bad in Larvik with Johan's credit card and actually drove her there after she'd fed the kids. She couldn't believe that I'd pay for her to stay the night at a fancy spa. *Thank you, thank you*, she kept chanting from the back seat where she sat next to Tobias. This is how far I'll go to get the hired help out of the house when I my want personal space. And date night *is* important, Johan is right. It's essential to keep that fire burning, they say. Still, my heart sinks a little at the thought of the evening ahead; we'll sit sipping champagne across from each other in soft candlelight, my homemade lasagna, Johan's favorite, on the table between us. I'll do that thing I know Johan likes; I run my index finger along the rim of the wine glass, then suck on it as though I'd caught a stray drop, meeting his eyes just when I do.

When I get home, Johan is already there, flung across the sofa like an unselfconscious dog. He looks ruffled, tired and old, but I can tell he makes a real effort when I walk in by brightening his expression, sitting up and smiling. I'm annoyed – I'd wanted to change before he got home.

'Hey, baby,' he says and pulls me down towards him on the sofa. I resist, but give him a peck on the cheek.

'Just going to change. The lasagna is in the oven. I'll be back up in a minute.'

'Oh, don't bother. You look hot as all hell. Come and sit with me.'

'No, honey. I want to change out of this. I've been wearing these jeans all day; I look a total mess.' Johan's grip on my hand tightens slightly and he pulls at me again, harder this time. I land across his knees and he pulls me close, rubbing his nose against my cheek, though I'm still struggling to get away.

'Hey. Hey, look at me. Stop trying to be perfect all the time. Just… just be with me.' Johan holds me really tight, and strokes the back of my head, like a baby's, until I stop struggling and am forced to just lie in his arms. I count down from a hundred, and surely that must be enough cuddle time, even for Johan. I get up.

*

By the time I get back upstairs with a full face of make-up and my new leather pants, I can tell by the way Johan moves about the kitchen that he's annoyed.

'The food's burning,' he says.

'It isn't.'

'It *is* burning. Can't you smell it? Where does that woman keep the oven gloves?'

'Honey, I've turned it down to eighty degrees. It isn't burning. Now, why don't you pour us each a glass of wine and we can sit a moment by the fire before we eat?' I slip my arm around Johan's waist and smile brilliantly up at him, feeling like myself again. He looks a little weary, but leans in to kiss me.

'Have you been drinking?' he asks, pulling away just before our lips meet and slightly narrowing his eyes.

'I had a glass of wine in the tub earlier.' Johan doesn't say anything, but he lets me go, and begins to open a bottle of champagne on the counter. We sit opposite each other in front of the fire, sipping gingerly at the animated bubbles popping in our glasses.

'I… I thought we should talk,' begins Johan, and though I'm staring at him hard with an expression intending to convey seriousness with an undertone of sultriness, I can't read him. My mind runs wild with different scenarios. He looks a bit sad; weathered, like life's been tough on him, which is hardly the case. He also looks slightly annoyed – he keeps clenching his jaw, making a muscly lump appear and disappear on his cheek. Is there someone else? I try to envision Johan with *her*; inching his way down a taut stomach, whispering in her ear, laughing in the dark, intertwining his fingers in hers, kissing her hard and joyfully. I focus on keeping my hand holding the flute completely still. He does travel a lot. London, Singapore, Frankfurt, Zürich – he could have a whore in every town and I'd never know about it. Unless he told me.

I take a big gulp of champagne, feeling the bubbles rise and pop at the back of my throat. Another thought briefly crosses my mind. What if my lie to Tobias is actually true? What if Johan *is* gay? I glance at him sideways, and take in the smooth, soft skin; his kind, mild eyes; the slightly vain hair carefully brushed back from his face and held down by expensive French hair oil. Could it be that when I said to Tobias that Johan is gay, it was because I subconsciously suspected deep down that he really is? I try to envision him with a man; wrapping his arms around a strong, tall figure from behind, nuzzling a broad neck, closing the gap between them entirely. This image is strangely unsurprising, like I've thought it before, or dreamt it, perhaps. *My husband is gay.* That's it. How could I not have realized this before? Perhaps I just didn't want to know. I wonder if he has a boyfriend, someone he exchanges suggestive messages with, someone who makes him smile, someone he thinks about when he's in bed with me. This must be the reason he stays with me. He doesn't want to be outed, and I can understand that. Johan is a gentle soul, someone who craves a normal life; he just wouldn't have the constitution for an all-out, flamboyant homosexual lifestyle. But on the side... I take another huge gulp of champagne, emptying my glass, and though I can feel Johan's eyes on me as I place the empty glass on the marble table with a loud clang, I avoid looking up at him. I need a moment to think.

I suddenly wish the kids were somewhere in the house, sleeping or playing quietly; unnoticeable but necessary, like good bacteria in the gut. Johan would never broach any big subjects with me when the kids are around.

'Cecilia,' he says, and I take a deep breath before looking up, smiling coolly, then gazing longingly at my empty flute. He takes the hint and refills my glass. I take another big gulp and when I finally look at him, he's studying me carefully, like you would a very rare and potentially dangerous bird. 'There's something I'd like to talk to you about.' I nod, finding that no words will come. I want to ask him for how long he's known, whether he has a boyfriend or just many casual acquaintances, and I guess I'd also quite like to know whether he really enjoys our sex life or if it was all just a show. I suppose I should be furious; God knows what illnesses he may have subjected me to over the years if he really has involved himself in gay sex, but then, I know I am hardly the person to be angry about this – it's hardly like I was always careful myself in those early years. I force myself to look at him and not look away again, even though it hurts, and I almost want to laugh out loud at the irony of it.

'What... what would you like to talk about?' I whisper. Even as he opens his mouth to speak, I will him to stop. There really is no need to bring all this out into the open. We have everything – the perfect life together; why fuck it up? He can be as gay as he wants as long as he keeps it quiet. Or maybe we could share this, somehow? After all, lots of couples do, and it's hardly like I'm a prude. We could find another couple and swap partners – perhaps there are even others in Sandefjord who are into that kind of thing. I wouldn't mind experimenting more with women, and I definitely wouldn't mind the other guy. We could have dinners together, perhaps even go on holiday with them – it will be just like our other couple friends, but with lots of hot sex. Most likely, Johan is into both anyway, it's not like he could have fully faked everything he and I have been to each other over the years. Or could he?

'Do you know what day today is?'

'It's... uh. November twenty-first?'

'Yup. What happened on November twenty-first, Cecilia?'

I look back up at him for clues, and his eyes are shimmering in the soft light from the open fire.

'Oh,' I whisper, and Johan begins to nod, then laugh.

'On November twenty-first, I married the love of my life,' he says, raising his champagne flute in a toast, touching his glass gently against mine. Oh God, thank God, it's just our anniversary! Of course Johan isn't gay. Why would I even think such a thing! The craziness of this past month must be taking me over entirely.

'I'm sorry,' I say, and I *am* sorry, but at the same time, I'm feeling angry and confused and even a little scared. How could I have forgotten?

'Did you forget?'

'No, of course not. I just… I just wasn't sure if that was what you wanted to talk about… You seemed so serious there for a moment.'

'I am serious.' Johan fumbles around in his pocket before pulling out a small, square box, placing it on the table in front of us. 'Open it.' Though the box is unwrapped, my fingers struggle with the smooth, soft leather. I wrench it open, and inside is an exquisite square-cut pink-sapphire ring, flanked by diamonds, set in a thin rose-gold band.

'It's the one you loved so much. In New York. Do you remember?' I nod, and this time the words won't come because I'm crying, and I wipe hard at the tears because I don't want to spend the rest of my evening with puffy eyes and mascara streaks.

'Cecilia, I've been thinking about this. I think we should renew our vows. Things have been… difficult – no, not difficult, but off-course – for a while now. I've had to travel more than usual this year, the girls have been really testing, then everything with Tobias happened. I want us to have something amazing to look forward to.' Johan slips the ring on my finger, where it slides around, too big.

'We'll get it taken in,' he whispers, and kisses my cheek, wet with tears, and then he must realize that my tears aren't entirely of the happy kind – I find myself sobbing and unable to stop. Johan doesn't flinch, just pulls me very close against his chest so that I can hear his heart beat, and I try to focus on the feel of the ring on my finger instead of all the other images rushing through my mind. Little boys alone in dark, abandoned houses. Long, limp hair rippling in dirty, dark water. Black splotches of blood on the ground. A thin, brown body shivering in steamy air, pool water studding his skin, loneliness emanating from him. Arms covered in cuts, perforations and scars, reaching for me through murky water. Johan running, fast, away from me. Me, floating in a bubble about to burst. When did my thoughts become so dark? Is my perfect life being slowly torn apart by one wrong turn after another?

'Shh,' says Johan.

'I'm sorry.'

'Don't be sorry.'

'We should eat. The food… it'll burn.'

'Baby, it's on eighty. It won't burn.'

'I'm sorry.'

'What are you sorry for?'

'For… for crying. And for being so awful.'

'I love you.' At this, I pull away and look at Johan even though my face is, without a doubt, completely messed up.

'Why?' I ask, the word catching in my throat and dislodging another bout of tears. *Why, why.*

'You want to know why?'

I nod.

'I love every little thing about you, baby, right down to your bones. You're funny and spirited and kind. You're a great mother and the best wife anyone could wish for.'

'I'm not perfect. I...'

'Shhh. Thank God you're not perfect.'

His words don't offer me much comfort; *au contraire*. I've always felt that much of my time and energy goes into putting on a bit of a show in life, and I've assumed Johan, eventually, would realize this and leave me for someone less empty inside. I have fretted endlessly about this, and spent vast amounts of energy making sure his eyes never strayed from me. In spite of me doing absolutely everything to prove to Johan that I really am the perfect wife, I couldn't be sure it was working. Once, back in the day when I didn't outsource that kind of thing, I was ironing his shirts, and he stopped me, putting a warm hand over mine. *You don't have to be so perfect all the time, Cecilia*, he said. *Come watch a movie with me*. And that was precisely the problem; nothing could have stressed me more than Johan telling me to stop being perfect. Being perfect is the only way I have a chance at stopping him from seeing how incredibly replaceable I actually am.

'Wait there,' I say, unpeeling myself from Johan's embrace and unsteadily getting up, walking towards the door. 'I got you something, too.' Downstairs in my wardrobe, I sit down on the floor and put my head in my hands. I feel empty from all the crying, even emptier than usual. I feel so confused. How do people know what's true and what isn't, even inside themselves? I dig out a small bag from an expensive boutique in Oslo. I bought it a while ago as one of Johan's Christmas presents, but it's not like he knows that, and I'm sure as hell not going to admit to forgetting our anniversary. Upstairs, I refill our champagne glasses and hand him the little bag. He peels the tissue paper apart, and again, I'm struck by how pretty Johan is, his soft skin more like a girl's than a forty-year-old man's. His face lights up sweetly as he takes in the monogrammed Gucci cufflinks.

'Thank you, honey,' he says, reaching for me again, but just then, the phone rings. It's past nine, and recent events have certainly taught me not to expect good news when the phone rings unexpectedly.

'You need to come,' says my mother, her voice thin and trembling. 'It's Tobias.'

'What is it? Has he run away?' Why is it that every time I seem to sit down to dinner, that kid runs off?

'No. He's here. But, Cecilia... Oh, Cecilia, he's hurt.'

CHAPTER 11

JOHAN DRIVES, TOO fast for someone who's just had half a bottle of champagne on an empty stomach. His jaw clenches and unclenches again. I call my mother twice on the way, but she doesn't pick up. I tell myself that she's tending to a fully conscious, slightly bruised Tobias, and that that's why she isn't answering, but I am overwhelmed by visions of her desperately performing CPR on that limp little body. *He's hurt*, she said before the line went dead. What does that even mean – a paper cut? Or decapitation?

Rounding a bend in the road, the car skids on ice and Johan has to pump the brakes hard to regain control.

'Fuck,' he whispers. An eerie mist is drifting out of the forest and across the road; not quite snow, nor rain, more like a carpet of tiny ice crystals.

'Drive slow,' I say and Johan stares at me like I'd just suggested something completely unreasonable. The tenderness between us as Johan gave me the ring is completely gone – I feel as though I'm in the car with a stranger. 'I shouldn't have trusted her,' I say. 'She's so self-absorbed, it's unbelievable! How could she let something happen to Tobias!'

'Call again,' he says, urging the Tesla fast along a straight stretch of road, crossing barren fields as we continue towards the southern tip of Vesterøya. I dial my mother's number again, and this time she picks up.

'Where are you?' she shouts.

'Five minutes away. We just passed Korsvik. How is he? Should I call an ambulance?' My mother is breathing hard, and there is no sound of Tobias in the background.

'Oh God. No. No ambulance. He's... he's fine. He'll be fine. I... I'm so sorry.'

'Please just tell me what's happened!' The car shudders over a speed bump and Johan swears loudly again. 'Mum, tell me!' She's crying and trying to calm herself down with long, exaggerated breaths.

'He... he's burnt himself. It's bad.'

'But how? How could that even happen? For fuck's sake, you'd think you'd be used to looking after little kids by now.' Johan shoots me a glance. 'I'm sorry. Please, just tell me how that happened. I think we need to call an ambulance.'

'No! No ambulance, Cecilia. You need to hurry. He... he did it on purpose...' My mother's voice trails off in an anguished squawk and then she hangs up.

*

Tobias is on my mother's bed, propped up by pillows, his eyes closed, slowly shaking his head back and forth, breathing in little puffs. He's wearing nothing but his red *Cars* underpants, and looks about five years old. His ribs are clearly visible beneath his skin, which is dotted with sweat, and his hair is matted down and damp, sticking to his forehead. On his chest sits a huge ice pack, directly above his heart, and it rises and falls jerkily with his strange breathing. Underneath the ice pack I can make out what looks like a wet kitchen towel. I make my way over to him quickly, turn on the bedside lamp and gently sit down next to him. Tobias moans loudly when I touch his arm.

'Jesus Christ,' says Johan. He has his arm around my mother, and it seems he practically has to hold her up; she is crying and breathing strangely fast like Tobias. I take her in; she's wearing a frumpy black housedress, and her dusty blonde hair is in a low French chignon, half undone. Her face is scrunched up, anguished, and her liver-marked hands clutch at Johan's arms. She suddenly seems ridiculously short, like she's shrunk without me noticing. I feel the most intense repulsion for her – how could she have let something like this happen?

Ever since my father walked out, I've regarded my mother with a kind of distant disdain; after all, she was the only woman on our street unable to hold on to her husband. She has always been the kind of woman whose ego really is quite astonishing – everything is simply all about *her*. She only ever talks about herself. If something bad happens to someone around her, she'll talk about how badly it has affected *her*. *Poor me, I've been so upset since Martha died of cancer*, etc. When my father left, it didn't occur to her that it might also have been difficult for me. Whenever I had a brief spat with the popular girls in school, she'd cry and beg me to fix it so it wouldn't affect her social life with the other girls' mothers. Even *this* she's claiming for herself, as if the burnt boy is something terrible that happened to *her* – I have to look away from her pathetic display of self-pity or I'm afraid I'll scream at her or even hit her for allowing this situation. This isn't about her; this is about Tobias, my poor unexpected little boy.

I very gently lift the ice pack off of Tobias's chest while making little shushing noises, but he lets out a wild, guttural scream at the sudden absence of the ice.

'Shhh,' I whisper. 'Oh, darling, what's happened to you?' I run my finger very gently across his eyebrows and he opens his eyes briefly, then shuts them firmly again.

'He needs an ambulance,' says Johan, his deep voice slicing into the intense atmosphere.

'No. We can't,' I say, very gently peeling back the kitchen towel, my other hand firm against Tobias's forehead to keep him from struggling. 'Look.' A purple-blue triangle the size of an adult's palm with raised, deep-red ridges is imprinted on Tobias's chest. On the insides of the edges are several darker-colored splotches, and in places the skin has opened, leaving moist red flesh exposed.

'Jesus Christ,' Johan says again, turning away from the bed.

'Tobias,' I say. 'I need you to listen to me. No, look at me, darling. That's it. You're going to be okay. Stay with me. I'm going to give you something that will make you feel better now, okay?' I turn to my mother, whose eyes are moist and desperate.

'What kind of painkillers do you have? Do you still have that OxyContin from your hip operation?' She nods, wide-eyed.

*

Tobias is fast asleep, breathing calmly and deeply. I go back downstairs to where my mother and Johan are sitting in the conservatory, lost in separate thoughts and staring out at the frozen, moonlit garden. I take the brandy Johan hands me and down it in one. He refills my glass and I down that, too. I give him a tired smile, but he doesn't return it, and his eyes are wide and afraid. I try to recall what it was like to be a child in this house, before my father left, and after, but my mind draws a blank. Only fragments come to me; sitting on my father's knee in this conservatory, watching rain hit the glass panes, listening to his deep voice reading me a story, punctuated by the deep suck of his pipe, followed by the hazy blue smoke spiraling towards the domed glass above us. My mother shouting upstairs, the sound of glass smashing, my father's averted eyes, like a dog's. And later – my mother and me, moving silently about the house, listening out for each other, like animals in the wild, needing to avoid one another. Her voice drifting up the stairs to my room from where she'd sit in the hallway cooing into the phone to some man or other, none of whom she managed to keep.

'We played Snakes and Ladders,' my mother says, cutting the cold air, 'and he was… just lovely. He's so beautiful, isn't he? Just… gorgeous. He didn't say much, but seemed to enjoy the game and kept smiling up at me every time it went his way. I gave him a bowl of vanilla ice cream with chocolate sprinkles and marshmallows. After that, he watched a couple of *Tom and Jerry* cartoons while I got on with some of the ironing in the utility room. I could see him from there, and after a while I noticed his eyelids getting heavier, so I asked him if he wanted to go upstairs to bed. He did, and we went upstairs so I could show him the guest room, your old room. He looked around, touching the little ornaments you'd collected as a child and lined up on the window sill. He pointed out of the window and said, *No moon*. I told him I was just going to go to the bathroom, then I'd come back in a minute to read him a story. I didn't hear a thing while I was in the bathroom, he must have tiptoed down the stairs, you know how they creak. It was just as I came back out that I heard it – the most indescribable howl. At first I thought it must have come from outside; it sounded like an animal caught in a trap. Then I heard a loud crash from the kitchen area downstairs and I rushed there as fast as I could. I saw Tobias, face down on the floor in the utility room, clutching the iron, which was on the floor beside him, still plugged in.

'I thought he must have come downstairs to look for me and touched it by mistake, but when I turned him over, it was clear to me that he must have done it intentionally. The iron had singed straight through his pajama top, and to do this kind of damage, he must have held it there awhile, not just a brief, accidental moment. I half dragged, half carried him into the bathtub and turned the cold water on him, because I'd read somewhere that that is what you're supposed to do.'

'I don't understand why you didn't call an ambulance. I still don't understand why we're not getting him a doctor,' says Johan.

'It would look like we've burned him, Johan,' I say. 'Nobody would believe that an eight-year-old would be capable of inflicting that kind of damage on himself. We'd go to prison. Seriously.'

My mother and Johan both shake their heads slowly back and forth like Tobias had done, delirious with pain, when we arrived.

'I thought he was doing okay,' says my mother. 'I'm just so... so upset and shocked.'

'Was there anything that happened while he was here that could have triggered this? Something he saw on television? Something you might have said that seemed innocent to you but which could have triggered something in him?' God knows she said a lot of weird stuff to me when I was younger. *Oh, Cecilia, if only you were different*, I remember as one of her favorite phrases.

'No. No, I shouldn't think so,' says my mother, but then, self-awareness was never her forte.

'How do we know a burn as bad as that won't kill him?' Johan asks.

'As long as we can keep it from becoming infected, he will be fine,' I say.

'How could he do something like this?' asks Johan, pressing his thumbs against the bridge of his nose, between his eyes.

'You can't be expected to look after someone with these kinds of problems, surely?' says my mother, her trembling hands clutching the tumbler. 'He could even be dangerous.'

'Mum, did he say anything at all? When you found him, was he crying or shouting or anything?'

'No, he was shaking and clutching his chest. He did say something when I put him in the bed.'

'What?'

'He said... he said *mama* a couple of times. The poor little thing. Maybe he can somehow remember something about the terrible mother who left him and briefly mistook me for her.'

'Are you... are you sure that's what he said?'

'Yes, absolutely. That isn't so strange in itself, is it? Most children would cry for their mothers in a situation like that.'

I excuse myself, saying I'm going to check on Tobias. I sit awhile on the side of the bed, and watch his tiny body twitch in his deep, medicated sleep. He's still sweating profusely, but he seems peaceful and pain-free for now. Thank the Lord for opiates.

'Why, Tobias?' I whisper and he lets out a long, shuddering breath as if in response. I need this boy. I take his hand in mine, but am struck by how cold and damp it feels. Again, I see Anni in my mind; those outstretched, icy hands reaching for me. I stand up and walk over to the window. The rain has let up, and the fog has evaporated, leaving behind a clear, cold winter night. A flush of stars climb towards a silver moon hanging low above white, frozen trees. I see myself out there, walking fast and silently through the birch forest until I reach the rocky beach at Vesterøya's southern tip. I could wade into the water, crushing shards of ice forming in between the rocks in the shallows as I go, gasping at the shocking cold as the black water surges into my boots. I'd stop when it reaches my waist, then I'd tip my head all the way back to see the stars again. Then I'd keep leaning back until my hair reached the surface of the sea and the sea would rise up to meet me and I'd just let myself fall back into it, until it would close over me forever.

I quietly step back onto the landing, and stand for a moment, listening to the faint murmur of Johan and Mother's voices from downstairs. I cross the landing and step into my old room, the room which held the first nineteen years of my life. My mother has strangely kept it exactly as I'd left it, and I find that rather creepy – it stands like a shrine to a child who no longer exists. Along the window sill the little glass figurines I collected in my early teens are lined up, and I pick one up, a tiny elephant, and am slightly taken aback by how my fingertips remember every curve and hollow of its glass body. I put it back down and run my hand lightly across a couple of the others – these, too, are intensely familiar. No dust has settled on or around them, my mother must still dust as obsessively as she used to when I was a child. I turn back around to leave the room and my eyes briefly pass across the bookshelves above the bed. Then they stop. A small object, completely innocent to unknowing eyes, and yet unmistakable to Tobias. Now I know why he did it.

CHAPTER 12

I SHOULDN'T HAVE done it. It's not normal to do things like cutting yourself or burning yourself, and I am normal, so I don't know why I sometimes do those things. Back in the Poland-house, when I first had to live with Krysz and Anni, I used to pierce the skin on my heels with a little fork I'd taken from the kitchen. At first it was to play with the very hard skin that was there because I'd run barefoot at the farm all my life, but then I realized it felt good to push the fork deeper and harder, until drops of blood appeared and it hurt a lot. It made everything go away – even Krysz and Anni's shouting and knowing that Moffa is dead, even if it only lasted a minute. Then I'd have to do it again, harder.

I'm better now but I'm still not allowed in school. *Maybe tomorrow*, says the mother in the house every day. I shouldn't have done it, but it was like for a moment somebody that wasn't me decided what I should do, and just did it. I'm afraid and I think maybe I'm angry, but they feel quite alike so I can't be sure. Because I burned myself, the family follow me everywhere. In the daytime, when the girls are at school, I'm not allowed to stay in my room, I have to be in the living room so Luelle can watch over me, or the mother, if she's home. Luelle comes from The Fipines and she's quite nice, but I think she likes cleaning more than children, even though she's not very good at it. Her name is Lu-Elle but the mother in this house calls her Luel as if it rhymes with fuel. When Luelle came to live here just after me, I asked the mother if Luelle was her sister. This made her laugh very loudly, the kind of laughing that is angry. She got a red splotch on her neck and a vein stood out on her forehead, that's how angry she was. I didn't know why it was a stupid question – in my school there's a girl from Norway and her little sister was adopted from Korea, but she's still the sister. Families don't have to look the same. Later, Nicoline came into my room and her face looked excited and a bit naughty, and she said, *Way to go. You really pissed off my mother when you asked if the servant was her sister.* She held her hand up in a high five. I said I didn't know Luelle was a servant and Nicoline laughed and said, *Same-same.*

I think Luelle likes me more than the girls, maybe because I pick up things and say hello to her and things like that. Or maybe it's because I'm brown, too, and not really in this family either. This morning when I was drawing in the living room and she was clearing up after breakfast, she stopped what she was doing for a minute and I noticed that she was looking at me. She left the room and then, after a moment, she came back and handed me a Toblerone chocolate bar. On the table in front of me she put a photograph. *My boy*, she said in English and I know quite a lot of English from TV so I knew what it meant. The photograph was of a bare-chested boy standing underneath a palm tree, holding a white kitten. The kitten was very white against his brown skin. He looked like he was my age, or maybe a little bit younger, and when he smiled, his front teeth were both missing. *Nice*, I said. Luelle nodded, and in her eyes were tears. *In Fipines*, she said, *two years*, and I think she was very sad to be here when her boy is there.

My body doesn't hurt as much now. It was very terrible for two or three days. The mother and the father in this house had fights about it and I know this because I could hear them in the night when they thought I was sleeping. *He needs to see someone*, said the father, many times. *No*, said the mother. She gave me pills to take the pain away. Some of them made me feel like I was dreaming. On the first day after I did it, she sat beside my bed the whole day after we came back to the house from the old lady's house. I tried to say something to her, but my mouth wouldn't say anything. It felt like everything, including me, had turned to a mushy jelly. It wasn't bad, more strange. The worst was that every day the mother would change the bandage on my chest. It hurt so bad that the first time, I pushed her off me and screamed and Luelle had to come and help her hold me down. She put a salve on it to stop it being infected. If it's infected, I can die, Nicoline told me. The mother had said it to her. On the third day, when she changed the bandage, she looked even more worried. *It's weeping*, she whispered.

A woman came. She said her name was Coco and that she's a nurse. The mother in the house looked very worried. She walked around and around in a little circle as Coco gently removed my bandage. When the burn was uncovered, she drew a sharp little breath and said, *Cecilia…* The mother in the house said, *Please, just do something.* Coco and the mother stared at each other for a long while and I think they were angry. *Please*, said the mother. Maybe Coco didn't want to do what the mother wanted her to, but I wasn't sure what it was. Coco took my temperature and sighed heavily, like it was my fault if I was too hot or too cold. After a while, Coco left, and I lay very still on the bed and listened to the sound of her car's tires crunching on the driveway. The mother sat on the side of the bed and asked if I needed anything. I shook my head and wanted to turn towards the wall, but it hurt too much to move that way so I just stared at the ceiling. Then, the door opened again and Coco was back, carrying a funny little white box. *I'm going to try to make you better*, she said.

Coco gave me many pills and then she spent a long time trying to make the burn better. It hurt, but less than when the mother in the house did it, probably because Coco's a nurse. At one point, the mother left the room for a while, and Coco leaned in very close to my face and said, *Tobias, tell me the truth, did you do this yourself?* I nodded. *Are you sure?* she asked. I nodded again. *Why?* she asked. *Because I was sad.* She asked, *Why were you sad?* and I opened my mouth to answer but just then the mother came back into the room, carrying a tray with three cups of the smelly red tea she wants me to drink. Roy bush, she calls it. She must have realized that Coco had asked me something when she wasn't in the room, because she acted strange afterwards.

Since then, Coco comes after lunch every day. The mother in the house calls her Cornelia, not Coco, and the girls call her Auntie Coco, because she's in the family. The mother has not left me alone with Coco again since that first day and I don't like that someone is always with me. I'm used to at least some time by myself and now I can't have it, so I wish I hadn't done it. I tried to tell the mother that I was sorry and that I wouldn't do it again and that it was okay for me to be alone a bit like usual, at least in my room, but she just looked away.

Today is a Tuesday and it's the mother who is here with me. If I hadn't burned myself, I could have gone to the pool with Hermine this afternoon. *Maybe in two weeks*, said the mother when I asked when I could go back. I *am* getting better, though.

I think Coco's pills were what helped me. *You're going to have an ugly triangle scar forever*, said Hermine yesterday. *Shut up*, said Nicoline. *Scars are cool.* Then Hermine shoved Nicoline. They fight a lot, and sometimes they fight about me. Like which one I like best, or which one's room I want to play in. I think I like Nicoline best, because she comes over to me in school and asks, *Are you okay?* sometimes. Hermine pretends like she doesn't know me in school and one time, a boy asked if I was her brother and she told him to shut the hell up and hit his arm then she had to go and sit in the head teacher's office for the rest of break time. Hermine is prettier, though. She has tight blonde curls that she brushes away from her face, and green eyes with very long black eyelashes. Her skin is quite brown but that's not how she really is, it's because the family went to Phuket in Thailand just before I came. The girls have pictures of nice beaches and palm trees on their phones.

The mother is typing on her computer. She likes to be on Facebook. Nicoline is on Facebook, too, and she showed me once how you can find the people you know and like their pictures and things like that. Once, before I burned myself and I was allowed to be alone in a room, I looked at the mother's Facebook because it was open on her computer and she had gone to the shop. It had many pictures of her and the father on the beach and in places other than Sandefjord. It also had some pictures of Hermine and Nicoline, sitting together closely on a giant blow-up banana in the sea. While I was looking at the pictures a little box popped up in the right-hand corner. It was a message from someone called Simon F. It said:

You were so hot at the gym. Sure you don't want to grab coffee? I'm hoping you'll say yes eventually.

I went back up and saw that Simon F. had sent many other messages and that the mother in this house had answered and said:

> You can look but you can't touch – I'm a respectable woman with a husband and two children.

I wish she had said three children because I live here now, too.

The next day, while we were all having breakfast, the mother in this house said to the father: *I'm off to the gym this afternoon. Can you take the girls to tennis?* He nodded and helped Hermine pour milk on her Cheerios. Luelle stood next to the table, just waiting in case anyone dropped something. For a moment I wanted to do something weird, just to make something happen. They're very odd, but at the same time, I think it must be how normal families are.

I look up now and find that the mother in this house is staring at me. *Do you want to come for a walk with me?* she asks, and it seems like a strange thing for her to ask, because I've never seen her go for a walk before. Outside, it is quite a nice day. Coco won't come for a while yet, so maybe the mother wants to walk around the neighborhood or something. I nod. I haven't been outside since the day I burnt myself. She closes the computer and walks around the kitchen, turning off all the lights. I watch her, like I often do, because she is quite weird.

She does many things which I haven't seen people do before. She takes away the hair on her eyebrows and then she draws it back with a pencil. She buttons the top button on her dress and then unbuttons it and then she says to the father in the house that she needs him to help her button her dress. She doesn't cut her nails even if it means she can't type on her phone. She hides the pouch of ready soup from the shop at the bottom of the bin and then she dips the head of the electric blender in the soup and leaves it dirty on the counter. She also sweeps up the crumbs on the table as soon as people start to eat, with a tiny dustpan and a brush, which Luelle, who isn't allowed to eat with us, has to empty. The first day I was here, Nicoline said, *My mother hates crumbs*, and the mother nodded. *They're like little rocks against the skin of your elbows, aren't they?*

We drive for quite a long time, and I don't know where we are going. I don't ask, because I think it's best to not say everything you want to say all the time. After a long while, the mother parks the car in an empty parking lot by a long beach. For a moment, I feel afraid. What if she leaves me here and drives away? Anni always said she'd leave me somewhere far away if I didn't listen. We get out and she smiles at me. I smile back but I feel a little strange.

On the beach, we pick up pebbles and little cracked shells. The waves are big because it's winter, and the light is pink even though it's only lunchtime. I'm wearing a blue woolen hat and mittens the old lady made for me. Around my neck is a scratchy scarf she also made, and I untie it, letting freezing air rush from the sea down my neck, but then the mother notices and ties it tight again. If Baby was here, she'd run like a crazy dog in and out of the waves, and she'd drag sticks along the beach for me to throw. If Moffa was here, he'd put me on his shoulders so I could be like a giant, and he'd pass me stones to throw into the waves. I pick up a rock and fling it to the sea, but my chest hurts with the movement and I'm not strong enough to reach the water. I write my name in the sand with a stick and watch the mother jump from foot to foot to stay warm as she stares out at the sea. Then I walk over to her, and say what I've wanted to say since the day I burnt myself with the iron, or before even, since the moment I saw the picture.

I know who you are.

CHAPTER 13

I'M DESPERATE NOW, that much is pretty obvious. It's like everything I've created, everything I considered solid and sustainable, has actually been constructed upon air bubbles that may pop at any time, one after another. Every day, I'm having to take tranquilizers just to function. The last few days, I've also had to take Adderall to stay focused, though it makes me jittery and even more nervous than usual. It's four o'clock in the morning and I haven't slept at all, just tossed back and forth in bed endlessly, staring at Johan's face in the dull glow from the streetlights. Again, I feel struck dumb by fear at the thought of Johan finding out what kind of situation I've placed us all in.

Tomorrow, we will pile all the kids into the car and drive to our mountain cabin in Hemsedal to open it up for the season. It's a long drive, but we'll give them each an iPad and hope for the best. I won't mind the road; I'm hoping it will distract me from the repercussions of what I'm about to do. It's been two weeks and Tobias has more or less healed, thankfully, but what he did and said has cast a dark shadow over his stay here, which I'd been beginning to hope could be manageable. I'd thought I would get away with what I told him at the squat house after he ran away, but now it has, of course, become clear that he's placed me in a very precarious position; I don't have much choice. *I know who you are*, he said, but what does that even mean? I need to know what he knows but I don't know how to get it out of him without potentially giving him information he doesn't have. He may be eight, but he can take me down, and I won't let him. At the same time, I've become fond of this boy, and the thought of losing him now hits me right in the heart. Tobias somehow reaches me deeper than anyone else.

I detangle myself from Johan, whose breathing is soft and slow, and go downstairs. Outside, the icy drizzle that seems to define this winter is falling, chased into dancing flurries by a brisk wind. I stand at the bay window in the living room, sipping from a mug of warm whiskey with honey and a dash of tea, when a curious idea forms in my mind. I go downstairs to the ground floor. Next to Luelle's bedsit is my walk-in closet – my wardrobe room, rather. On a high shelf, wedged in between boxes of summer clothes, is a little basket containing soft blue yarn that I bought a few years ago on a whim to knit a hat for Hermine. The hat never materialized and I'm not exactly the kind of mother who knits, though I like people to think I do – but seriously, why bother when I can discreetly buy homemade things online? I sit down on the bare floor, buzzing with determination. It won't take me more than an hour – it's a simple little thing I'm making, just a small gesture, a Band-Aid for a gunshot wound, perhaps, but still. I want him to have something of me. It's therapeutic, watching the knitting needles move around and through, over and over, and it is with some satisfaction I hold the little object up to the light when I've finished. A little blue bear for Tobias, no larger than the palm of a child's hand, with stitched black crosses for eyes. I return the yarn and knitting needles before going back upstairs to make another rosehip and booze concoction. I take a few deep breaths, and drink the tea quickly. It's just after five a.m.

I knock very lightly on Tobias's door. I was half expecting him to be awake, sitting on the floor and drawing, like he sometimes is in the night, but he's fast asleep, his chest rising and falling rapidly, as though he's distressed. What might this boy dream about? I lay a gentle hand on his shoulder and sit down on the edge of his bed. He immediately tenses up but doesn't turn around.

'Tobias,' I whisper. He's awake now, I can tell from his deliberate stillness. 'I have something for you.' He turns around slowly, mindful of his burn. I press the tiny bear into his hand. A cry of surprise escapes from Tobias. He holds it up to see better in the faint light streaming in from the corridor. His face is flushed with wonder, but his eyes look tired and confused.

'Go back to sleep,' I whisper.

'How… ? How did you… ?' I hold a finger to my lips and Tobias seems to resign himself to this strange moment. He reaches his arms up to me and I draw him close, breathing in his sweet, sleepy scent, smoothing down his thick hair, kissing the top of his head. How am I going to manage to do what I have to do? I ease him back onto his pillow and sit awhile, stroking his hair, watching as he drifts back off to sleep, his little mouth dropping open, exposing the soft pink lining inside. I steel myself, breathing slowly and deeply. I will do this just like I managed all those years ago – because I have to.

I had a plan, a perfectly decent plan, and fucking Anni went and royally fucked it up, and I can't see that I'm left with any other options when it comes to Tobias's future.

I go back downstairs to the lower level, open Johan's study and sit down at his old computer, the one Nicoline and Hermine use for Minecraft and YouTube tutorials, and wait as it chugs noisily to life. I activate 'incognito' mode, then go to Vike.no. I create a new account, yogamumsandefjord@vike.no – I'm pretty sure nobody would try to log in to that even if they somehow were to come across it. It's almost six a.m. by the time I've done this – I'm taking much longer to complete these simple tasks than I normally would, but then, I'm exhausted this morning and can't help procrastinating. I'm so tired and the whiskey and the Adderall make me feel like I'm moving through water. I can't believe what I'm about to do, or the events I may be setting in motion. How do you even go about finding someone you've spent almost a decade pretending doesn't exist? And what could come of it? But, let's face it, I'm desperate. Truly desperate.

I must have passed out or fallen asleep, because I wake slumped over the closed laptop. I listen for a while, but the house is still silent, and outside the sky is pitch black. The events of this morning rush through my mind, but they are disjointed and murky, and I can't immediately recall everything – the less sexy consequences of mixing spirits with Diazepam and Adderall. Did I really do what I think I did? I open the computer and log in to my new Vike account. In the sent folder I find what I'm looking for – an email sent at 6.11, with the subject 'Punta del Este March 2008, Scandibelle'. My heart begins to thud hard, and a bitter taste of bile shoots up into the back of my throat. I can never take this back. Never.

He wasn't hard to find, not when I finally let myself look. I can't even begin to imagine what it would have been like, back in the day, trying to find someone in a different country, someone you've only met once, who you know nothing about – or almost nothing. A first name, a remembered smile, a couple of bits of exchanged information – it's enough, these days, to track someone down. LinkedIn came up dry, like I thought it would. Facebook, too. Instagram, on the other hand... There he was, easily found with the hashtag #DJSoulo. His account linked to a website, and on the website I found the email address.

Tobias will never know the circumstances of his early life, but as he's lived in my house for almost two months now, and this situation is taking an incredible toll on me, I have come to the conclusion that I am left with little choice but to come forward with what I know. He knows that I knew Anni, and while he promised he'll never divulge the reason to anybody, he's eight and likely to let slip to someone like Laila Engebretsen. This situation has escalated completely out of control, and the only choice I have is to divert attention away from myself, and the secrets I've had to keep to save my marriage and my family. A contributing factor is also that, in the time Tobias has stayed here, I have grown fond of the boy, and while I'm under no illusions about what I could offer him, I would like to give him a chance at a life better than being shuffled around different foster families. I am the only person alive who holds the key to this, because, once, I knew his father.

*

The cabin was a wedding gift to us from Johan's parents, and over the years we have extended it several times, so it is now one of the bigger cabins in this area. Obviously, it has also been impeccably styled, with charcoal slate floors, walnut walls, huge open fireplaces and pared-down, antique French chandeliers. During the winter, we generally spend at least every other weekend up here, and under more normal circumstances, it's the most relaxing place I know. Though I'm not much of a morning person, I like to sit wrapped in blankets on the terrace at dawn, watching the sun stain the rounded mountains pink. I breathe easier up here in the thin mountain air, but not this time. I walk from room to room as if in a daze while the children play outside in the snow and Johan goes off on his twenty-kilometer cross-country sprints. Every hour or so, I walk out of the cabin and down to the main road, holding my iPhone above my head until it finally picks up a weak signal. I check the yogamumsandefjord account over and over, but there is no reply. My work emails I ignore entirely. It's like I'm itching from within. No response as of today. Two days have passed since I sent the email and it's highly unlikely that it has not been read. I should never have sent it; I must have been struck by a moment's madness. But what was I to do? It isn't human to be stuck in this kind of situation. When I get home, I am going to delete yogamumsandefjord@vike.no and pretend that this whole thing never happened.

'Mommy,' screams Hermine, cutting into my thoughts, making me look up from where I'm making a coffee in the kitchen. It's a bright, beautiful day and I squint as I step outside. 'Mommy, you have to see this,' she shouts. The kids are tobogganing off the garage roof – that's how much snow has fallen here in the mountains in the last couple of weeks – the lowest part of the sloped roof is now level with the ground. They're red-faced and shrieking with laughter, and I watch them for a while. Tobias looks like any other boy, carefree and happy, not like a troubled child who would burn himself with an iron. His burn has finally healed, and the plan is for him to return to school on Monday. Watching him, my heart picks up its pace as it often does; there is something about his smile that just clutches so very hard at my heart.

Nicoline throws a little snowball at Tobias and he laughs, running away up the side of the roof, ducking. He hides behind the chimney, his little hands working hard at packing a suitable snowball to send back down at Nicoline, who's jumping from foot to foot, laughing and chanting, 'Tobias can't get me.' But then something strange happens. At first, I confuse the bolt of fear in Tobias's eyes with him being blinded by the sharp winter sun or something; he's come out from behind the chimney and is holding a large snowball between his hands, as if about to fling it down towards where Nicoline stands, but it is as though he has suddenly been struck dumb. The happy smile of just moments ago has faded to a strange, anguished expression and his face is ashen.

'Tobias?' I say, taking a couple of steps towards him, but it is as though he can't hear me. Has his burn suddenly caught on something, causing him pain? Nicoline and Hermine, too, have fallen still and stand staring up at the boy on the roof. I clamber up the steep incline of the snow-packed roof and touch upon his shoulder, and only then does he respond. He turns slowly towards me, and then drops his gaze to the big snowball still held in his hands.

'No,' he screams, suddenly – his voice echoing down the valley. He drops the snowball, then stomps on it until nothing but trampled snow remains. Then he rushes past me, hops off the roof and runs up the track behind the cabin to where the dense fir forest begins. He disappears between the trees so fast that the girls and I barely manage to react, and by the time we reach the forest, he's nowhere to be seen. We spend over an hour walking slowly about, screaming Tobias's name, listening out for any sound, but it is as though he has been sucked up into thin air. How long could he survive out here? It's minus eight, and darkness is only a couple of hours away. Nicoline and Hermine begin to cry, and I realize I must take them back to the cabin where they'll have to wait for Johan while I continue the search. I help them out of their soaking wet snowsuits and put a cartoon on before heading back out.

I see him immediately – he's followed us silently back out of the forest and is sitting back up on the garage roof, staring down at me. I approach him slowly, the way you might a sea creature who's still deciding whether to fear you. When I reach him, I pull him close, and he falls into my arms like a limp, unconscious body. He cries for a long time and I rock him gently back and forth.

'I'm sorry,' he whispers.

'It's okay.'

'Can… can I please call you Mommy?' he asks suddenly, in a very thin voice. I'm still holding him, and I pull him even closer to me, because I dare not expose him to the expression on my face.

'Tobias…' I begin.

'Please,' he says. 'Just once.'

'I'm not sure if that's a good idea, sweetheart,' I say, wishing my violently thudding heart would slow its pace down.

'Please.'

'I…'

'Mommy,' he whispers, and as he speaks I feel the most vicious dread spread out in my stomach like acid, turning everything it touches into pulp.

'Shhh,' I say, and we stay like that a long while, until I can be certain my tears have stopped.

CHAPTER 14

IT'S TUESDAY, AND in my world that means it's usually a shit day. In an attempt to change this trend, I've decided to try something new today. I am at the pool with Hermine and Tobias. Usually I sit on a chair and read a magazine, but today Nicoline is at home with Johan, and I'm doing laps in the empty lanes on the far side of the pool, away from the children. I used to swim, and for some reason I stopped many years ago. As a teenager, it was how I managed the noise in my head, especially after what happened with my father, and now, as I gingerly take a step into the turquoise water, I'm filled by that same calm. I wasn't going to put my hair under – I've curled it earlier today and for once this winter, it isn't raining – but I do, almost instinctively, and immediately the hoots and laughter of the swimming club kids is muted, and the world is blue. I swim until my arms ache, mostly underwater. The years peel back and all the things I've become are irrelevant and here, under the surface, I can just be the very core version of Cecilia.

In the last few days, ever since I sent that email, I have been swallowed up by the most intense turmoil. It has been like being dragged under by wild, gray waves, then briefly expelled to the surface, before being pulled back under, spluttering and gasping for air. One moment, I touch upon some perspective, and reason with myself that much of the craziness is in my own head, but then, the next, the reality of the situation hits me again full force and I want to throw myself to the floor and wail until someone kind gives me a sedative.

I've been drawn repeatedly back to thoughts of my childhood in these last few days. Perhaps unsurprisingly, those thoughts make me feel like I'm drowning, too; though my childhood was largely happy, it was marred by some difficult times. Looking back, it's the little things I remember; the lock on the bathroom door of my house, which was unusual and made to look like a padlock; my mother's favorite rosewater scent lingering in the darkness of my room after she'd kissed me goodnight; the shapes thrown by the waves breaking against the cape in the distance; the feel of my leather satchel slicing into my shoulders as I walked alone through the birch forest to school; the way my glass figurines twinkled when the sun shone on them. When did I know that my life as I knew it was breaking apart? I don't remember the day my father left, or my mother's face when she told me. When did I become who I am now? Was my future persona added to childhood Cecilia layer by layer, like brush strokes to an oil painting? Or, did one Cecilia become another as a result of certain episodes? And if so, which episodes were the most influential?

The water is so chlorinated, my eyes begin to sting and hurt after a while, though I've kept them firmly shut underwater. I come back up to the surface and rest awhile, holding on to the edge, settling my breath, when something catches my eye over by the diving board. Some*one* rather – it's Tobias, shivering slightly, standing at the back of the long line of children. He looks lost in thought, and his eyes seem to focus on something in the water to the left of where I am. He looks exactly the same as the first time I saw him: small, different, afraid. I try to give him a little reassuring wave, but he doesn't see me, and I feel overcome by a violent sense of dread and confusion. It's as though I can't trust myself, or even my own feelings and reactions. Have I told so many lies, both to myself and to others, that I have lost the ability to recognize the truth? I don't know what's real. I haul myself up on the edge of the pool and sit with my head between my knees, trying to remember my breathing exercises. *It's in your head*, I tell myself. *Everything is in your head.* I look up briefly, and he's still standing there in his Batman swimming shorts, and he's looking at me now, alarmed. His face angular, exotic, beautiful, familiar, unreadable.

When did I know? I try to think, try to force the one moment I knew for sure out from my memories, but my mind is murky with fear and exertion and regret. Or did I always know? Did I know Tobias's face before I ever saw him that first night? I can't isolate one thought from another and it is as though they pile on top of each other – good thoughts like Johan and wine by the fire and swimming fast and alone, but bad thoughts, too, like lost boys, split-second madness, façades toppling down, leaving the stark emptiness beneath exposed to the world… Pool water shoots from my mouth, though I am not immediately sure that that is what it is. My first thought is that it's blood, and that it's coming from inside me, broken free. Someone says something, careful at first, then loud, and then someone else begins to lift me, up, up, up away from the water, but a woman is screaming, screaming so loud that every other noise in the vast hall falls away. *Blood*, she's screaming. *My blood!*

Four days later

I've always thought that madness is something that happens to other people. Most people think that, I imagine, mad people included. The problem is that once you have been there, on that stretcher, shouting disjointed gibberish and throwing up and tearing at your skin, it is very hard to explain to people that it was just a bit of a funny turn. *I feel better now, off I go.* What made me really angry was the kindness. The professional, calm attempts at understanding. *No, Mrs Wilborg, of course we understand that you're not crazy.* Nobody will use the c-word, in fact. It's all *a cognitive setback* and *emotional confusion* and *stress-induced psychosis.*

Nobody will say, *Sorry, Mrs Wilborg, you went completely fucking batshit crazy there for a while, but fear not, here is the pill that will cure you.* For a loony bin, they are remarkably restrained with the drugs here. Not that I've ever been to a loony bin before, but I'd imagined they'd like you nice and mellow during waking hours, and out cold at night. All I get is one pill in the morning, and one at night, and I can't say I feel that either of them makes much of a difference. My thoughts still feel interwoven and inseparable, like a tight, tangled ball of hair at the nape of my neck.

'How long have you been feeling overwhelmed?' asked the female doctor who came to see me the morning after I came here.

'Who says I feel overwhelmed?'

'Don't you feel overwhelmed?' That is how these people carry on.

'I feel tired.'

'Okay. How long have you been feeling this kind of tired?'

'For a very long time.'

'Cecilia, your journal says you are currently prescribed Zoloft and Xanax. Do you take any other medications? Have you made any recent changes to your dosage?'

I take Adderall and Diazepam and a couple of other helpful pharmaceuticals, but as I get them off the Internet I am certainly not going to inform Dr Nielsen about this. 'No.'

'Have you at any point previously experienced hallucinations, internal voices or unusual visual disturbances?'

'Look. I know you think I'm crazy. You're probably right. Now can you please run some tests and find out what kind of crazy I am, so I can get the right cocktail of drugs and go home? You can't hold me here against my will.'

'You're right about that, Cecilia, and nobody will hold you here against your will. The standard procedure after a panic attack with psychosis is to keep a patient in for at least a day or two, before making a longer-term therapy plan, most likely in combination with medication.'

At the end of the second day, the same doctor came back and said I could go home if I wanted. Johan was ready to pick me up at any time, and I could come back the next morning for counseling. I sat perched on the window sill as she spoke, looking out at Tønsberg. Snow was falling in drifts, chased by a strong wind and settling against the sides of buildings in steep crags. I watched Dr Nielsen's face as she spoke, at first thinking that I kept mishearing what she was saying, but then realizing that it was much worse than that; underneath her voice, another voice was speaking, inside my head. *You ugly, stupid girl*, it said. *Everybody hates you. You're going to die soon. Make it so, Cecilia; hurry up. What a waste of skin you are. Spare the world having to put up with you any longer.* Ugly, stupid, crazy – those were the only words I could hear as the doctor spoke, and in the end, I closed my eyes against them, and began shaking my head vigorously.

'No,' I whispered, and then, louder, 'Shut up!'

'Excuse me?'

'Shut up!' It sounded very loud when I shouted inside the small room. 'Sorry,' I said, trying to catch Dr Nielsen's eye to reassure her that I'm not an actual crazy woman, or at least, not like most of the people she probably sees, but she wouldn't meet my eye. 'Sorry. I wasn't talking to you,' I shouted. 'I said sorry! I didn't mean to say shut up to you! When everybody's talking at the same time it isn't so strange that I become confused. Sorry.'

So now they won't let me go. It's not so bad. I have my own bathroom and TV. The food is nasty, but I needed an incentive to diet anyway, so it doesn't bother me much. What I want is for Johan and the children to come and visit me, but Johan said in a message the doctors showed me that he thinks it's best if he waits until we can be certain there won't be new 'episodes' as the children, and Tobias in particular, were so unsettled by the episode at the pool. I know there is something I need to do, something to do with Tobias. I have little recollection of the days leading up to that Tuesday – all I can remember clearly is taking a lot of my pills and feeling constantly on edge. I remember other things, too, but they are less clear; pacing up and down the stairs late at night, feeling Tobias's eyes on me across the table, thinking I could hear the scratch of his pencils in the dead of the night, Hermine or Nicoline speaking to me and me feeling unable to decipher what they were saying. I remember the night I drove to Østerøysvingen 8 and, looking back, I wonder whether that was the start of whatever is happening to me now; it was hardly a sane thing to do, sleeping on the bare floor of an unheated house in Norway in November, wearing a cocktail dress and with only a small, lost boy for company.

And later... I recall the intense conviction that I had to contact someone, to tell them something of utmost importance, taking a long time composing an email, but I can't quite touch upon the details – it is as though every time I get close, the truth edges away from me.

I have slept for many hours and just woken up. Soon, they will bring me the little white pill to take. What if... what if it's the pill that is making my head so heavy and strange? If I just don't take it, perhaps clarity will return to me again. I sit up in the bed, and outside, the snow is still falling like it has all week, but heavier now. Even though it must be morning, I can barely make out the faint glow of the streetlight across the road through the white haze. There is a knock at the door.

'Yes?' I say, and Johan's sweet face appears. It's etched with worry, and judging by the blue circles around his eyes and the deep frown lines, you'd think he'd been up all night several nights running. In his hand is a small bunch of supermarket tulips, and for a short, sharp moment this makes me really angry.

'Hey,' he says nervously, glancing back out into the hallway, as though he were stepping into a lion's lair and not his wife's hospital room.

'Hey,' I say, but as I speak, my words are drowned out by a loud voice shouting 'Fuck off!' and it is as though I have no control of myself, or my mind, because it would seem that I shout it out loud. Johan stares at me.

'Sorry,' I say, and then, 'No! Shut up! Just shut the fuck up!' because the other voice is so loud that I can't hear what Johan is saying, never mind my own thoughts. Johan takes a step back, so that he's barely in the doorway and his mouth is moving like he's talking to someone out there in the hall, and then Dr Nielsen and two nurses appear and they say 'It's okay, Cecilia.

It's okay. You are going to be just fine. Now, you're going to go back to sleep for a while, and when you wake up, you're going to feel a whole lot better.'

Several days later

We drive in silence, but I can feel Johan's eyes on me frequently, as though I'm suddenly going to go nuts again and jump out at a red light, running down the street babbling incoherently.

'There's, uh… there isn't that much food at home, I didn't get a chance to shop on the weekend. Okay if I stop at Meny now?' asks Johan.

'Can't you just go later? I want to get home to the kids.' The thought of wandering around the brightly lit aisles of the supermarket fills me with dread – at this hour of the morning I'd be likely to bump into one of the other mothers from the school, or one of my friends from the tennis club. Do they all know? Sandefjord is a small town. You can't have a public meltdown and be sectioned here without everyone knowing about it. I'll be a pariah from now on – the crazy lady who went berserk and threw a fit in front of a group of children. We'll have to move. Johan seems to read my thoughts, because as we drive down the last bit of road by the sea before turning up the hill towards our house, he takes my hand from my lap and strokes it.

'Nobody knows about this, by the way,' he says.

'What about the people at the pool? The other parents? They know about this!'

'A couple of people called and I told them you'd had a severe allergic reaction to mercury that can lead to intense confusion.'

'Jesus, Johan.'

We've come to a stop in front of the house and I'm about to get out of the car, when Johan stops me. 'Cecilia, wait.'

'What?'

'Just... Wait... wait a moment.' His eyes are pleading with me, but this is typical Johan, getting all worked up about something, and making me feel like something terrible has happened, when actually what he's trying to say is he forgot to take the bins out.

'For God's sake, just say it.'

'It's Tobias.' I hear myself draw a sharp breath. Tobias. I haven't even thought about him for several days, but now I feel a strong yearning for him, as strong as for Nicoline and Hermine. I want to be inside, upstairs, in my favorite chair, drinking my tea while the house hums with the activities of the kids.

'What... What... what about him?'

'Cecilia, he's gone. They took him away.'

'What do you mean? Oh, God, what are you talking about?' I'm shouting now, and opening the door, but Johan reaches over and closes it hard. I glance at the house and can make out a faint rustling of the curtains in Hermine's room.

'Look. This was only meant to be a temporary arrangement, Cecilia. I know you've grown increasingly fond of him, and so have I, but it's in his best interests that they find a more stable long-term home for him.'

'When? Who did this?'

'The day after... after the pool. Laila Engebretsen called me. She explained that it wasn't possible for Tobias to remain in our care when you were in a psychiatric hospital.'

'That fucking bitch!' I'm crying, in spite of myself, and the old, ugly fury returns – the same fury I felt all those weeks ago when Johan agreed to take Tobias in the first place. How everything has changed since then. He's got under my skin; the serious, lost boy. And I want him back.

'Cecilia...'

'No! Don't "*Cecilia*" me! That goddamned bitch has never liked me. She was always out to get me. I'm going inside to have a shower and change my clothes, then I'm going straight down there and have her immediately return Tobias. For God's sake, it's less than ten days to Christmas! All his presents are in the attic with Nicoline and Hermine's!' Johan doesn't speak for a long while, merely stares down at his own hands still resting on the steering wheel.

'Try to see it from their point of view, honey. He's not our child, and it is their foremost duty to shelter an already vulnerable boy from unstable influences.'

'Unstable influences? Is that me?' Silence. 'Shelter? *We* have given him shelter when he had nowhere to turn.'

'Yes, but the plan was always for him to move into a permanent home in the longer term, Cecilia...'

'So have they now miraculously found him a permanent home, is that what you're saying? That Tobias has been placed in a loving home, where he can live until he is eighteen, in the custody of foster parents, who will treat him like their own?' No answer from my husband. Obviously.

'Now, if you'll excuse me. I'd like to have breakfast with my daughters, and then I'm going to go down to Laila Fucking Engebretsen's office and get Tobias back.'

'Cecilia, it isn't going to work. They have access to your medical journals. Social services is never going to give us Tobias while you are undergoing psychiatric treatment and are medicated on lithium, among other things.'

'Wait and see.' I step out of the car, taken aback by the bitingly cold air. Less than ten days until Christmas, and they have removed Tobias from our family and placed him in another temporary foster family, or worse, an institution. I turn back to Johan, who just looks forlorn and stressed, grabbing my holdall from the back seat. I could open my mouth and say the words – the words that would change everything.

'Johan,' I say, and he looks up. 'I… I'm sorry I screamed at you. I just… I feel like Tobias has been a good addition to our family. Hell, maybe we should even talk about applying for permanent custody of him.'

'Cecilia, I would. But they won't let us, not now. No way.' I open my mouth to let them out, the impossible words, but in the exact same moment I am about to speak, I remember the yogamumsandefjord email. I have to check it, right now.

*

Trying to behave like a vaguely normal person when you are sedated and upset about the fact that a small boy has been removed from your care is impossible. I try to log in to yogamumsandefjord@vike.no but keep getting the same message – 'account disabled'. Did I delete the account? My thoughts are sparse, obscure and darting about – I just can't remember. I'm trying to determine when the last time I checked the account was – it was after Hemsedal but before the pool, and there definitely hadn't been a response then. I don't understand how that is possible – anyone would have responded to that email at the first opportunity. What if he didn't get it? What if it isn't really him? I close the computer and blink back tears. I should never have sent that email in the first place, but I can't determine whether no response is a good or bad thing. And now I'll have to live forever with not knowing. I might be clearer than I was a few days ago, but I'm still confused, especially about how I can solve this situation without ruining everyone's lives. I run into Tobias's room, and Luelle is there, dusting, though it is already spotlessly clean.

'Ah, Mrs Cecilia, did you have a nice holiday?' she asks. I nod. 'Shall I… shall I take the sheets off the bed? Mr Wilborg told me to leave the room for the time being and to ask you when you came back…'

'No. No, leave them. For when Tobias comes back.' Luelle nods and gives me a kind, small smile.

The girls are on their iPads, but for once, I'm thankful. Every now and again Hermine looks up from the screen at me, and then quickly away when I notice her. I sit in my favorite chair by the window and drink Earl Gray. The harbor is busy, with both Color Line and Fjord Line loading their ferries, gushing black smoke into the white sky. Their chimneys are strung with fairy lights and the fjord is covered in patches of ice. I've taken my pill, and I feel fine. The voices subsided after a couple of days, but I must now live in fear of them suddenly starting up again, screaming abuse into my ears from inside my own head. The doctors said that with trauma, these things can happen and it doesn't mean you're crazy, though they didn't use the c-word. Permanently destabilized, they said.

I have a hot shower, but as soon as I step under the jet of rushing water, I am reminded of those terrible moments at the pool, when I was throwing up water, thinking it was blood, and feeling my control of myself slip away like stray droplets scarpering for the drain. I step back out of the cubicle, though I still have frothy shampoo on my head. How will I manage to live this new life, knowing that I'm nuts? Is this what it was like for Anni – that one bad thing happened and then that led to another bad thing, until everything was completely shit? And how can it be that I so badly miss someone I never wanted in the first place?

*

'Laila Engebretsen is unfortunately unavailable,' says the young, acne-ridden woman behind the desk at Sandefjord social services desk.

'Where is she?' I ask.

'She's in a meeting.'

'Here? In this building?'

'Well, yes, but she can't be disturbed while she's in there.'

'I think you'll find that she can. Could you please go and tell her that Cecilia Wilborg needs to see her right now, or I will call the police.' She rises slowly, like she doesn't understand the meaning of 'right now', looking at me apprehensively, but I slam my handbag down on the reception desk so hard she jumps and scurries off down the corridor. Through the glass doors, I can see Johan waiting in the car. He wanted to come in with me, but I made it very clear that he's more likely to get a date with a Hadid sister. A moment later, the young receptionist returns with Laila, whose face is etched with worry, and her customary sad half smile. I want her to look angry and shout that I can't just barge in here, but she just looks sympathetic, because now she knows that I'm craaazy.

'Come, Cecilia,' she says, and takes hold of my elbow, guiding me towards her office a couple of doors down. I do my very best to maintain my usual cool, calm expression – this bitch sure as hell isn't going to throw me. I have a sudden memory of her at school, standing alone at the edge of the playground by the fence, staring out at the fields, occasionally being whacked intentionally by the skipping rope of one of the girls playing nearby, who never let her join in. That girl, quite often, was me.

'How *are* you feeling?' asks Laila with what would appear to be genuine concern.

'Never been better,' I retort, but I know I have to play this right to beat this bitch once and for all. 'Look, I know you've heard about what happened to me. I understand that it's your job to protect Tobias, and ensure that he is in the care of capable and nurturing adults. He's been doing very well in our family, and though I wouldn't have imagined it, I think it has benefitted all of us to have him around. We'd like for Tobias to be returned to our family as soon as possible, and I'm also willing to discuss the possibility of us becoming his permanent family.' Laila nods as I speak, but slowly and sadly, as though she's trying to prepare me for the fact that whatever I say, her response will be 'No'.

'Cecilia, I'm very happy you came to see me. And I'm so glad you are feeling better. I can only imagine what an overwhelming time you have had recently, and it's only human to fall apart sometimes. I'm afraid, however, that there is no possibility of returning Tobias to your family.'

'And why is that, exactly?'

'Like you said yourself, Cecilia, it is my job to ensure he is taken care of in a stable environment. It is strictly against our guidelines to allow a child to remain in a short-term foster home if one adult is sectioned under the Mental Health Act, or receives anti-psychotic medication.'

'What about all the children who live in their *own* families who have a parent with a *temporary* problem which is being managed successfully? Does social services show up at the door and take those kids away?'

'I'm sure we can agree that's rather different.'

'Why is it different? We are the only family Tobias has now.'

'Cecilia, we are working very hard at the moment to find a permanent, suitable family for this child. I can assure you that we will not hand him over to anyone who isn't considered a very good match for him.'

'Where is he now?'

'I'm afraid I can't tell you that.'

'He's in an institution, isn't he?'

'Cecilia, I am not authorized to tell you where Tobias is.'

'It's Christmas in just over a week and you've stuck a traumatized nine-year-old in a fucking orphanage! There always *was* something wrong with you...'

Same sad smile, composed expression, ugly purple glasses teetering on the bridge of a long, thin nose.

'I'm afraid I'm going to have to ask you to leave. There are strict regulations about the treatment of social services staff, and it is illegal to physically or verbally abuse any staff member...'

'Listen to me, Laila,' I say, and my heart begins to pound very hard in my chest. I didn't say the words earlier, but I will now – I knew it as soon as I walked through the door. I will stop at nothing. 'You are going to tell me where Tobias is, and then you are going to return him to my family. Okay? That way, I can return to taking care of my family, and you can return to eating or whatever it is you do here all day. If you don't, I'm going to have no choice but to contact my lawyer and file a police report against you and Sandefjord social services.'

'Cecilia, please. I am not trying to upset you, I...'

'You're not upsetting me! You're breaking the law!'

'Excuse me?' Quick glance towards the closed door. She's afraid.

'I'm Tobias's mother.' A stunned silence hangs between us, and Laila exhales hard several times.

'Look. I've been trying to tell you that I'm very sympathetic that things have been hard for you recently. And I am very pleased that you bonded with Tobias, he will have benefitted from that. But...'

'I'm his biological mother, Laila.' I burst into tears, not only because it's true, but because I've finally said it out loud. 'If you don't believe me, why don't you commission a DNA test?' Laila nods, but weakly now, and that ugly half smile is finally gone from her face. She picks up the phone.

PART THREE

PART THREE

When you think about most women who have gone from having an okay life to having a terrible life, or worse, if they end up dead, it is usually because of some man. Women who get beaten or killed aren't usually abused by their female friends – it's always the lover, isn't it? When I was Oliver's girlfriend, I was sometimes bored. Often, I'll be honest. He was sweet and normal, but the things that excited him were things like magazines about power tools and watching ice hockey, so we didn't have that much in common. Perhaps because only one thing has ever excited me. Sometimes I was also sad when I was with him, because I felt alone, and it is actually worse to feel alone when you are with somebody else than when you're really alone. But I was never afraid. With Krysz I am, all the time, but on the upside, I'm never bored and I never feel alone.

When I first arrived in Krakow, I decided to try to help some of the many junkies I'd seen lying slumped in doorways and on park benches. It felt wrong to walk past them in my new, clean clothes and give them a friendly smile, showing off my even white dental veneers. I'd been there, right there on the bare ground, and I'd sworn to myself I'd never forget it. One early evening I walked from this bedsit on Wygoda Street, along the river and then across it, to Bednarskiego Park. It was getting dark, and most of the daytime park-dwellers had gone home, leaving a few dogs and their owners, and the junkies emerging from the shadows. I approached a couple of girls my own age who stood underneath a stone bridge, chain-smoking and rubbing their gloved hands together against the cold.

'Hi,' I said in English, and they turned slowly towards me, narrowing empty eyes.

'Buy?' asked one, and I shook my head.

'My name is Anni,' I said. 'I... I just wanted to talk to you.' The girls stared at me, and I realized how crazy it seemed to just walk up to a couple of drug addicts in a park for a chat.

'*Policja?*' asked the younger of the two, a skinny brunette with a chunky nose ring and heavy eyeliner.

'No,' I said, 'not *policja*. I just want to talk.'

'Talk?' The second girl spat the word out, and it occurred to me that they might rob me. I glanced quickly around me, cursing myself for having been so stupid, but there was no one nearby, just the charcoal silhouette of a man in the distance.

'Yes. I wanted to talk to you.'

'Fuck you,' said the brunette, and they both began to laugh, turning away from me. The older of the girls turned back around after a minute, and when she saw me still standing there, she lifted her eyebrow and threw her hands up in the air, presumably to someone behind me. I turned around, and there stood a tall man with sandy blond hair and expressive dark eyes. He was thin, unlike so many of the men I'd met in Poland so far, who seemed to subsist entirely on pork dumplings, but not gaunt like a drug addict. He looked at me with a serious expression, not hostile, but not exactly friendly either.

'What are you looking for?' he asked, in heavily

accented English. There was something about his eyes; an intensity in them, which made me feel even more nervous than I already was.

'Sorry,' I said. 'I... It's stupid. It's just, I used to be a heroin and crystal meth addict and I managed to get clean. I wanted to see if I can help someone, or...' The man laughed, and the girls began to titter again, too, though I doubted they'd understood anything I said.

'Did you find Jesus Christ or something?' he asked, and the girls laughed simply at the mocking tone in his voice.

'Excuse me,' I said, but the man took a quick step to his left, blocking my way.

'*Svenska?*' he asked. *Are you Swedish?* I nodded. 'I spent nine years in Gothenburg,' he continued in Swedish, which was much better than his English.

'Listen, walk with me,' he said, and started off down the path in the direction he'd come from. I could have made a run for it then, and might have made it to the gates before he managed to catch up with me, but there was something about the man that drew me in and made me want to speak with him.

'Fuck bitch,' I heard one of the girls shout after me as I followed the man down one of the lanes, which was completely deserted by now.

Suddenly he turned around and faced me. 'Look, I can't have you showing up here and offering to help any of my customers, do you understand?'

'I... Sorry.' He watched me intently, as though trying to figure out whether I had some more serious intentions, but seemed to decide I was harmless, as he strangely raised his fist in the air and motioned for me to touch it against my own, like they do in American high school movies.

'Bye,' he said, and started walking away from me, my fist still held in the air.

'Wait!' I said, and half ran a couple of steps after him. 'Who are you?'

'I'm somebody you want to stay well away from if you used to be on smack and managed to get yourself clean.'

'I'll never touch it again,' I said, 'No matter what.'

He nodded seriously. 'I'm Krysz,' he said.

'We could drink coffee or something,' I said, and even in that moment, I knew that this was one of those wrong turns, one moment's lapse of judgment, that can lead to your whole world breaking apart. How right I was. But there was something about his eyes that suggested kindness, or sympathy, or maybe there wasn't, and I just told myself that because in his presence my skin began to prickle with a wild heat. Krysz laughed, and stuck his arm out for me to take.

I'm writing about this because women like me, we should always write down what is done to us, not because we might one day want to read about it, but because it may save our lives. Or someone else's, if they find it and read it after he's done away with you.

*

Unfortunately, Krysz is the smartest person I know. He didn't suddenly say, *Oh, here you go, Anni. Why don't you get back on the heroin?* He broke me down slowly and so subtly that when everything I'd built up for myself was slipping from me anyway, all he had to do was one terrible thing to get me begging him for the one thing in the world I didn't need. It has been almost a year since I met Krysz now, four months since I shot up again, and one month since I left my bedsit and my studies, and went to live with him in his campervan. How could I do this to myself, I ask myself every single day, but the answer is very simple, like the truth often is. I fell in love. From that first evening in the park to later that night when Krysz stayed over at mine, to the delirious days and weeks that followed, I was head-over-heels infatuated. It was like I came alive every time he touched me, it was better than anything I've ever known, even better than the cleanest, hardest hit of smack.

It only vaguely bothered me that my new boyfriend was a drug dealer; I reasoned it didn't have anything to do with me, because back in those days I was still completely certain that for me, there would be no way back. It didn't occur to me that I had placed myself in a world where no one lives peacefully, where love is nothing but a cruel illusion, with a man who could only ever be my executioner.

Krysz lives in a purple VW campervan which he parks in various quiet streets off the canal, and now I live here with him. It might be a strange place for a drug dealer who makes good money to live, but Krysz has a five-year-old daughter, Magdalena, who lives in Sweden with her mother, and who has a blood disease that could kill her. Krysz saves almost all his money so she can go to America and get stem cells from somebody else because it is the only thing that will save her. Next year Krysz and I are going home to Sweden so we can give Magdalena the money, but sometimes I dream about not going with him, because it isn't like it was before anymore. At the time it seemed to me that it started without any warning, none at all, but now I know it isn't true. Before that first terrible night in January, Krysz had been acting differently for a while. He'd be loving and affectionate one moment, and cool and disinterested the next. Sometimes he'd criticize me in a cruel way, saying things like, *You are dirty inside and out, junkie whore* so many times I'd burst out of the van, clutching my shoes or jacket or whatever, running down an empty street in the middle of the night, towards my bedsit, Krysz shouting mean things after me. Now, of course, I have nowhere to go.

Even at the beginning I knew that Krysz worked most nights in a club where girls dance naked and that kind of thing. I'd never been, and back then, I was still spending all the time I wasn't spending with Krysz on my studies. I preferred to ignore the details of his business, focusing instead on the fact that he was only doing bad things to make enough money for Magdalena to go to America. When she gets better, he's going to sell used cars to people, because that's what he did before.

One night Krysz came to my house unannounced around eleven. He asked me to come with him to the club and help him out because there was some kind of problem. When we got there, it seemed all closed, and we walked down several dark, hushed corridors, towards the muffled sound of dance music playing in the distance. We walked into a softly lit space with an empty stage. I'd imagined girls twirling to the music, up and down a pole, *zlotys* sticking out of their tiny lace underpants, but there was no one there. Krysz turned to me.

'Four of the girls are off. Vomit bug. I need you to help me out.'

'Help you... with what?'

'Private clients,' he said, pointing to a black door faintly visible against the dark red wallpaper. 'Through there.'

'No,' I said, my voice strong and calm, but there

wasn't even enough time to turn towards the exit before his fist slammed into the side of my head, filling my ears with the sound of bone crushing. Again, and again. When I came to, one man was pushing his way hard into me while another held my legs up against my chin. I began to struggle, and noticed yet another figure standing in the shadows next to the sofa bed I was on. It was Krysz, and he smiled at me and held a finger to his lips, the way you'd hush a baby. On either side of the man holding my legs stood other men, laughing and smoking, some of them stroking their penises, waiting their turn. After a long time, they left me alone with Krysz and he told me to go to sleep on the sofa. I didn't want to, but I fell asleep with exhaustion and shock, and the intense pain in my head. When I woke up, Krysz half carried, half dragged me to a toilet with a wheelchair sign on the door, and brusquely cleaned me from head to toe with a dirty towel. Then, there were more men.

On the third day, Krysz helped me place a shot in the crook of my elbow, where some of my veins had become visible again after so many years of being completely destroyed. It was fine then. All of it. I didn't mind. That's how smack works, that's what it does to your mind; it makes everything okay, as long as you've got it.

*

Sometimes Krysz stays away for many days – three days, four, and on a few occasions, a full week. When he's away, I have played with the idea of just driving off in the campervan and going somewhere new. If I could get clean once, perhaps I could get clean again. Even while I think those kinds of thoughts, I know it isn't true or possible. I know why Krysz stays away – because by the time he returns, I've finished all the drugs he left me, and miss him so badly I will do anything, absolutely anything he says, without kicking up too much of a fuss. *We're a team*, he's always said. *What the fuck did you think – that I'd just support you and look after you without you bringing anything to the table?*

About a week ago, I passed Oliver on the street. I pressed myself against a building and tried to make myself merge with its limestone walls, but his eyes met mine and widened in horror. I wish I'd had sunglasses to disguise my watery, red eyes, or a hat to hide my lank, greasy hair tied back in a tight bun every day. I don't know what I'd expected, but I suppose I would have thought he might have said hello. Instead, he swiftly crossed the road, pointing out something in the distance to Åsa, whose hand he was holding, to distract her. She laughed at something he said, and her glossy ponytail swished back and forth as she walked. Over her shoulder was a nice leather handbag, and she wore cropped navy jeans and a pink Ralph Lauren top, the kind old ladies wear to golf.

After I had the misfortune of seeing Oliver and Åsa, I went back to the campervan and got out some crack I'd been saving. I walked to a wasteland behind a warehouse where I sometimes meet some other people like me, but that day, I was alone. I lit the pipe and drew the acrid smoke deep in my lungs, waiting for the first rush. I looked around me – at the gray, abandoned warehouses, the factories across the river spewing smoke, at a ripped billboard advertising some kind of amazing station wagon, and it all felt so wrong and foreign. For a very brief moment, I let myself think about Ellen, and Josef and Sofia. Did they know by now? I wondered. Up until I met Krysz, I spoke with Ellen two evenings a week. When I became so engrossed in Krysz I could barely sleep or eat or think straight, so our calls became more irregular, and I could tell that Ellen was becoming increasingly worried about me. She kept asking if something was wrong. *Come home if you need to*, she said several times, but I coolly reassured her that everything was just fine.

That day, after seeing Oliver and his preppy perfect girl, I took a shard of glass I found on the ground and sliced it along the inside of my left arm, making blood rush from me. I began hallucinating, seeing grotesque shapes grow forth from the upturned bodies of wrecked cars, and the sky went from a dull gray to a plethora of shimmering colors. I must have passed out, and when I woke again, my mother stood in front of me. She was crying, and I would have done anything to make her stop. *No more*, she mouthed.

*

I'm better now. I had to go to the emergency room even if they look at you like you're vermin there, and make you wait much longer than anybody else even if you're sicker than they are. I had miraculously missed my arteries, mostly because my arm was black and blue in the first place and I didn't know how to cut it right. I don't want to die. But I'm tired. The doctor who stitched me up – forty-four stitches in total – was kind and insisted on me sitting with him and talking for a while before I was allowed to leave.

'There's a whole world out there,' he said. 'So much more than this town, and your problems and your history.' I nodded. 'You could be anybody. You don't have to be like this forever.' I nodded again, and felt a sorrow so deep and ugly because I've lost Ellen and Josef and Sofia. I would have given anything to be back there, at the *torp*, making birch-root baskets and pulling fat, squirming lake fish from the clean, dark water.

'Do you have a family?' asked the doctor. I shook my head. 'Anybody?'

'Boyfriend.'

'Would he be helpful if you wanted another kind of life?'

A small puff of disbelief escaped my mouth at the thought of Krysz helping me. 'No.'

The doctor stood up and rummaged through his desk, which seemed to be full of papers. He pulled out a card and handed it to me. 'Nowa Kobieta – it means "new woman". It's an organization that helps women in desperate life situations. They can help with methadone, shelter, education, legal aid and so forth. I think you need to get in touch with them.' I took the card, knowing I'd throw it away as soon as I left the medical center – if Krysz found it among my things, he'd beat me to death. That night, I called Ellen, clutching the phone to my ear, and sat sobbing silently at the sound of her voice.

'Annika,' she said. 'Annika, darling, I know it's you. Please, please talk to me. It doesn't matter where you are or what you've done, honey. Just talk to me.' I put the phone down and it was a very long time before I was able to get back up off the mattress in the back of the van, I was crying that much. At the beginning, Krysz always called me Annika, but even then, when loving him was easy, I didn't want him to. Only my mother and Ellen have ever been allowed to call me Annika. I don't know why – maybe I've always sensed that there was some part of me that should only be for those who have really cared about me without an agenda.

Tomorrow morning I am going to Nowa Kobieta. I didn't throw the card away, after all, and I managed to hide it in the inside pocket of the wash bag where I keep things like tampons and tweezers. I called them two days ago and a woman who spoke American said that they will help me even if I'm a junkie and a whore and pursued by a man who will want to kill me, as long as I'm willing to get clean. I am, though I know how awful it is. Sitting here tonight, with my last smack and a little lump of weed, it feels like I'm going to war tomorrow and having to say goodbye to those I love most. Krysz has been away two days and nights already, and I hope to God he will stay away another – I doubt I'll make it to Nowa Kobieta if he comes back with drugs and more tasks I have to do for him.

Annika L., Karlstad, March 2015

If I hadn't made it to Nowa Kobieta when I did, the baby would have died. I would have unknowingly killed it with my endless cycle of drugs and abuse. I didn't even know it existed when I arrived there late one night, having walked cautiously all the way there along the river. They gave me a room to share with two other women: Debra, a very young Romanian girl covered in cigarette burns who'd been trafficked and managed to run away, and Sofi, a Ukrainian girl who'd been living on the streets since she was nine, and addicted to smack for as long. A doctor came and examined me, taking a urine test and a blood sample, and weighing me, before prescribing me methadone. The next morning, when I woke up in my middle bunk, the woman I'd spoken to on the phone – Macy Decker from Pennsylvania – stood by the side of my bed, and when she saw that I was awake, she took my hand and whispered, 'Oh, Anni, did you know you're having a baby?'

I got clean for him, and it wasn't as hard as the first time. I spent my days walking in circles in Nowa Kobieta's walled garden with Debra, drawing in this journal because I wasn't ready to write, taking my vitamins, learning to cook with the nuns who volunteered at the shelter and just trying to heal my broken heart and body.

After five months at Nowa Kobieta, I was encouraged to return to Sweden, and a residential place was arranged for me in Karlstad at a foundation that supports vulnerable mothers and their children. Before I went home, I wrote a long letter to Ellen, explaining what had happened to me in Krakow. I wrote that I understood that she wouldn't be able to see me again if I relapsed, in spite of the extraordinary things she and her family had done for me. I tried to explain that it had been difficult for me in Poland, away from home and the routines I'd built in Karlstad with Ellen and her family, and that it had been like being untethered again. I left before she could have responded, even though I didn't think she would, but when I arrived at Karlstad's red-and-white-brick train station, blinking at the impossibility that everything here was exactly the same when I was so very different, I heard someone call my name.

'Annika,' the voice shouted, 'over here!' It was Ellen, whose hair was shorter and grayer than before, and the next thing I knew, she was hugging me close, my protruding stomach strangely wedged in between us. She realized this and pulled back, staring down at my tummy – I'd just reached thirty weeks then and was unmistakably pregnant.

'Oh, Annika,' she whispered. 'Dear, dear girl.'

At the new women's shelter, the Marieholmhemmet, I continued much the same as at Nowa Kobieta – eating green things, exercising in the garden, reading books in bed, stroking my belly and feeling the baby nudge me from within in response. A team of social workers and doctors looked after me, praising me for my commitment to stay clean for my baby, and every few days, Ellen came to visit me. We'd sit out on the terrace in the cold winter sun, or walk to the bakery down the street for a *kanelbullar* for old times' sake. Everyone said to me that I might be able to keep the baby and that they would help me. Ellen even said that after the baby was born, I could come back to the red house in Sternvegen and live with her and Josef and Sofia, and they would help me with him.

The new life was beyond anything I could have imagined, in those difficult days in Krakow, when I was just waiting for Krysz or another overdose to kill me. All the kindness I received, it was astonishing. My baby would be welcomed into this world, even though he came from me. It all made me thankful that I didn't die that day I cut myself with the glass shard, high on crack. I knew the reason I'd made it was because my mother appeared. For so many years, I'd prayed that she would come back, just one time, that I could see her face one more time, because in my memories she'd become blurred, and that was almost worse than her not being there, but I'd lost hope that she ever would. That day in Krakow at the wasteland, smoking crack and cutting my arm open, was hardly the first time I was close to death, and yet, that was the time she chose to come back to me. She was the same, and the greatest gift I am left with after seeing her apparition is that my memories of her have been replenished, so now when I think of her, her face is clear in my mind again, as clear as though I was still a child.

In spite of all the offers of help and rehabilitation and promises for the future for me and my baby, I made a decision the moment I learned I was pregnant, and that was that I'd give that baby every chance at a decent life. And that meant he couldn't stay with me. Ellen tried to convince me that I may live to regret giving my baby up, but I always felt that it wouldn't be giving him *up*, but giving him an actual *chance*. Adoptive parents were found; a lovely couple from Uppsala in their mid-thirties who'd tried to conceive for a decade. They came to visit me every fortnight at Marieholmhemmet and would stare in awe at the visible kicking of their baby, wiping at tears, laughing and holding hands. They had good jobs, a shiny new Volvo, a house with a big lawn, a cute little dog, and a sincere wish to raise a child. It was the right thing to do. I maintain that even now that I've known his tiny clasped fists, his fuzzy forehead and mop of black hair and his puckered little pink mouth, and looked into his ocean-blue eyes. I could never have given him what his new parents can, and I only want him to have everything.

'We'll send you a photograph every year on his birth-day,' they promised on the day they took him home with them, but I shook my head and said I'd rather they didn't. Of course, there isn't anything in the world I'd rather have, but sometimes it's better to see someone in your mind and heart than in real life. The mother, Ulla, nodded solemnly, and drew me into a close hug, and I think she actually understood.

'I will protect him with my life,' she said, and Ellen and I watched them drive away from the orangery where we'd sat drinking tea every few days when the baby was still inside me. I think she was worried for me then, and that I would break down over giving the baby away, but all I could feel was overwhelming relief. I'd been upset and worried before because I wasn't sure that my body, which had been abused so much and for so long, would be able to carry the baby safely into life.

It's not like I don't miss the baby, or that I wouldn't give anything to hold him one more time, but I always knew that he was bigger than me, better, more important; and that if I could do right by him, then I'd have done at least one thing right. The strangest thing about right now is that my life is so very empty. There is no Krysz, no big belly, no baby, no drugs, no studies, no anything other than me. I'm almost thirty now, clean, lost. Ellen says I can be anything and go anywhere, like she's always said, but I feel like I can't see anything ahead, except an infinite whiteness that's neither good nor bad. The truth is, and obviously I can never discuss this with anyone around me, I miss Krysz so much at times that I want to walk into the river or throw myself off a building. Of course, I don't miss the bad things, the destructiveness and the abuse, but I miss *him*, or rather, the person I know he could be. That is why I still write to him.

It was me who wrote first. After all, he wouldn't have been able to find me. I did it a few weeks after I'd arrived at Nowa Kobieta, and walked a couple of blocks to a post office and posted a letter addressed to him at the club. I also rented a postbox, and that was the return address I used. I didn't tell him about the baby, but I told him that I would love him forever and that I felt sorry for him for having to live in such darkness. He wrote back after a couple of days, not angry like I'd thought he would be, but apologetic and seemingly sincere. He blamed his childhood, his shitty parents, the situation with his daughter, and his dreadful ex-wife. I should have left it there, considered it closure. But I responded, again and again, simply because I loved Krysz and still do. The reason I didn't tell Krysz about the baby was that I didn't believe it to be his, and also, even if he had been, I knew they'd never meet.

A new letter arrived from Krysz today, to the postbox I keep here in Karlstad. It was posted in Gothenburg. He wrote that Magdalena had taken a turn for the worse, and though she'd been treated in America last year, she might die from her blood sickness. He said he had moved to Sweden to be near her. He said he quit selling a long while ago, and that the combination of losing me and his daughter being so ill had given him a new perspective on life. He works on a large farm and believes the manual work helps him to stay sober and to be constructive. Like in every letter he's written to me, he begged for my forgiveness, saying he'd give anything in the world to see me one last time and make his apologies to my face. Some ideas are good and some are bad, and the problem is, of course, to be able to distinguish between them, something which hasn't come easily to me. But even as I wrote my reply, saying that perhaps we could meet sometime, I knew it was another wrong turn. I hesitated a long while by the postbox, and I could have just turned around and gone back home, dumping my letter into a bin along the way. I stared at my trembling hand holding the letter – the letter that could kill me – a long while as it hovered at the mouth of the postbox. Then I put it in. What's wrong with me? There are easier ways to die. But… Krysz clean – I can't even imagine it. Could it be that he's just a different man now, like I've become a different woman? Is it that unreasonable to believe that people really can change?

Annika L., Karlstad, June 2015

He met me at the station, leaning against a nice black Volvo, the kind my baby's parents have. A normal-person car, and Krysz looked like a normal person indeed. His hair, which used to be shaggy and matted, was cut short and neat. He wore discreet glasses, and was cleanly shaven. His T-shirt was black and nicely cut, and stitched above his heart was a little white cross and underneath, it read 'Jesus'. At first I thought it must be meant ironically, but then I noticed he was also wearing a black leather bracelet with 'I love Jesus' spelled out with white beads, and a new tattoo of a cross on his wrist. He was the same and he wasn't. I walked towards him slowly, feeling like my legs might buckle both from fear and longing. My skin, too, reacted to the sight of him, just like it had that first time I met him; it began to tingle all over, yearning for his touch, but fearing it also.

At his house, which was a small one-bedroom basement flat on the outskirts of Gothenburg, he'd framed a photograph of me, smiling and eating an ice cream by the river Vistula. I don't remember it being taken, but then, there are a lot of things I don't remember. It looked like he'd gone to IKEA and indiscriminately picked all the cheapest furnishings, but everything was clean, if completely impersonal. Looking around, I couldn't see a single object that I could remember having seen in the purple van. On the coffee table lay a well-thumbed Bible. On the kitchen counter was a stack of brochures that read '*Guds ord*' – God's word.

'I hand them out,' Krysz said, his voice startling me. 'At the supermarket and things. For the church.'

'But when... when did you become religious?'

He shrugged. 'I guess when I lost you, I realized there wasn't anything left. And then, with everything with Magdalena, well – I just had to feel some warmth or love from somewhere, and the church was where I found it.'

Krysz drank herbal tea and made me a vegan curry. He made no attempt to touch me or kiss me, but kept saying he would always be thankful that I gave him a chance to say how sorry he was. He slept on the sofa bed and gave me the freshly made bed in the bedroom, but I found it impossible to sleep, overwhelmed by the incredible strangeness of the situation, and this new Krysz. I felt the scars on my arms in the dark and watched roaming shadows from cars passing outside. I listened to the kitchen clock ticking so loudly I could hear it through the closed door. I tried to reconcile this new docile, God-fearing Krysz with the violent drug dealer who forced me into prostitution and repeatedly beat me unconscious, and while I couldn't, I realized I was no longer afraid of him, nor angry. I was tired of running.

Now we talk every day on the phone. For hours, and in a way we never used to before. Back then, it was all about getting high and getting money, but now, Krysz has returned to his interests from when he was younger. He is reading a lot, especially philosophy, and he is particularly interested in Nietzsche and Kierkegaard. *Life can only be understood backwards; but it must be lived forwards*, he quoted to me recently, crying down the phone as he spoke. They are saying Magdalena doesn't have long to live. Was I wrong for allowing this increased communication? Can it really be wrong to have faith in a person's ability to change and emerge from awful situations stronger and saner? I can't imagine the pain Krysz and Magdalena's mother must be going through; how could it be wrong for me to be there for him at this time? I wish I could have met his little girl; her plight has also touched me very deeply, but you can't introduce new people to a dying child.

I made it back to the *torp* with Ellen and Josef and Sofia, though I'd never dared dream I would. I live alone now, in a council flat in a block where a district nurse is always on duty, but every now and again Ellen invites me to join them at the *torp*. Though I am clean, this time for longer than ever, everything was different. The water in the lake was murkier than I remembered, my annex felt claustrophobic and my fingers would no longer comply with the birch-root coiling. The food, which used to taste incredible in its fresh simplicity, now struck me as boring. The soothing peace I felt before, far away from mobile reception and computer screens, made me feel like I was itching within, desperate for the nightly phone call with Krysz. All these sudden reservations about spending time at the *torp*, which had once been my very definition of heaven, were of course to do with Krysz. Not only his reappearance in my life, but because I was in love and knew of something so much bigger than myself.

Perhaps it also had to do with my baby; ever since I'd handed him out of my arms for the last time, I had felt a most profound emptiness. I wasn't sad, exactly; rather, I was proud of having managed to do what I did for him. I had safely carried him into the world and ensured he would be raised in a loving, safe environment. Hopefully my flawed genes won't cause him too much trouble, but maybe my shortcomings have little to do with my genes – after all, I came from my parents and there wasn't anything wrong with them except that they didn't manage to live for very long.

Even Ellen doesn't reach me in the way she used to before. Back then, it had been enough to just have her near, to know that I could call her if I needed to. I still love her as much as I always have, and Josef and Sofia, too, but they aren't enough anymore. I need to have Krysz, too. Even if it kills me. Tomorrow I'm going with Ellen and the family to the *torp*, and I am going to find a way to tell her that I am going to go and stay with Krysz in Gothenburg. It will only be a couple of weeks at most, but he has begged me to be there for him just for a little while.

I don't know what will happen when the little girl dies. I don't know how anyone can keep breathing when their baby stops. When he speaks of what is going to happen, Krysz says that Magdalena is going home to Jesus. He says he will never go back to what he was, because that would be to mock his little girl's life, and that the only way he can do right by her is to become a good man.

I am writing this at my desk in my apartment. I have so much now, so many things I couldn't have dreamed of. I have this home, filled with things either given to me, or chosen myself because I liked them, and a fridge full of food and a closet full of clothes. I'm not on the street, or slumped in a doorway somewhere, or underneath yet another stranger. I'm just me, right now, Annika, and I am steering the ship that is my life humbly and in awareness. My ocean has always been tumultuous, but miraculously I've found a safe harbor at the eleventh hour, over and over. It is clear to me now that the star I steer by is Krysz, and it always will be. Once it was my mother, and it might still have been, had she lived. Then it was Ellen. But the brightest star, the one I can't seem to turn my gaze away from, the one I follow faithfully, even if I know it will lead me to destruction, is Krysz. I'm going to stop for tonight; it is a wonderfully warm evening and I'd like to sit on the balcony for a while, looking at the stars against their pink midsummer night sky.

CHAPTER 15

I DON'T KNOW what this home represents anymore. I thought I did; all the years Johan and I have built a family and a life together, it was always to give Nicoline and Hermine what I didn't have – a stable home life. When my father left, he said, *I just can't live with your mother anymore*. What about me? I wanted to scream, but didn't. *What about me?* It became the biggest rejection of my life, and I know I've been marked by it ever since. People felt sorry for me. I was no longer one of the girls I'd previously identified with – the good-looking, preppy girls with the big houses and seemingly happy parents; I was one of the *others*. I probably placed more weight on this fact than anyone else ever did, but I certainly developed an inferiority complex over my missing father, and the fact that my mother and I could no longer go on the kinds of holidays everyone else seemed to go on so that we could afford to keep the house. Perhaps that was why I was so determined to get Johan Wilborg in the first place, and why I've held on to him beyond what might be considered reasonable. I won't have my façade shattered again. In Sandefjord, I finally enjoy the kind of social status I felt eluded me in my earlier life; I look how a lot of people would like to look, I'd imagine. I live in a huge, beautiful home. I work here and there, because I want to, not because I have to. I have two little girls who I will protect against the vicious, envious gossip and judgment this kind of little town can bring.

I've told so many lies. Most of them I've told to save myself, to preserve the life Johan and I have built together. All I ever wanted was a normal family, the kind of family others may look to for inspiration. Does that make me bad? All my life, I've worked hard. Perhaps not so much in paid employment, but then again, I haven't had to. I've worked hard at being the perfect wife and the perfect mother, though I could never have anticipated how difficult being a mother really is. Some people make it look easy. Like you're always overwhelmed by intense love for your children, or like you wake up every day just gagging to see those little beaming faces. Even though I've found it difficult, to put it mildly, I have worked hard to protect what I have. I suppose that is why it has felt violently unfair that one wrong decision should have set in motion such a devastating chain of events. I've done everything, I really have, to avoid placing my family in the current situation, but that was all before I realized that I love Tobias. It is a love I thought I'd been able to bury so deep it would never rise to the surface, but from the moment I realized who the little lost boy really was, it has fought its way into my heart, into my very bones. I thought his presence would be the end of this family, but I know now that it is the only outcome that can save it. I have to get him back, even if it means losing everything else. But first, I have to find a way to tell Johan.

Laila Engebretsen called Inspector Ellefsen and I told them everything. Well, almost everything. I'm not sure they believed everything I said, but they agreed to arrange a DNA test of Tobias. Inspector Ellefsen warned me not to leave Vestfold County as I have most likely breached several counts of the law and an investigation will be launched. I assured him the only place I'm going is the psychiatric ward in Tønsberg for my counseling session this afternoon. He stared at me, clearly thinking I was making some kind of odd joke, but I stared back levelly, and eventually he looked away, shaking his head slightly.

I was going to tell Johan last night, after my conversation with Laila. I didn't manage it, and went to bed at seven o'clock with a hot water bottle and a tea mug full of red wine. I suppose Johan just concluded my meeting with social services didn't go very well. I decided to save the conversation until we were in the car on the way to Tønsberg, because then, at least, he'd have to keep his eyes on the road and not on me.

Now I'm at home, looking around at all the familiar things one last time before Johan comes home on his lunch break to pick me up and drive me to Tønsberg. I've taken my pills and my head feels heavy and muddled, which is unfortunate. I'm sitting by the window, looking out at the empty harbor. It is a beautiful winter day, cold and crisp, the kind when you want to go cross-country skiing in the forest, listening to the silence. Tonight, everything will be different. This house will no longer be a safe haven for my children. Johan will leave me – fact. Perhaps Nicoline and Hermine can live with him and Luelle here full-time, and I'll get a small apartment nearby – that way their lives won't change so much. I guess I never was much of a mother.

I imagine Johan in this exact moment, getting up from his desk at the *Skandinaviske Forretningsbank*, walking down the stairs and outside to his car, turning his open, kind face to the weak rays of the sun. On the way home, he'll fiddle with the radio, his mind blank and calm. He may be slightly nervous about my hospital appointment, and upset about Tobias and the way I reacted yesterday when I found out they'd taken him away.

But he will be completely unable to even imagine the bomb I'm about to drop on him. I'm going to run through them again, the moments that set all of these current events in motion. I thought I'd got away with it, I really did. But maybe my mama was right, after all. She always used to say that whatever you create will come back and give you the attention it deserves.

*

The blazing sun on my pale winter skin felt better than anything I'd ever felt before, especially after my pregnancy and the diabetes. I'd spent close to a year on the sofa with my feet up, becoming bigger and angrier by the day. All I'd wanted was to get the kid out so I could get my life back. Now she was out, but it was beginning to dawn on me that I'd never get my life back. I loved Nicoline and the feel of her sweet, dense little body against mine, but not a day went past that I didn't intensely regret motherhood. *How could we have done something like this to our perfect lives?* I'd sob to Johan. During my pregnancy, I'd developed gestational diabetes and prenatal depression, and after Nicoline was born, I didn't get any better, as I'd assumed – I got much worse. Johan had to take several months off work because I was so fragile I wasn't able to take care of the baby by myself. I cried all day, most days, and so did Nicoline. She had colic, and writhed in pain much of the time, while I stared emptily into the air and Johan did his best to take care of us both.

I felt ugly, fat and old, and every attempt from Johan to come close to me was instantly rebuffed. Our relationship, which had been mostly happy, became fraught with all the things that weren't said, and strained by my intense unhappiness. I became convinced Johan would leave me; after all, why would someone as attractive and successful as Johan Wilborg stay with someone as utterly vile as me? Looking back, it is clear to me that I'd always thought like that, and that's most likely why I did what I did. Ever since the beginning of our relationship, when I was still infatuated with the man I'd always wanted and we started to build a life together, there were others. Many others. One man just couldn't give me all the attention and reassurance I craved. The year we lived in France before we went to university, I used to go home with random men at the end of a night out with my girlfriends. At university, it was easy to meet men for sex. And later, when we'd married and settled back down in Sandefjord, I'd find them on the Internet and meet them in various anonymous hotels on the outskirts of Oslo or Drammen. It didn't mean anything, and I'm hardly the first person who's allowed herself a few indiscretions outside of the boundaries of matrimony. Perhaps Johan has as well, I wouldn't know, and frankly, I couldn't care less as long as he stays with me. That has always been my number-one priority, and why I did what I did when I realized that my indiscretion in Uruguay would have permanent consequences. And it's not like I didn't learn my lesson – I have never again risked my marriage in any way – I'm faithful in body and mostly in spirit, and I really have tried unbelievably hard to be the perfect, best wife in every way.

Back to Uruguay. We went to Punta del Este when Nicoline was four months old, on an extended family holiday and paternity leave. The thought behind it was that perhaps getting some winter sun would lift my mood and fix our family situation. The very thought makes me want to laugh now. At first, it seemed like a good idea. The sun's rays on my skin were amazing, and even the baby seemed to cheer up in the warm sea breeze. She didn't scream all the time, and I managed not to cry all of the time. Unlike Sandefjord in early spring, in Uruguay there were so many colors everywhere; the incredible blues of the ocean, the verdant trees, the golden sunlight everywhere. I began to breathe properly again.

One night, Johan stayed with Nicoline at our rental villa, while I went to a beach party with some Swedish girls I'd met. It was the first time since I became pregnant over a year before that I'd felt like anything that vaguely resembled myself. I drank one cocktail after the other, danced in the sand under a huge moon to the set of an up–and-coming Cuban DJ, DJSoulo. I laughed, smoked thin French cigarettes and wished on the myriad stars that my life would be good again. One of the Swedish girls pulled me into one of the bathroom tents, and together we snorted a couple lines of coke. The rush of clarity I'd yearned for, that I hadn't had since before my pregnancy, washed over me, and I walked down to the ocean and sat in the sand, letting the wavelets lick at my toes.

'Hi,' said a man's voice. I looked up and saw the DJ from earlier, DJSoulo.

'Hi,' I said.

'You looked like you were having fun out there on the dance floor.'

'Yes, it was amazing. Great set.'

'You okay?'

'Sure. Just needed a moment – it's busy over there.'

'Tell me about it. I'm on again in half an hour. Mind if I join you?'

I didn't mind one little bit and shook my head. 'I'm Cecilia.'

'I'm Thiago.' Thiago was the kind of handsome most people only ever see on a movie screen, and even I, who'd certainly had my fair share of attractive men, was taken aback by his sheer beauty. He was of indeterminable ethnicity – there was something Cherokee and Johnny Depp-esque about his high cheekbones, but his skin was a rich brown and his eyes a playful, dark amber. I fought the urge to make excuses for the way I looked, but from the way Thiago looked at me and laughed at everything I said, it would appear he hadn't noticed that I was a chubby, sad mother. Maybe he thought I was like one of those Swedish girls – a young, rich jetsetter travelling the world on yet another gap year. Less than ten minutes after he sat down beside me, Thiago was inside me, moving frantically, kissing me passionately, breathing hard in my ear, grabbing me by the back of my neck and my lower back. We were up against some rocks further down the beach, but frankly, I wouldn't have cared if we were doing it in front of the whole beach club – just looking at the man made me tremble with lust.

And afterwards, well, he was gone. He went back to do his set and I danced for a while longer, gazing at him flirtatiously and laughing as he winked at me, still weak in the knees from the sex. It would have ended there, like all my other little dalliances have. Since my period had not returned since the birth of Nicoline, and since it all happened so fast, we had not used any protection. With hindsight, that was obviously a stupid thing to have done, but personally I have never met anyone who hasn't made a decision like that in the heat of the moment. And it really was hot; I've never forgotten it. I haven't forgotten Thiago's warm smile and killer cheekbones either, and when I first saw Tobias there was something intensely familiar about his smile. Though I didn't immediately put two and two together, I was unsettled by how I felt like I'd seen him before. I think I knew it was him when I met the swimming pool receptionist that rainy day, but I couldn't be absolutely certain until the last time I saw Anni.

My thoughts are interrupted by the door shutting downstairs and the sound of Johan kicking his shoes off.

'Cecilia,' he calls, and though I have been expecting him, I feel suddenly thrown by the prospect of seeing him, and what I'm about to say. 'Hey, babe,' he says, walking into the room. 'You ready?' I swallow hard a couple of times, and stand up from my chair by the bay windows. I nod.

In the car, I feel as though my thoughts are running wild, and my heart is beating so hard I check my pulse with my fingertips several times; it feels as though I'll have a seizure. Johan asks if I'm okay every few minutes. I nod and stare out the window at the early afternoon traffic moving freely towards the E18 motorway. It's almost completely dark and it's not yet three p.m. The longer I wait, the chances are I won't manage to tell him before we get to Tønsberg, and I have to tell him now, before someone else does.

'I... I have to tell you something,' I say, and just like I knew he would, Johan's face takes on his serious and concerned expression which makes him look like he's eight years old.

'Okay. Are you okay, honey? You seem agitated. I know it's been hard on you, that Tobias...'

'Johan, I know who Tobias's parents are.' A stunned silence follows and Johan fixes his gaze on a lorry in front of us, as though hypnotized.

'But... but they said the Lucasson lady definitely wasn't biologically related to Tobias,' he says. 'They haven't been able to connect Tobias to anyone else, have they?'

'I'm Tobias's mother,' I say, but my voice comes out barely a whisper.

'Cecilia... you need to stop this now. He's gone. But they *will* find him a mother, I'm sure of it...' Johan removes his hand from where it was on the wheel, and tries to take mine from my lap, but I pull it away aggressively.

'Listen to me, goddammit! I am telling you that I'm Tobias's mother and that is a fucking fact!'

'Did you take your pill?' says Johan, face still open and kind and concerned.

'Tobias is my son!' A thick vein appears on Johan's neck and pulsates ominously. He drives faster than usual, faster than he should in the dark on icy roads. But he doesn't say anything.

'I'm sorry,' I say, over and over. We exit off the motorway and only moments later we are parked outside the psych ward.

'You do realize that you're going back in there, don't you?' says Johan.

'What?'

'What you are saying is beyond crazy, Cecilia. It's completely insane! Don't you think I might notice if we'd suddenly had another baby?'

'You need to listen to me. He's not yours. And I am so sorry for hurting you, and I hope there is some way we can work through this...' Johan interrupts me by slamming his hand down on the steering wheel incredibly hard, and this startles me because Johan is never angry.

'Cecilia, shut up for a moment, okay? Just shut up. Listen to me. You need to stop, right now, with this crazy talk. If you talk like that when you get inside to Dr Nielsen, she's going to lock you up and throw away the key.'

'No, you need to listen to what I'm saying!'

'Stop,' says Johan, so sternly I actually comply. 'Please, please, listen to me, for your own sake. For the sakes of our children. You will be detained here, in this place, if you tell the doctors what you just said to me. Do you comprehend that?' I shake my head. 'You're not Tobias's mother, Cecilia. That is crazy babble. Now, please tell me, did you take your pill?'

*

They won't let me go. Which is illegal, and I'm going to fucking sue this hellhole for incompetence and violation of basic human rights as soon as I get out of here, which will most likely be tomorrow, when Tobias's DNA results have been processed and everybody knows that I'm his mother.

'The erratic behavior has escalated again today,' Johan told Dr Nielsen. 'Disjointed tirades, obvious inconsistencies, twisted reality, that kind of thing.' Dr Nielsen wrote something in her book as Johan spoke. I chose to not respond to anything Johan said, telling Dr Nielsen I'd happily tell her everything once my treacherous husband had gone home. And, now, a whole day has passed, and I'm still here and nobody has come to hear what I have to say. It is obvious to me that they are giving me some other medication, because holding on to my thoughts is as difficult as it would be to pick up a droplet of water.

It is snowing again today and apparently I'm supposed to entertain myself for hours on end in my claustrophobic room, angry and medicated. Some well-meaning soul has left some magazines behind and I'm rifling through one when there is a sharp knock at the door. It is Inspector Ellefsen accompanied by Dr Nielsen. After inquiring about my general well-being and so on (fucking fabulous), Inspector Ellefsen draws up a chair and sits down next to the bed I'm in. Dr Nielsen hovers by the door, but seems to have no intention to leave.

'If you feel well enough, could we have a quick chat, Cecilia?'

'Never felt better. What do you want to discuss?'

'Considering recent events and some preliminary evidence, I would like to informally question you about Annika Lucasson's murder.'

'Oh,' I say. 'You mean the drug addict?'

'Mrs Wilborg, there are some fairly substantial inconsistencies in the account you told us previously. While some parts undeniably seem true, there are other parts I just can't make sense of.'

'Such as?'

'You say you've never met Annika Lucasson. Is that correct?'

I need to think, but my mind is like a dense, slippery stone in rushing water. 'Yes,' I say.

'And yet, Tobias maintains that you two know each other. He insists you were friends.'

'Friends! Hah. That's crazy. But no, to answer your question, I didn't know her.'

'You asked us to run a DNA test to determine whether Tobias could be your biological son. We've done this and naturally cross-checked the DNA with what we recovered in the Lucasson case.' Ellefsen pauses a long moment, looking up at me wryly from underneath his bushy eyebrows. I make my expression completely empty – a skill I've honed over the years. I stare straight ahead, focusing on the blue-and-white flowers on the washed-out duvet cover. I will tears to my eyes, but it isn't easy to cry on command in spite of my nerves and the strange situation.

Finally, I feel them sting and look up at Dr Nielsen, and then Inspector Ellefsen, pleading. 'Inspector Ellefsen, could you please confirm the results of the DNA tests?'

'I am afraid I am unable to do that at this point.'

'Why?'

'Because recent developments in this case have led us to reassess the nature of the investigation.'

'Yes, well, I know that I am.'

'I appreciate that you have had a tumultuous time recently, and I certainly hope your condition will improve… When it does, I will need to bring you into the station for further questioning.'

'Questioning for what?'

'For the murder of Annika Lucasson.'

'Like I've already told you, I've never met the woman.'

'And yet, your DNA was underneath the deceased's finger-nails. It was the only clear DNA evidence we were able to secure from the body.'

'I won't say another word without a lawyer present.'

'That's fine, Mrs Wilborg. I'll confer with Dr Nielsen about when she anticipates you to be well enough to leave, and I shall see you in Sandefjord.'

CHAPTER 16

I COULD MAKE a run for it. Perhaps I'd make it out of here – after all, people have done it before, and as far as I know, they can't convict me of murder just because my DNA was found underneath Anni's fingernails. I could go back to Punta del Este; I've heard Uruguay is lenient with the criminally pursued. Or maybe I could go to Miami, where DJSoulo would appear to live now, judging by his Instagram account. I could find him, and... *And what?* I ask myself. I study DJSoulo's face intently, alone in the downstairs lounge, after they finally let me come home tonight, two days after Ellefsen came to see me. Johan has finally, reluctantly, gone to bed, like I'm some irrational child that needs to be watched over. Meanwhile, DJSoulo is out there, posting on social media, living his life, now presumably fully knowing he once fathered a child with a stranger, and he doesn't care. Like me, before. I've been trying to pinpoint the exact moment that something changed, the moment I let it slip and began to take apart the walls I'd so meticulously built up.

I could get in the car right now, and go to my father on the farm. I can practically see it in my mind; the long driveway from the main road north from Munkfors, the rambling old farmhouse, the black lake at the bottom of the hill, the old, brown horses my father likes to keep in the field, the stern pine trees surrounding the farm as dark and isolating as an ocean to an island. I can see myself stumbling from the car, paranoid and desperate, into my father's arms, and he'd fix everything. Like the last time. No. I can never go back there; not now, not after what I did to him. And to Tobias... He'd turn me away, make me get back in the car, driving into the night, a lone fugitive.

I could stay here and maintain my innocence. I can blame any inconsistencies in my story on my newfound mental illness, and everyone knows there's no point arguing with someone who only just escaped the psych ward. I return to the images of DJSoulo on the screen, scrolling through his Instagram posts aimlessly, compulsively, as though I might suddenly uncover something that would make a difference in this hot mess. He looks like a nice man, and that is also how I remember him from the half hour we knew each other. There is warmth in his eyes – a certain air of reliability, and he looks like he has a sense of humor, judging by the occasional witty captions on his posts. It would seem he has friends, and a girlfriend, too; in several of the images he is posing with a slim brunette with a toothy grin who gazes up at him adoringly. I pore over the pictures for some clue to why he never responded to my email, but my mind flits back to my father, the farm, and the last time we met.

*

When I became pregnant with Nicoline, I knew within two weeks of her conception. My body hadn't yet begun to change on the outside, but the changes within were noticeable from very early on. My moods, which have always been volatile, started to alternate between jet-black and completely blank. My breasts felt tender and swollen, and my mouth tasted of metal, as though I'd just sucked on a rusty nail. I felt constantly nauseated; not bad enough to need to throw up, but as though I'd just smelled something violently unpleasant. After the pregnancy, however, around the time we went to Uruguay, when I was struggling to recover control over my body, many of these symptoms were still present. A persistent taste of metal remained, I'd often feel phantom kicks from my womb, I carried excessive weight I could not find the motivation to get rid of and not even a cocktail of antidepressants could keep my depression at bay. This was the state I was in at the time Tobias was conceived, and bearing this in mind, it is perhaps not so strange that I didn't understand that I was pregnant again until far beyond the point when one can legally end a pregnancy.

I shut the computer. I want a moment, just one moment's break from the thoughts jostling for space in my tired head. The thought of lying down to sleep next to Johan after everything that has been happening is impossible. I consider sleeping in one of the guest rooms, but this unrest I feel isn't a need for sleep. My mind is still muddled from the medication I have to take, and I'm not sure what it is that I want or need. Usually, I'd pour myself a large glass of wine and sit in the dark by the bay windows, watching the hushed, silent town outside. I can't mix alcohol with the new anti-psychosis drug I'm on, apparently under any circumstances, and so I am just standing here, in the quiet night, in the middle of the floor. I decide to tidy.

The thing about a home like mine is that I've always felt it has to be presented to the very highest standards. People aspire to achieve my kind of housekeeping. This is not the kind of house where flowers hang their heads, or where clouds of dust gather in corners, or where a visitor might open a kitchen drawer and find piles of old receipts and bits of broken utensils. I suppose not everyone is able to keep a home the way I do, in part because they have less impressive spaces to work with, and in part because they just don't have my eye. This house is always full of people, because Johan and I are a sociable kind of couple. I'm not sure whether it is subconscious or intentional, but I always notice that my guests study the house, and the food, and that day's floral displays carefully, taking note. And then, when I go to Cathrine's or Silje's or Fie's, wouldn't you believe that there's always a new detail, stolen from my own home? A violet orchid, a new metallic Missoni throw I bought first, a fine Nebbiolo only available by special order, first served at my table. This doesn't make me angry, exactly; it just makes me a bit exasperated sometimes that I'm not fortunate enough to be surrounded by inspirational people.

The problem, if you could call it that, is that most people don't know what it takes to create a well-thought-out ambience. You can't just buy the candlesticks of the moment or plonk a marble island in the middle of your kitchen or buy violet flowers because Cecilia Wilborg buys them and so they must be great. Oh no. You have to have a strategy. Every morning I inspect Luelle's cleaning and tidying after the children have left for school. It is obvious to me that certain aspects of housekeeping are very different from a Filipino point of view, but I suppose you can't expect an au pair to understand the kind of strategy we're talking here. Most days, for example, I have to take a few moments to turn all the cups in the cupboard so their handles face outwards, ready to be picked up. Luelle wouldn't think to do that. She thinks it's enough to take them from the dishwasher and place them in the cupboards.

We make ourselves busy for so many reasons, don't we? Tonight I fear long moments looking out onto the town, the sea, the black sky. I think of last summer when the rat that plagued us suddenly disappeared. The poison must have finally got him after all that time. I found myself missing the ritual of checking for the overnight damage he'd done to my fruit. I begin to organize all the cupboards, though they are already so tidy that it's a matter of running my fingers along neatly ordered shelves, trying to find a speck of dust. I find one of Tobias's Pokémon cards underneath a box of Cheerios, slightly crooked, as if loved a lot and kept in a jeans pocket. I crush it and throw it in the bin, then take it back out and place it on top of some newspapers in the recycling bin, then pick it up again, smooth it out and put it in my back pocket. How can you miss someone you never wanted so much? I wish there were some dirty dishes or some laundry to wash or books to order alphabetically, but everything is beautifully in its place and this makes me irrationally angry. Am I supposed to just sit here thinking? I pour ammonia into a bucket, letting the smell a little too deep into my lungs, and head back downstairs to begin scrubbing the washroom tiles.

The scent of the cleaning products throws me straight back to that strange, unmistakable metallic taste from my pregnancies. I can't seem to escape the memories of that second pregnancy tonight – the one that wasn't supposed to happen. Some incompetent postnatal nurse told me that I was highly unlikely to conceive again while I was breastfeeding, but it's not like Johan and I had been at it like bunnies since the terrible experience of becoming parents had happened to us. Every time he so much as insinuated he might appreciate some form of sexual interaction, I'd swat his hand away and turn towards the wall. It wasn't until we'd been in South America for a while that some remnant of the old me began to resurface, and as Tobias is a living reminder, the reappearance of my sexual feelings did not benefit my husband, but rather a Cuban DJ.

I thought the stay in Uruguay had done us a world of good, and that I'd gotten away with my one little indiscretion. By the time we returned to Norway six weeks later, Johan and I were coping marginally better with life as new parents. We'd begun speaking normally to each other again, rather than merely grunting instructions through gritted teeth, avoiding each other's bloodshot eyes. Nicoline, too, had settled into being a fairly content baby. And yet, several of the physical sides of the pregnancy I'd so loathed lingered on. I remember one morning, around three months after we'd returned from our holiday, when Nicoline was eight months old. It was early summer, and I woke up feeling strong and a little more like myself. I sat up, listening to the chirping of birds from outside, drawing crisp, fragrant air into my lungs, when I suddenly felt a sharp tug from within my stomach. I instinctively placed my hand on the spot I'd felt this strange rumble, so like the somersaults Nicoline had enjoyed subjecting me to when it was her I carried. My skin felt taut, and I remember wondering whether it could be that my body was finally beginning to tighten naturally after so many months of podgy, loose skin.

A few weeks later, I was at Cornelia's house for a dinner party with the girls. I kept lifting my champagne glass to my mouth and lowering it again, unable to take even a single sip. I was wearing a dowdy kaftan dress to disguise the fact that I hadn't managed to lose much of the weight; in fact, it seemed to me that I may even have put more on. I jealously studied Silje, who was also breastfeeding at the time, and she had the body I had fully expected to have immediately restored to me after birth; skinny, angular, almost boyish, were it not for her not-so-real large D-cups. That was what I'd looked like before, and what I'd just assumed I'd snap back to after expelling the alien child that had made me a fat, depressive wreck. And yet, there I was, most likely the laughing stock of the tennis club – perfect Cecilia, not so perfect anymore in her elasticated tights, floaty kaftan and bloated, prematurely aged face.

The day after the dinner party was the day when everything went to hell. To this day, I cannot remember ever returning to the memories of those desperate moments when I set everything that happened later into motion; it was as though I was acting on pure instinct. I scrub harder, trying to keep my mind sharp, accepting that they are coming now, those memories. I run an old toothbrush along the satisfyingly dirty grouting behind the tumble dryer, forcing myself to breathe slowly into the pit of my stomach, like Dr Nielsen taught me.

It was a late-summer evening; it must have been early August by then. Johan and I had been invited to a work colleague of his for a crayfish dinner at his country house just south of Sandefjord. Nicoline was at my mother's for a sleepover. It was a cool, beautiful evening – one of the first nights of summer when it had actually begun to get dark again – we'd been so used to months of midnight light. We sat outside, watching the peaceful back-and-forth dance of a buoy out in the bay rocking on dark, shimmery water. A plump moon sat high above us, and the scent of the day's hot sun lingered on the yellowing grass. After the meal, the men had gathered at one corner of the table to watch something funny on someone's phone, and we girls gathered together at the other end. I didn't know the other women well, and I'd be damned if I had to pick any one of them out of a crowd now, almost a decade later, but they were pleasant enough ladies and the conversation flowed easily around the usual subjects: work, kids, travel. At one point, I went into the kitchen behind the hostess as she'd begun to clear some dishes and I thought I'd help her. We stood side by side rinsing the discarded pink legs of the shellfish from the plates into the basin, when she suddenly said casually: *So, how many weeks is it now? They'll almost be Irish twins, your two, I'd imagine?*

The sensation of being unable to speak was truly physical. I tried. I shook my head and handed her a half-rinsed plate rather too forcefully, and glanced outside at where the men were huddled together, laughing drunkenly. *Excuse me*, I said finally. She nodded, and the last I ever saw of that woman was her standing there, rubbing at an ugly red rash which had appeared on her neck, as I made for the door. My aversion to alcohol had come and gone in the past few weeks, and that night was one of the nights when I'd been unable to drink even a single drop, in spite of the fact that I really wanted to. For this reason, the car keys were in my bag and I half ran across the gravel courtyard to our car, tears flowing freely now. How could I not have known? I placed a hand on the tight drum of my lower abdomen and screamed from the pit of my stomach inside the warm air of the car. I was crying so hard I could barely make out the road in front of me as I merged onto the empty main road, pushing hard down on the accelerator.

I was going to go home. I would sleep off the shock, and then the next day, I'd go to a private clinic and make the necessary arrangements to get rid of it. I racked my brain for dates. When did we last have sex? And when was the first time since Nicoline's birth? The truth was, Johan and I had only slept together once since she was born, and that had been just a few weeks ago. If it had been him who'd impregnated me, I wouldn't be far enough along to be starting to show. The only other option was DJSoulo, just over six months previously, in Punta del Este. I drove past the exit to central Sandefjord, continuing towards the E18.

Thought after thought washed over me, pushing against each other in my mind, blocking out any sliver of sane reasoning. I had to get rid of the baby. Instead of an immediate rush of maternal affection, which I actually had felt in the early days of my pregnancy with Nicoline, I felt a deep and vicious repulsion for this impossible child. I knew that I'd get rid of it one way or the other, even if I had to do it with my own bare hands.

I drove and drove, past Drammen and then Oslo, aimlessly, and at times recklessly fast, but the roads were empty and I needed to still my heart and the dreadful rolling movements from within my belly. How, how could I not have realized? I could only blame the unbelievably awful aftermath of Nicoline's birth and how it turned me into a deranged ghost of my former self; it was as though I was stunned for months by the sheer hell of parenting.

Near Oslo Airport Gardermoen I drove past a sign for a Best Western hotel and, on impulse, exited off the motorway. I lay atop the hard bed, staring up at a blinking red light on a fire alarm on the ceiling, running my hands over what was now undoubtedly a baby bump. To my horror, something within seemed to nudge back in response to my touch, but not even for a split second did I empathize with the creature growing inside of me. I just had to find a way to get it out. I knew I couldn't go for an ultrasound to find out how far along I was; any pregnancy would obviously have to be registered and monitored. My only option would be to go into hiding.

I think it speaks volumes about what a resilient character I have that I found a way to deal with such a horrifying situation. I've never been someone with many enemies, but I suppose you could say I've also never been someone with the kinds of friends one may consider calling upon in a real emergency. But I did have someone; one person who owed me a hell of a favor, and now it was well and truly payback time. I didn't close my eyes for a moment that night in spite of the fact that I ached all over and my eyes were bleary both from the crying and the hours of driving. I got back up and left again as the first early morning flights began to take to the skies from Gardermoen. Luckily, my aimless drive had actually brought me almost halfway to my destination. As I merged onto the E6 heading north, I glanced at my phone and its twenty-six missed calls. I rolled the window down as the car began to gain speed and tossed the phone into the roadside blur, feeling immediately saner and lighter. I could do this. *I can do this*, I told myself, *but I only have one shot*. One.

It's the same now. I have one shot. Though my mind is muddled and it is the middle of the night, I have finished scrubbing the washroom, and as the grimy dirt has disappeared, the beginning of a plan has started to form in my head.

CHAPTER 17

THERE ARE MANY things I don't understand, but usually, if I sit and think about them for a long time they become more clear, like strange things at the bottom of puddles when the grubby water has dried up. Now there are some things I can't understand even if I think about them the whole time, which I do. The mother in the family I lived in became very afraid and very sad, they told me, and that's why I can't be in that house anymore, even though that's what I want and what the family wants. *Please don't think they do not want you there, Tobias*, says the lady I hate, whose words I try to block out by closing my eyes and making a low humming sound. *They are very upset you can't stay there anymore, but the reason it has to be like this is that we have to protect you above all.* But I'm not afraid of the mother in the family, I'm afraid of this place. And I don't understand why the girls can stay there but not me. Why do they have to protect me but not Hermine and Nicoline? Nothing they say is true.

I think it's my fault. Maybe it's because of what I said. It made the mother in the house afraid, I could see that. What was a nice time on the beach wasn't nice anymore because her face got angry and she put her hands on the side of my face and forced me to look in her eyes. Then she held a finger to her lips for a long time. It wasn't true what I said, though. It wasn't true that I know who she is. I only knew where I'd seen her before. The picture on the shelf above the bed in the old lady's house was the same picture as the one Moffa kept in the desk drawer in his bedroom. I'd found it, when I was maybe six, and turned it around and on the back a name and date was written. *Cecilia, 1994*, it said. I know what it means, but I also don't know, so I shouldn't have said that I know, and now I'm here.

This house is bad. Not because it's ugly but because they pretend like it's a real home and not a house with orphans in it. There is a framed drawing in the hallway of two adults and three children of different colors, all holding hands and smiling, and behind them is a neon rainbow and some trees and a stupid sun with a face, and underneath them it says 'Healing Families Everywhere'. I have my own room which has been made so that almost any kid would like something about it; one wall has fire engine wallpaper, one wall has Queen Elsa and Olaf dancing through falling snowflakes, the third wall is painted blue, and the last pink. The bed is made of wood and it's the only thing in the room I like. It's nice wood, too, the kind you can run your fingertips across in the dark, feeling every ridge and swirl.

They brought all my things from the family's house but it made me cry and then they wouldn't go away, they stood in the room for a long time as if that would make me happy. Here, I don't have a cool desk like the one with the drawers, so I have to keep the cards and the marbles at the bottom of the wardrobe in a tin box the man in the family gave me.

There are more things I don't understand. The mother in the family gave me a bear, just like the one Anni took from me, the one Moffa said my mother made for me because she loved me when I was born. But I hadn't told her what it looked like. Maybe all mothers know how to make those bears.

The other strange thing is, she knew my birthday. It was just a couple of days before the day they took me away after what happened at the swimming pool. It was the day after we came back from Hemsedal. She was sitting on the side of the bed in the very early morning again. Usually, I'd be awake before the family knocked on my door to say it was time to get ready for school, but that day I was still sleeping because I'd been drawing for many hours in the night, which is my favorite time. *Happy birthday*, whispered the mother. I didn't think to ask how she knew it was my birthday, but I wish I had because I know I have not told anyone my birthday, even when they asked. One of the first days after Anni left me, someone asked me my birthday, and I said it was December fourteenth, even though it is December fourth. I'm not sure why. Which is why it is so strange that the mother sat by the side of my bed on December fourth and said, *Happy birthday*. She then handed me a heavy, round object wrapped in green tissue paper. Inside was a kind of large hollow, shiny stone, shaped like a jagged heart. *Is it a diamond?* I asked, and she smiled and said, *No, honey, it's a white amethyst. I found it myself in Yosemite National Park in America when I was just a little bit older than you. It looked like an ordinary rock, and I happened to kick it, and it split open to reveal this unbelievably beautiful core. And strangely, it broke into two pieces that looked a bit like hearts. So now you have one and I have the other.*

Perhaps even stranger than this was that my birthday wasn't mentioned again that day, and the mother said over dinner, in front of the others, *So, Tobias, what do you want to do on your birthday next week?* By then, I was of course already here. Two women and a man who work here and call themselves 'family members' came into the room in the morning with a cupcake like the ones they sell in 7-Eleven with a single purple candle stuck into its middle. They sang 'Happy Birthday' and handed me a teddy bear wearing a red woolen sweater. Across its chest, someone had stitched 'Tobias'.

I'm not allowed to go to my school because it's too far. Instead, a man named Karl-Henrik comes every morning for a few hours and we sit together downstairs in the kitchen, doing math and Norwegian and English on his Mac. Karl-Henrik is not old, but not exactly young either. He speaks in a low voice and never laughs. He does smile, but only with his lips pressed closely together. I think it's because his teeth are very, very small and he doesn't want to show them. If I want something, they usually let me have it. *Help yourself*, they say, and point to the cupboards and the fridge in the kitchen, which looks like the kitchen in a normal house except for the fact that everything has a little label on it saying what it is. *Cereal, milk, cookies*. Outside is a garden, and in the garden is a little fenced-off section where the 'home' keeps some animals. There are two bunnies named Pepper and Viggo, and one of the 'family members' told me that they are so shy because some of the children who lived here before were so angry and sad that they hurt the bunnies. You're never allowed to hurt an animal, no matter what. Anyway, I've never really seen their faces, only their fluffy round bottoms sticking out in the air as they always hide when I approach the cage. There are also five chickens in a tiny enclosure, but I don't like them and their fleshy pink necks, or the fact that they stand around all day in chicken shit, so I don't bother with them.

There are two other children living here, and the adults say that they are my 'house sister and house brother'. The boy, Hamed, is much older than me, almost fourteen, and he came from a country with war and bombs that killed his mother and father and many sisters. He came here alone and now he must live here until the adults can find a family for him. He is very quiet, but very kind, and all the time he says, *Merci, merci.* Sometimes, we kick a football around outside in the garden, but it has suddenly got very cold and Hamed doesn't like cold or snow. The girl is also much older than me, and very strange. Her name is Sigrid and she has lived here for many years. She hates me but I don't know why. *What are you looking at, you little fucker?* she shouts every time I look in her direction, even if I didn't know that she happened to be standing there. When she does this, a woman called Pia, whose job it is to follow Sigrid everywhere, places her hand on Sigrid's arm and says, *It's okay, Sigrid. It's okay.* They tried many times to find a family where Sigrid could live, but she had to come back here every time and now it's been decided that she can live here until she's eighteen.

There are more things I don't understand, no matter how much I think about it. Like who killed Anni. When I lived with the family, the mother and father once sat me down on the sofa by the big windows and explained to me that I didn't have to be afraid, and that whoever did it would be caught and put in prison, and that the police thought it was Krysz who killed her so they were looking for him in Poland where he'd run off to. They asked me questions about him, like did I maybe know where he was, or the names of his friends or anything at all that might help the police to find him, but I just looked down at my hands and said nothing, and they gave up. What I don't understand is why they haven't found him.

*

I didn't love Anni because sometimes she was very angry with me and sometimes she forced me to do things I didn't want to do, like finish all the food on my plate and on Anni's and on Krysz's when I was already full. It was also her fault that I'm not with Moffa at the farm anymore. I know she was sad about many things and that was why she was sometimes horrible to me, but it's like those bunnies in the garden and those other kids. I didn't love Anni but I didn't want her to die. That's why it happened. It was easier than I had thought it would be. And I had thought about it before, not in the kind of way like *I* might actually do it, but in the kind of way like it would be good if *someone* would do it.

It started the way it usually did – they were shouting at each other and Krysz suddenly hit Anni hard across the face, so she was bleeding from her nose and crying. That was when Krysz said, *I'm leaving* and Anni said, *You're leaving?* and laughed that laugh that wasn't happy laughing. He was shoving things into plastic bags, swearing and kicking the walls when they got in his way. They argued about who would take the fucking boy and Anni said that Krysz should take me, and then I felt really afraid. I thought about Krysz taking me to a new house, and then another, and another, and always screaming in my face. I was standing in the stairwell, quiet but shaking, when Krysz suddenly burst from the bedroom carrying his bags, pushing past me and suddenly seeing me as if he just hadn't noticed me before, and screamed, *Get the fuck away from me!*

I ran out of the house and climbed up the rocky slope opposite, where I could sit quietly on a little patch of moist moss and wait for the bad time to stop. I heard Anni scream loudly once, followed by a series of thuds from inside. I felt my hands curl into fists at the sound and thought that maybe I should run in there and try to help her, but I knew that he'd turn around and then hit me. He'd hit me before, many times, and once he even threw me at a wall, but Anni always tried to stop him. After a little while, Anni burst out the door. Her lip was split open and black blood ran down the side of her face from a big cut over her eyebrow. *Come!* she shouted to me. *Come down, Tobias.* And then, *Oh God, hurry!* I felt as though I'd been frozen, and couldn't move from the spot I was sitting on top of the boulder, because Krysz had appeared in the doorway, smiling the way wolves do, baring teeth. Anni turned slowly towards him, and maybe she relaxed for a moment because he didn't throw more punches at her right away, but from where she was standing, she wouldn't have been able to see the knife he was holding behind his back. I stood up. I remember shouting something, maybe it was *No!* or *Run, Anni!* I don't remember picking the rock up, but I remember every nanosecond of throwing it and watching it fly through the air; the way its weight went from snug and dense between my hands, to the dull crack as it struck Krysz right on top of his head, towards the back.

Afterwards, it was as though the world had stopped. I just stood there holding the empty space between my hands where the rock had been. Anni's face twisted in a wild scream but no sound came out. Krysz fell face-forward and the big rock, almost as big as a football, lay right next to his broken head. The back of his head where the rock had hit him was open and dark and wet. Suddenly his body violently shuddered, but that was the last movement he made and I just knew that he was dead then. *Come*, whispered Anni through her bloody lips. I climbed down slowly, as though I was someone who didn't know every crack in the stone and every root that crept across it like the back of my own hand. *Stay there*, she said, and went inside the house, so I stood beside Krysz and tried to not look at him, or the big knife which had been knocked from his hand, or the big rock. I looked up at the gray, low sky and began to whisper the prayers that Moffa taught me, I'm not sure why. After a little while Anni came back outside carrying a tarpaulin I recognized from when we lived on a campsite in Poland for a while. She moved strangely slowly, like her head didn't yet know what her body was already doing. She flung the tarpaulin across Krysz's body and as it landed perfectly, covering him completely, she let out a little cry, like Baby the time I stepped on her tail.

We went back inside and Anni did what Krysz had done just a half hour before – walking fast from room to room, shoving everything she saw into black bin liners. She went upstairs and shut the door to their bedroom and I listened at the door. She sobbed and wailed and it took me a while to realize she was talking on the phone – every word was followed by hiccupping and jagged breath. She was speaking in Polish and I caught only a few words: *hurry* and *please, please!* Then it went quiet for such a long time I almost wondered if she'd fallen asleep, but then I heard a long, slow draw of breath and realized she was smoking crack. I went downstairs and then outside to where Krysz still lay underneath his tarpaulin. I nudged the big rock with my foot and had to use real force to get it to budge at all, that's how heavy it was. I made it roll all the way over to the side of the house and the dark bloodstain on it seemed to disappear as it traveled across the wet gravel.

Pawel came. He's very bad. He has grooves on his face like someone cut him with knives, and maybe they did even. He has very small pig eyes and every time he waves his hand so I'll go away and if I don't he kicks me. They closed the door to the living room and were in there for a long time, whispering. When they came back out, Anni stepped outside for a moment and returned with Krysz's car key, fished from his pocket. She handed it to Pawel. Pawel then went down to Krysz's red Skoda station wagon, which was parked by the side of the road, and reversed it up the narrow track to the front of the house, very close to where Krysz lay, just out of sight around a corner. He opened the boot, and then he and Anni half dragged, half hauled Krysz into it. They stood looking at each other seriously for several long moments, then Pawel placed a hand on Anni's shoulder. She turned quickly away, as though this hurt her, and again her face looked like it did in the moments after the rock tumbled through the air – empty, mouth half open like a scream in a dream, watching Pawel drive away. Then she did something strange. She dropped to her knees in front of me and held me in a hug for a very long time. *Come*, she said again, and together we left the house. Walking along Østerøysvingen, half running after Anni, who seemed strangely calm and like nothing was wrong, I kept turning and looking back at the house and every time I couldn't believe that it could just stand there like nothing had happened.

Now that I'm here in this 'home', thinking about these things feels like a dream, just like the first while after Anni and Krysz took me away from the farm had felt like a dream. Every day I'd wake up and it would take me a very long while to really understand that my whole life had disappeared and I now had to live with these two people who were so crazy and mean. I would look around the unfamiliar walls of whatever house we were staying in that night and really pray that I was still asleep, that I would wake up and I'd be in the carved wooden bed in the old farmhouse, Baby sleeping on her similar bed next to mine, the only sound the wind outside or Moffa snoring through the walls. But every day I'd wake; back then most days in a new bed somewhere, in a different country, surrounded by strangers who all hated me, and I started to do many strange things, like biting my wrist, tugging at my hair, stabbing myself with a little fork and staying silent for several days, just to stop myself from screaming.

CHAPTER 18

TO HIS ETERNAL credit, my father did not seem the least bit surprised to see me after nearly fifteen years. I arrived just after eight o'clock in the morning, and the air still had that violet, milky glow, with ribbons of mist rising from the fields. I left the car with the engine running in the space between the barn and the main house, and took a couple of tentative steps towards the building, which looked empty. I even left the car door open – that was how ready I was to just turn back around and return to the road, heading God knows where. As I approached, a light came on in the window immediately left of the entrance door, and then it swung open to reveal a man I didn't immediately recognize. Rationally, I knew that it had to be my father, but he just didn't much resemble the man I remembered. This guy looked relaxed, healthy and much younger than sixty. The man I remembered had always been stressed, fidgety, drawn-looking and evasive. He took one look at me and said, 'Oh, honey.'

When my father left my mother and me in Sandefjord, I was fifteen years old. I was so angry that, to this day, I believe that fury manifested itself in my mind as a kind of black fog every other experience and feeling had to be seen through. He went to live with a Swedish woman who was in her twenties at the time, and this obviously did not help. They bought a farm near Munkfors, and in those early years after the divorce, my father used to write to me frequently, asking me to please come and visit him and Helén, but I never responded, considering the thought of visiting him and his Swedish slutty child-bride at their hovel in the middle of nowhere was about as tempting as chewing off my own leg. Then, out of the blue, Helén drowned at twenty-nine in a freak accident while walking on a frozen lake, and my mother began to prepare for my father to come running back, begging for another chance. She'd turn him down twice, she said, then she'd welcome him home. But he never came.

That was the background to the day I turned up, out of the blue, aged twenty-nine, six months pregnant with a stranger's baby, desperate for help. I did what I had to do, just like I will do what I have to do now. That's human. That's how this species has survived and evolved through the ages. If nobody had the balls to do what has to be done, even when that is highly unpleasant, then the simple fact would be that the human race would have disappeared a long time ago.

I assumed we'd have to talk everything through in depth immediately; that there would be the frenzied activity of accomplices, that he'd want to know every single detail of the events leading up to the current situation, but it wasn't anything like that. My father brought me into an old-fashioned farm kitchen where a voracious fire burned in a huge open hearth. He placed a large bowl of milky coffee and some rye crackers in front of me, and only then did I realize how hungry I was. When I'd finished, I looked up at him and he was looking back at me, seriously, but not without a glint of humor in his eyes. *You have to help me*, I whispered. *Okay*, he said.

And like that, we settled into a routine. My father dealt with Johan, telling him that I'd had a serious breakdown as a result of the aftermath of the postnatal depression with Nicoline, and that I had come to him desperate for help. He told him that he'd been able to secure a place for me as an outpatient at a progressive clinic near Munkfors with fantastic results in treating mental health problems. Johan called several times a day, insisting on seeing me, understandably upset at the very difficult position my sudden disappearance had placed him in, but my father was able to talk him around to the notion that I just needed time, and peace, to process the difficult year I'd had.

My father had a friend called Rolf, who was a retired doctor. Rolf came to the farm on several occasions during my stay, and on one of these occasions, he brought with him an ultrasound machine. We watched the baby dance on the screen in flickering neon darkness as Rolf ran the device across my distended belly. He wrote a statement saying I was undergoing acute psychiatric treatment in his clinic, and that the long-term prognosis for my particular challenges was very good, provided I'd be given the space and peace to complete the course of treatment.

Every day my father and I would go for long walks around the farm. Ironically, I was in much better shape than I had been during my pregnancy with Nicoline, and over the course of the three months I spent in Sweden with my father, I believe we became friends. He liked to walk around the lake and once I asked him if that was where Helén had drowned, and he'd nodded slowly, gazing out over the frozen blue sheath stretching out between towering pines. I asked him if he hadn't considered coming home after she died and he said that of course he had, but he'd always felt like he couldn't leave her here.

As November neared its end, it was apparent that it wouldn't be much longer now. From my calculations, I must have gone over the due date. The baby sat tight and high inside me, moving only occasionally and slowly, as if his movements were thought through and necessary – nothing like Nicoline's wild, unpredictable tumbles. What a strange time it was; I'd gone from being a wife and mother at home to being a kind of daughter in exile at my estranged father's home, but the strangest thing was perhaps that I was happier there than I had been at home during the past year. It was decided that Rolf would assist with the birth, though in the end it didn't turn out like that. I was adamant that the baby would be put up for adoption immediately after his birth, and that Rolf would take the child away with him and hand him over to social services, saying he'd helped a young, vulnerable teenager with the birth and that he'd promised never to reveal her identity. My father and Rolf were equally adamant that I should wait for the child to be born before making that decision final.

One night I sat down and knitted a little blue bear for the baby. I tried to make it similar to one I'd had as a child, which my paternal grandmother had made for me. While I was fully committed to giving my baby away at birth, I liked the idea of sending with him one little thing from me. It turned out rather lovely and I sat holding it to my chest a long while by the roaring fire, my tears dripping onto the little wooly thing.

Nicoline's birth had taken twenty-four hours and I truly believed that eternity in hell would have nothing on childbirth, so I wasn't looking forward to another round of self-slaughter. Värmland at that time of year is a rather bleak place, and that year it was particularly cold. The lake had been partially frozen since mid-October, and every day my father and I walked around it, increasingly slowly. I just couldn't understand how he could bear looking out over the shimmery blue ice, knowing how Helén had been held beneath it. The last day we did that walk, we were halfway round our usual circuit when I felt a sudden, unbearable twinge in the lower-right part of my stomach, and had to grab on to my father's arm for support. It was the middle of the day but it wasn't fully light – the bleak sun didn't seem to properly rise above the enormous pine trees that surrounded the farm. The air was so cold that every breath hurt. We went back up to the farm and I half sat, half lay on a sofa my father pulled up close to the fire.

Should I call Rolf? he asked, every time I winced at a contraction, by early evening, they were coming thick and fast. *Not yet*, I whispered, having learned the hard way just a year earlier that this could take forever.

Outside it had started to snow heavily, and after less than two hours it had covered the cars, leaving white, eerie mounds where they'd stood. I remember biting hard into a damp cloth, then having it taken from me and wiped gently across my forehead. I focused on the fast-falling fat snowflakes and on not screaming; even then, I was intent on not losing control. My father became increasingly worried as the night wore on – he'd tried to call Rolf constantly for several hours by then, but thought the phone lines were down because of the incredible snowfall.

Ten minutes past midnight on December fourth, Tobias was born. In my mind, all those months leading up to that moment, I'd imagined I wouldn't look at him or hold him, or spend even a moment drinking in his tiny, perfect features. It didn't happen like that. He didn't cry much, not even when my father slapped his bottom firmly to get him to breathe, but he was most certainly alive, alert and with black, alien eyes. He had thick, black hair and little pink fists he clenched and unclenched. He kept smacking his lips as though he'd just been given something delicious and wanted more. I laid him to my breast, because what else could I do? And I cried so hard my whole body shook and the baby kept losing his grip, but he was a persistent little thing, and that was how we sat that whole first night, by the fire. The next day, and the day after, I didn't let go of the baby – I found that I couldn't. Unlike with Nicoline's birth, I felt strong this time, and by the third day, physically well. *I need to go soon*, I told my father, and though he'd known it all along, I could tell he'd thought I'd change my mind. *You need to give him a name*, said my father, but I shook my head. *You do it*, I said, and so I never even knew his name. On the morning I was leaving, when Tobias was five days old, my father sat me down in the kitchen and told me he intended to keep the baby at the farm until he was six months old. In that moment I was holding the boy, my boy, and I just nodded. I didn't need to ask why, because I knew my father felt sure I'd come back for him. But I never did. I went home, bleeding and dazed and hardened inside in a way I'd never thought possible.

*

Melancholia doesn't have much of a function, I've always found. No point in dwelling on that which cannot be changed. I think I've transcended regret, even. It's occurred to me, having watched my life disintegrate entirely, that there is so much freedom in destruction. I can just *be*. Obviously, everyone's lives would be less complicated at present if I hadn't gone and gotten pregnant with a random stranger on a beach in Uruguay, but then there would be no Tobias. And if there's one thing that's become very clear to me over the course of the last few months, it is that that kid is supposed to be here. Something feels strange and liquid inside me to think of those first few days when I clutched the baby to me, watching his trusting, gentle face by the light of the flames my father kept going day and night. And to think of driving away, my foot on the accelerator, the wheels crunching on gravel as the car began to roll away from the house when my baby was still inside it, sleeping in his wicker crib by the hearth, the bear next to his heart, not knowing that his mother didn't want him and had just left him forever; well, it makes me want to break something. It is the middle of the night now, and I think I've worked out most of what I need to do in my mind – it is difficult to think much at all through this medicated sludge. I stand up and sit down several times, suddenly angry with myself for having cleaned the washroom, because it means that now there is absolutely nothing to do except sit here, alone with my thoughts. Or… or I could go out. It's a free country. I'm a free woman. Yes, that's it. I need to retrace my steps of the night when Anni died. I can't believe I haven't thought of this before.

Quietly, I find a down jacket of Johan's, a torch and some mountain boots – it's ten below zero outside, according to the thermometer by the basement door. If Johan were to stumble across me now, dressed like a yeti, getting ready to go outside at three o'clock in the morning in mid-December, to go walking around Sandefjord's harbor basin retracing my steps of the night a junkie was murdered, he'd surely have me sectioned again.

*

The freezing air hits me like a clenched fist, and I half run down the driveway, concentrating on not turning back to look at the house; it would be too tempting to go back inside if I saw the soft glow from the windows. My heart is beating wildly, though it is hardly dangerous to walk around little Sandefjord in the middle of the night. Unless you're Anni, then it is dangerous indeed, but I don't have enemies like she did. Or do I?

Even in the middle of the day, Sandefjord is sparsely populated, and it is perfectly possible to drive along for several minutes without seeing a single soul. At night, it really feels post-apocalyptic, but tonight this suits me just fine. It isn't a long walk from my house to the frozen inlet behind Meny, the food shop, where Anni was found – past the international school, past the pizza restaurant that burned down last year, across the parking lot behind the gas station. I find this part frightening – in the winter, the parking lot is used to store boats on land, and they are towering above me underneath swathes of tarpaulin, creating myriad hiding places for potential assassins. I stand completely still between two large sailing boats, listening. Though it is cold, there is no wind, and I feel as though I could pick out the sound of a pin dropping. The water is a solid black sheath of ice, probably thick enough to walk across the bay now. I think about Helén, whom I never met, who was four months beneath the ice before they managed to recover her body, but the image of Helén bleeds into that of Anni – and I can practically see her floating before my eyes, face down in black water. I don't think that one could say I killed Anni. Like many other things, I suppose it is a matter of perspective. I'm not sure why I'm here tonight, when I could be home in my bed, next to Johan, in my silk pajamas, cozy with our state-of-the-art heating. Then again, Johan most certainly doesn't want to sleep next to me, and may never want to again, unless I manage to pull all the strings in the right order, absolving me of all blame. One shot. And that is precisely why I am here, to piece together the night Anni died, step by step; I can't afford one more incriminating lie.

I stood approximately where I am standing now, in between two large boats. They'd probably been pulled up from the sea just a few days earlier – they still carried the stench of decaying seagrass on their hulls. It was ten thirty at night, and she kept me waiting the way she often had. I clenched and unclenched my fists in my pockets and shuddered as lashings of rain struck my face underneath the hood I'd pulled over my head. In my pocket was fifty thousand kroner in five-hundred-kroner bills. I rocked back and forth on my heels, trying to keep warm, or maybe just steeling myself.

I felt extremely nervous and jittery at the prospect of seeing the boy for the first time. The day before, when I bumped into the receptionist in town and had a sudden panicked feeling that Tobias was my son, I texted Anni and insisted that she confirm everything was okay. She responded immediately, assuring me everything was fine. I tried to believe her, but needed to see him with my own eyes.

Suddenly she appeared, walking fast from behind the Shell station, cupping her hands, trying to shield a cigarette in the torrential rain. She was alone, and I felt a surge of wild anger at the realization that she'd disregarded our agreement. *Bring the boy*, I'd said. What part of that had she not understood? But it wasn't that she hadn't understood. It was that she'd lied to me. *Everything is fine*, she'd said in her text. *Meet me tomorrow.* I'd desperately worked out a plan to solve the situation with Anni and Krysz, which had spiraled completely out of control. I'd drive the kid back to Munkfors to my father, and he'd just have to stay there.

Her face was bare and her ugly teeth jutted out of her mouth as she opened it to speak. She looked even more deranged than usual and kept looking over her shoulder. She opened her mouth to speak and I silenced her with a finger to my lips and desperately tried to think. She'd fucked me over by not bringing the boy. The boy was the whole point, but I realized in those moments why she hadn't. She no longer had the little boy I'd abandoned as a baby – I did. When she hadn't picked him up from the pool, he'd ended up with my family. And now Anni had tried to extort me for fifty thousand kroner by pretending she still had Tobias. As if in slow motion, I felt my right hand stir in my pocket, then emerge into the cold, rainy air, pulling back, gathering force, then slamming as hard as I could into the side of Anni's face, making a cracking sound. She dropped straight to the ground, and at no point did she even attempt to defend herself. I hit her again and again.

CHAPTER 19

'ARE YOU SURE you are really able to do this?' asks Inspector Ellefsen, gazing at me seriously across the long table. Next to him is that dreadful lesbian, Camilla Stensland, and next to her sits another man whose name I can't remember. Unlike Ellefsen and Stensland, he is wearing a full police uniform, but he has scribbled all over the back of his left hand, which I find highly unprofessional. I sit across from them, and next to me sits Johan, though he's deliberately placed himself so that there is a big space in between our chairs. To my right sits Laila Engebretsen, who'd seemed touched that I asked her to be here. Every now and again she gives me her sad, tight smile, and I force myself to return it – I need her on my side now. Also present is my mother, sitting alone on a green sofa next to the table, crossing and uncrossing her legs nervously. I nod solemnly. I've taken care with my appearance today, and instead of dressing like a sexy Scandi gym-bunny fashionista, which is the look I usually go for, I'm wearing a demure knee-length black skirt and a roll-neck white sweater. Part nun, part waitress, but my goal is to appear as harmless and proper as possible.

'As you'll be aware, there are so many holes in your previous accounts that we are at a loss to establish what information is true and what isn't.' Ellefsen pauses, and I nod again. 'This is now a formal investigation, and I am obliged to inform you that everything you say in this room will be recorded and subject to further investigation. Do you understand?'

'Yes,' I say, keeping my voice low and even. I glance at Johan, who, although he was looking at me out of the corner of his eye, quickly looks away. He thinks it's insane that I should speak to the police today already, when I've just been released from the hospital and am 'clearly confused'. It's as though he fears that I will make up some fantastical story for fun, like he thinks I made up the fact that I'm Tobias's mother.

'Do you have any questions before we begin?' asks Camilla Stensland, clasping her meaty manlike hands together atop the table.

'I would like to know the results of the DNA test,' I say. I can feel my mother's eyes burning into my back – God knows what Johan has told her of all this, but she insisted on coming to support us. Stensland lets out an incredulous little whistle and opens her mouth as though to speak, but Ellefsen discreetly quiets her with a quick move of his head.

'Certainly, Mrs Wilborg. Are you happy for me to tell you the results now, or would you like to be told in a separate room, alone?'

'Now's fine.' For a brief moment, I imagine that Ellefsen opens his mouth and says that the test was negative. That would mean I truly am insane, and that I've imagined all the events of the past ten years. Sudden goosebumps prick at my forearms and I take a deep breath. Do crazy people ever know that they are crazy? Ellefsen and Laila exchange a long glance, or maybe I'm imagining it, because I may very well be truly mad. I hold on to the underside of the chair as if to tether myself to it – I fear I'd bolt from this room if I didn't.

'The results of the DNA test confirm with a ninety-million-to-one certainty that you are Tobias's biological mother.' The room is deathly silent, as though everyone is holding their breath. *Told you so*, I want to shout, but I'm looking at Johan's stricken face. My mother looks as though an aneurysm has just burst open in her brain. I take another deep breath; I need to stay calm now. One shot. I nod seriously. I think about Tobias's baby face, how his black hair started almost at his eyebrows, like a little monkey. I think about how being his mother is imprinted not only in my DNA, but in my bones, and almost laugh out loud at the thought of trying to run away from it.

'Thank you for confirming that,' I say. Everyone is looking at me.

'What I would like you to do, Mrs Wilborg, if you still feel up to it in light of this new information, is run us through everything, from the beginning, and Inspector Stensland or I will stop you if we have any questions. Does that sound okay?'

'Yes.'

'Excuse me,' says Johan, and stands up, a little too fast, knocking his bony knees against the table. 'I'd like to leave.'

'No!' I say. 'Please, no!' He hesitates for a moment, and looks at me pleading with him. His eyes are empty. 'Please don't go, Johan. I can explain everything.'

'Cecilia, for fuck's sake! What they're saying is that you had a baby with someone else, then abandoned it, and quite possibly murdered a junkie. I think I've heard enough.'

'I can explain, Johan!' I try to scream, but my voice comes out a mere whisper. I bring the tears to my eyes from the thought of placing five-day-old Tobias in my father's arms and turning away from him. 'I was raped at knifepoint,' I say, louder now, letting my voice crack at the end of the sentence. Everybody grows stiller yet. Johan, who has reached the door, turns around slowly. A big vein is pulsating at his jaw, and for a long moment

I both hate him and love him. I love him because I always have; it's like something I was born with, a part of my basic construction, like arms or intestines. I hate him because I've sacrificed so much for him and now he might take it all away from me. Johan walks slowly back to his chair and sits down.

'The beginning, please, Mrs Wilborg,' says Camilla Stensland, but even *her* voice has softened slightly. I let myself cry all those tears I've held back over the years, and at one point my mother stands up and hovers by my side, patting my back, before sitting back down. Between sobs, I tell them of the desperation of postpartum depression. I woke every morning praying I was dead. I hated my child and feared I'd fling her into the sea when I strolled along the promenade with her. I'd look down at her little face looking up at me from the stroller and fantasize about smothering her. The dark fog didn't lift for several months, and that was why we went to Uruguay. At this point, I focus on calming the crying down, so that only an occasional tear drops from my eye onto my hands.

'I wasn't myself,' I say, rubbing at my swollen eyes with a tissue Laila handed me when I burst into tears. 'If I'd been myself, it would never have happened. None of it.' I turn in my chair, towards Johan. 'Johan, I was broken. You remember how broken I was. I was literally falling apart. I truly feared I'd kill myself, or worse, Nicoline. I didn't want to, but it felt like something dark inside of me was compelling me to. I couldn't even slice bread for fear of turning the blade on myself. Or the baby.' I pause. Johan winces. Laila gives me a very sad, small smile. 'I began to drink secretly. Every morning, I'd pour myself three or four vodka shots before continuing with my day. It took the edge off, but by the time we arrived in Uruguay, I needed something more than just alcohol. We'd met some other young people at the beach clubs, and when some Swedish girls invited me to a midnight beach party, I decided to go.' I catch Ellefsen's eye and he doesn't flinch. I feel like he doesn't believe me. I need tears, more tears. Tobias latching on to my breast that first night, when the chubby snowflakes were falling heavily outside, when the wind howled, and I held my baby until dawn. Knitting that little bear with shaking hands and streaming eyes. I burst into tears again.

'I didn't see anyone,' I whisper. 'I'd gone down to the water's edge because my head was spinning. I'd taken cocaine and amphetamines. I didn't even hear anyone approach. I was sitting in the wet sand, watching colorful swirls grow out of the waves and move towards me like strange clouds, when I felt something sharp and cold pressed to my neck.' Blow nose, rub eyes, hiccup. Repeat. 'My face was held hard into the sand and I remember feeling certain that he'd suffocate me or stab me when he'd finished. I was wearing a dress and he just pulled it up and tore my underwear.'

'May I stop you for a moment?' asks Camilla Stensland gently. I nod. 'Did you attempt to call for help, or struggle in any way?'

'I… I cried "no", and tried to wriggle free, but he was so strong. The whole time he held the knife to my neck, it's what I remember most. How cold it was. And he hurt me, of course… down there. He was brutal. Afterwards, when I finally dared to stand up, I felt his come run out of me and waded into the sea to try to wash him off.' At this, I pause again, and stare down at my hand holding the soaked tissue paper.

'Did you tell anyone what happened to you, Cecilia?' asks Ellefsen.

'No.'

'Why did you not report the rape?'

'I felt so incredibly stupid. I guess I was afraid of the police finding the traces of drugs in my system if they ran tests... I thought that nobody would believe me and that they'd make it out like I'd wanted it and got cold feet the next day and cried rape.'

'I'd have believed you, honey,' Johan whispers and takes my hand. I nod and a teardrop falls from my eye onto his hand intertwined with mine. He squeezes it. I tell them about how I didn't realize I was pregnant for such a long time because I was still reeling, both physically and mentally, from the arrival of Nicoline.

'Did you not at any point think the baby could be your husband's, after you realized you were pregnant?' says Ellefsen. I shake my head brusquely, glance tenderly at Johan, and smile a sad little smile, like the ones Laila uses.

'Johan and I weren't making love at that time,' I say. 'At all. I was so traumatized by what happened in Uruguay that I just couldn't bear it. Please understand that I love my husband.' I look at Johan. 'I love you so much, and that's why I did what I did. I was so shocked when I realized, it was as though I completely lost hold of myself. I unraveled. I wasn't thinking straight. I'm so ashamed... I...'

'Shall we break for five minutes?' says Laila, and Ellefsen nods. The guy with the scribbled hands flicks the 'off' button on the tape recorder on the table. Laila and Ellefsen leave the room. Camilla shoots me a vaguely sympathetic glance, then pulls a phone from her pocket. My mother is crying silently. Johan traces little shapes in the palm of my hand and looks at me as if I just did something wonderful and touching. Laila returns and places a steaming-hot black coffee in front of me. She squeezes my shoulder.

'Are you feeling okay to continue?' says Ellefsen, and I notice that his sausage-like bloated fingers are wet. He must have just gone to the bathroom and the thought of that makes me shudder.

'Is everything okay?' asks Laila.

'Yes… It's just… It's… it's so hard reliving everything. I've repressed it for so long. I just pretended it never happened, and it has been so difficult.'

'It seems to me like a strange thing to do,' says Ellefsen. 'To run away from everything when you found out about the pregnancy. Many women might have tried to pass the child off as their husband's. Did that ever occur to you?'

'Uh, no.'

'Why not?'

'Well, I presumed it would be colored and so it would be very obvious.'

'But you never saw the rapist?' asks Camilla, her eyes colder again, as though she'd slipped up and believed me for a moment, even though she didn't really.

'No. Like I said, my face was pressed into the sand.'

'Why did you then assume he would be colored?' asks Ellefsen. 'As far as I know, Uruguay's population is of predominantly European heritage.' I swallow hard. I let out a bitter little half-laugh.

'I… I guess I thought it would be likely because statistically speaking, let's face it, most rapists are not predominantly of European heritage.'

'I know of no such statistic, Mrs Wilborg,' continues Ellefsen, 'but I will make note that this was your personal belief.' I nod, forcing my features to remain neutral. I feel my cheeks burn, and rub hard at my eyes again so the redness will be ascribed to the rubbing.

'What did you do next? How did you come into contact with Annika Lucasson and Krysztof Mazur?'

'I went to my father in Sweden.' At this, my mother gasps. Ellefsen and Stensland turn to look at her. 'My mother will be surprised to hear this, because as far as she knows, I haven't spoken to my father since I was fifteen.' I turn to my mother. 'I'm sorry I never told you.' My father convinced Johan to tell my mother that it was he who'd taken me to the clinic in Sweden – she would never have believed I'd seek my father out for any reason, and so might have become suspicious.

'Why is that?'

'Well, it doesn't have anything to do with anything, but he left my mother and I, and I was very angry with him.'

'And yet it was him you turned to when you found yourself in this desperately difficult situation?'

'Yes. I knew he felt guilty about how he'd treated me, so I assumed he'd help me, no questions asked.'

'Where is your father now?'

'I don't know.'

'You don't know?'

'No. Presumably he is at home, in Värmland.'

'But you are not in touch?'

'No. I left the baby with him. He was going to give it up for adoption. He didn't do it like I'd wanted him to. He's only been in touch with me a couple of times since then.'

'So how did the child end up in the hands of Lucasson and Mazur?'

'I have no idea.'

Ellefsen clenches his jaw, and looks briefly angry. I glance at Laila, who is hanging on my every word. I know she believes me.

'Returning to the time immediately before Tobias's birth,' continues Ellefsen. 'How long did you stay with your father?'

'For almost nine weeks in total.'

'And where did you think your wife was at this time?' Ellefsen asks Johan, who looks as though he's just been asked to perform a circus trick.

'Uh. Uh. I thought she was receiving help for her depression at a clinic in Sweden.'

'Why did you think that?'

'Because her father phoned me and said she'd come to him, completely desperate. They sent me information on her treatment and… uh, I spoke with her father many times.'

'And you believed him.'

'Well, yes. She was… she was in a very bad place before she went there.'

'Did you not at any point suspect that your wife may be pregnant again?' asks Camilla Stensland.

'Of course not. Like Cecilia said, we hadn't been making love for a long time. I'd tried a few times, but… but Nicoline was a difficult baby and I could see that Cecilia was still struggling a lot after her birth.'

'And when Cecilia returned from Sweden, did you feel like her condition had improved?'

'Yes, very much so. She was warmer, somehow. Like every little thing touched her very deeply. I liked this change in her. She'd been so numb for so long. I assumed she'd missed me and Nicoline a lot, and that she was finally making real progress towards recovering. And almost as soon as she came back, she started talking about wanting another baby. I tried to say that we should wait a while, especially since our first experience with parenthood had been so dramatic, but she was adamant about needing to hold a new baby, and well, I generally like to give Cecilia everything she wants. Four months after she returned from Sweden, she was pregnant with Hermine.'

'So, you gave birth to three babies in pretty much exactly three years?' asks Laila.

'Yes,' I whisper.

'Returning to your account, and bearing in mind that we need to resolve several serious discrepancies here, I'd like you to explain to us how you first came into contact with Mazur and Lucasson.'

I take a deep breath. I need to keep my version of events streamlined here, juggling both truths and modified truths. 'I first met Annika Lucasson around a year ago. I had just come out of the gym when she approached me in the parking lot. She asked if I was interested in buying cocaine.'

'You have previously stated, on several occasions, that you had no prior knowledge of Annika Lucasson.'

'Yes.'

'Lying to the police is a serious offence, Mrs Wilborg. It is, in fact, punishable.'

'Yes.' I nod miserably.

'Why did you deny your connection to Lucasson and Mazur?'

'Because I was ashamed. In the years after giving up Tobias, I had expected the fog to lift and that things would eventually go back to normal, but they never did. It was as though what I'd done had become a huge black hole inside me that just sucked all joy, all life out of me. I began to travel to Oslo to buy drugs...'
I'd still rather be thought of as a cokehead than a mother who purposefully abandoned her baby.

'What kind of drugs?' Camilla Stensland interrupts.

'Mostly coke. Occasionally LSD.' Both my mother and Johan gasp at this. Too late to stop now. 'I drank in secret, and combined the alcohol and coke with Xanax and Zoloft, occasionally Adderall, Ritalin and Diazepam.'

'Jesus,' says Johan.

'Did you have any inkling of Cecilia's substance abuse, Mr Wilborg?' asks Ellefsen.

'Well, I sometimes thought she drank slightly excessively. But nothing that wasn't within the accepted amount within our social circle, I'd say. I knew she was taking some antidepressants and was under the impression she'd have to take them for years to come, considering her history. But Jesus... No, I had no idea that she'd used cocaine and LSD.'

'So, back to that day when Annika Lucasson approached you and propositioned you with cocaine? What did you do?'

'I bought the drugs from her.'

'How much?'

'A gram.'

'And when did you see her again?'

'I think it was later that same week. I wanted more. I was tired of having to go up to Oslo all the time for coke. It suited me to have someone dealing locally.'

'Were you afraid of being found out?'

'Of course.'

'How did you manage to hide such a substantial drug addiction? Cocaine isn't exactly cheap,' says Camilla Stensland.

'Well, in our family, Johan manages most of the common costs, like house, cars, food, etc. I work freelance, so whatever I make every month is my pocket money, so to speak.'

'And this goes into a separate account?'

'Yes.'

'What, besides cocaine, do you usually spend this money on?'

'Clothes.' Camilla Stensland raises an eyebrow at this, the jealous bitch.

'On average, can you please confirm what kind of amounts you were paying Annika for cocaine monthly?' I swallow hard, trying to guess how much coke would cost on the streets these days; after all, I haven't bought any since I was at university.

'I would say I might have been spending around twenty thousand kroner a month.' I'd have to have been doing a hell of a lot of coke to roughly match the payments I've been making to Anni. Ellefsen whistles softly between his teeth. Johan stares at me.

'What?' he says. 'Are you serious?' I nod and burst into tears again.

'How did you withdraw this money?'

'I'd do it a little at a time. A few hundred cash back every time I shopped, a thousand here and there.'

'Let's take a break there,' says Ellefsen, adjusting his belt, squirming slightly in his seat. 'Afterwards, I'd like for us to continue with what led to the events of October nineteenth. Please bear in mind that this is still primarily a homicide investigation, and the fact that the deceased had your DNA underneath her fingernails places you in a very serious position, Mrs Wilborg. I am, however, pleased with the progress we've made this morning, and feel confident you are in a position to continue this account. Can you please confirm that you are happy to proceed after the break?'

'Yes, I am.' I stand up fast and move towards the door, so I don't have to face Johan or my mother just now. Cecilia the cokehead, Cecilia the rape victim.

'Bathroom?' asks Camilla Stensland. I nod. 'I'll take you there,' she says. Being a dyke, I bet that's her favorite part of her job.

CHAPTER 20

THE MAN WITH the scribbled hand presses 'record' on the tape recorder.

'Continuing the account of Cecilia Wilborg, in the presence of family members Anne-Marie Dysthe and Johan Wilborg. Cecilia, returning to your initial contact with Annika Lucasson, could you please confirm when you first became aware of Tobias being in the custody of Lucasson and Mazur?'

'Oh, I never knew,' I say. 'I found out that they'd had him at the same time as everybody else, I suppose.'

'Wait, Annika never told you that they had your son?'

'No.'

'Did you ever see her with the child?'

'No, never.'

'Do you think that Annika knew that you were Tobias's biological mother?' asks Camilla Stensland, narrowing her eyes as though she thinks that might help her read me better. And perhaps it does; I'm fighting off a faint touch of panic. I knew they would ask me a million questions, and though I've gone through my story over and over in my head, I realize now that any slight deviation from the version I've memorized throws me off course.

I touch my index fingers to my temples, wincing visibly to buy some more time. 'No. I can't imagine she would have known that.'

'It seems like a very big coincidence that Lucasson and Mazur should have removed the child from your father's care and then turn up in Sandefjord without the intention of making contact with you.'

'I suppose.'

'Do you think your father had a connection to Lucasson and Mazur?'

'I wouldn't know,' I say. 'You'd have to ask him yourself.'

'We are trying to establish contact with him at the moment, Mrs Wilborg. I can assure you that we are most interested in speaking with your father at his earliest convenience. So. The boy somehow ended up in the care of Mazur and Lucasson, who for some reason showed up in Sandefjord, where you began to buy large amounts of cocaine from Lucasson. Is this correct?' continues Ellefsen.

Fear; gray, impenetrable, ugly. 'Yes.'

'When exactly did you learn of Tobias's disappearance from your father's farm?'

'I never knew.'

'You never knew?' Camilla Stensland's voice trembles with indignation as she speaks. 'I'm sorry, but I find it extremely hard to believe that your father, who presumably had been taking care of this child for several years, did not get in contact with you when the child was taken by a pair of junkies.'

'He tried to contact me about a year ago. It was just before Christmas, in fact. He called and emailed me repeatedly.'

'What did he want to discuss?'

'Inspector Ellefsen, I put the phone down every time he called. I deleted his emails as soon as they arrived. Then, he showed up at my house, coming towards me as I was getting in the car. This was around a week after he'd first called. I'd assumed his efforts to get in touch were to do with Christmas or something. You, know, old people get lonely and I just assumed he was trying to get an invite. I began to drive away, but he said, "I need to talk to you about the boy."'

'And what did you say?'

'I said...' I pause here, for dramatic effect. They are all staring at me. I feel ill, like something is boiling in my blood. 'I said, "That boy never existed," and then I drove away.' I didn't really say that. My father got in the car with me and we drove around aimlessly for over an hour, him sobbing as he spoke of the boy going missing in the middle of the night. We tried to come up with a plan to get the boy back to Munkfors. My father would go to Poland, try to track down the kidnappers who were blackmailing him. We'd have to sort this situation between us without police involvement, that much was clear. *What if they kill him?* my father said, looking at me with wild eyes. *Then they kill him*, I said, but I hadn't even finished speaking before my father slapped me hard across the face. And now, I need to maintain that I never knew he'd been taken at all; the truth would surely land me in much worse trouble. If I didn't know, then the only bad thing I've done was having an illegitimate child and leaving him with my father.

'Mrs Wilborg. You do realize that elements of your account sound quite hard to believe? Did you never, at any point, reconsider your actions with regard to Tobias? Did you never think it may be easier to come clean and face the consequences?'

'Of course I did. I should have come clean as soon as I was raped.' I burst into tears here, though the tears don't come easily now because I'm afraid, so I rub my eyes hard and blink sadly, taking several long moments to regain my composure. 'I was just so disoriented and out of myself. And when I realized

I was pregnant, I became convinced Johan would leave me. I couldn't bear that. I would have killed myself.' I turn to Johan. 'I wouldn't have been able to bear it,' I say, pleading with him with my eyes again, but his face is unreadable now. He has heard too many difficult 'truths' about his wife for one morning.

'Another question, Mrs Wilborg,' says Inspector Ellefsen. 'I wonder why your father didn't telephone the police if and when the child was removed from his care?'

'You'll have to ask him yourself.'

'Very well,' says Ellefsen. 'I would have thought his primary concern would be the safety of his grandchild, not an old and frankly criminal promise he'd once made to his estranged daughter, wouldn't you?'

'Well, we don't know the circumstances, do we?' I say. 'Like I said, I never knew. Perhaps he handed Tobias over to Lucasson and Mazur for whatever reason that made sense to him at the time. Or perhaps they were threatening him to stay silent. Or maybe he was just very afraid of getting into serious trouble for the role he'd played, and was trying to find Tobias himself.'

'Can you think of any reason why your father would have handed a seven-year-old boy over to two drug addicts with an extensive criminal record?'

'Yes. Perhaps he didn't know that. Maybe they befriended him and managed to pretend that they were a normal, caring couple. He is a lonely man, my father. Maybe they wanted to adopt Tobias and my father reluctantly agreed because he knew the situation was unsustainable.'

'Did your father at any point express concerns to you about the fact that the situation with Tobias was unsustainable?'

'Yes.'

'When was that?'

'When Tobias was around six months old. I made contact with my father to make sure he was going ahead with the adoption plans. He said he was horrified by my lack of remorse, and believed the boy should be kept in our family. I said that that simply wasn't possible, and he maintained that he would raise the boy himself. I think he always believed that my maternal instinct would prove stronger than my will to preserve my marriage and family, though I don't know how he imagined I'd solve the situation. He became bitter at how things turned out, even though they were his fault for not doing as I said. Had he turned Tobias over to the authorities as soon as I left, none of this would have happened.'

'And when were you next in contact?'

'When he tried to speak with me around a year ago, but, as I said, I refused to hear him out.'

'May I ask,' interjects Stensland, as if I don't realize what they're doing here – firing away question after question to throw me, 'at which point exactly did you realize that the child living in your house was in fact the same child as the baby you'd left with your father all those years ago?' I catch my mother nodding out of the corner of my eye, as though she, too, would like the answer to this question. Had I known it would be like this, I would most certainly have brought my lawyer. They advised me to bring legal counsel and I coolly informed them that that wouldn't be necessary as I'm an innocent woman simply giving my version of events. I feel Johan's eyes on me as well, and silently curse him for just sitting there when I'm being subjected to the third degree by this goddamned buffoon and his butch henchwoman.

'I realized that Tobias was my son that day at the pool when I had a complete breakdown. Before then, when he first came to live with us, he'd occasionally give me a slow, sweet smile and that smile reminded me very much of something or someone, but I couldn't quite put my finger to it. Nicoline once pointed out that even though Tobias has dark hair, he actually looks like her and Hermine. I laughed it off at the time, but it was something I thought about a few times after she'd said it. It was so many little things, I guess, and they all hit me at once in that moment when Tobias turned to look at me at the pool.' This was, of course, strictly untrue. That first, devastating suspicion came when I met the receptionist from the pool in town that dreary, rainy day, when she told me the boy had been to the pool with a woman who sounded very much like Anni, my shaking hands as I texted her asking if everything was okay, the tingling feeling of vodka in my stomach as I walked home in the rain, a niggling feeling of impending disaster spreading throughout me. I knew for sure when Anni turned up at the boatyard without the boy, that's why I did what I did to her. I still didn't want to believe it, of course. Or maybe I knew even before then, that night we arrived at the empty house. I tried to look for proof that it wasn't true, that it couldn't possibly be him, but in my heart I knew that it was. Then I tried to convince myself that it didn't matter who he was; soon he'd be sent off to another family anyway, a permanent family who'd take care of him forever, and nobody would ever know. The mistake I made was that somewhere along the way, I had allowed myself to love him.

This continues for at least another hour and they ask me endless variations of the same questions; how had I communicated with Mazur and Lucasson? Setting up appointments by text message, meeting and talking in person. Thank God. Had my husband never noticed tens and thousands of kroner going missing? Nope. They'd be looking at my accounts, they said. Go right ahead, I answered. Why had I spoken up when I did? Because I had a nervous breakdown at the swimming pool, obviously. Did I have any further information that may prove of interest to the investigation? Yes. And so we continued to the night Annika Lucasson died.

'Traces of your DNA were found underneath the fingernails of Lucasson. Can you offer any explanation as to how it got there?'

'Yes. We had a fight.'

'A fight?' Camilla Stensland looks like she might laugh. Just because I'm rather less manly than her doesn't mean I can't throw a punch.

'Yes.'

'Can you confirm the date this took place?'

'I, uh, think it must have been about two days after Tobias was left at the pool.'

'So, the evening of October nineteenth.'

'Yes.'

'Are you completely certain about this date?'

'Yes, it was definitely that night. October the nineteenth. I had arranged to meet Anni.'

'Where, exactly?' Clearly nobody has taught that Stensland bitch that it's rude to not wait your turn.

'In the boatyard behind Meny. It was around ten thirty at night. Anni was late. When she finally showed up, she looked terrible. She had a big bruise at the side of her head and her lip was cracked open. She was literally shaking as she approached me, drawing repeatedly at a cigarette that had gone out. And then... I hit her.'

'Why?' asks Ellefsen. Johan's eyes, sharper than they've ever been on me before.

'Because she hadn't brought what I'd asked for.'

'Did you give her any money?'

'No.'

'What was it you'd asked her to bring?'

'Two grams of coke.'

'And why hadn't she brought it?'

'I don't know. She started trying to explain, but she seemed completely out of it. She kept mumbling "Oh God, oh God" and "You've got to help me." She was such a mess. I shouldn't have hit her, but I just completely lost it with her.'

'How did you hit her?' asks Camilla Stensland. 'Closed-fist punch, or a slap?'

'Closed-fist punch. Side of the face. She fell straight to the ground. It was almost like hitting a mirage, she already seemed half dead. Immediately I felt bad because I knew I shouldn't have hit her. I crouched down next to her and checked that she wasn't dead, and then she grabbed hold of me really hard, by the neck of my rain jacket. I could feel her fingernails slice into the skin on my neck and pulled her off hard. I hit her again, a hard slap across the mouth. And then...' I pause here for a moment. I'm not sure if I should actually say what I said to Anni next, the last words she'd ever hear as it turned out. I decide to say it. 'And then I leaned in to her ear and said, "Anni, why don't you just go kill yourself? I mean, come on. You are such a fucking waste of skin. Please, Anni, please just kill yourself. God himself would applaud you. Come on. Tonight is the night, you fucking disgusting whore."' As I speak, I realize I've raised my voice in memory of my furious, vile voice that night. Everyone is staring at me in a stunned silence. I'm almost enjoying the attention.

'Cecilia...' says Johan, but then just stares at a spot on the wall behind Ellefsen and Stensland.

'The last I ever saw of her,' I continue, making my voice thin and remorseful, 'was around ten minutes later. I'd left her on the ground and walked away. I stopped in between two large boats on the far side of the boatyard, by the road that leads out to Vesterøya. I could see her from there, and watched as she slowly got up. She was crying, and the sound of her sobs rose above the rain, which was still falling heavily. As far as I could tell, we were definitely alone. She walked towards the water, hobbling and clutching her face. I did feel bad, I want to say that. Really bad. I almost called out to her and said, "Hey, Anni. Come over here and I'll give you a hot coffee and a dry bed for the night," but I guess I'm just not that person. I suppose at the very least I could have said I didn't mean what I'd said to her. And I didn't. I've never said anything like that to anybody before, it was completely out of character. But you must understand I was frustrated and upset that she hadn't brought what she was supposed to, and also, I was under a lot of pressure...'

'What kind of pressure?' asks Stensland.

'You know. Keeping a home. Working and taking care of the children. And the little boy had just arrived in my family.' *Paying tens of thousands of kroner every month to get a couple of junkies to shut up about your seedy past.* Just the usual. 'I have a question,' I say.

'Go on,' says Ellefsen.

'Can you tell us how Anni Lucasson died?'

'The post-mortem showed that she'd suffered a couple of substantial blows to the head, but they were not the cause of death. She died from drowning.' I nod, weakly. I guess we're all thinking the same thing – I'd basically killed her. Me who has everything, feeling the need to encourage someone who has lost everything and more to commit suicide. I feel like adding something else, something that will make me be seen in a more positive light, but it's a little late for that, let's face it.

'We'll stop there for now,' says Ellefsen. 'You're free to go home, but don't leave town,' he adds. I let out a little laugh to humor him, but realize that he's completely serious.

'How are you feeling?' asks Laila.

'Fucking fabulous,' I snap, then realize what a mistake it is to alienate her even further. 'I'm sorry,' I say. 'It's just, in the middle of all this, I miss Tobias so much I don't know what to do with myself. I want my son back.' Laila nods and smiles that dumb, sad smile that means 'no'. Johan grabs me by the elbow as we leave the police station, my bewildered old mother in tow.

*

At home, my mother sits on the sofa by the bay windows with a huge glass of Pinot Noir and reads a magazine about property in France, as though nothing has happened and she's considering a nice little apartment with a balcony and sea views in Port Grimaud. Johan rubs at his eyes and makes an excuse about catching up on work before disappearing downstairs. The girls sit at their grandmother's feet, watching little American girls plaster their faces in make-up, talking their fans through contouring, step by step. I want to disappear. I wish somebody would talk to me, even if it's just one of the girls asking if I've washed something they'd put in the laundry bin. But nobody does. I go into the kitchen and take my medicines. Even the ritual of popping the pills out of their foiled shells feels calming, like it doesn't matter what they contain. My head is spinning and my heart feels slow and old. I want my head to be clear, but I don't want to remember anything else, not tonight.

On Tobias's birthday I gave him half of the amethyst I found in California as a teenager. He liked it, I could tell. As I was about to leave his room and wake the girls, he whispered, *Wait*. Then he jumped out of bed, rummaged through some clothes that lay in a heap by the wardrobe, clearly found what he was looking for, then pressed a small object into my hand. *What is it?* I asked. *It's a key*, he said. *What does it open?* I asked. Tobias shook his head. *I don't know*, he said. I turned it around in my hand and realized it looked pretty much identical to the one we have for the postbox we keep in town. That same afternoon, I went there, parking further up the street, as though being seen at the post office was something suspicious, like being spotted at the police station or social services. On the key's green plastic grip was the number eighteen. Inside box eighteen was a big fat mess of notebooks and loose sheets of paper. I don't know what I'd been expecting, but I suppose it wasn't that. In the car I spent several minutes putting the journals together by date, then I began reading. It was almost dark by the time I finished, and then I drove home, heart hammering, and fed every last scrap to the flames. No one will ever know her thoughts, or how she came to be who she was. Except for me. And I suppose I am someone who is able to keep big secrets.

There is a part of me that would like to someday tell my son what little I know of his father. But I never will. I'll never tell him what I remember, and I really do remember him in great detail; the way his smile slashed beautiful vertical dimples in his cheeks – our son has them, too – and the way his hair curled at the nape of his neck just like Tobias's, and the way his laughter seemed to flow from him at almost everything I said that one night our lives crossed paths, leaving a new life behind, forever. I'll never tell Tobias about long, loaded smiles, or about intense kisses, or about how, in those few moments, it felt as though I came alive with his touch after being so very close to dead for so long. He'll never know he was born out of beauty. Instead, I'll tearfully recount the sensation of mouthfuls of sand and twisted limbs and ice-cold, sharp metal, should he ever ask. *Not even a glimpse*, I'll whisper, should he wonder where he came from. If I get my way, and I am fairly confident I will, as I normally do, Tobias will come back and live with us. Laila, unbelievably, pities me. She's jealous, just like she always was, but I believe that in this situation, she feels that I really got served a raw deal. Johan, with time, will become Tobias's father. He'll forgive me. He has to, because what kind of man could leave his wife because she was raped at knifepoint? The ladies at the tennis club will whisper frenziedly behind my back, and this little town will doubtlessly be rocked by the scandal of it all; after all, it is no little feat to single-handedly bring junkies, drug abuse, abandoned children and murder to a small, wealthy town in Norway. And then, someday, they will find something else to talk about, because that's how these things work. I have to remember this in the next few months, when gossip will be rife, when people will steal long glances at me and my dark-haired boy with the deep dimples in Meny. At least, this way, I can keep my head held high.

From time to time, my mind might wander to Anni's last moments; desperate and confused, bleeding and concussed by the frozen harbor, needing just one kind word, one outstretched hand, but finding none. I can see her, reaching down towards the still, dark water, perhaps intending only to touch it, then falling in, falling silent, falling still; finally. She wouldn't have fought it so much. We will pray for her, my family and I, for her soul's rest. In a week's time it is Christmas Eve. I only want one thing, and as soon as the dust has settled from today's exhausting interrogation, I shall set about getting it. Laila looks up to me, for whatever pathetic reason. My father's account will match mine. I have a very expensive lawyer. What Cecilia wants, Cecilia gets.

CHAPTER 21

I'M NOT SURE what I expected, but I guess it wasn't this. Nicoline and Hermine are furious with me, even though Laila and a child psychologist explained the whole story to them in the most pedagogical way people like them can cook up. My daughters ignore me, and Hermine even had the cheek to insinuate that I'd 'sold' their little brother to bad people. *Please bring him home*, said Nicoline, and burst into tears for the first time I can remember that doesn't have to do with screen time. Furthermore, my lawyer has lent me little hope of getting away with lying to the police. Twice he asked me whether I was absolutely positive I hadn't known that Lucasson and Mazur had the child I'd abandoned, and I maintained that of course I hadn't known that. My lawyer isn't confident we'll manage to get Tobias back either, but is meeting with Sandefjord social services tomorrow, together with Johan, who apparently is considered more able to negotiate with the authorities than me. In spite of all this, I've invited the tennis club here for dinner. The show must go on, as they say, and this is especially important in the face of the kind of turmoil this family has endured in recent weeks.

A strange thing happened this morning. While I'd sent out a text message a few days back inviting the tennis club members over, I hadn't heard back from Silje, though she would have heard about my terrible ordeal – I had Johan call around to tell everyone the truth to avoid speculation. Some friend, not jumping at the chance to support me after everything I've been through. Then, this morning, I was at Meny, and while waiting at the fish counter, I spotted Silje over by the bananas. I gave her a little wave and she visibly hesitated before smiling tightly and walking over to me, holding a huge bunch of green bananas.

'Hi, Cecilia,' she said. 'How are you doing?'

'Did you get my message?' I asked. 'Are you coming this evening?'

'I did. I'm sorry I haven't got back to you. I won't be able to make it tonight, I'm afraid.'

'Oh,' I said, feeling suddenly dizzy and odd, like I was reacting to something she hadn't yet said.

'I don't want to, if I'm honest with you.'

'What? Did you not speak to Johan?'

'I did, and I'm pleased for you that he believes your story and stands by you. But I don't.' She smiled that tight little smile again and walked away from me. I was so shocked I could feel my heart tremble in my chest. I should have screamed at her or at the very least told her exactly how many fucks I give about her, but I ended up just meekly clutching the parcel containing the long, wet salmon to my chest and walking to the checkout as though in a daze.

On top of that, I came home to find Johan in the kitchen, reading a newspaper.

'Why aren't you at work?' I asked, feeling like I'd been caught out with something rather more grave than a shopping bag full of salmon.

'I thought you should see this,' he said, sliding a newspaper across the marble island.

It was *Dagbladet*, one of Norway's biggest newspapers. On the front page, in the top-right corner, the headline read: '*Police Appeal for Information in Sandefjord Murder*,' accompanied by a small picture of a much younger, almost normal-looking Annika Lucasson.

'What the fuck?' I said, grabbing the paper and opening it to page eight. The police, apparently, wanted anybody who'd known Lucasson in the last five years of her life to immediately come forward. I threw the paper down on the counter, but it struck a vase full of roses and brought it crashing to the floor. Johan stared at me with a perplexed, frightened gaze.

'Oh, that poor, poor woman!' I said, attempting a small, sad smile. 'I just get so angry thinking about how people like her are treated.' Johan kept looking at me as I bent to pick up the vase shards; my hands were shaking violently, my head swimming with thoughts about what a disaster it would be if some busybody came creeping out of the woodwork, desperate for five minutes of fame.

*

I've calmed down, thankfully assisted by some quality substances. I walk around the house, which is looking immaculate, fluffing cushions and checking for dust. It would seem Luelle has allowed herself to take a more relaxed stance to housekeeping over the last couple of weeks – one of my daughters probably informed her of what's been going on, and she decided to take advantage of that. I'm not sure how pleased she'll be with herself when she finds herself on a flight back to Chiang Mai or wherever she came from, and that's exactly what will happen if she doesn't get her act together. The doorbell rings and I smooth down my skirt and smack my lips together. I look tired and slightly less put together than usual, and that is precisely the look we're after tonight. That odd little woman Silje might have decided she's too good to spend time with me, but at least all the others have RSVP'd and are ready to be there for a friend in need. They are decent enough to support me rather than second-guess my gruesome ordeal.

Fie and Tove are at the door, worried expressions on their faces, as though they'd arrive at the Wilborg residence and find it to be changed, sullied somehow. But no. The candles are lit, the sashimi is sliced, Johan and the girls are at his parents' for the night, the champagne is in the cooler, and I'm looking skinny and polished, with a slightly tired, deliberate undertone.

We hug, and Tove whispers, 'You poor, poor woman.'

That's more like it. Within minutes, Cathrine and Cornelia have arrived as well, and I've unwrapped all my new orchids and poured everyone a glass of Perrier-Jouët. I notice Cornelia glancing at me when I raise the glass to my lips, probably wondering whether I should be drinking when I'm on medication and also apparently have a history of severe substance abuse. I smile coolly at her. We all sit around on the sofa, and at first it's just like before, when my life was simple and uncomplicated. We talk about things such as upcoming city breaks, how to make low-carb cake pops, whose cabin would be the most suitable for our annual girls' ski trip in February (mine, for sure). Then Fie brings the conversation around to the reason we're all really here – to hear about what I've been through.

'Darling, you are so brave having us all around so… soon. I really want to say that it's incredible how well you're holding up, considering the circumstances.'

'Oh, thank you,' I say, making my voice thin. 'Well, I must say, it has been difficult. I mean, I'm not sure you'd even be able to imagine what I've had to endure over the past few weeks.

But it does seem like it will all be resolved fairly soon.' They all nod, and Cornelia squeezes my knee.

'If you don't mind me asking,' says Cathrine, and as she speaks, I can feel the hairs on my arms prickle and stand up, 'did you know that Tobias was your son the last time we were here? When he ran away?' Fie nods faintly.

'No, of course not. I only found out much later.'

'But you did know you had a son?'

'Well, yes. But I certainly didn't know that the baby I'd given up was the same kid as the one who'd come to live with us.' I empty the champagne glass, and stand to refill everyone's, but then I realize that my glass is the only empty one. Cornelia is looking at me again, and the way she watches me makes me feel nervous.

'God, it must have been so shocking. I mean, I wish you'd felt you could talk to us after what happened… in Uruguay,' says Tove. 'We're your best friends, we're here for you.'

'I know, and I appreciate that. It's just… it was just too much. I tried desperately to forget about what had happened. It was a very difficult time.' They're all looking at me and I feel as though I should continue speaking, but I don't know what to say.

'Do you think you could press charges now, like maybe even find the rapist?' says Cathrine.

'What do you mean?' I ask, blinking theatrically.

'Well, now that Tobias has been found, perhaps it could be possible to trace his genetic father. You know, like a DNA test? Chances are that creep would have raped before and after, and perhaps he's been caught by now and is on some kind of sex offenders' register?'

'I suppose that could be possible, but I'll be honest with you, Cathrine. This whole ordeal has just brought me so much pain and heartache, and I just can't face dealing with it anymore. I just want to forget.'

'What about Tobias?' asks Cornelia, trying to frown. Ever since the episode with the burn, Cornelia has been constantly asking about him.

'What about him?'

'Well... what's going to happen to him now?'

'He'll be coming back home, of course. As soon as it can be arranged.' I register that the girls look faintly surprised.

'Oh,' says Cathrine. 'Wow. Well, that's good news. I didn't realize that had been confirmed.'

'Well, it hasn't. Not yet. But that's obviously what's going to happen. I'm his mother. We're his family.'

'Yes, of course,' says Fie, her stringy hair falling into her eyes, 'Just... I mean, you didn't want him... Are you sure you'll definitely get custody of him?'

'This isn't a question of custody,' I say, having to focus on keeping my voice level and calm, but even so, I can hear it tremble. 'This is a question of a small child being returned to his family.'

'Don't be upset, sweetie,' says Cornelia. 'What Fie means is that it might get complicated since you abandoned him when he was a baby...'

'Abandoned? What the hell do you mean, abandoned? I gave him up. I intended for him to be adopted into a loving, safe family. If my father had done what he was told, this whole situation would never have happened in the first place!' Nobody says anything for a long while and both Fie and Cornelia finish off their champagne in one long glug. I don't refill their glasses.

'I was raped. Raped at knifepoint. I don't think any of you can even begin to fathom what that's like. I had no choice whatsoever when it came to Tobias.'

'I know that,' says Cornelia, and takes my hand. 'You poor thing,' she whispers.

'I guess I just wondered whether Johan wouldn't have forgiven you back then. It's not like it was your fault. And it seems like he's been pretty amazing about all this now.'

'I think that's beside the point. And anyway, what was he supposed to do? Divorce me for having been raped? It's Sandefjord, not Islamabad.'

'I bumped into Silje at the tennis club the other day,' says Fie. 'She, uh, seemed really odd. We only spoke for a little while but she was quite mean about you. Rest assured, I immediately came to your defense, of course, but it was very strange.'

'To be honest with you, I've always found her to be an odd woman. Cold, you know? Jealous, I imagine,' I say, giving a little laugh and glancing around my beautiful living room tellingly. My heart is hammering and I'm afraid they can actually see that through my blouse. 'Anyway. What did she say?'

'She... she said that she'd seen you with Annika Lucasson before.'

I raise an eyebrow. 'Well, I'm not sure what Johan told you, but I gather you all know that I've had some personal problems due to the terrible ordeal I've been through...'

'She also said that Annika had approached her outside the shopping center once, a while back, and asked if she knew you. Though she tried to get away from Annika because she was so clearly high, Silje had said yes. Then, Annika had said to her that she should know what kind of person you are and that you were paying her "lots of money" to keep your illegitimate son away. Silje thought at the time that it was the ramblings of a madwoman, but I guess after everything that's happened, she thought it might be true or something...'

Everyone stares at their feet, except Fie, who has the nerve to look straight at me.

'And you? What do you think?' I ask pleasantly, as though I was asking their opinion on curtains, looking at each of them in turn. Nobody looks up, and even Fie drops her gaze to the floor.

'Listen, girls,' I say, after several long moments of silence. 'This was really fun. We should do it again sometime soon. Or actually, let's not. Now, get the fuck out of my home.' I stand, slowly, smoothing down an imaginary crease on my skirt and picking up the empty champagne bottle. Then I lift it above my head and make sure they all see it, enjoying the sharp, wild fear in their eyes. I throw the bottle incredibly hard at the window behind where they're sitting, shattering it and spraying the tennis club ladies with tiny, razor-sharp shards of glass. I walk slowly backwards, laughing at the pandemonium I've caused – the screams, Fie's bloodied shoulder, the frenzied scramble towards the door, Cornelia's wide-eyed expression of horror, the glass crystals in Cathrine's hair catching the light and twinkling like little stars where she remains on the sofa as if in a daze until Tove pulls her up and away. When they've all left, I pluck another bottle of champagne from the cooler and pop it open. I'm guzzling it straight from the bottle when Luelle walks in. She looks terrified.

'There's been an accident, Luelle,' I smile widely at her, as though I was explaining some spilled Cheerios. 'You're going to have to wipe that up,' I say, pointing to the unbelievable mess of the pulverized window, someone's blood on the beige sofa, and the upended champagne glasses dribbling onto the Missoni rug. She nods but doesn't make a move. I snap my fingers an inch away from her face, and leave the room. I need to lie down. I feel strangely riled up, like I want to hit someone or drive really fast or place a big bet at the roulette table. I lie down on Tobias's bed, and as soon as I rest my head on the pillow and draw in the lingering scent of him, I burst into hysterical tears.

*

I wake up and Johan is sitting by the side of the bed. I sit up, but when I do, I realize that I'm soaking wet. I can't possibly have... Then, Johan holds up the second champagne bottle, empty.

'You fell asleep on this,' he says.

'Right.'

'Cecilia—'

'Don't.'

'Look—'

'Just... don't.'

He gets up, and rubs his eyes hard before turning back to me from the doorway. 'I'm off to meet with Laila at social services.'

'Fine. Bye.'

'You do realize that this kind of behavior isn't going to help your cause if you want Tobias back, don't you?'

'I said, don't.' I turn towards the wall and actually have to laugh a little bit at the memory of last night, and the expressions on the girls' faces when I threw the bottle. It passed Cathrine's head by less than two centimeters. The unbelievable nerve of some people. I should consider suing them for defamation and emotional distress. I hear Johan shut the door behind him, and am still chuckling to myself when he comes back a couple of minutes later.

'For you,' he says, handing me my phone, which I'd left in the kitchen. Its screen is flashing with an incoming call and Johan presses 'accept' as he hands it to me.

'Hi, Cecilia,' says a woman. 'This is Camilla Stensland calling from Sandefjord Police. I was hoping you could come down here this morning. We've had some new developments with regards to the Annika Lucasson murder.'

'Right?'

'Can you be here in an hour?'

'I guess so,' I say miserably.

'Please bring your legal counsel.'

CHAPTER 22

CAMILLA STENSLAND HAS shaved a line down the side of her head, unbelievably making her look even more butch than before. I give her a tight smile, but she looks coolly back at me, rising to shake my hand. I picture her off duty, wearing some kind of baggy sports outfit, watching a rugby game on television, drinking beer out of a can, her feet wide apart – that is the kind of person she is. Also present is Inspector Ellefsen and another police officer I don't recall having seen previously. I've brought my overpaid lawyer, Georg Sylling, a deceptively meek-looking man who generally manages to crucify his opponents.

'Hi, Cecilia,' says Camilla Stensland. 'Thank you for coming in at such short notice.' She gestures for Sylling and I to sit, and as I do, the atmosphere strikes me as particularly tense, even considering the circumstances.

'This is not a formal interrogation, Mrs Wilborg, but we do want to ask you a few further questions. Since we last met, we've had some significant developments in the Annika Lucasson case, particularly after we appealed to the public to come forward with any information.'.

'That's… that's great,' I say.

'As you can imagine, there are a couple of questions we feel need to be answered to be able to determine your role in the events that led up to Annika's murder.'

'Of course.'

'Late last night, as a direct result of a tip-off from the public, we discovered the remains of a second body, burned and buried on private land near Kjerringvik.'

'A… a second body?'

'Yes. Do you have any idea who this person may be?' asks Ellefsen, holding my gaze.

'Excuse me, how is this relevant to my client's case?' asks Sylling, just as I say 'No'.

'What does that have to do with Annika Lucasson?' I ask.

'Do you know who this individual is?' asks Camilla Stensland, sliding a photograph across the table, her fingers briefly brushing against mine. I glance at the photo, and immediately feel wildly relieved to see that it is a complete stranger. The man in the photo is a heavy-set man in his forties with a pockmarked face and thinning, brown hair.

'No, I don't,' I say. 'Is he the dead person?' Stensland and Ellefsen exchange a quick glance before Stensland slides another photograph over to me. This guy I know.

'I know him,' I say. 'I don't understand…'

'Can you please confirm the identity of this man?'

'That is Krysztof Mazur,' I say. 'The guy who must have killed Annika.' I let out a hollow little laugh.

'We believe that it was Krysztof Mazur's remains we found last night,' says Camilla Stensland. 'This would tie in with our theory as to who killed Annika Lucasson, and why.' I swallow hard a couple of times, my mouth feels unnaturally dry and strange. They think I killed both Anni and Krysz. I try to think when the last time was that I saw Krysz with my own eyes. Several months ago. I mostly spoke with Anni, though he'd occasionally hover in the background, a glimpsed face in the shadows, momentarily lit hazy orange when he drew on his cigarette.

'Can you please explain your relation to this man?' says Camilla Stensland.

'I knew him only as someone who'd accompanied Annika a couple of times when I met with her for the... the, you know, drugs. I had the impression he was her boyfriend.'

'Are you certain that you never saw Annika Lucasson with the other man?'

'This guy? No, never.' Again, Stensland and Ellefsen exchange a glance and I peer down at the man's crude face again, but I really cannot recall having seen him before.

'But if you've found Mazur dead, how can he have killed Annika Lucasson? I thought you said he was in Poland.'

'We found CCTV footage of his car on the ferry from Larvik to Hirtshals the day after Annika was murdered.'

'But Mazur wasn't in the car?'

'We now believe that it was this man, Pawel Karlowski, who was driving the vehicle.'

'We also believe that Karlowski was with Annika Lucasson on the night of her death.'

'The... the night I met with her.'

'Yes.'

'She was alone when I met her,' I say. I shudder at the sudden thought of us back there in the boatyard in the dark. How frightened she'd looked.

'You are absolutely certain that Lucasson was alone that night?' I nod. I think about the way I hit her, how she dropped to the ground, how I stood over her, telling her to die. If somebody else had been present, it certainly wasn't somebody interested in helping her.

'I'd like to move on and ask you a question of a slightly different nature. It is very important that you think your reply through well and answer truthfully to the best of your ability,' says Stensland, and I glance at Sylling, whose mild eyes are staring at her. I nod.

'Were you at any point prior to October nineteenth, 2017 aware of the fact that your biological son, Tobias, was in the custody of Mazur and Lucasson?'

'You've asked me that question before,' I say, but my voice comes out thick and wobbly, like I'm speaking underwater.

'Yes. And we need you to answer that question again.'

'I'd like a moment with my client,' says Sylling, standing up. We are shown into a small interrogation room across the hallway.

'Look,' says Sylling, 'the point here is that they know that you knew. I can tell – they have proof. If you lie and say you didn't know and they can prove you did, you're looking at a prison sentence for perverting the course of justice.'

'I didn't know,' I whisper meekly, and attempt a very slight eyelash flutter at Sylling.

He stares at me like I'm insane, and then he actually says it out loud. 'You're going to plead insanity.'

'No. Why should I? I didn't know. I had no idea they had Tobias! If I did, I wouldn't have just continued like before, would I?'

Sylling very slowly raises an eyebrow. 'Come on, Cecilia. I'm a lawyer, not a judge.' I open my mouth to tell this man to shut up and do his job rather than taunt me, but only a faint little cry escapes. Maybe all this was just… madness. Insanity. Yes, that's it. Of course. I'll just tell them the truth and blame madness.

Back in the room with the others, the same tense, odd atmosphere remains.

'I did know,' I whisper as soon as I sit down.

'My client will not answer any further questions concerning Tobias today. She is continuously undergoing medical assessment for her persistent health problems, and her psychiatrist will be able to provide the police with a full report with regard to how her illness is likely to have affected her previous account. Now, are there any further questions with the exception of anything pertaining to Tobias?' I stare down at my hands as Sylling speaks; I don't want to see Stensland's sharp eyes or Ellefsen's intertwined sausage fingers.

'Mrs Wilborg, were you aware of Annika Lucasson's diaries?'

'Excuse me?' Everybody looks at me, and I realize I spoke too soon, too loudly.

'She kept a series of journals over several years.'

'Oh,' I say, more controlled now. 'I didn't know that.' How can they possibly know this? I fed every last scrap of her insane words to the flames and watched the paper curl and crumble.

'In her last week, Annika Lucasson wrote about a series of events that give much more of an indication why somebody might have wanted her dead. When we went to the media with our public appeal which presumably you saw, a woman named Ellen Egedius of Karlstad, Sweden, contacted the police and came forward with some information. Information which turned out to be crucial to our investigation. Egedius was Annika Lucasson's social care worker over many years, and remained a devoted friend to her into adulthood. Lucasson lived with the Egedius family for long periods of time, and they were very fond of her. In spite of this, Lucasson kept relapsing and, well, you know much of the rest. It would seem that her relationship with Mazur really was her downfall. In her final account, Lucasson refers to a postbox in Sandefjord where she kept her diaries, presumably out of fear that Mazur, who was extremely violent and unstable, would find them. We have opened that postbox and found it empty, and for that reason we need to establish whether anyone else might have had knowledge of the journals.'

'I certainly never heard of any journals.'

'As I'm sure you'll understand, Mrs Wilborg, we will be going through the CCTV footage from the post office over the next few days to establish who might have had access to postbox eighteen, so we're confident we will gain clarity with regards to this.'

'Great,' I say, forcing a tight smile. I feel Sylling's eyes on me. I want to knock the table over and bolt from this room or smash the window above Stensland's head. Suddenly I think about last night – the shattered glass, the spiteful ladies scarpering, the look of horror on Luelle's face. I can't stop a little laugh escaping. They all look at me, and I return my gaze firmly to my hands resting on the table, and use all my focus to keep them completely still.

'Fortunately for us, Lucasson had the foresight to send a copy of her journals, all the way back from 2010, to Ellen Egedius, along with a goodbye letter.'

'Oh,' I hear myself saying.

'We'd like to take a break now. Your husband has arrived, he's waiting for you in the foyer. Afterwards, we'd like you to read through certain parts of Annika Lucasson's account so that we can ask you some further questions.'

'Sure.'

October 18th, 2017

Dear Ellen,

I've fought myself, endlessly, about whether I should post this to you. I ~~want~~ need you to know that I'm absolutely not doing this to hurt you, or to make everything even worse. I'm doing it because you once told me its always better to know the truth, no matter how painful. I want to tell you the truth. Everything thats happened. A few weeks ago I wrote you a long explanation telling you everything I've done and explaining why things came to be the way they are. I based it on my diaries and I spent a long time on it because I wanted you to maybe understand. I didn't post it then, I decided to only post it if it doesn't look like I'll live for very much longer. And that's how it looks now. I'm in a bad way. If I don't die, I will disappear, so completely that you'll never hear from me, or have to see me again – that I promise you. You can read it below, I dont know how I'm going to get this to you, Ellen, but I know I have to find a way. You will wonder what the mass of paper in the enclosed folder is. It's a copy of my complete journals from the last few years. Most of this letter, the parts that are most important for you to understand what's happened, is based on my diary entries. You don't have to read any of it, Ellen, but I thought you might like to have the option.

I won't lie – not a single lie, I swear, so I'll tell you right away – I'm high, writing this. I wouldn't otherwise be able to. I'm so high, but so lucid. Hundreds of episodes and feelings and memories and thoughts are coming to me all at the same time and I will try to describe them as best I can. Good smack can be like that, but thank God, you'll never know a thing about smack, dear Ellen. I wasn't high when I wrote much of what you'll read below though – I stayed pretty clean in the last few months up until like a week ago. I had a little boy to look after. I miss him. I want you to know about how that happened and that I never meant to hurt anyone. In case I forget to say later or in case you won't read further because you are upset, and I totally understand that, Ellen – I don't

300

have the right to ask anything of you – I will say it right now – I am so sorry. I am so very sorry. I am sorry for everything I've done, for all the stress I've caused, for disappearing, for making you look a fool, for repaying your endless love and support with nothing at all.

It's been almost three years since we last spoke. Even after I went to live with Krysz again in Gothenburg, you tried to contact me. You wrote to me saying it wasn't too late, that it would never be too late and that you and Josef love me like you love Sofia and Vicky and that you and Josef have three daughters, always will, but I didn't answer you. The last letters I burned, unopened. Maybe you thought that it was easy for me to leave it all behind, but it wasn't. I need you to know that.

I love you.

Annika Lucasson X

'That poor woman,' I say. Johan blinks and blinks theatrically, like he just can't believe that he's reading the dead woman's words.

'Keep reading,' says Camilla Stensland. 'It would seem that the rest of this letter has been composed over quite a period of time. It's fragmented, but she probably felt a strong need to confess to Ellen Egedius in some way and didn't have the confidence to post it until her final days.'

You said that writing about my life was a good idea, because I'd be able to read back and see that everything wasn't as bad as I might have remembered, but I don't think I realized back then that by writing and then reading it, it becomes very clear that things are cyclical. At least in my life. Had I known that sooner, perhaps I could have avoided a round or two of the eternal circle-dance of getting clean, picking up the pieces, leaving Krysz, before getting back with Krysz, back on smack, watching the pieces scatter to the ground again. And again. I haven't written much in my journals in the past two years, mainly because I have been afraid of my notes being found by someone who'd alert the police. We're always on the move; it's hard to keep track of all my things. A little notebook could be left behind and then everything would be terrible, so I'm usually scribbling on some random paper which I then hide as well as someone in my situation can. Before, I'd never done anything so bad as to get into real trouble with the law. I'd done a great deal of drugs obviously, but most of what I did, I did only to myself. Since what has happened in the last year, that has changed, and I now know what it feels like to always look over your shoulder. I haven't written to you either, Ellen, because what would I say?

I've been more or less clean for close to a year now, and though I'm being supported with methadone through a women's charity here in Sandefjord, it has been increasingly difficult of late, as Krysz is in a bad place again. His daughter Magdalena died. After he lost her, he lost his God, too. I'd feared that this would happen – that no God could provide solace for a man burying his child, but Krysz had seen that same God give comfort to others in similar situations, so I dared to hope. I want to write again; I need to try to make sense of everything that has happened, but first I want to write to you. Things are spinning out of control here fast and it has even occurred to me that these words may very well serve as a kind of testimony in the event of my death.

The first year after I left you and moved to Gothenburg, things were going okay, considering the circumstances – Magdalena was gravely ill by then. I was squeaky clean, so was Krysz, though he was never half the user I have been. Then Magdalena died, after several weeks of devastating suffering, veering between lucidity and terrible pain. It was too much for him. Of course it was. He began waking in the night, screaming. This quickly escalated to drinking and pot-smoking in the evenings, followed by occasional violence and frequent verbal abuse. In the mornings he'd be sorry, so very sorry, and he'd go back to the church and try his best to find meaning in Jesus's words. His apologies had stopped reaching me by then; I'd become equally numb to both violence and repentance. It wasn't long before I was shooting up again, but even before then, I was so very, very tired. I still am. In those days, I thought often about my little apartment in Karlstad where a district nurse was always on duty, where I'd watched the plants I'd planted on the balcony grow green and strong, where you came to visit and I proudly poured us tea in the sweet little pink cups I'd bought for myself at Åhlens. Nothing fancy, but it was mine. I'll never forget the moment I left it.

I went into the bedroom and lay down on my back. I didn't want to get up again because I already knew I was going to do what I shouldn't do; that I'd walk out of that hard-earned apartment, that I'd never return, that all the help I'd received would be in vain, that I'd disappoint you and all the others who'd shown me kindness, that whichever road I chose, it would inevitably lead back to Krysz, back to smack, and then, to death. I tried, as a last resort, to summon you to my mind, studying your calm face in my memories. You never tired of trying to save me. So many memories. At the country house, you spent every morning weaving little baskets out of birch roots, and though you never asked me to join you, you must have known that eventually I would; there just wasn't anything else to do. Sometimes you'd start a conversation, and sometimes you would not, but either way, it always felt like the air between us was clear. Back then, you always seemed like some kind of actual saint – I presumed you had to be, to take someone like me on. Now, I realize you were just an extraordinary woman who tried to show me how to be whole.

The bed was hard, and I thought it had been made that way to force people to get up. I didn't want to get up, because it would mean setting the next chain of destruction into motion. You stayed on in my mind awhile longer, and I tried to see you as you might have been long before I knew you; you told me you were born after the war, when Europe was still burning, when children played freely and learned to weave wicker baskets from their mothers. If you had been my mother, maybe my memories and my imaginings and my guilt would have been enough to keep me on that bed. But you weren't; you were a stranger who'd tried everything to save me, and who I would now disappoint so bitterly. I wish that you were my mother.

I got up, and by then, the corners of the room lay in purple shadows. It was still light outside, but gloomy now, with dispersing, wispy clouds stretching across the sky. In the park across the road, a child flew a wild red kite which ended up caught in the branches of a tree. The father was still standing there, trying to untangle it, when the moon appeared, yellow and full, behind the trees. He's an ordinary father, I thought, and a good one. I got up and looked around the apartment. Even the photograph of you and me, laughing together by the lake, holding a fish with a swollen white belly, couldn't stop me from picking up my handbag and softly closing the door behind me.

I want you to know what happened afterwards.

The summer after Magdalena died, Krysz was practically tearing at the walls. I decided he needed a change of scenery from the apartment we'd lived in during those last terrible months of Magdalena's life; where he'd come home every day having watched her become less and less, and so I began looking for a summer job for us on one of the many farms requiring seasonal help. I'm not quite sure if it was intentional or coincidental, but one day as I read the advertised jobs in *Göteborgs-Posten*, I turned the page beyond the jobs nearby and glanced at the ads for Värmland. And there it was. My parents' farm was looking for ten to fifteen people to help out with the strawberry fields. I remember my hands shook so hard I barely managed to dial the number.

So I came home again. I didn't tell Krysz that it was the farm where I'd grown up, because a part of me suspected that he'd then refuse to go, just out of spite, because sometimes he can be like that. Of course I knew how incredibly overwhelming and painful it would be to return to the farm, faced again with the loss of my father, my mother, Besta, and of course – my home itself, but I hadn't considered how *good* it would feel, too. It felt mostly good. The man who'd bought the farm was fair and seemed kind, though he had a slightly shifty, sad look about him, as if he personally felt all the sorrows of everyone around him. And I suppose we were a rather sorrowful bunch – the people who take strawberry-picking jobs in Sweden today are generally either addicts of some kind, or illegal immigrants, and that was certainly true of those who'd arrived at my parents' old farm for a summer's hard work.

I think the reason I came to develop more of a relationship with our employer that summer than any of the other workers was that he soon realized what was happening between Krysz and me, though we were staying in a tent behind the barn and not in the main house. Our employer noticed my many bruises, and did not approve. *You're not much of a man if you hit a woman*, he said to Krysz one evening. Krysz just nodded and looked away, clearly concentrating hard not to reciprocate – we couldn't afford to lose the job. When the older man had retreated and we'd gone back to the tent, Krysz pressed his hands together around my neck and whispered, *I can't fucking wait to kill you*.

On the farm lived a small boy called Tobias. He was a serious, wild little thing who you could tell had spent a lot of time alone in nature. He spoke unselfconsciously to the rocks and the trees as though it was the most natural thing in the world, always trailed by a little white dog – it was like they were one being. He wasn't half as interested in people. He reminded me of myself when I was little. Our employer told me once when I was helping him in the barn that the boy was his daughter's son and that he was visiting for the summer. The old man was clearly very fond of his grandson – he always gave him a ride on his back, or chased him around the lawn, and smiled lovingly as the boy trundled off to play in the forest with the dog. The boy never spoke to us workers, but he did sometimes sit on the steps outside the main house, watching us with a serious expression as we came in from the fields. There was always something quite un-childlike about him.

Towards the end of that summer, Krysz and I had a very big fight, and though we were taking care to keep our voices down, I guess Krysz had grown more reckless as we were leaving soon anyway. The old man interfered and pulled Krysz off me, and it took several of the other men to stop Krysz from killing him. The old man's nose was broken and he suffered a nasty cut above his eye, but it was nothing compared to the words Krysz screamed at him, even in front of the child. He called him a fucking pedophile and said he'd call the police on him and have his fucking shithole of a farm repossessed. He tried to pull me into the car, but the old man said *stay*. I don't know why I did, but like I said, I was tired. So tired. Though I wasn't using as much at that time as I have in the past, mostly occasional cocaine and crack and very occasionally heroin, it took me several weeks to come clean. I spent those weeks in a pleasant yellow attic room, and the old man more or less took care of me. When I began to feel stronger, I started to sit in the kitchen with the old man in the evenings, watching the curling flames in the hearth he always kept going, even though it was still summer. He seemed lonely, though I think it was company he was after, rather than conversation.

I'd stare right into the flames, blocking out anything else, and then I'd be back there, in that same kitchen, with my mother. I'd have given anything to stay at the farm, and for a while, I considered trying to interest the old man in a romantic relationship, because then, when he died, the farm would be mine again, and just the thought of that made my insides go weak. At the same time, I knew I couldn't do it. Firstly, I just didn't have the confidence to try something like that – though I'd only just turned thirty, I looked like I was over fifty. And though the old guy seemed to like me well enough and probably appreciated the company, I don't think he ever considered me in that way. Who would? It was pretty obvious to anybody that I was a hard drug user. A few weeks after I was clean, I realized September had arrived. And that the boy was still there.

*

I've been mostly clean for a long while now, though there are some modifications to that truth – I smoke a fair bit of pot, and we've both been drinking a lot over the past few months. Today is a Friday, and Krysz has gone to Sweden for the weekend with Pawel to buy cigarettes and meat. Pawel is Krysz's friend from his teens and basically the reason why Krysz got into bad stuff in the first place. He's violent and dangerous and I'm always on edge when he's around. We just got a new sum of money yesterday, and he likes to take off whenever that happens, to blow off some steam, as he puts it. He tends to come back in a better mood, so perhaps that will happen this time also. It's just the boy and me until Tuesday, and I am in part looking forward to that, and also dreading it. I wanted to take this opportunity to write to you, dear Ellen, though I can't imagine ever posting it. But I want it off my chest, everything that has happened. I want you to know my story.

*

It took a while for the old man to begin to really talk to me. When he did, I think it might have been because I didn't say much back, so he felt there was more space to speak freely. He told me that he'd left his first wife and their teenage daughter in Norway many years ago, and come to the farm because he *needed to learn to breathe again*. That's what he said, and I know what he meant by that, because it is how I have felt so often over the years – that I just can't breathe. That, and that I'd like to sleep until I'm dead. He said his daughter was so angry with him for leaving that she swore she'd never speak to him again, though he had tried everything to remain in contact with her. His letters were returned unopened, and he'd even driven to see her on many occasions, but the girl had refused to come to the door and his ex-wife had shut it in his face. He'd married a woman he loved madly, he said; a Swedish veterinary assistant who was much younger than him. His new wife loved the outdoors, and dreamed of a place where she could keep horses and dogs, and that was why they bought my family's farm. They loved it there, and I was glad to hear that at least it wasn't sold to someone who didn't much appreciate it. As the old man told me of his life, night after night in the kitchen, I found that I couldn't hate him for owning my farm. I became fond of him, and I enjoyed the new roles we began to take as I grew stronger – I cooked for him and the boy, cleaned the house, running the cloth tenderly along the floorboards put in place by my ancestors.

Less than a year after they bought the farm, the man's young wife drowned in the lake. She'd gone out onto the ice to help an injured bird and fell through the ice. It was at that point in winter, late November, when the temperatures had suddenly risen, and then plummeted almost overnight, so though the ice had appeared strong, it had cracks underneath. By the time the old man realized she was missing, the hole she'd fallen through had frozen almost all the way back over, and though they hacked holes all over the lake, her body didn't reappear until March, floating one morning in the brown shallows. It must be the worst way to die, drowning. Or perhaps it isn't; I'm used to feeling like I can't breathe. Perhaps falling from a great height is worse.

The old man stayed on at the farm – he said he felt close to his wife there. When I'd grown stronger, we sometimes walked around the lake together, and I almost told him, then, that his farm was once my farm. I didn't because I was afraid he'd think I had some ulterior motives in coming there, other than just being there and feeling at home again. I don't think Tobias liked it when his grandfather and I walked together, or when we stayed up in the evenings, talking. I can understand that; he was used to having his grandfather all to himself, just like I'd had my mother all to myself for so many years, and I hadn't liked sharing her either. Though I was curious about how the little boy had come to live with his grandfather at the farm, I didn't ask because I figured he'd tell me himself when and if he wanted to. And he did.

The daughter had shown up after many years, pregnant and desperate for help. She told him she had to keep the pregnancy from her husband no matter what, or he'd leave her, and her life would be over. It was agreed that she'd give birth to the child and that it would be given up for adoption. When he spoke of this, I felt a sudden, stinging sensation in my gut at the thought of my own baby, whose name I never even knew. Though the plan had always been to give the child up for adoption, the man said he felt with every part of him that it was the wrong thing to do, that his daughter would come back for the child; he'd watched them together those first few days of the child's life, and felt that the bond between his daughter and her baby was unbreakable. He had only intended to keep the baby for a few months, but the daughter didn't return, and he grew increasingly fond of the boy, and found he just couldn't give him away. He'd pleaded with his daughter relentlessly over the years, but she refused to discuss the matter and told him she wanted nothing further to do with him or the boy. Those were the problems the old man found himself dealing with that summer when I'd arrived on the farm. It seemed to me like a lot to carry, I said, and wasn't there someone who could help? The old man said that it had gone too far, that by not reporting the boy's existence to the authorities he'd committed a bad crime and Tobias would surely be taken away from him if anyone found out, and the old man couldn't bear that. *But you can't hide him forever*, I said, and the old man just looked at me as though that thought had never before occurred to him.

Krysz came back one early morning in December, a few days after the boy's birthday. Tobias and his grandfather were still asleep upstairs, and I was lighting the fire and brewing coffee the way I did every morning. I heard the purr of the engine and saw a flash of the red car between the bare trees as he approached, and felt my heart drop to the pit of my stomach. He didn't drive all the way up to the house, but parked in between two huge oak trees at the top of the long driveway and just waited. It was a strange moment; to realize that I was choosing between the farm and the little life I'd begun to establish there, and Krysz. I walked upstairs as if in a daze, and picked up the old valise on the chair. I stood and listened, but the house was still. In the end, I walked out of the house with nothing. I wanted to leave all my things behind to make the old man understand that I hadn't entirely wanted to go.

Krysz was sober and somber. We made love in the car, right there, in the driveway. Nobody else has ever made me feel anything much, at least not since I was twelve years old. Taking Tobias was all Krysz's idea. People always say that, don't they? There is a part of me that is aware of you reading this and passing it on to the police or whatever to be used as some kind of evidence if I die, and I remain conscious of that, and so this isn't entirely a matter of writing a letter to a dearly loved friend. I shouldn't have told Krysz the things the old man told me – I find it difficult to live with, sometimes, that I did. If I hadn't, Tobias and his grandfather would probably still be there at the farm, going about their lives. Krysz stared at me for a long time after I'd told him everything that had happened in the months he'd been gone; about the wife under the ice, the daughter who didn't want her baby, what the boy was like, how kind the old man had been to me. His eyes went from deliberately sympathetic to ice cold. *We'll take the boy*, he said, *and get the old man to pay for his return. Then, we'll make the mother pay to make us go away.*

You'll be horrified to read these words, Ellen. I know that. I'm sorry I've done these things and that you'll now know about them.

At first, I don't think I quite believed that we'd really taken him. I still don't, sometimes, and now it has been seven months. The other day, I woke in the night, and he was standing there, at the end of the mattress, looking down at us. I catch myself forgetting we have him, then I suddenly jump when he walks into a room, in that quiet, catlike way of his. I think he must have learned it from those years he spent out in the forests at the farm; he really does move in the cautious, studied way of a wild animal. He doesn't say much, but he cries in his sleep. He's smart enough to mostly stay out of our way, and it's a bit easier here in Sandefjord where he spends most days in the forest behind the house. The good thing about having the kid is that there's less pressure on me to bring in money. Apart from on a few occasions, Krysz hasn't asked me to pull tricks since we took him.

On the night we took Tobias, we drove fast through the night to Trelleborg, and then on to the ferry to Świnoujście. The kid was out cold because Krysz had given him Rohypnol, and on the ferry we left him in the back seat of the car under a huge old tarpaulin. When we arrived in Świnoujście, Krysz bought a new phone off a man in the harbor, and took a picture of Tobias, his face only just visible under the tarpaulin, and sent it to the old man with instructions on how to keep the kid alive. No contact by SMS from this point forward, email only, one million Swedish kronor cash left in a postbox in Trelleborg. When he'd sent the message, Krysz dropped the phone into the gray water.

Tobias didn't wake up until late afternoon the next day. At that point, Krysz had been getting stressed and kept saying things like, *We've gone to all this trouble, why won't the little fucker wake up?* and *Fuck, I've given him too much*. When he finally did come to, Krysz stuck his face very close to the boy's, who seemed groggy and kept blinking comically, as though he couldn't believe his eyes, and said: *If you're not a good boy, I'll fucking break every bone in your body*. The boy cried, *Moffa, Moffa*, and Krysz told him the farm had burnt to the ground and that we'd saved him. *Can't you remember the fire?* he asked. I turned away, I didn't want to see the boy's eyes, then. I thought of

Magdalena, and how it seemed impossible that Krysz had once been a father.

After three days, an email arrived from the old man. Krysz read it at an Internet café in town, and brought it back to show me. He said he couldn't get a million kronor together that fast and begged for more time. *Please don't hurt Tobias*, he said, *I'll do anything*. Krysz responded that if he wanted to stop us from killing the kid and burying him in a forest somewhere he'll never be found, he'd have to pay twenty thousand a month until he could remortgage the farm or find the million elsewhere. *You've got a week*, Krysz wrote. The following week, Krysz returned to Trelleborg with Pawel, and sure enough, there was twenty thousand in the postbox. And that's how it has continued – the old guy never did manage to find the million, and Krysz thinks he's probably in some kind of debt or something, but at least he's coughing up monthly, and now the daughter pays, too.

It was strange being back in Poland. I could barely get my head around everything that had happened since I last left – I had the baby in my belly when I arrived in Karlstad, and I had you waiting for me, though I didn't know it. For Tobias, it must have been very hard. In Poland, there weren't any forests or any outdoor space where he could go, so he just watched television every day. We went to live in the house where Krysz had lived with his mother in his teens, after his father died. He'd inherited it a few years before when his mother had a heart attack and went into a care home. It was a dirty, over-furnished, freezing house, but Krysz said we'd be unlikely to be found there.

Gorzów Wielkopolski seemed like an all right enough place in itself, though I didn't see much of it in the few months we spent there; I mostly stayed inside the house with Tobias, sorting through loot Krysz and Pawel brought back, or smoking pot, or crack if I could get it. I hadn't touched heroin since the summer before on the farm. On the few occasions I left the house, which was a squat bungalow in an anonymous neighborhood on the north side of the town, it was in the car. Once, Krysz brought me to a big warehouse where they sold paint and building material and told me to choose some paint for the house. He said it would be nicer for everybody if we at least tried to make the house look okay. It made me happy, because I didn't think Krysz cared about that kind of thing anymore, but I did remember the vegan, straight-laced Krysz with the pristine apartment in Gothenburg, and there must be a part of me that believed he could one day be that guy again. Don't we all try to believe that things will turn out ~~good~~ okay, Ellen?

It took me about a week to paint the house. It did make a difference, when the walls stopped being stained yellow and brown, and were nice and white again. Tobias had, until then, slept on a shaggy rug in a small single bedroom that was stacked high with boxes, but after I'd done all the painting I felt quite inspired and decided I'd make it nicer for him. Just because I didn't want him there didn't mean I couldn't try to make some parts of it easier for him. I dragged the boxes into the entrance area and then pushed them one by one into another room which had just been used as storage. We didn't have a hoover, but I swept all the huge clusters of dust out from his room and all the way out of the house. I told Krysz he had to get a bed for the kid, because he could catch a chill sleeping on that filthy rug on the floor, and get pneumonia and die, and then where would our money come from? He came back with a baby's travel cot a few days later, the kind you can fold down to a rectangle and take on holiday.

I placed it beneath the window and put the rug over the hard plastic mattress at the bottom, then brought a couple of old, embroidered cushions from the sofa. Tobias liked the bed, and started spending a few hours in the morning in it, after he'd had his biscuit for breakfast. He'd sit at the bottom of the bed, shielded from view by the high mesh sides, and draw for hours. *Fucking weirdo*, Krysz would mutter, but left him to it. He still does it sometimes, in this new house, which has a tiny loft space filled with insulation material, but for some reason, he likes to sit up there, doing God knows what.

He didn't cry much, even those early days in Poland, or ask for stuff. He just skulked around like a little ghost. I constantly had to ask him to stay away from the windows, because the last thing we needed was some neighbor seeing a kid standing there staring out, and alerting the authorities. Once, a few weeks into our stay in the house, a man who buys loot off us for his second-hand shop stopped by the house. With him he had a small terrier in a hand-knitted pink frock. It sat in the crook of his arm, delicately licking its little nose every now and again. I'd told Tobias to stay in his room to draw while the man was at the house, but suddenly he stood there, in the middle of the room, reaching for the dog. Krysz laughed nervously and explained that Tobias was my nephew visiting from Sweden. *From Pakistan, more like it*, said the man and guffawed, blowing blue smoke towards my new white ceiling. The man let the kid hold the dog, and it seemed to enjoy the company of a child, jumping about on the sofa, slithering underneath Tobias's knees, yapping and play-biting. The boy laughed for the first time since we took him from the farm.

I tried to give the kid some experiences that were okay, I really did.

One weekend, Krysz went to Trelleborg. The kid and I were alone and played around with the idea of doing something other than just sitting around in front of the TV. I actually asked myself – *What would Ellen do?* It was early spring but quite warm outside, and I'd seen a TV program about Poland that said there was a kind of national park near where we were, with lakes and fields – it looked quite a bit like southern Sweden. Krysz and Pawel had taken Pawel's car to Sweden, so Krysz's old red Skoda was parked outside, though I hadn't driven a car since Josef taught me years ago back at the *torp*. Remember how he insisted on giving me driving lessons? At one point, I was pretty proficient. Would it be so bad if we went?

I made Tobias crouch down, hiding under a jacket, to creep to the car. I said he had to lie down on the back seat and then I covered him with the tarpaulin, just like on the way from Sweden. His eyes were wide open and fearful, like maybe he was afraid I'd take him somewhere to kill him. I smiled at him, but that might have been even more frightening because of the state of me, and he turned away from me, covering his eyes with his hands. It was not yet six in the morning, and the town was quiet and dark as I drove the Skoda quietly through the streets. Tobias lay completely still in the back, and after a while, I began to relax even though driving a car was unfamiliar and nerve-racking. After less than an hour of driving along an empty dual carriageway, I took off onto a smaller road, following signs towards

Barlinek, until we reached our destination, a large lake with a beach and a campsite. On the opposite side of the lake from where we'd parked was Barlinek, and it looked like a sweet little spa town. I peeled the tarpaulin back and found Tobias fast asleep underneath. I stood watching him a long while – he seemed older, suddenly, after I'd cut his hair close to his scalp just a few days earlier. I'd had to – he'd gotten head lice, most likely from sleeping on the disgusting old cushions with no pillowcases.

Hey, I said after watching him awhile, *wake up*. He did, and looked around. At the sight of me standing over him, his mouth dragged down in a sad line. Then he sat up, suddenly realizing we'd left Gorzów Wielkopolski and were somewhere entirely new. *It's a national park*, I said, before he had a chance to speak. *Shall we try to have some fun?* He looked around, and I could tell he was wondering whether I'd taken him back to Värmland – the landscape was very similar. I held my hand out to him and he took it, and moments later, he dashed off into the woods, which were dripping with intense orange morning sunlight – it felt like summer though it was only March. I sat and watched him from a bench by the lake, and every now and again his little face came peeking out from between tall trunks, making sure I was still there, or maybe hoping I wasn't. I so wished you could have been there, in those moments, Ellen, and in a way it felt like you were.

He stayed in the little wood for hours. I watched him stand completely still, his head thrown back, his hands pressed to the trunk of a tree. Later, he sat on the forest floor with his legs crossed, moving something back and forth in his hands as though he was about to toss dice. I sat gazing out at the wide, silvery lake, which had a couple of wooded islands in the middle. It was a good place to be. In my mind, I played with thoughts such as – what if I just got up and drove off, leaving the boy in the woods? He might be found by somebody who'd offer him a home and a normal life. I could drive due south as fast as the Skoda would go until I ran out of money. Maybe I'd end up somewhere nice, and I could just do what I've done before – pull tricks, make enough money for drugs and a roof over my head. Who's to say it would be any worse? Krysz might never find me.

After a while, Tobias came and sat next to me on the bench. I handed him a Snickers bar and a Coke I'd found in the car; I hadn't thought to plan this trip very well and hadn't brought any other food. When he'd finished, he stood up and unselfconsciously peeled off his dirty old sweatpants and Mickey Mouse T-shirt. He ran into the lake, splashing about in the shallows, throwing water in the air, running in and out of a field of tall reeds swaying on a warm breeze.

We drove home when the sun hung low on the sky and we were so hungry we couldn't have stayed any longer. On the way back to Gorzów Wielkopolski, I stopped at a gas station and bought us huge, greasy bacon burgers. When we'd finished, Tobias settled back onto the seat, lying flat with the tarpaulin covering most of him, in case anybody should happen to peer into the car if we stopped at a red light. I gave him a smile before gently shutting the door and he smiled back, his face glowing from a day in the sun.

When I turned the corner onto Wiejska Street, I realized something was wrong. In the bungalow's driveway stood a white van – Pawel's car. I should have turned. Perhaps I'd have gotten lucky and they'd never know we'd come back at all, but I didn't. Krysz had said he'd be back in two days. I suppose I must have known he'd be angry I'd taken the car, but in those moments, it didn't fully occur to me to be afraid.

Krysz went insane. The kind of insane where he might have killed somebody, and he nearly did. Before I even realized what was happening, he came out the door and grabbed Tobias from the back seat, tarpaulin and all. I ran into the house after them and watched Krysz fling the bundle with the boy inside incredibly hard at the wall. Pawel was nowhere to be seen. I screamed, grabbed at his arm and his clothes, but he was wild, swearing at the child. Then he turned to me and said, *The old fuck hasn't left the money in Trelleborg.* Then: *Let's see how he likes this.* He pulled out a phone I'd never seen before, opened the camera, and pressed 'record.' Then he squatted down next to Tobias, pushing his face right next to the boy's, who was whimpering and shaking. He held the camera out at arm's length and said calmly: *It is nine o'clock in the evening on Thursday, March twenty-first. If the money isn't in Trelleborg on Monday morning I will drown this kid. Do you understand?* Tobias stared straight ahead apathetically, as though he'd been struck dumb.

Krysz got up, and walking past where I stood in the doorway, frozen with fear and crying silently, punched me incredibly hard in the stomach. When I was able to straighten back up, I half crawled, half walked over to where Tobias lay on the floor, his lower body still wrapped in the tarpaulin. I pulled him close to me and he neither resisted nor responded in any way. I stroked his short, spiky hair and my hand came upon two large bumps at the back of his head. Why hadn't I just left him there, in Barlinek's peaceful woods? He might have been tucked up in a clean bed somewhere by now, his stomach full of food, and I'd be on the road, driving fast away from Krysz and everything else through the night. Or I could have even taken him with me. We could have gone north, to Norway, and I could have dropped him at his real family's door. I even thought about coming to you – ringing the doorbell and standing in the shadows on the porch listening to your soft footsteps approaching. But I'd never do that to you. Never.

Sometimes, in Poland, I'd stand at the window and look out at the empty street. There were other houses like the one we were in; modest bungalows with a patch of neglected front garden, a couple of low-rise apartment buildings, and beyond the busier road that crossed our road, a fringe of pine trees. It all looked so normal; the kind of life any person would want to live. A home on a safe street in a country where most people have food. A home you lived in with the man you loved. A little boy, tucked up and asleep in his bed. How those images lied. That house, that man, and the little boy – oh God, it was the very definition of hell. My life truly is hell.

*

We had to flee from the house in Gorzów Wielkopolski. One day, a week or so after Tobias and I went to the lake, the doorbell rang. Krysz opened it, and I watched from the hallway. The unseasonably warm weather had completely disappeared and fresh snow had fallen in the past few days, and because we hadn't left the house at all, Krysz had to shove hard at the door to get it to open, and a flurry of snow whirled into the house. On the doorstep stood a pale little boy, perhaps eight or nine years old. He had wild blond curls which haloed his face, barely held down by an old-fashioned knitted cap. Krysz stared at him, his lips curled back in a disgusted grimace. *Who are you?* he asked. *I'm Gregorz*, said the boy. *I live next door. Can the boy come and play with me in the snow?* I could tell from Krysz's hunched shoulders and white knuckles gripping the doorframe that he was trying to think fast. *What boy? There is no boy*, he said finally, and began to close the door. *But I've seen him*, said Gregorz, *every day, in the window*, his voice silenced by the thud as Krysz pressed the front door shut and turned to me.

I braced myself, waiting for him to scream and shout at me, and glanced at Tobias in the living room, perched on the armrest of a chair, watching a game show. Krysz ran a hand several times through his hair, which by now had thinned to thin, greasy strips on the top of his head. *Let's go*, he said, and I saw then how very tired he was, too. People do crazy things when they are our kind of tired.

Within two hours we were on the road, that's how little we had to pack. I was so relieved that the episode with the boy at the door hadn't resulted in a huge argument that I wasn't even stressed out or sad at the prospect of another move. I didn't even ask Krysz where we were going, though I noticed that we were heading north. *The police would have been next*, Krysz kept saying. After a couple of hours, he stopped the car, and though it was dark outside, I could make out lights from boats on the sea and realized we were in Świnoujście. On the ferry, Tobias lay still on the back seat like the last time. Krysz and I went up into the ship to find some food and a coffee. We sat on hard blue plastic chairs and watched as the lights from Poland's shore became smaller and smaller until they were indistinguishable from the little stars. Then Krysz told me that it was time to put the next part of the plan with Tobias into motion. We'd go to Sandefjord and contact the woman, Cecilia Wilborg, Tobias's mother. We'd get her to pay us a one-off sum or we'd go to the police. When she'd paid, we'd get the old man to pay as much as possible and then we'd take the boy back to Sweden. *What if she wants the kid?* I asked. Krysz snorted into his black, watery coffee. *Trust me*, he said, *she won't.*

*

Now it's summer, and we've been in this house in Sandefjord for a few months. Every day I think about you. The problem with living our kind of life is that you're always waiting for the knock on the door to come. Though maybe the police don't knock at all, I don't know. The reason I'm dreading this weekend is because the boy has started to become a little difficult sometimes, especially when Krysz isn't around. He probably senses that it's a good idea to lay low when Krysz is here.

He wants to go to the swimming pool. He knows such a thing exists, because before we came to Sandefjord, he watched TV all day and sometimes all night, too, and so he's seen most things, really. He has wanted this for a long time now, and the last time he asked, a couple of days ago, I must have hesitated a little bit too long because his face lit up in such a wonderful, unguarded way that it seized me right in the heart. I've explained to him that it's too dangerous for us to just prance around this town, that Krysz and I are trying to solve this situation without actually ending up in prison, but I can tell he just doesn't get it. Often, he starts a sentence by saying, *Other children do this* or *Other children can.* But he isn't other children. Often I wish we could go back to the way things were before Krysz had the brilliant idea of taking the boy. He's brought us more money than any of our other activities combined, that's for sure, but I'm just not sure the stress and difficulty of it has been worth it.

I'm going to stop for a while now. I am actually going to take Tobias to the swimming pool. I'm not sure how much it can hurt for him to go there. A few weeks ago I bought him some swimming shorts from H&M. He hasn't seen them yet, and I think he'll be very pleased. I do want to give him some good experiences, because he sure has had some pretty bad ones, and they're because of Krysz and me. We told him his grandfather was dead. He still cries about his Moffa at night sometimes, which makes me feel terrible. Krysz tells me to get the little idiot to shut the fuck up, so then I'll go in there and sit by his mattress and stroke his damp curls down while he cries, but it isn't enough, is it? He's annoying sometimes, but it isn't really his fault because he's little, so Tobias will go to the pool. Sometimes when I'm with Tobias, I wonder if it's a little bit like it was for you when we met? Like you feel that you just *have* to take care of someone even if you might not really want to or know how even. I'm telling you all this because I want you to know that I tried to do some good.

*

It's very late at night now, but it is still light outside, and I can hear Tobias shuffling about upstairs in the smaller bedroom from time to time. He's probably still on a high from the hours we spent at the swimming pool. Nobody paid us much attention, and I'm not sure why I'd imagined they would. I guess that's what hiding does to you. I chose Saturday morning to go, because I knew it would be packed, so we were less likely to stand out. Thankfully, it was raining, too, after weeks of hot weather, and it seemed like half of Sandefjord's population had gone to the pool. I found myself scanning the crowd for Cecilia, but then I remembered they have an outdoor pool at their house, so she wouldn't be bothered with a dirty public pool, at least not in June. I imagined her, wearing a fancy kind of beach kimono, supervising her children, her *other* children, that is, tottering about on silly high heels and sipping from a glass of white wine with ice cubes in it. I have never been able to understand why she has done what she's done. I think I am somebody who has a lot of understanding for how sometimes life can just happen to you as though you played no part in its outcomes whatsoever, but there are some things you just don't do. Like paying two junkies to keep your own child away from your so-called perfect family. I think it's disgusting and I don't think I'd ever really hated someone before Cecilia Wilborg. Not Roy, or even my disgusting uncle, or all the men I've met over the years who were happy to be inside my body but didn't even want to know my name. What Krysz and I have done to Tobias is nothing, *nothing*, compared to what Cecilia Wilborg has done.

Tobias already knew the basics of swimming; his grandfather taught him in the lake at the farm. I often think of that day I took him to Barlinek, too – he liked playing there. I wonder who his father is, it sure as hell isn't that pale, ruddy-faced husband of Cecilia's, and that is probably the very reason why she did what she's done. Tobias's face lit up at the sight of the turquoise water, and he gazed up at me with such gratitude as we approached the steps leading to the shallow end that I had to look away. There was a box full of pool toys that people could borrow, and Tobias chose some red goggles and a little blue stick to dive after. I sat by the side of the pool watching over him as he dived for the stick again and again, staying in the shallow end. Every now and again he'd stand still for a moment and lift the goggles to the top of his head, and he'd look around in awe, as if he couldn't believe he really was at the swimming pool. The goggles were tight and left a deep imprint on his face. He smiled more freely than I've ever seen him smile before, and it was in that moment that I decided to take this situation into my own hands if Krysz doesn't manage to solve it within the next few weeks. The boy needs a family. He needs to go to school. And he needs to smile like that a lot more often.

*

Camilla Stensland's eyes are hard on me, and I stare back, unflinchingly. I carefully raise one eyebrow slightly, using all my strength to ensure my face is perfectly composed.

'Would you keep reading, please?'

I swallow hard.

'This is clearly nuts,' I say. 'I mean, this woman was so crazy she even lies in her own journals and letters.' I laugh, but everyone is serious and unamused. They can't possibly believe Anni over me. She was a crack-smoking junkie, and I'm a respectable, successful mother who made a single mistake years ago. I'm not going to let that woman take me down. I stare at the next section, the hairs on my arms standing up at the thought of the crazy allegations and lies I'll have to read next. I don't dare look at my husband, but his shock emanates from him. 'I mean, this can't possibly be considered proof. She could have written this crap just to frame me. And who is this Ellen character anyway? She could be a criminal, too!'

'Mrs Wilborg,' says Ellefsen sternly. 'Let's move forward. We'd like you to finish reading the letter.'

It's nice here. Things have settled into a pretty comfortable existence, though not exactly as Krysz planned it. Pawel knew of someone who'd come here for a winter's work last year and they'd stayed in an empty house, and so when we arrived we went there, and thankfully found it empty still. We don't have much, just a couple of mattresses and some clothes. The house sits back from the road on a little hill, with the distinctive rounded cliffs that are everywhere in Sandefjord towering behind it. A small dense wood next to the house hides it from view, and so we feel pretty safe here. From the first floor, you can see the sea. Tobias likes to play in the wood, and we let him do it here because we have a clear view of the road and if a car approaches, we can see it from far off, and he knows to lie down or run inside.

I've opened a postbox in the town, and that is where I keep my journals. For so long now, I have toyed around with the idea of writing to you, wanting nothing, asking for nothing, just forgiveness. The thing I want the most in the world would be for you to read these words and somehow manage to forgive me. I thought maybe I could send you the spare key to the postbox, so in case anything was to happen to me, then at least you could read this and the rest of my journals and then you'd know everything.

Just after we arrived here a couple of months ago, Krysz and I found Cecilia Wilborg. It wasn't difficult; this is a small town – all we had to do was look online at 1881.no and it gave her full address. Late one night, when Tobias was asleep, we drove over to the Wilborgs' house on Vesterøya. It was a huge, newly built house with sweeping views of Sandefjord's inner harbor, just above a big international school down by the water's edge. It was late, but all the lights were on, and we didn't want to take any chances, so we just drove slowly past. When we got home, Krysz and I drank beer and smoked pot, laughing into the house's cold air, excited because the Wilborgs clearly had even more money than we'd dared hope. A couple of days after that, we made our move.

We'd found out that Cecilia Wilborg went to the gym in the former industrial buildings down by the water most mornings after dropping her daughters at school. We decided that it would be me who'd approach her, she'd be less likely to scream or make a scene if it was a woman. Krysz drove me to the parking lot by the gym, and sure enough, there was her Range Rover. It was a kind of bronze color and on the wheels were expensive-looking pinkish gold alloys. Like her house, it was extravagant, and I found I couldn't actually envision sitting in a car like that, or living in such a home. She probably has matching cutlery and ironed sheets, I thought to myself, waiting in the freezing cold morning. After less than ten minutes, Cecilia emerged, her face bare of make-up, but beautifully smooth, like she spends every day rubbing expensive oils and creams into her skin.

'Excuse me,' I said, just as she opened the car with

the key fob, and only then did she notice me standing there, in between her car and the one next to it. A look of disapproval passed over her face and her eyes were cold. She hesitated before answering.

'Yes?' she said at last.

'I need to speak to you.'

'Sorry,' she said breezily, opening the boot and throwing in her gym kit. 'I'm in a rush.' She made for the driver's door, but I blocked her, leaning against the car. Her eyes narrowed in anger and she shoved me, then tried to open the car door, a huge diamond on her ring finger glinting in the sharp winter sun.

'What the hell do you think you're doing?' she said, pulling harder at the door, but my body weight was against it, and she couldn't get in. 'Who the fuck are you?' she whispered, looking around the parking lot, most likely terrified at the thought of being seen with some shabby stranger.

'My name is Anni. Word on the street is, you're looking to buy.'

'Buy what?' she hissed, her cold eyes blinking repeatedly.

'Coke,' I said, and again, she glanced around, though the car park remained thankfully empty.

'You must be insane.'

'Why don't you meet with me tomorrow night, at ten thirty, in the boatyard behind Meny.'

'Look. Anni. It would seem you find yourself in a difficult situation or something. This is not a town that has a problem with vagrants or druggies or criminals or anything like that, so I must say I'm surprised to bump into someone like you here. But listen. I'm going to give you ten seconds to get your fucking dirty hands off my car or I will immediately call the police.'

'No. I will call the police, in fact.' At this, she laughed. Though it was a spiteful, mean laugh, I could see how beautiful her smile was, how even and well-maintained her teeth were.

'*You* will call the police?'

'Yes.'

'And why would you do that, Anni?'

'Because I have your son.' The exaggerated mock-smile died on her lips and she visibly shrunk where she stood.

'What did you just say?' she whispered.

'I said, I have your son. A lovely kid, actually. And I will call the police unless you play ball.' She didn't speak for a very long time. Her hands were held in tight fists against her body, and I think she was fighting the urge to hit me. Just then, a voice broke the silence.

'Cecilia?' it said. I remained where I was, with my back turned, so whoever spoke didn't see my face. Cecilia forced a wide smile back onto her face.

'Oh. Oh, hey, Silje.'

'You okay?'

I stared at Cecilia, whose eyes went quickly from Silje to me and back again, the smile still frozen on her face.

'Yes. Oh yeah, just uh... yeah. Great.'

There was a slight silence before Silje spoke again. 'See you at tennis tomorrow, then.'

'Yep,' said Cecilia, waving at the woman behind me with the fist holding the car key. A moment later we heard the other car start up and pull away, its tires squealing on the snow.

'How fucking dare you,' she said.

'How fucking dare *you*,' I replied, meeting her gaze.

330

'If you bring who you say you have anywhere near me, I'll fucking kill you with my own hands,' she whispered.

'Meet me at the boatyard tomorrow night. Bring twenty thousand kroner.' She snorted hard.

'What? Why would I do that?'

'Otherwise I'll hand the kid over to the police and suggest they run a DNA test on Cecilia Wilborg, that's why.'

'Say I do what you're asking, which in itself is practically impossible, then what?'

'Then we'll explain the full terms and conditions to you. Once you've done your part, we'll return the boy to Munkfors.' At this, she let out a sharp little exhalation and I saw that tears had sprung to her eyes.

'Okay,' she whispered. 'Fine.'

*

She came on time, walking fast across the boatyard to where I stood leaning against the wall of some abandoned workshops by the water. Fifty yards away, to the side of the gas station, Krysz sat in the Skoda, smoking and watching. All the lights were off, but Cecilia passed less than ten meters from him and would easily have seen him had she turned her head. Her face was fully made-up this time and as she approached me, her lower lip trembled with fury. She looked like she was going to hit me, but focused on restraining herself.

'Where is he?'

'Who?'

'The boy.'

'I can't tell you that.'

'Fuck you.'

'Now, let me explain. We want five hundred thousand kroner.'

Cecilia stared at me hard. 'I... I can't get that. I don't have it! You said twenty thousand.'

'Yes. You've got a month. The twenty thousand is for this month. And then you find the five hundred thousand.'

'It's impossible.'

'I'm sure you'll find a way.'

'How do I even know you've got him?' I'd thought she might ask me that. I reached into my pocket and pulled out a small item I knew she'd recognize. It was a tiny knitted bear, as small as a child's palm, which she herself had made for the baby before she'd given birth to him and abandoned him. The old man told me this. Cecilia looked at it for a long moment, reached out and touched upon it lightly, before recoiling as though it had burned her.

'Jesus,' she whispered softly. 'Please don't hurt him.'

*

So now we're waiting for Cecilia Wilborg to find the money. In the meantime, Sandefjord has been kind to us. There's a daytime center for recovering drug users and I go there most days. They give you methadone and food and whatever medicines you need. The house we found is small but cozy. Tobias is much happier than in the Poland-house, I can tell, though he doesn't speak much. Sometimes I think about what we'll do when this situation has resolved itself. We'll have lots of money. Krysz says we will go back to Gothenburg and get a nice apartment like the one he had before Magdalena died, and we'll do things like go to the cinema and get gym memberships.

He says he'll get properly clean, and go to therapy even, and then we won't fight or anything because there isn't much to fight about when you have money. I think maybe those things won't happen even if we do get the money; I worry that it will all just go on smack and there we'll be, still sleeping on mattresses in other people's houses.

I have so many regrets. I regret most of what I've done. I don't know how I can make up for the things I've done, I just don't think it would even be possible. I wonder what you are doing tonight. It's summer, so maybe you are at the *torp*. Maybe you're looking out at the same bright, pink-streaked summer sky as I am. We haven't spoken since I went to live in Gothenburg when Krysz was a vegan Christian. But inside, I talk as if to you, all the time.

Taking a kid to the pool isn't much in the way of atonement, I realize that, but I'm trying to think of more things I can do. This afternoon when we left the swimming pool in the early afternoon, Tobias's fingers had become all crinkly from so many hours in the water. He kept looking at them and smiling. A young girl stood in the middle of the reception area handing out fliers and I walked straight past her, but Tobias took one and handed it to me outside. 'Children's swimming club starting August fifteenth,' it read. Tobias kept his eyes on the ground, not daring to look at me. *Do you want to go to this?* I asked. He didn't answer at first, he probably thought it was a trick question, like when Krysz asks him if he wants chocolate and then slowly eats the whole bar in front of the boy, laughing. Then he looked up at me, nodding boldly, and I noticed his eyes were full of tears. *Okay,* I said.

These are little things, I know that. But maybe those little things are better than nothing. I think, if you didn't know me, and you were just another person at the pool this afternoon, and you'd happened to observe me with Tobias, you would have thought I was his mother. Not one of those perfect, healthy, energetic mothers, but someone who really *saw* their child and tried to give him a fun day. You might have thought I was a little rough around the edges and that the little boy was a little scrawny, but you might still have thought I was an okay person. Thinking of you watching me with the little boy has me really happy, like if everything was different and you knew where I was and you'd happened to come look for me, you might have stood there watching us and smiled.

Oh, Ellen, I wish you could know these things. I wish I could just go and post this letter to you but you'd hate me and you wouldn't believe that I could have done what Ive done, not to a little kid – youd never have thought that about me. Would you? Maybe you would. Often when I write to you I get myself all upset and very sad about how much I have messed things up and how much Ive lost because we came so close there for a little while, didn't we. So close to everything being okay. I know i said I'm not using and its mostly true, I swear but on nights like tonigt when im writing to you and thinking about everything and knowing that it doesn't even matter what I write because I will just put this away like all my other letters to you, it's just too hard to not smoke up.

'You can stop there for a moment,' says Camilla Stensland.

'I don't understand the point of any of this,' I say, and glance briefly at Johan. I'm taken aback to see that he is crying, and not even bothering to wipe away the tears running down his face. A sudden, unexpected twinge of real sadness hits me. Where can I go from here? I can't go to prison and lose Johan. I just can't. If I did, all of my sacrifices, all of my suffering would have been for nothing.

'I'm sure we can agree that this brings new light to the circumstances of Annika Lucasson's last few months and subsequent death.'

I don't respond, but pointedly stare at my hands for a very long time.

'Mrs Wilborg?' asks Inspector Ellefsen. 'The next section, please. This part was written less than two weeks before Annika's death and is taken from her journals. It will fill in a few gaps from her letter to Ellen Egedius.'

Annika L., October 14th, 2017

Things have changed here. It is dark and rains all the time and Krysz hates Norway and wants to go back to Poland. He is trying constantly to get more and more money from Tobias's mother. I've done something that was probably both stupid and dangerous. If Krysz knew, he'd break every bone in my body. For so many months now, I've felt that this situation just can't go on, so I contacted Cecilia secretly and told her I will hand the boy over to social services and tell them who his mother is, unless she pays us one large final amount, and then either takes him, or finds him a place to go. To my surprise, she agreed, but said she'll never give us another penny unless I show her the boy. *I'm not even sure I believe you have him anymore*, she said. Usually it's me who goes to get the money from her. We meet somewhere quiet, late at night, she hands me the cash and I walk away, and that's it. We're due to meet again soon, and I'm going to gently tell Krysz that she wants to see the boy in person to be sure of the fact that we really have him. Then I'm going to hand him over to Cecilia, and he'll be hers to do as she pleases with. I imagine she'll try to return him to her father. She'll give me enough money so that Krysz and I can go back to Poland and lay low for a long while, and I'll tell Krysz that she threatened me and stole the boy. We just can't keep doing this. It isn't even so much that I feel sorry for him, though I usually do, but more that it is absolutely exhausting, and at one point Cecilia might decide she'd rather face the music than keep paying us.

Also, I feel mostly sorry for the old man. I was surprised he didn't call the police immediately when we took Tobias, but Krysz just laughed at the suggestion and asked what he'd have said to the police. That he'd kept an unregistered child at his home for years and years? He was fucked and he knew it, Krysz said.

Today is a Saturday, and it is almost completely dark by five p.m. I feel a melancholy so strong I don't quite know what to do with myself. Tobias is outside in the forest behind the house like he usually is, and Krysz is sleeping upstairs. Yesterday it was terribly cold and Krysz smashed the old sofa that was here when we came and burned its legs in the fireplace, though he's always said we shouldn't use it because someone will see the smoke. We sat on the floor in front of the flames, the three of us, eating Maryland cookies and drinking freezing beer. Tobias likes beer and I don't think he knows children aren't supposed to drink it. Krysz thinks it's really funny, and always laughs mockingly when Tobias asks for one. *It'll make the little idiot sleep well*, he'll say.

Now I'm going to walk into town and put this diary into the postbox I have at the central post office, which Krysz doesn't know about. The key I will place in the pocket of Tobias's only jeans like I usually do, telling him to never ever give that key to anybody, unless I'm dead. Then he can give it to whoever he wants.

CHAPTER 23

I REMAIN COMPLETELY still in my chair, but push the mass of paper slightly away from me to indicate that I have finished reading. Both Camilla Stensland and Inspector Ellefsen are staring at me. I look over at Johan, who is still staring at the pages of the letter and the journal, brow furrowed, hands tightly clasped, eyes red but dry now. I resist the temptation to sneak a glance at Sylling – he, too, has been given a copy of the journals. They've been photocopied from the originals and each page is individually stamped 'Sandefjord Politi'.

'As you can imagine, we have quite a few questions for you with regard to the information brought to us through Annika Lucasson's own words. We've selected one further section we'd like you to read before we move forward. The last she'd ever write, as it turned out.'

'Fine,' I say. I wonder what prison will be like. I glance at Sylling now, and judging by the way he is pursing his lips and pressing his thumbs into his eyes, it's pretty clear that the reappearance of Anni's journals is a straight-up catastrophe. He turns and looks at me and I widen my eyes the way a crazy person might, to show him that I agree; I really will plead insanity. Camilla Stensland pushes the last section of Anni's account over to me, and I stare down at the table where the mad words swim before my eyes. I won't give her the satisfaction of meeting her eye now she's caught me in yet more lies. Georg Sylling sighs heavily.

'Look,' says Johan, breaking the silence, making everybody turn towards him. 'Is this really necessary? I think my wife has had enough for today, don't you?' He pointedly looks at Camilla Stensland. My husband is a very sensitive man, and I'm certain he perceives the negative energy this woman directs towards me.

'Mr Wilborg, this is a police investigation. We have a lot of material to cover, and really need to push forward today.'

'It's fine, Johan,' I say, trying to find a brave smile. 'Really.'

'No, it isn't, really,' he continues. 'Whatever the circumstances here are, I'd quite like some kind of legal justification for forcing my wife to sit here and read through all this. Like she said herself, it could all be made up.'

'Thank you for raising your concerns, Mr Wilborg,' says Thor Ellefsen. 'I can assure you that we are well within our rights to request a suspect to read through the first-hand account of the murder victim.' Georg Sylling nods, raising his eyebrows in an exasperated expression.

'Whether you are within your rights or not, I think this is morally wrong. Look at her! My wife is a normal person. A mother. A wife. Every single day of her life, she does good things for other people, and has, up until all this started, been a highly functioning member of society. She's made one mistake. A single mistake. Have you never made a mistake in your life? Not one? The poor Lucasson woman can never be brought back, no matter what. What are the chances of you finding her killer? And we all know it sure wasn't my wife. It's time to lay this case to rest and give us a chance to recover.'

'Johan,' I begin, but Camilla Stensland interrupts me.

'Mr Wilborg, you'll appreciate that this is a murder investigation.'

'Yes, I do. But what you're playing at here is morally wrong. And I am fully entitled to say that.' The room falls silent, and both Stensland and Ellefsen stare down at their hands for several long moments. My heart is beating fast and hard – I've never before been so proud of Johan in all my life. After a while, Camilla Stensland looks up at me, then points to the rest of the journal, open on the table in front of me. I drop my gaze to the densely printed sheets of paper, and as I do, a couple of fat teardrops spill from my eyes and land on Anni's words.

Annika L., Somewhere near Sandefjord (Kjerringvik?), October 16th

This is a wake. I don't know if I can do this. I can't find the words to do this. This is a wake, the only one he'll ever get. This is his eulogy, words to keep him in the world forever. My journal will end up somewhere, and in it, Krysz will continue to exist. That's why I have to do this. I will find the words. I will sit here all night until I do. I am writing this by the light of a single candle at a kitchen table overflowing with newspapers, old, yellowed books, crusty plates, mugs soiled with years of bitter, black coffee, overflowing ashtrays and empty cigarette packs. Pawel says it's some woman's house, that she has another house in somewhere like Lanzarote, where she spends winters, so it's okay for him to live here while she's away, though she sure as hell doesn't know about it. It's very late and so cold. Writing this on the back of an old electricity bill – stacks of bills have been left on the table so I've got plenty of paper. Over by the terrace door is Krysz. I've pulled the tarpaulin back so that most of his face is showing.

Came here yesterday night. After Pawel took Krysz away in the car and I'd left the kid at Fatma's, I went back to the house and packed the rest of the stuff, but throwing most of it away in the bins down the road at Co-op Extra. I usually never go into the shops near the house, but I went into Rema then, in the middle of the day, and bought a cucumber and some cookies, as though I'd eat them, as though I hadn't just watched Krysz die. The girl behind the counter didn't meet my eyes, but I felt her staring at me when I was picking the coins out of my purse. On the back of my hand is a large cigarette burn; black, bloody and ugly, a last souvenir from Krysz, and that was probably what she was gawping at. Or maybe it was my bloated, twisted face – I couldn't seem to find a remotely normal expression even when I was consciously making an effort to.

Late in the evening, Pawel picked me up, and drove me here. I don't know where exactly this house is, but we drove for a while in the direction of Larvik on the 303. We passed a sign for Kjerringvik. *Where is he?* I asked after a while, avoiding Pawel's blunt, pockmarked face, looking instead at the trees by the roadside, imagining a freshly dug grave among them. *Where the fuck do you think?* he asked, sucking hard on the soggy end of a roll-up. *He's in the goddamned boot, Anni. What did you think I was going to do? Wave my magic wand to get rid of a fucking corpse?* I couldn't stop the tears that began to flow, and I didn't try to. Pawel didn't say anything else, but I could feel his eyes on me occasionally. Just behind where I was sitting, Krysz lay, dead. I thought Pawel had taken him out. I twisted my nose stud around and around to stop myself from howling.

When Pawel finally stopped the car, neither of us immediately got out. I could see a building in front of us, but it was so dark I couldn't tell how big it was, or which color. *Look*, he said, finally, *I have a plan*. Inside the house, it was very cold, and Pawel said we couldn't turn on the heating because then the owner would receive bills and realize someone was in her house. We couldn't use the wood-burning stove either, because someone might see smoke curling from the chimney, even though it was the middle of the night and we were miles away from anywhere. I went into a bedroom and took a purple fleece jacket, some woolly socks and a ski jacket from the top of a closet, and that is what I'm still wearing now.

We ate some rice crackers with raspberry jam, and the cookies I'd bought at Co-op. Pawel said he will help me for fifty thousand kroner. He will get rid of the body, then we will go to Poland on the ferry. *It's easy to hide in Poland*. I told him that I don't have fifty thousand kroner, all I have is just under two thousand kroner left over from the last time Cecilia paid us, almost a month ago. Pawel burst out laughing, a mocking bark, like a wolf's, then he slammed his fist very very hard down on the table, sending several loose sheets of paper sliding to the ground. *Are you fucking stupid or something? You will go to the Wilborg woman and get the money from her, tell her whatever the fuck you have to. Say we'll hand the kid over to the police, or that we'll kill him, whatever it takes!*

I was going to go to bed. Tiredness had seeped into every hollow in my body, filling me like lead. Or maybe that was grief. I stared into the candle's flame, focusing on blocking out Pawel's voice as he rambled on about what a fucking mess I'd landed him in. Then Pawel brought out the crack pipe. I've not done much for almost a year now, with the occasional exception of coke when we've had money, but when he held the pipe out to me I took it. I don't know why, I didn't want to, really. Once, Ellen said to me that people always want to live, no matter what, that survival is programmed into our DNA, but that can't have been quite true because what about all the people who kill themselves? It might have been true for me, though; because even when things were awful, and they have been mostly awful, I've still always wanted more time. But last night when I took the pipe from Pawel and pulled the sour, dense smoke deep into my lungs, it occurred to me that it doesn't particularly matter whether a part of me still wants to live – it just feels like one way or another I'll be dead soon anyway. So I might as well smoke crack and whatever else Pawel can get me.

When I did go to bed, hours later, high as hell and still crying at the thought of Krysz out there, in the boot, Pawel followed, and without a word placed me on the bed, face down. It was too cold to take any more than the absolutely necessary items of clothing off, so he just pulled my jeans down to my knees, and his own, too. On the wall hung an old-fashioned cuckoo clock, and I kept my eyes on this, trying to block out Pawel's cold, fleshy hands gripping my hips. I half expected the clock to suddenly spring open, revealing little wooden figures and playing merry music. It still worked, because I watched several long minutes tick by. He was rough and took a long while, probably because of the crack and all the beers, and he put it into both places, which made it much worse. I couldn't stop myself from crying out in pain after a very long time when he still hadn't stopped. *You like that, don't you, you whore?* Pawel said, bending forward, grunting into my ear.

When I woke this morning, Pawel was standing over the bed. *Make contact with the Wilborg woman,* he said. *I'm going to Oslo, and I won't be back until tomorrow.* I nodded, swallowing hard. Bile rose from my stomach at the thought of last night. *I need you to bring Krysz inside,* I said. *No,* said Pawel. *Yes,* I answered. We stared at each other for a long time, but I did not flinch, and finally he walked downstairs and I heard the door slam shut behind him. I watched Pawel cross the little courtyard to where Krysz's Skoda stood, dripping with the overnight heavy rain. He opened the boot and stood staring into it for several long moments, then he turned and saw me at the window and threw his hands up in exaggerated exasperation. I ran downstairs and outside, and by the time I reached them, Pawel had managed to haul Krysz, still covered in the tarpaulin, onto the gravel. His eyes were narrow and cold, and he motioned for me to pick up the feet end.

Krysz was so heavy I doubt Pawel would have been able to carry him alone. We half carried, half dragged him over to the house, then up the wooden stairs on the outside that led to a large terrace which wrapped around the entire first floor of the house. It was bigger than it seemed from the inside, painted a light gray, with white shuttered windows – it reminded me of one of those American beach houses you see in the movies, but in a run-down kind of way. From the terrace I turned back towards the car and tried to make out anything at all that could tell me where this house is, but there wasn't anything. Besides the red car, everything was gray; the bare, somber trees that surrounded the house on all sides, the sky, the silvery stretch between the trees to the left, which looked like a lake or perhaps even the sea.

Pawel dragged Krysz through the terrace door into the living room, then turned to me. *Now what are you going to do with him, you sick bitch?* He spat at the floor, in between my feet and the head-end of the tarpaulin, then walked back outside to the bitterly cold, gray morning. A moment later I heard the car start. I don't know why he went to Oslo, nor that he'll actually come back. But I expect he'll want the fifty thousand.

Tomorrow we are going to get rid of Krysz's body, and Pawel has said I'll have to help him. I don't know that I can do it. But he's here, now. In the house, with me. I've never been to a wake before, so I don't know exactly what it is I should do, but I think it must have something to do with sending him off in a respectful and loving way. After Pawel left, I walked into the forest in front of the house, towards the water until I reached it and it was a lake indeed. A thin sheath of ice covered it, so fragile a thrown pebble would have cracked it. I stood awhile, looking at the black water beneath. I found some small pinecones and some smooth, light gray stones. The kinds of things Tobias would have brought home with him. I walked slowly back towards the gray house, my old running shoes squelching loudly in mud covered in ice crystals. I stopped a few times and just let the tears fall from my eyes. How do I grieve someone who hurt me so deeply and so constantly? How?

Back at the house I pulled more of the tarpaulin back, but there was something very frightening about how Krysz didn't yield at all, even when I pulled quite hard on the tarpaulin. I don't know what I'd expected, nor why I'd insisted on Pawel bringing him inside. I just knew that I had to do something. I placed the pinecones in a circle around his head and placed a coin over each of his eyes. I lit a couple of tea lights I found in a kitchen drawer and placed them into wine glasses because I couldn't find any holders. They looked kind of beautiful and I placed one on either side of Krysz's head. I placed one little stone in his pocket, one in my own, and the remaining few around him, like the pinecones. Then I just sat there for hours. I talked to him, I touched his face, I recited the only prayer I remembered from school, though I didn't know all the words. It was almost completely dark by three o'clock, and it was then, in the violet, hazy light that it really hit me; I will live the rest of my life, however long it may turn out, without Krysz. I felt so intensely furious with Tobias for doing what he did, that I imagined snapping his thin neck with my bare hands or smashing a rock in his head, just like he did to Krysz. But then, I thought about the man my heart had chosen, and I felt briefly relieved he was gone, and then, ashamed at my own relief. *God damn you*, I whispered. I began praying again, but this time, it wasn't a vaguely remembered prayer from childhood, it was as though words appeared from inside my very core, intended for God himself.

This was somebody's baby, I whispered into the cool, quiet air. *He was somebody's daddy, and now they are together. He was somebody who never found peace, and that is what I wish for him, now. Please, please, please give him peace.*

Throughout the evening, I sat by him, smoking crack, crying, cutting myself with a little penknife and letting the blood drip onto Krysz's navy shirt. At one point I was so angry with Krysz for everything – for leaving me, for hitting me, for being dead, for having been alive at all, that I ran the knife down the side of his face, leaving a dry pink line like a scar. I screamed loudly and pummeled his still chest with my fists. A couple of times, I felt the phone vibrate in my back pocket but I didn't even glance at it, I was so high and so consumed by giving Krysz his wake. And now it is the early early morning and I've been here all night and only now is the high wearing off, leaving behind this dreadful, cold nothingness.

This is his eulogy, these words are everything that will be left of him, and perhaps of me, too. It is my greatest wish that Ellen one day will read the letter I wrote her and my diaries and forgive me. Maybe she can sit on that same bench at the cemetery in Eckfors where she once sat with me when she took me to see my mother's grave, and maybe by then I'll be buried next to her, and maybe Ellen would find that to be quite comforting.

Back to now, and to Krysz. He's here tonight. Here with me. And tonight is all we've got.

CHAPTER 24

I WISH THEY pretended it wasn't Christmas instead of pretending like we are going to have a nice family Christmas. Hamed looks confused and says *merci* every time someone hands him a cookie. Yesterday he walked around and switched off all the fairy lights and said, *S'il vous plaît, non*. Sigrid looks like she wants to stab someone, and because she might actually do that, there aren't any knives in any of the drawers. The bunnies are hiding and the chickens are gross. The 'family members' are talking constantly about the big meal we will have tomorrow, but secretly I bet they are angry about having to sit here on Christmas Eve with the orphans instead of with their actual families. They're not going to cook, though, because I have seen the cardboard boxes of ready-made Christmas dinners in the fridge. I'm not dumb just because I'm short. I said that to Hannah, one of the nicer 'family members', but then she made me sit and draw and the man with glasses whose name I can't pronounce sat and watched and brought my drawing with him when he left. I drew a bird with a smiling face and a big smiling sun to confuse him.

Today is the twenty-third of December and two thousand and seventeen years ago, Jesus Christ was about to be born. That's cool. I know that we are celebrating Christmas because he was born and because he brought so much light and love to the world – that's what Moffa always said. He also said that even if you have nothing else, you'll always have Jesus if you believe in him. Karl-Henrik didn't come today because it's Saturday, but it wouldn't have been a school day anyway. There isn't anything to do here. I've been on my iPad since I woke up, and here, nobody says, *Tobias, that's enough screen time. Why don't you go outside to play?* like the mother in the house always said.

If Moffa hadn't died and I was still at the farm with him and Baby, I'd play in the snow today. Maybe Moffa would have made me hot chocolate with tiny marshmallows, and maybe we would have walked around the lake together in the afternoon, me on the wooden skis that were Moffa's when he was a kid. If I'd been allowed to stay with the family, I don't know what Christmas would have been like. I think there would be many presents because they're rich. The mother and the father would have wine, and the girls and I would draw or watch YouTube videos. If I'd still been with Anni, I guess we would have been in the house at Østerøysvingen 8. It would be very cold without any heating and it would be just Anni and me, but I'd get some chocolates and she might let me play Candy Crush on her phone. Someone is knocking on my door.

'Tobias, sweetie, you have a visitor who has come from Sandefjord to see you.' I sit up fast, and place the iPad on the floor next to the bed. Downstairs, the woman with the sad smile, Laila, who I hate, sits on one of the blue wicker chairs. She smiles sadly. She is the one who took me away from the family, so I turn to run back upstairs to my room, but Hannah, the 'family member', is blocking my way in the doorway. Upstairs, Sigrid is screaming and thumping something against the wall. Laila pretends like she doesn't notice.

'Tobias,' says Laila, her voice soft like she is whispering to a baby. I shake my head. 'Will you come back to Sandefjord with me?' I shake my head again. I know what this lady is. She's a liar.

'I have to tell you something, Tobias. Many things, in fact. But first, will you please come back to Sandefjord with me? Some very bad things have happened to you, and I understand you are angry. But your family is waiting for you, and they are hoping that you will come home for Christmas.'

In the car, I say nothing. Laila made me bring everything I have with me in a suitcase that Hannah packed for me. I guess this means I'm not coming back here, and that makes me happy. Unless it's like with Sigrid, where they've found me a family, but they might send me back here if they don't like me that much after a while. I want to ask lots of questions, but I don't want to speak with Laila. We drive away from the 'home' and I look around the little town. It says '*Notodden*' on a sign and there is a gray lake and some mountains in the distance. Nobody ever took me out so all I've seen of Notodden is the garden of the 'home' where I played football with Hamed. Maybe I'll miss him a little bit. When I left, he came to the car and said, 'Bye bye, *mon frère*.' It means *brother* because he's told me that.

I have to sit up more straight and watch the road because I feel sick. The road is windy. Maybe Laila thinks that means I want to talk, because she keeps looking at me in the mirror and smiling, and it's not a sad smile anymore. It's a very happy smile and I don't think she knows that I'm not happy about being taken somewhere else today, even though I wasn't happy about being at the 'home' either.

'The girls need your help decorating the tree,' she says. *What girls?* I say nothing, but try to picture them, these new sisters. 'Hermine has made you something special,' she says next, watching me. For a minute, I wonder whether it could be a joke, and that she said it to be cruel, but nobody who works with children is allowed to say or do mean things, they write that everywhere. I look at her and now I actually want to say something, but I can't. I open my mouth, but a low cry comes out – the screaming cat noise again.

'Oh, honey,' says Laila, and her eyes are filling with tears that she doesn't wipe away. 'Oh, sweet boy, they can't wait to see you.' I don't want to cry in front of her, or laugh or anything, because I hate her, but maybe I don't so much now. I begin to laugh, a strange giggle that I can't stop, it's a bit like popcorn popping in the pan – when you think it's over, there is another pop, and then another. I want her to drive so fast the car lifts a bit off the ground. She *does* drive fast, and after a while we leave the windy road and merge onto the motorway that leads to Sandefjord – I recognize it because the family took me to Tønsberg to buy things in a big shopping center once. And then we are in Sandefjord, driving through the center, and I recognize everything like maybe it's home. I am so happy I want to shout out of the window. When we approach the family's house, I can see many cars in the driveway.

Laila slows down and says to me, 'There is another very big surprise for you inside, Tobias. Are you okay?'

I nod, and even give her a big smile. 'Thank you,' I say, and then the door is opened and the mother in the family almost pulls me out of the car and lifts me up and hugs me. The father is there, too, and he rubs my back. The girls are waving from a window upstairs.

'I love you,' the mother whispers in my ear, and I wish I didn't cry in front of them, but they are crying, too, so it's okay. The mother slowly puts me back down on the ground by the front door. I look at the wooden heart sign next to the door, the one that says 'Welcome to the Wilborg family!' Underneath, it now says: 'Cecilia, Johan, Nicoline, Hermine & Tobias.'

'Tobias, there is something I have to tell you.' She looks up at the father, who nods. 'So many terrible things have happened, but it's all over now. You're home now. I will explain everything to you, my darling. But first, there is someone upstairs who can't wait to see you. It's my father.' I feel confused because I don't know her father, and maybe I want to go to my room first and put the marbles and the cards back in the three drawers, but I feel strange, like all my thoughts are being thought at the same time, like I don't know how to move my arms and legs. I think of the swirls in the wood on that table, how they reminded me of the pattern on the tree stub at Moffa's farm. The father lifts me up in his arms and carries me up the stairs. There is a loud repeated sound coming from upstairs and when we come into the big living room a small white shape comes flying towards us and I cry out but then I realize that it's a dog and see it has a brown spot on its back and it really is Baby and then I look up and standing there is Moffa and he is crying like I've never seen an old man cry before and I hold Baby to my chest, and Moffa holds me to his chest very hard and we just stay like that.

CHAPTER 25

IT'S FUNNY HOW, with time, most things really do come together. I've always believed that, I really have. Yes, everyone was very angry. Still are, I suppose. The police, my father, Georg Sylling, Johan, and so on, but let's face it, how angry can you really be with someone who has suffered as much as I have, and who on top of it actually has the statement to prove she is mentally unstable? I can't leave town, and am still under investigation, but prison looks unlikely, according to Sylling. Even after they produced the CCTV footage from the post office. Insanity, said Sylling. Completely insane, no doubt about it.

More importantly, Tobias came home. My father and my mother spoke for the first time in over twenty years, and as mad as it sounds, he is now staying with her in the house that was once their marital home, so he can spend time with Tobias every day until we work out what happens next. Johan, well, Johan is very tired. I think a part of him has always feared me; like his gut instinct had always told me that one day, I'd be the one to burn his heart and life on the bonfire. He said he might need to go away for a few days because it's like he can't *see* me, only what I've done. *Please don't leave me*, I said then, my head in his lap, the winter sunlight picking gray out of my husband's hair. *I'm not leaving*, he said and I have to believe him, because now, more than ever, I need to keep this family together. The girls and Tobias have become incredibly tight-knit – it's like he's the glue that finally made the family whole.

It has been decided that no further action will be taken with regard to Tobias having killed Krysztof Mazur. He will receive intensive counseling and support from social services in the years to come, and it is my hope that he himself will grow up to forget his part in that awful man's death. Camilla Stensland, for all her shortcomings, managed to put two and two together in terms of Anni's murder, and uncovered CCTV footage from the Shell gas station next to Meny. While it doesn't show the spot where Anni and I met, and where I hit her, it does show a red Skoda parked behind the car wash, all the lights off, a man matching Pawel's description smoking inside, and then, at 10.47 p.m. leaving the vehicle and walking towards the boatyard, where I'd just left Anni.

Tomorrow is the last day of 2017, and it is my intention to go into the new year cleansed and absolved of everything that's happened. It seems like I will avoid a prison sentence thanks to Sylling's relentless campaigning to assert that I've been mentally unstable ever since my first pregnancy with Nicoline, and so not really responsible for my actions in the years since. The police, on the other hand, seem to believe that I did everything I did calculatingly and in cold blood, and only became mentally unstable this autumn, when Tobias turned up. The thing is, these people know very little about me and the internal processes I've been through. I will win. I always do. Fact. As long as I have Johan and the children, I can overcome anything.

*

Tobias runs off as soon as my father has parked the car, trailed by a wildly excited Baby. My father looks momentarily alarmed but I smile reassuringly at him, and we walk over to a bench at the top of the beach. For December, it is mild today, and there are a couple of other families walking dogs on Vøra Beach. We sit on polystyrene seat pads I've brought from home, and drink strong coffee from a thermos, watching Tobias throw a stick for Baby, whose hysterical barking hollers up and down the beach. Words don't come easily in my father's presence. It feels impossible that we haven't spoken properly in so many years; now that he's here again, it is as though he never left, as though we are just another father and daughter taking a small boy and his dog to the beach early one morning.

'I'm sorry,' says my father suddenly, and he catches me off-guard, because it's not like he is the one who needs to apologize here.

'No,' I say, focusing hard on keeping my voice calm and even. For days now I have felt like I'm likely to burst into tears at any unpredictable trigger. 'Please. It is me who should apologize. You only did what you believed was right for Tobias. And maybe it was.'

'I don't mean in terms of Tobias. I'm sorry for what happened when you were a girl. That I left you.' If I was feeling less vulnerable and less overwhelmed, perhaps I would have managed to stop the tears that begin to sting in my eyes. The winter sun is thankfully sharp and I pull my sunglasses down from where they'd sat on the top of my head, keeping my eyes on my son and his little white dog.

'It's fine,' I whisper, but it isn't, and we both know it. 'I'm angry,' I say.

'I know,' says my father. We stay silent a long while, watching the sun rise above the sea, trailing pink and red wispy clouds. 'Do you think we can begin to repair our relationship, Cecilia?

I've made some terrible mistakes. Maybe we could really talk in the next few days? I'd like that.'

I force myself to turn my gaze from Tobias and the dog to my father, and nod.

*

I try to push this morning's trip to the beach to the back of my mind as I pull up in front of a nondescript office on Rådhusgata. In this new life, it seems I'm always being shuttled around these various institutions – social services, the mental health unit at the hospital in Tønsberg, the police station and now this – Vestfold council's rape counselor. 'Ada Hagemo' reads the sign on her office door, and I raise my hand to knock, but just then, it is opened.

'Cecilia Wilborg?' Ada Hagemo smiles widely and shakes my hand, as though I am here to discuss something rather more pleasant than my brutal rape on a beach in South America. She looks how one might imagine these therapy types to look – she wears a purple, organic-looking kaftan with half-moons stitched in silver thread around the bottom hem, and her dark-brown hair is streaked through with vivid smears of gray. Her skin is supple and glowing in that smug, wholesome way of gluten-free vegans, and her mild, brown eyes study me carefully from behind Harry Potter glasses. This woman seems to be the kind of person who'd discuss her aura in all seriousness.

'Take a seat,' she says, and ushers me into a subtly lit office overlooking the Scandic Hotel park. The lovely weather of this morning has given way to another onslaught of bitter, windy rain, and I watch a gust of wind shatter droplets against the window, like marbles flung to the ground. This makes me think of crystals like the ones favored by various therapy types and

I discreetly glance around to see if I spot any, but I don't. Ada Hagemo has a neat desk, on which stands a deep red poinsettia and a photograph of a smiling little girl sitting atop a handsome man's shoulders. I let my eyes wander, determined to uncover at least one incriminating thing; something to prove that this woman can't possibly be quite… all right.

'I was thinking we could start off with taking a moment to talk about the things we're grateful for in life. I often find that when dealing with very difficult subjects, it can be immensely helpful to start off a therapy session rooted in the present, and on a positive note. So. Cecilia. I've read your referral form, and it would seem that while you have faced some huge challenges, you also have a lot to be grateful for.' Here she smiles encouragingly at me, and I slowly raise an eyebrow, focusing on keeping my face blank and unreadable.

'Would you like to mention something in your life for which you are particularly grateful, Cecilia?' I open my mouth to say something sarcastic, like: *The fact that I have three Gucci Indiana bags when most people in this town only have one*, but just then I see Johan's face in my mind, the way he stood up for me in the meeting with Sylling and the police. I wanted to lightly touch his arm, make him calm down, but I could tell that he needed to do it. *One mistake*, he said, his voice level and strong, but I could tell how nervous he was by the scattered red rash along his neckline. *Have you never made a single mistake in your life, Inspector Ellefsen? Not one?*

'Cecilia,' says Ada Hagemo kindly. I close my mouth and open it again, but still, no words will come. Only tears. I stare hard out of the window but the falling rain just makes it worse; it reminds me of the night when Tobias appeared, when my life began to go to hell.

'It's okay, Cecilia,' says Ada, handing me a tissue and squeezing my knee gently, but for a brief moment her hand becomes Anni's dead, cold outstretched one. I swat her hand away, and stand up to run from this room, but I'm so tired of everything, maybe most of all myself. I also want to answer her question, but the problem isn't that I can't think of anything I'm grateful for – it's rather that there are so many things. And I've treated all those things abysmally and neglectfully, caring much more about myself and my immediate satisfaction than the people around me. I'm embarrassed, frankly, but I'm sure as hell not going to admit that.

'I'm sorry,' I say. 'I don't know what to say.'

'You don't have to say anything at all if you don't want to. We'll be meeting regularly for a long while, you and I. Not everyone finds it immediately natural to discuss intensely personal matters with a stranger.' I nod and give Ada Hagemo a little smile. She has, after all, done nothing wrong.

'I hate myself so much,' I say after a long silence, and even this doesn't seem to throw her.

'Feelings of self-hate are very often prevalent in rape victims,' she says softly, but I interrupt her.

'It's not because of the... rape. I hate myself because I've done so many shitty things. I've lied constantly to people I love. I'm a terrible mother.'

'Everyone has done bad things, not just you. Sometimes we need to bring our focus to the future, and to forgiveness. You can't change the past, no matter how much energy you spend wishing you could.' I nod, and again, we sit in silence for a long time. I decide that I quite like Ada Hagemo, in spite of myself. I entertain a mental image of the two of us, meeting for a glass of wine, chatting away like old friends. Her kaftan is actually quite cool; it's clearly handcrafted, and at least she's someone who dares to dress the way she wants to, unlike my generic, clone-like group of yummy mummy friends. Ex-friends. I close my eyes, and more tears drop from them.

'Do you have any questions about how these sessions will proceed? Or any other questions?'

'Are you a vegan?'

'Excuse me?'

'Sorry, I realize that is probably not a relevant question. I just... It just occurred to me.'

Ada Hagemo smiles, then actually laughs a little. 'No, I'm not a vegan, to answer your question,' she says. 'Look, why don't you head home for today, and I'll see you same place, same time next week.'

*

Sometimes, we just have to pull it together. After the session with Ada Hagemo, I just had to put certain things into perspective. I stood awhile in the rain by the car before unlocking it, letting icy droplets take tiny stabs at my skin. I breathed deeply, clenching my teeth together. It's true what I said to Ada Hagemo – I've jeopardized my family. I've shocked and hurt Johan. I've endangered and traumatized a small, innocent child. My child. A child who was treated better by a junkie kidnapper than his own mother. But in those moments I decided that if I am to hold on to this life and the people in it, I've got to forgive myself. It's not too late, because I still have it all. *One mistake.* One wrong turn. I've only ever really made one mistake, albeit a very big one. I have to forgive myself for that and turn my gaze very firmly towards the future.

I stop for fuel on the way home, making a conscious effort to look at the fuel pump rather than beyond it, to the boatyard where Anni's life ended. A voice slices through the gurgling sound of the flowing petrol and the hammering rain.

'Hi, Cecilia.' It's Fie, who's nervously fiddling with the petrol cap on the Range Rover that just pulled up next to mine. I give her a tight smile and retract the nozzle from the fuel tank, though it's less than half full. I'm not going to stand here being told again what an awful person and mother I am – I meant what I said about looking towards the future. I get in the car fast, and am about to turn the key in the ignition when Fie knocks on the window. I close my eyes and swallow hard, needing all the focus I can muster to keep the tears that wouldn't stop flowing earlier from returning. Then I lower the window an inch and turn to face Fie. To my surprise, she has a faint smile on her lips and her eyes are soft.

'I want to apologize to you for the other night,' she says. 'We were hard on you. It wasn't fair. And it wasn't our place to judge you.'

'Yes, well, I'm sorry I tried to kill you all by throwing champagne bottles around,' I say, and we stare at each other for a long moment before Fie starts to laugh, and then, surprisingly, so do I.

*

I wake in one of those black pockets of night when the deep silence is both exhilarating and frightening. I disentangle myself from Johan and lie awhile, looking at the faint contours of his face in the near-darkness. I smile at him and hope he can feel it in his dreams. I get up and creep quietly across the hallway to Hermine's room. She is splayed out on her bed, face down like a starfish, duvet flung to the ground, and I gently cover her again, tucking in the sides. She stirs and smacks her lips the way hungry babies do. I smile at her, too. In Nicoline's room, she and Tobias are sleeping head to foot, the way they have started to do sometimes, and Baby is on the floor next to the bed. When I enter, she looks up at me with her little black eyes and thumps her tail lazily on the floor.

I'm about to head back to bed, snuggling in next to my sleeping husband, but am drawn to the window looking out onto the harbor. It is a moonless night, and though the rain has let up, the streets are wet and shining with frost. The inner harbor basin is faintly lit up by the glow of Vesterøyveien's street lights, and I can see the exact spot where Anni was found from here. I feel suddenly and violently unhinged at the thought of her, again, bloodied and alone, out there. I walked away from her. Would I have turned back for her if I'd known she'd be murdered moments later? It frightens me to realize that I wouldn't have. Here I am, safe and warm in my house; a woman who has everything. And there she is – I imagine her out there in the frozen water – cold, dead and alone, a woman who has nothing and never did.

CHAPTER 26

I WALK UP the long hill to the house. I've been down to the gym; I believe it's important to keep to your routines, especially at times of upheaval, although Johan seems to think I should just lie about on the sofa and get chubby. When I left, the girls and Johan were getting ready to go to my mother's house for lunch, but strangely, the Tesla is still parked in the driveway, so they must have not left yet, or come back for something. Tobias and Moffa are off somewhere with that crazy little dog, as usual, inseparable.

'Hello?' I say, taking my shoes off downstairs, but the house is completely quiet. The hallway is a huge mess of winter boots and shoes flung about – nobody is here to tidy now that we paid for Luelle to go home to the Philippines for Christmas and New Year. This makes me angry, and combined with the strangeness of the quiet house and the car in the driveway, I feel immediately anxious. 'Hello?' I say again, climbing the stairs to the first floor, but still, there is no response. I walk into the kitchen and stand awhile by the central marble island, warming my frozen fingers under the tap. They must have taken a taxi, Johan might have wanted to have a glass of wine with his lunch. If nobody is here, I suppose I could try to sneak a tiny glass of wine; I've had to sit out the entire festive season with San Pellegrino – my whole family watching over me like hawks, even peering into my glass to check it really is filled with water. I walk over to the integrated wine cooler and squat down to look inside, and only then do I see him, reflected in the glass door. Johan. I jump, and my heart begins to pound hard in my chest. He's sitting silently on the low sofa by the bay window, in the last of the day's natural light. I turn around.

'Hey, baby,' I say, but he doesn't react. It's like the figure on the sofa is a Johan-doll rather than the real thing. I walk slowly over to him. 'Honey,' I say, 'What is it? Has something happened?' On the low marble table in front of Johan is a stack of papers. I suddenly think back to that night just a few weeks ago, when Johan had said he wanted to speak to me, and I thought he was leaving me, but he ended up giving me the beautiful pink sapphire ring. This will be like that. The papers could be a printout of an amazing holiday he's booked. Yes, that will be it. He's so clever, my Johan; always knows exactly what I need, and then just goes and does it. I wonder whether it will be the Caribbean this time – I do hope so, I certainly made it clear that I didn't much appreciate Thailand when he booked that back in September without even consulting me. I reach for the papers, but he swiftly pulls them out of reach. I then try to touch Johan's shoulder, but he takes my hand, hard, and pushes it away. Fear, so very familiar by now, flaring up in my gut.

'Jesus, Johan, what is it?'

'You received an email. I printed it out for you. Why don't you read it?' My eyes won't move from Johan's frightening, empty ones, to the piece of paper between us.

'I said, read it!' It feels like my heart has dropped into the corrosive bile in my stomach.

From: Santiago.Romero@icloud.com
To: Wilborgs@Wilborg.com
Date: December 28th, 3:38 p.m.
Subject: Attempting This

Dear Cecilia,

I received your email of November the 30th, and while you can imagine it was a big shock, I tried to respond to you to the same address three days later, but received an 'undelivered' message. I hope it is okay for me to contact you here, I have spent some time on Google, trying to find you, but without a last name, it was rather difficult. Hopefully, this is your address. Anyway.

I was shocked to read your email. I did, of course, remember you, though I'm sure we can both agree our first and only meeting was short but sweet. I wish I'd known before that a child had come from it. I can assure you that it is my intention to be there for the boy. Thank you for attaching the photograph of the boy, he is very beautiful, and he looks incredibly similar to my other son, seven-year-old Xavier. I am divorced from his mother, but we remain friends, and my son is a huge part of my life. I want Tobias in it, as well. As you may have gathered, I live in Miami. Can you please get in touch again at your earliest convenience to confirm that you have received my message, and perhaps we could arrange a time to speak on the telephone?

Dear Cecilia, I am embarrassed to say I did not remember your name, or perhaps I never even knew it in the first place. But I do remember this; you were incredibly beautiful, though your smile was sad. I remember the dress you wore, and the droplets of seawater on your ankles, and your gorgeous green eyes. I am hopeful that life, in spite of unforeseen developments, has been kind to you, and that we can meet again, to find a way of supporting this lovely boy together.

Very best regards,

Santiago Romero

Johan stands motionless, watching me, and before I manage to say even a single word, he pushes hard past me, knocking my hip against the side of a chair.

'Wait,' I manage to shout. He turns around in the doorway.

'Fuck you, Cecilia.'

'Johan, I can explain!'

'Do you see those other papers over there? They're divorce papers. You can explain yourself in court.'

He rushes down the stairs, and I just don't have the strength to run after him – it's as though every drop of energy has drained from my body. *No. No, no, no.*

EPILOGUE

1.

I CAN CALL the mother in the house Mommy now. She said. It's because she's my mother. She loved me when I was born but decided it would be best that I lived with Moffa and I'm not angry about that because I loved to live with Moffa. I still can if I want. Everybody's talking a lot about what is best for me. I know this because they told me and because they asked me. I said to the tall lady with the glasses who brought me back here that I wanted to live here but also with Moffa at the farm and I want Baby with me all the time and she said that sounded really great.

Every day when I wake up, Baby is in my bed. Sometimes Nicoline, too. She's my big sister and she loves that I'm in the family. Most days Moffa comes after breakfast and we take Baby for walkies together. Moffa cries when he looks at me because he is very sad that Krysz and Anni stole me from the farm. If they hadn't died Moffa says they would be in prison until they were really old, or dead.

Moffa is here now and we are going to walk Baby by the sea and then we will go to McDonald's because children love it there. It's very cold and the sky is blue-white, like ice, so I'm wearing a lot of clothes. The long hill from the house is very slippery and I like to hold Moffa's hand in one hand and Baby's lead in the other and slip-slide down it. We're almost at the bottom when we hear strange noises – it's like a very loud roar, then a whiny cry, like a dog that's got stepped on. But it's not a dog, it's a car and it comes very fast past us down the hill, and on the bend it has to brake hard and that's what the whiny noise is. It's Mommy's car but that's strange because she is at the gym like every morning, and I want to say to Moffa that it's strange but he's already half running very fast the same way the car went, dragging me and Baby behind him.

Across the road, slippery, so fast, Baby panting, Baby carried by Moffa, Moffa's face very strange, me saying *look, look*, pointing at the car in the distance. It's stopped in the middle of the wide-open space by the gas station behind Meny, and the door is open and the engine is still on and warm smoke comes out of it, making the cold air crumble. *Cecilia*, shouts Moffa, but we are still far away and she can't hear us. She is running away from the car, falling a bit, then running more and from here she looks a bit like Anni. I get angry if I think about Anni so I look away from her, to the quiet gray sea. It has ice on it now and for two days the boat to Sweden couldn't go because of it. *Cecilia*, shouts Moffa again, so loud his voice hollers across the road and down towards the water. He drags me along and I want to open my mouth to shout something but the air is just too cold and I can't get a single word out while I'm running, too, not even *Mommy*.

SANDEFJORD IS A summer town; the Hamptons of Norway, they call it, but I can't recall those long, white summer nights – it feels like this winter has stretched on and on. Like it has been dark forever, inside me, and out. I left the Range Rover in the gas station parking lot, and ran around the back to the boatyard, passing the spot where Pawel sat in his car, watching, that night I hit Anni. Over and over. He sat there, watching, waiting. And when I was done, he walked over to where she sat, crying and bleeding, realized she hadn't got any money off me and tossed her into the water.

So this is where I am. Alone. Doomed, destined for the dark ocean floor. I glance around – it's still only mid-morning, but the town is quiet, stunned by the extreme drop in temperature that has resulted in most of the inner fjord freezing over in the last couple of days. I walk over to the exact spot where Anni lay as I smashed my fists into her face, the same spot I stared down at from the hallway window last night, when I still had everything. I think about how Anni's life started – quite happily, it would have seemed, on that farm with parents who loved her. Her mother would have peered with wonder into the same face I struck with pure hate, shattering bone. She would have whispered sweet words into the same ear I'd whisper into, thirty years later, imploring Anni to die. Her mother would never have imagined that her baby would end up a murdered, heroin-addicted child-snatcher. My own mother would never have been able to imagine her only daughter in these moments, either – indistinguishable from the broken, bleeding Annika, crying silently, shaking with cold, reaching down towards the glassy surface of the ice-covered fjord, down, down… The surface of the sea is a mirror and the person staring back up at me is Annika Lucasson.

I could swim. People do it all the time. I've seen them in the papers. Ice-bathers. They stand around afterwards, red-faced and laughing, rubbing stunned limbs. I could be like them. Or I could be like Anni; finally still, quiet, at peace. Yes, I could be her. The ice snaps easily enough into sharp, thin shards, and the water is not even that cold, but there is a loud noise, one that superimposes itself on top of the sound of my heart pounding, my jagged breath, the hiccupy sobs I can't stop even though this is a joyful occasion; this is a return to where I'm supposed to go, yes, this is a chance to be at one with everything, to be at peace. It is the sound of a dog yapping, and it follows me as I swim further and further out from the boatyard, though the going is slow, because my arms are leaden. The silly animal runs alongside the harbor basin between where I am and a little jetty empty of boats that juts out in front of me around twenty meters away. On the jetty I can make out the outline of a person. It's Tobias and he's shouting. Behind him, the dog is spinning around and around, hysterical. I become aware of other voices and I would say something, but I can't talk or even move; all I want is to close my eyes and let myself be carried off to sea on the current, but that doesn't happen, and suddenly strong arms close around my waist and begin to drag me towards the shore.

ACKNOWLEDGEMENTS

I have a lot of thanking to do – this book would not have been conceived, written or published without the incredible support of these wonderful people:

A very big thank you is due my wonderful agent, Laura Longrigg at MBA Literary Agents. Your support and enthusiasm for this book has been wonderful. I am so lucky to have you as my agent! Thank you also to Louisa Pritchard, and to Jill Marsal of Marsal Lyons Literary Agency. Your fabulous work is very much appreciated.

Thank you to my wise and insightful editors in the UK and the US – Madeleine O'Shea at Head of Zeus and Michelle Vega at Berkley – I am very fortunate to work with you both.

Thank you to all the lovely people at my publishers' who have contributed to making this book a reality.

Thank you to Tricia Wastvedt, whose creative guidance and friendship over a decade has meant so much. And a big thank you to my writing workshop friends and colleagues, whose opinions and company I greatly value – Christine, Diane, Fiona, Jane, Mary, Mina and, of course, Tricia – what a lovely community we have – total soul food. Thank you to my fellow writers and friends Barbara Jaques and Katrine Bjerke Mathisen, who have both read and re-read many drafts of this and other works, providing amazing support and advice. Thank you to my tutors and fellow writers at Bath Spa University's MA in Creative Writing – I wish I could do the MA every single year. Thank you also to all my other friends for the laughter, the support and the occasional force-reading… you know who you are.

Sia, Lana del Rey, London Grammar and Laura Pausini – thank you for the music, I rarely write a word without you.

A big thank you to my grandmother, Kari, who was a writer too, and who showed me a world of words and wonder. To my father, Henning, who would have loved to hold this book in his hands – I wish we'd had more time. To my mother, Marianne, who has gone above and beyond in her unwavering support – thank you for believing. I love you and this book is yours.

To my children, Oscar and Anastasia, who inspire me and spur me on every day – I love you forever.

And last, but definitely not least, a very big thank you is due Laura, my love, my queen and my rock; for everything.

A letter from the publisher

We hope you enjoyed this book. We are an independent publisher dedicated to discovering brilliant books, new authors and great storytelling. If you want to hear more, why not join our community of book-lovers at:

www.headofzeus.com

We'll keep you up-to-date with our latest books, author blogs, tempting offers, chances to win signed editions, events across the UK and much more.

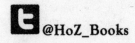 @HoZ_Books

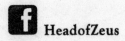 HeadofZeus

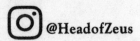 @HeadofZeus

🦉 HEAD *of* ZEUS